# Undead and Unwary

*Anthologies*

CRAVINGS
*(with Laurell K. Hamilton, Rebecca York, Eileen Wilks)*

BITE
*(with Laurell K. Hamilton, Charlaine Harris,
Angela Knight, Vickie Taylor)*

KICK ASS
*(with Maggie Shayne, Angela Knight, Jacey Ford)*

MEN AT WORK
*(with Janelle Denison, Nina Bangs)*

DEAD AND LOVING IT

SURF'S UP
*(with Janelle Denison, Nina Bangs)*

MYSTERIA
*(with P. C. Cast, Gena Showalter, Susan Grant)*

OVER THE MOON
*(with Angela Knight, Virginia Kantra, Sunny)*

DEMON'S DELIGHT
*(with Emma Holly, Vickie Taylor, Catherine Spangler)*

DEAD OVER HEELS

MYSTERIA LANE
*(with P. C. Cast, Gena Showalter, Susan Grant)*

MYSTERIA NIGHTS
*(includes* Mysteria *and* Mysteria Lane, *with P. C. Cast, Susan Grant,
Gena Showalter)*

UNDERWATER LOVE
*(includes* Sleeping with the Fishes, Swimming Without a Net,
*and* Fish out of Water*)*

DYING FOR YOU

UNDEAD AND UNDERWATER

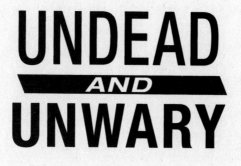

# UNDEAD AND UNWARY

MaryJanice Davidson

BERKLEY SENSATION, NEW YORK

**THE BERKLEY PUBLISHING GROUP**
**Published by the Penguin Group**
**Penguin Group (USA) LLC**
**375 Hudson Street, New York, New York 10014**

USA • Canada • UK • Ireland • Australia • New Zealand • India • South Africa • China

penguin.com

A Penguin Random House Company

This book is an original publication of The Berkley Publishing Group.

Library of Congress Cataloging-in-Publication Data

Davidson, MaryJanice.
Undead and Unwary / MaryJanice Davidson.—First edition.
pages cm.—(Undead/Queen Betsy ; 13)
ISBN 978-0-425-26344-0 (hardback)
1. Taylor, Betsy (Fictitious character)—Fiction.   2. Vampires—Fiction.
3. Hell—Fiction.   4. Humorous fiction.   5. Paranormal romance stories.   I. Title.
PS3604.A949U5277 2014
813'.6—dc23

FIRST EDITION: October 2014

PRINTED IN THE UNITED STATES OF AMERICA

10  9  8  7  6  5  4  3  2  1

Cover art by Don Sipley.
Cover design by Lesley Worrell.
Interior text design by Kristin del Rosario.

*For Benedict Cumberbatch, on whom I have the most undignified crush. So undignified I'm dedicating a romance novel to the man. The delicious, delicious man. Also, I was into this guy way before the Star Trek movie, unlike some of these Johnny-come-lately jerks. I stand ready to abandon my husband of two decades to be at his side. Also, I'm going to require role-play. Like, a lot of it. I'll be his Moriarty. And his Kirk!*

*Anyway. This one's for you, Ben! (In my fake relationship, I call him Ben when I'm happy with him and Dict when I'm not, like if he doesn't want to go to Missouri to visit my folks, or didn't pick up milk on the way home. This is a partnership, Dict. You have to meet me halfway.)*

## Author's Note

The St. Paul Winter Carnival is a thing. They've been doing it for over a century, it pulls in almost a half million people a year, and the city makes millions. There really is a Snow Slide, a Queen of the Snows, an Annual Snow Stomp, a Moon Glow Pedestrian Parade, a blood drive, a castle, an outdoor baseball game, and beer.

My feelings on this phenomenon are mixed. On the one hand, I'm proud my fellow Minnesotans not only endure winter, they embrace it. Minnesotans *own* winter, okay? They have made winter their bitch. It is a glorious thing to see.

But, and not to be a traitor to my state, I don't go near the festivities. I went once, and once was enough. It was cold. There was ice and snow all over the place, and the fact that it had been molded and/or sculpted into interesting things made it no less unbearably cold. Lines for hot beverages were torture ("I can see, I can see the steam rolling off the hot chocolate so close and yet so far and, ahhhhh, can't this line move any faster? I can't feel my face! I have not felt my face in half an hour! Oh, face, come baaaaaaack!"), most of the activities seem to be designed to make a person even colder, and I just . . . no. I admire the effort, and I want nothing to do with it. St. Paul Winter Carnival, I apologize. I just don't get you.

Stoli Elit Himalayan Edition is also a thing. It really does come in a beautiful brown and gold bottle in a keepsake dark wooden box, and it really costs three thousand dollars. And on a list of most expensive vodkas in the world? Stoli doesn't even come close. Man, if I have a few grand to burn, I'd never blow it on a bottle of vodka. I'd blow it on Coke and Funyuns.

Scribbling on babies with Sharpies is not cool. Seriously, just don't. Even if they're scented. Perhaps especially if they're scented. The Sharpies, not the babies.

The state of Minnesota is shockingly cavalier about enforcing a timeline for its citizens to name newborn citizens.

The dreadful jigsaw puzzle Marc worked on can be found on Amazon and it's actually called the World's Most Difficult Jigsaw Puzzle. There are two kinds of people in the world: those who like jigsaw puzzles and those who hate and fear them. The World's Most Difficult Jigsaw Puzzle is the thing of my nightmares. Proceed with caution.

Referring to Laura Goodman as the Anti-Antichrist isn't mine; *TV Tropes* (tvtropes.org) did it first. And it was wonderful. I am filled with grinding envy that I didn't think of it first. Grinding envy, however, provides the lubrication for my ambition. And, ugh, I just talked about lubricating myself.

I am determined to make *zangst* a thing.

The Game is a thing! One I lose all the time and, if you're reading this, you have, too. Check it out here: http://en.wikipedia.org/wiki/The_Game_(mind_game).

The baggie of diamonds Betsy stumbles across are red diamonds, the rarest in the world. Also, am I the only one who thinks jewelers should just stop rhapsodizing about "Chocolate Diamonds"? Guys: they are brown. You're selling rocks the color of mud. You are selling fancy gravel. Which is fine, but just . . . just own that, okay? Okay.

Silver Lamborghinis absolutely look like giant electric shavers. I've got nothing against the good people at Lamborghini (who are actually the good people at Volkswagen), but Betsy is quite right to mock Sinclair's purchase.

I have nothing against Giada De Laurentiis. I think she is a lovely woman and a wonderful cook. I regret that my characters do not agree.

Finally, no matter how tempting it may be, faking your death is not cool, not least because of the inevitable paperwork nightmare.

"Dee, are you seriously bragging about sleeping with a married man?"

"I'm not the one who's married. I didn't do anything wrong."

"You let him buy you a car."

"Well, Frank, I'm not going to go passing on free cars."

—FRANK AND DEE, *IT'S ALWAYS SUNNY IN PHILADELPHIA*

"I was visiting Carol in Las Vegas and there was . . . a performance issue."

"I'm Reaganing, Lemon. Let me solve this."

"It's not him, it's me. I'm the one with the performance problem."

"What? What are you talking about?"

"I freaked out and my junk closed. It's like Fort Knox down there."

—LIZ AND JACK, *30 ROCK*

"My father loves this car more than life itself!"

"A man with priorities so far out of whack doesn't deserve such a fine automobile."

—CAMERON AND FERRIS, *FERRIS BUELLER'S DAY OFF*

"Blood and gore all over the floor / And me without a spoon."

—OLIVER SPURGEON ENGLISH, *FATHERS
ARE PARENTS, TOO: A CONSTRUCTIVE GUIDE
TO SUCCESSFUL FATHERHOOD*

"Okay, gross."

—ELIZABETH "BETSY" TAYLOR, QUEEN OF
THE VAMPIRES

# Undead and Unwary

# CHAPTER
# ONE

**You know how you see someone you love stuck with a job** they don't know how to do? Or maybe they do know how, but they don't like it, maybe even hate it? And you watch them struggle with a kind of dread because you know if they can't pull it together you'll end up offering to help them, even if the job's over *your* head? Even if you know you'll probably suck at it but you can't just leave your loved one stuck with something awful? Even though you're pretty sure it might devour your lives?

Yeah, that's how I ended up working at Walmart the summer my friend Jess and I were eighteen, which was just so stupid. Among other things, neither of us needed the money, and also, Walmart is evil. I knew that long before I became a creature of the darkness. But that's a whole other story and we come off pretty drunk in it.

Also, it's why I'm cobitch in charge of Hell.

I'm just too nice, dammit. It's one of my biggest character flaws.

Fortunately I've been able to avoid my cobitch responsibilities for a couple of months now, and I had my brother/son's—the vampire king's—new churchgoing activities (he's on the Historical Preservation Committee and running the cookie exchange, which—I can't even), my dead dad, the never-ending quest to housebreak Fur and Burr, and the entire household being a slave to Thing One and Thing Two to thank for it. (Off topic, lately I've realized we are dangerously close to being outnumbered by babies. Which just . . . yikes.)

All this to say it's pretty chaotic around here. Our normal is other people's chaos. Actually, it's other people's fever dreams. I was legitimately busy. Which I told myself as often as I could. It's not like I just lolled around the mansion, talking my sexy husband into role-playing Scarlett and Rhett having passionate, pre-rape foreplay on our sweeping huge staircase. I *loved* scooping him into my arms and darting up those stairs only to ravish him in our bedroom and talk about how, frankly, my Sinclair, I don't give a damn.

Lots to do, no time to hang around Hell. Except Hell had shown up in the form of my sister, Laura. Half sister, technically; we had the same dad, but Laura's mom was Satan, making my little sister the Antichrist. Or the Anti-Antichrist, I guess, since she used to rebel against the devil by being good. Because how else would you do it? How can you outdevil the devil? It'd be like trying to outvapid any one of the Kardashians: no matter how determined and driven you are, no matter how much time you devote to what you suspect is the impossible, it cannot be done.

And I had to give my little sis props: Laura never once tried outdeviling the devil. Instead, she was (and is) a fixture at various local soup kitchens, food banks, church banquets, shelters, and the occasional Democratic fund-raiser.

Plus, there was no need for passive-aggressive maternal

rebellion anymore, because I killed Satan (crazy week—don't get me started). If nothing else, there was no point in rebelling against the devil when you *were* the devil.

Anyhoo, Laura was here, she wasn't queer, and I'd better get used to it. Or however that was supposed to go.

"Share," she said again, tapping her Payless-shod foot on the faded peach-colored carpet. Black flat, rounded toe, made of some horrific plastic/pleather hybrid; I reminded myself that it wasn't nice to tackle the Antichrist for the purpose of confiscating her shoes and then blowing them up.

Mind you, this was a woman who could literally travel through space and time using only the force of her will, a woman who, it was foretold, would take over the world, and she can't bring herself to wear footgear that isn't wretched.

Also, round-toed shoes have creeped me out ever since I read Roald Dahl's book *The Witches*. The way Mr. Dahl tells it, witches *have* to wear round-toed shoes because . . . they have no toes! Their feet just *stop* at the end of the . . . whatever the bones are just before the toe bones start, that's where their feet *stop*. They just *stop*! Even thinking about it summons my vomit reflex. "We agreed. Sharing, remember?"

Eh? Oh, right. I shook off my case of the creeps and tried to focus. Running Hell. *Sharing* running Hell. Which was an unfortunate word choice, since I had been an only child for most of my life (my half sister/work buddy/occasional nemesis didn't pop up on my radar until I hit thirty—an age I'll be for centuries, so it's a good thing I never got that tattoo), so "sharing" wasn't something I'd had much practice with.

"We agreed," she continued, being as dogged as I was when I tried to talk her into some decent shoes, "we'd run Hell together."

Agreed? Run it together? Hmm. Didn't sound like me. I tended to avoid work, not blithely agree to it. Unless I was trying to get back on someone's good side. Which, given that I'd killed my sister's mom, was something I would have had to do. Dammit. I probably *did* agree to share. The things we do in moments of weakness: recycling in a desperate attempt to save the earth, obsessively updating Amazon wish lists, agreeing to run Hell with the Antichrist.

"We agreed"—ah, cripes, she was *still* going on about this—"it was the least you could do after murdering my mother."

That irked me, but not for the reason you'd think, which is why many people are (rightly) convinced I'm a bad person. "First off, the least I could do is nothing." Huge pet peeve of mine, along with people using *amongst* and *towards* and *synergy*, and people mailing Christmas letters instead of cards. And I'm saying that as someone who used to do the letter thing; I actually thought people were genuinely interested in the promotions I didn't get, the shoes I did, the guys I didn't marry, the babies I didn't have. But even my puffy vanity couldn't keep convincing me people wanted an envelope full of Who Cares, I've Got My Own Problems for Christmas, so now I don't send anything.

Ironic, because I actually have cool (cool = weird/terrifying) stuff to write about now. *Well, we picked out our tree—had to go at night, obviously, and then helped ourselves to half a pint of B neg from a would-be Christmas tree thief. BabyJon is learning to walk, his parents are still dead, and I killed the devil. Happy holidays from all of us at Vamp Central! In lieu of gifts, donate blood. Because the Red Cross shouldn't be able to hog it all, dammit.*

"Okay?" I needled. " 'The least I can do,' by definition, is nothing. Ergo the word *least*. Ergo the word *ergo*."

"Which you've been doing! All across the board, nothing but nothing."

"All right, fair point. It's just I hate when people say 'the least I could do' without acknowledging—"

"Stop talking. Right now."

"—that the least I could do *is* nothing."

"It was really naïve of me to hope you'd stay on track for this."

"You bet it was. Also, if the shoe fits."

"That makes *no* sense."

"And while we're on the subject of shoes—"

"We aren't!"

"—those things on your feet could make it through a nuclear winter, which, believe it or not, is not a selling point. That plastic/pleather doesn't look like it would ever break down. Cockroaches and those shoes, that's all that would remain on the poor scorched earth." The thought was so sad, I had to shake my head. "Also, killing someone in self-defense isn't murder. Right, Dickie-Bird?" It was handy to have a cop in residence, and this wasn't the first time I'd had that thought. "Not murder?"

"Justified homicide, yes, it *is*. Yes, it *is*." Detective Nicholas Berry, one of my several thousand roommates, was perched on the peach-colored love seat as he cradled Thing One and cooed to him. We were surrounded by peach, which is why our nickname for the peach-colored parlor was Peach Parlor.

(Sometimes we had no imagination. Of any kind. Peach Parlor, my God.)

It was at the front of the mansion, just off the entryway, and we usually used it to entertain welcome guests and occasionally corner uninvited guests. But Dick and his full-time sweetie, Jessica, had taken into their heads that the color peach soothed their weird babies, and if it was true, those babies were probably going to be the most relaxed and laid-back on the planet because *everything* . . . couch, wallpaper, love seat, overstuffed chairs . . . peach. One hundred percent peach. All peach, all the time. We're having a special in the Peach Parlor, and the special is peach.

Meanwhile, the Thing That Sired Lovers of Peach was still cooing at his baby. "Not a jury in the world, no, there isn't, not a jury in the world and oooh! Look, she's yawning. Come see, you guys."

Damn . . . that was Thing Two, then. Dick had knocked up my bestie (which Jessica loves to pronounce "beastie" and

which, since she is as sleep deprived as a POW, I let slide) with
twins and even though they were fraternal, they looked identical to me. Except for the boy having a penis and the girl not,
I mean. They were pale, like Not-Nick, with Jessica's not-pale
features. Same dark eyes (their besotted parents claimed the
babies had big pretty eyes but whenever I looked, said eyes
were squinched up in a yawn or a yowl or in sleep . . . they
could be cross-eyed for all I'd been able to see), same teeny
nose, same pointy chin, same weirdly gangly limbs. Yes, I will
be the one to make that particular announcement: Thing One
and Thing Two were pretty hideous.

"Guys? C'mere, loooook!"

Laura, still standing in her patented "arms akimbo in judg-
ment" pose in the parlor doorway, didn't move. I didn't, either.
"I'm not crossing the room to watch your kid do something
she does at least five dozen times a day." Yeah, Not-Nick and
Jessica were doing that annoying thing parents did, to wit:
come see my ordinary kid do ordinary stuff that we totally
think is the opposite of ordinary and we're sure you'll agree,
rinse, repeat. Repeat × 1,000.

Pass.

"You know how I know I need to get more sleep?" he asked
and, since I was pretty sure it was rhetorical, I didn't reply.
Which worked out fine, because after a pause he kept going.
"I couldn't find the babies last night. Jess was asleep, and the
babies were asleep, and you guys were out hunting, and I went
to look in on them and for a few seconds . . ." The exhausted,
slightly dazed smile fell off his face and I saw with a start that
he was afraid. Not "what if they don't get into a good college?"
afraid but "I didn't know what to do and was scared" afraid.
"I couldn't find them. I knew they were in the room—where
else would they have been?—but they weren't there. At least,
it seemed like they weren't. Gave me a hell of a start."

"You're right," I decided. "You need more sleep. Your lazy
babies are hogging it all."

"I don't think sleep works like that," he said through a yawn.

Laura was now gazing thoughtfully down at father and daughter. "Maybe we shouldn't discuss this in front of the baby."

"Trust me, the baby doesn't give a shit." I chortled. "Except, of course—"

"Don't even."

"—when she shits! Heh."

"Scatological humor," Laura commented, unimpressed. "A mark of true class."

"I'm full of surprises." Scatological. Probably something to do with poop, right? Scat = poop, taught to me many years ago by my mom (she hunts; geese, deer, ducks, and wild turkeys are not safe from her). Which wasn't even true, since I don't even like poop humor and if I ever did, *Family Guy* would have killed that part of me long before now. If there had been no *Family Guy*, *South Park* would have taken care of the job. But there's no level I won't sink to in order to get the Antichrist off her "you promised, and also it's 'bring your sister to work' century" thing. If that meant poop references, I was fully prepared to make them. It was, after cornering my husband and banging him senseless, my number two priority. Ha! Number two. Get it? (It's possible I need professional help.)

I'd been lucky so far, and I knew it. This place, our St. Paul mansion (dubbed Vamp Central about a day after we moved in), was a madhouse even on good days. Normally I disparaged that. Normally I bitched about it like I was getting paid. I never wanted the queen-of-the-vampires gig, but was slooowly becoming used to it. (Used to it = dead inside.) Or resigned, I guess—that's probably a better word. And I sure never wanted to live with assorted vampires, werewolves, and babies, but again: resigned. Didn't want to be married to a vampire, didn't want to go time traveling. Didn't want to be haunted, literally haunted, by several ghosts (spirits? shades? life forces? pulse challenged?), including that of my loathed stepmother. Didn't, couldn't, wouldn't.

And now, when it was too late to fix it and too early to properly mourn my pulse-accompanied lifestyle, I missed the normality of everyday life. Predeath my biggest problems had been not strangling my boss, saving my hard-earned pennies for the new Louboutins, avoiding my stepmother while trying to get my father to pay attention to me (yes, pathetic, and yes, thar be daddy issues ahoy), watching Jessica go through more boyfriends than a cat through cat litter, and trying to vote Republican without feeling like a traitor to every female ever conceived. All those things were a huge pain in my ass back in the day (back in the day = about three years ago), but now that I had to worry about death threats, death attempts, navigating a timeline I screwed, kind-of-sort-of raising my half brother/ son, accepting that my mother is (groan, shudder) dating and (argh!) possibly having sex, and now cohosting Hell with my half sister, it seemed like my old life was laughably carefree.

It wasn't, of course, but that's how we are about older, smaller problems when faced with newer, awfuler ones: ah, the good old days! Which weren't *so* great, and certainly not all the time, but I'm going to pretend they were perfect.

"But that's enough murder talk around my baby," Not-Nick continued, reminding me that I was in the middle of a conversation, kind of. "Not a sentence I thought I'd be saying ever," he added cheerfully. "I was pretty convinced I'd die alone."

"That's the spirit, Dick-Not-Nick."

A word about Nicholas Berry and his annoying name. In the old timeline, we'd known him as Nick. Which made sense, since it was shorter and more efficient and short for Nicholas, *his actual name*. For some unexplained, illogical, silly-ass reason, when I returned to the changed timeline, he informed me no one ever called him Nick, no one ever called him by his full first name, and furthermore, his nickname was and always had been Dick so I'd better get with the program, and also, we're out of milk so the next time I'm out and about could I please bring home a gallon of skim?

Outrageous! First of all, skim? That's white water. That's all skim milk is: they take out all the wonderful stuff that makes milk taste like milk and replace it with white water and people actually drink that shit. Second, Dick? How? How did his family get Dick from Nicholas? It makes no sense. And nothing against the Dicks and Richards of the world, but I always disliked that one. Call me immature if you like— I've earned it many times over—but come on: The word. Is slang. For penis. If he was a woman named Virginia, would he insist we refer to him as Vag? I think not! (God, I *hope* not.)

Old habits were hard to break, and I had enough trouble remembering people's actual names, never mind their nicknames both pre- and post-timeline-fuckery. Trouble was, for some silly reason Nick disliked being called Nick and called me on it. A lot. (My vamp queen title never seems to impress or intimidate the people I *want* it to impress or intimidate.) Which was his prerogative, but I dunno. Seems like his time could be spent on pretty much anything else.

"Sure, she doesn't understand now," the Roommate Formerly Known as Nick was saying, "but it's never too early to get into the habit of watching absolutely everything we say all the time around the babies constantly."

*Oh, goody.* "Yeah? Well, let me give you a tip, No-Longer-Nick—"

"God, will you *stop* with that?" Exhausted, but not too exhausted to glare and correct me. I had to admire that. "You know what year all your favorite shoes came out but can't remember which four-letter word I prefer being called?"

"—it's kind of hard to accept your authority on anything when you're dressed like . . . um . . ."

DadDick was dressed in a stunning ensemble of gray sweatpants (which I suspected had been black about a decade earlier), vomit-stained T-shirt (I assumed it wasn't *his* vomit, but here at *Casa de los Weirdos* you could never be sure), and bare feet. And God, did his toenails need trimming, and don't get me started on how much his heels were crying out for a pumice stone. The bags under his eyes told the world that he hadn't slept in a thousand days. The smell coming off him told the world that he hadn't showered in a thousand days. I didn't know how it was even possible, but he was barely even cute anymore. The babies had sucked all the cuteness out of him.

"Are you honestly telling me you've got no need in your life for an internal censor of any kind?" he argued, pretty coherently for a zombie. (Not a real zombie, of course. That was Marc, one of my other roommates.) "Think of watching what you say around the babies as excellent practice for future vampire queenery."

"Making the horror that is now my life complete," I finished.

DadDick rolled his bloodshot eyes. "Don't talk to me about horror. You got more sleep in one night than I've had in a week. Do *not* talk to me about horror."

"Fair point," I conceded. It was. Jessica had told me it wasn't that the babies didn't sleep for long; they'd known that was coming. It wasn't the three a.m. feedings or the multiple daylight naps or the midnight diaper change. It was never knowing, when she or DadDick did get a chance to lie down, if they would get a twenty-minute nap or six blissful uninterrupted hours or something in between. *It's the not knowing that exhausts you,* she'd told me. I had listened in horrified fascination; all she needed was a flashlight to shine in her face as she finished her story with, "And the call was coming from *inside the crib*!"

"Look, we don't have to talk about this now," I conceded while trying to make it look like I wasn't conceding a damned thing. "Let's wait until the babies are out of earshot." And maybe puberty. How long could I stretch this out?

Unfortunately, the Antichrist was not only too nice (when she wasn't killing serial killers, proving an overreaction is not always a bad thing even as she terrified me) but she saw through me too well. Which wasn't *that* impressive; it's not like I was some inexplicable force whose every thought was cloaked in mystery. Laura found me as mysterious as a dartboard.

She pointedly shifted her gaze from the baby and speared me with her blue-eyed gaze. "Do you know how many people die every day?"

"I know it's more than twenty."

"About one hundred fifty thousand."

"At once?" I asked, appalled.

"It works out to about six thousand people an hour."

"That," I said, "is a lot. Let me guess where this is going . . ."

"Yes, *please*. It would be so great if you knew where this was going."

". . . at least some of those dead people end up in Hell?"

"At least," she replied dryly. "The backlog since you murdered my mother—"

"Justified homicide!" I yelped and pointed to DadDick, who was nodding and droopy-eyed. I thought it was cool how the sleepier he got the tighter his grip on the baby, like even his subconscious was devoted to its safety. He could be snoring and still have her cradled safely in his arms. I couldn't multitask for shit, so I found that impressive. "He said!"

"—has been immense. Black Plague immense."

"I don't get it."

"Immense means gigantic and—"

"Jeez, I'm not that dim." Polite silence was my response. I decided DadDick's was because he was dozing and Laura's was because she could be an immense bitch. Don't tell me about pots and kettles; I know all about pots and kettles. "I'm not," I finished, trying hard not to whine.

"Then you get it. How this is an *immense* problem. And you understand that regardless of whatever nonsense is going on around here, it likely doesn't trump sorting six thousand souls an hour."

"I don't think you can generalize that," I argued. "What if there was a nuclear bomb in the basement that only I could defuse? That'd be more important. That'd be loads more important."

Laura closed her eyes and kept them closed. Counting to ten, maybe, or reminding herself that killing her sister/colleague would be bad for workplace morale. Or maybe thinking about investing in a pair of shoes that weren't horrible; I dunno. I was a vampire, not a telepath. "Is there. A nuclear bomb. In the basement?"

"Not that I know of," I admitted, "but obviously I need to make checking it a priority." And anything else I could think of. "Safety first! That's our new motto." Which, come to think of it, we should have implemented the minute I woke up on the slab in pageant makeup and horrible shoes. "In fact, you—huh."

"What."

Yikes, the flat "what." No upward inflection; it's not so much a query for more information as a statement of being pushed too far. Kevin Spacey set the precedent in *L.A. Confidential*, the best movie ever based on the worst book ever. And now the Antichrist was picking up the "what" torch; I never should have made her watch it. Though her crush on Exley was super cute (I was a fan of Bud White, because a man who would kick the shit out of a wife beater hits my "isn't that romantic?" buttons every time). Also, is it me or does the older Guy Pearce get, the more simian he gets? Watch *L.A. Confidential* and then watch *Iron Man 3*. Heartthrob to monkey. Weirdweirdweird.

"Nothing, it's just . . . I think Jessica's back." I'd been able to hear the car pulling into the driveway, of course, but the slow, plodding footsteps didn't sound at all like Jess's usual springy stride. Sleep deprivation could be an explanation, but I didn't think . . .

The front door creeeaked open. We should offer to rent out that sound for Halloween.

. . . that explained . . .

Jessica wandered in, not bothering to close the door.

. . . everything.

"Uh. Jess?"

No answer.

DadDick stirred on the couch, instinctively tightening his grip on Thing One (or Two . . . the whole *problem* was that I couldn't keep them straight), which caused her to let out a small squeak. He absentmindedly soothed her as he rose to his feet. "Hey, babe. You okay?"

"Hmm?"

"Where'd you go?" I asked, curious. She was acting like she was in a trance or had been mojo'd by a vamp. I knew it wasn't the latter because it was daylight hours and also, no vampire would *fucking dare* because I would kill them *so much*. And who'd want to put her in a trance if it wasn't vamp related? "Jess? Where were you?"

"Oh, I took the babies to see your mom." Jessica had a peculiar expression on her face, a combo of impatience and worry and fatigue. Like, *I didn't think I'd have to talk about this, you poor thing, and stop bugging me and boy am I tired.* "That's what it was. Where I was. Yeah."

"The babies are here," I couldn't help pointing out. "Remember? Marc's watching Other Baby in the kitchen while he . . ." *Dissects things*, but that was no way to end a sentence around Jess. The world's biggest hypochondriac isn't as paranoid about germs as a new mother. ". . . does stuff." Also, DadDick was holding one of her babies. Five feet from where she was standing. Standing *without* the babies.

"Yeah, I know."

"You—you do?"

"So we didn't stay long, obviously."

"You and the babies you didn't actually bring," I couldn't help adding because *weirdweirdweird*.

"Right!" she finished with a touch of her prebaby snapitude. Then she turned around and walked out. But it wasn't Jessica's brisk got-to-get-going-quick pace that she used everywhere. She just sort of . . . wandered off.

Laura shook her head, a resigned expression on her face. "I don't know what that is, but it'll be more than enough to keep you occupied for a few days."

"You think?" I managed to keep the hope out of my tone.

"My point! What*ever* it is—she's on drugs, she's exhausted, she's been mojo'd by a nasty vamp, she found out she's being audited—you'll seize on it as an excuse to avoid your responsibilities from Hell." She smiled a little, and who could blame her? Responsibilities from Hell, heh. Maybe the "I've got the [*fill in the blank*] from Hell!" thing will make a comeback now. "All right, yes, I hear it, but it's true, and you're slacking."

"Look, obviously something's going on," I began.

Laura's beautiful face (the Antichrist has never had a pimple) remained unmoved. "Something always, always is."

"Someone could have attacked her!" *Argh, dial back the excitement, Betsy.*

"In broad daylight? Without leaving a mark on her?"

"Okay, someone might be . . ." I cast about for what "someone" might do. "They could be blackmailing her!"

"Who would?" Laura asked, displaying a shocking display of callousness when everyone in the house knew being a callous asshat was *my* job. Nagging and now poaching on my territory! My torments were endless. "She's a billionaire who lives with murderously protective vampires."

"She is not!" I snapped back. "The economy has sucked so hard and so long, she's only a millionaire now." The vampire thing was harder to argue.

"Like I said. It doesn't matter what this is. You've got your excuse du jour to avoid keeping your word."

"Boy, you just don't care about anything but yourself, do you, Laura? I'm sorry to say it, but it's shocking to see."

The Antichrist, usually pale as milk, started to blush. It only made her more dazzling, which was just annoying. Tall, slim, with blue eyes and long blond hair (until she lost her temper, then it went red and her eyes poison green), looking better in faded jeans and a Livestrong T-shirt ("Just because Mr. Armstrong cheated doesn't mean the charity isn't a worthwhile endeavor," she says) than I did in my wedding dress . . . I didn't like being the ugly sister *and* the mean one.

So I kept up with the nagging, because artless beauty must be punished. "It's just me-me-me with you these days. Meanwhile my best friend might have gone insane, or she's being blackmailed or hypnotized or audited, or some awful combination, and I'm going to get to the bottom of it. Because that's what a good friend does: she pushes her troubles—nay, her responsibilities!—aside and helps. No matter what the cost." I swept toward the door and pointed toward the foyer. "Good day, madam!"

"Oh, Jesus jumped-up Christ on a crutch," she muttered, which, for her, was about the most shocking epithet ever uttered. This was a woman who considered *shoot* over the line, swearwise. "Fine. Let the record show I tried." She followed my pointy finger and exited with a huff and a glare. I vowed to make it up to her. Just as soon as I broke my other vow and figured out what was wrong with Jessica.

"Okay, great!" I practically cheered. "Let's get to the bottom of this! Hoo—"

"Don't cheer; you can be really obnoxious in victory," DadDick warned.

"I was going to say 'whoever did this to her will be sorry,'" I managed with hardly any dignity. I managed to keep myself from jumping up and down in sheer glee. Something was wrong with my best friend and she obviously needed my help! Thank God something was wrong with my best friend and she obviously needed my help!

Like I said: bad person. That's me all over.

# CHAPTER
## TWO

*"Hey, Jess! Wait up!"* Before I could track down wherever she'd wandered to (wandering was also new behavior; Jess did not *wander*, she favored a "help me or move" stride), I nearly fell over Tina exiting the kitchen. I checked my watch—three o'clock in the afternoon. Sunset was still two hours away (winter, blech), so she was stuck in the mansion for a bit unless she stowed away in Marc's trunk. But that was a whole other thing, and they only put Operation VampTrunk into action when it was important.

Of course, important—like everything around here—was relative. Important could mean Tina had a five p.m. craving for sorbet-flavored vodka. (Don't get me started on the vodka. She had her own freezer for the vodka. She didn't care to share the vodka. I didn't even like vodka but knowing I couldn't have it made me crave it like a diabetic craves insulin.) And Marc loved the whole trunk setup; said it made him feel like he was in an action movie. I managed not to point out that, as a zombie, he was definitely in a movie, just not the genre he thought.

So when he got twitchy or cabin-fever-ey, he'd occasionally pretend an errand was more urgent than it was ("We're down to a half-pint of raspberries, Tina; get in my trunk stat!"—this from a guy who wouldn't say *stat* if everyone around him was going into cardiac arrest) so she would climb into the blanket nest he always had ready, then they'd chat or text on their phones while tooling around town doing whatever it was they did . . . and why was I only now realizing that I kind of wanted them to do a buddy movie?

"Majesty," was how Tina greeted me, which was typical. We'd lived together for years and had saved each other's lives more than once, and she loved me not for my (symbolic . . . if the queen gig had come with an *actual* crown I might have been more amenable) crown but for what I had done for Sinclair, the *other* person she loved more than life (death? undeath?) itself. I know my husband would have been lost without her, not just on a weekly basis but decades before I was born, and I was starting to suspect I'd be lost, too. I'd gone from not knowing what a majordomo was (I'd assumed it had something to do with the military) to wondering how I'd ever gotten along without one.

All that love and devotion and it was still "Majesty" and "My queen" and "O dread majesty" and "Dearest sovereign, if I catch you in my vodka stash just once more, I shall set you on fire, however much it will hurt me to hurt you."

Very much a stickler for propriety, that was Tina. She was a recovering Southern belle—she'd been turned during the Civil War, or born during the Civil War; I forget which—and maybe that was why. Tact and politeness were as much her style as her habit of dressing up like a dirty old man's dream. Short plaid miniskirts, crisp white blouses, the occasional demure headband holding back waves of blond hair (which only emphasized her dark-dark eyes), the occasional pair of kitten heels. She usually went for "mouthwatering" and tended to hit the nail without hardly trying. It was my curse in death to be surrounded by women much prettier than I was. If my husband didn't (almost literally) drool at the sight of me, it could have been awful for my ego. And my ego is the strongest bone in my body. *Wait, that isn't right . . .*

"Did Jess come through here?"

She shook her head and, as it was a headband-free day, her pale, pointed face was momentarily obscured by hair. She tossed it back like the Sexiest Cheerleader Ever and replied, "No, but I'm aware she returned just now. Does she require an infant?" I loved how she said that—*an infant*—as though any random one would do. As though we had a room full of random babies just in case someone needed one. Oh God, what was I saying? That day was probably coming.

"You'd think, because she apparently took the babies to visit my mom but forgot the babies, but no. I don't know what she requires but I'm going to find out. I swear on my filthy polluted soul that nothing will get in the way of me solving this mystery." All I needed to do was add a superfluous "Jinkies!" and I'd be Velma in better shoes.

"I also heard Laura Goodman arrive and then depart." Tina's expression was carefully neutral in the way only an old vampire could pull off. Here's a hint: never ever play Statues with an old vamp. "You were, ah, unable to assist her?" The *again* went unspoken, for which I was grateful.

Because the thing about Tina and also my husband was, their attitude was, "Why *wouldn't* you be exploring the hell out of Hell every chance you got? Why wouldn't you be honing brand-new previously undiscovered power number six? Why would you go out of your way to do anything *but* that, you silly bim?" That attitude was also, fortunately for them, largely unspoken.

"Laura's fine; Hell's fine," I replied with an impatient gesture. "Place has been there for a billion years but suddenly things are out of control and just crying out for *my* steadying hand?" I couldn't even say that without grinning; the whole idea was beyond dumb. "But something's up. And where's Sinclair?"

Tina smiled at me. "Outside."

Her one-word answer told me everything at once: *Outside, he's outside because he can brave the sun now because of you, he's outside and he's the happiest he has ever been because of you, he's outside and I am so, so grateful because of you and would follow you into death, and would you like tea? A smoothie? Not my vodka, but anything else you desire.*

"That," I replied, "was a dumb question." And bless her sideways, Tina didn't agree out loud or even nod. Because of course I should have guessed. Outside could be anything and everything, because my husband was almost a century old and most of that time he'd had to hide from the sun the way Republicans had to hide from talking about rape.

Long story short: the devil granted me a wish, and I wished for that before I killed her. And Sinclair was wallowing in it and took every chance to get out of the house. Bringing one of his five cars in for a tune-up? "Of course." Swinging by the farmers' market to grab fresh fruit for one of our designated smoothie blenders? "Of course." (Even though it was winter, and precious little was in season.) Shovel the driveway? "Do we have a shovel and if so, where do we keep it?"

He volunteered to go to the DMV for Jessica, who gently pointed out that the State of Minnesota frowned upon citizens sending proxies to renew their driver's license. "Are you quite certain?" had been the disappointed reply. "Perhaps they have changed the rule. I had better check, just in case, don't you think? You need your rest; I will find this out for you."

"If you really want to help, you could change the babies'—"

"Nothing will prevent me from aiding you in this," he'd declared, snatching his keys. "I swear it."

"Please don't try to bribe anyone in the DMV," Jess had

replied, not even trying to hide the horror. "It doesn't work. It makes everything all the more awful. I *know*." Not that Jess was speaking from personal experience; her dad was a shit of the highest order and did all sorts of unsavory things. He was in Hell now, which was excellent. That wasn't a guess on my part, by the way. I saw him there. His stupid wife, too.

Eric Sinclair, vampire king and devoted pet owner, former creature of the night and current creature of the day *and* night, was also a huge fan of alfresco sex. Me, not so much. Sex, yep; my husband was (almost literally) a demon in the sack. Bedroom sex, counter sex, basement sex, attic sex, bathroom sex, hallway sex, even stair sex (*argh, my back! this carpet needs to be thicker*). But outdoors? In January? Why?

We lived in a mansion people would pay to bang in. (I think it used to be a B&B, even, so people literally have paid to bang in it.) It was like living in Honolulu and then going to Honolulu for vacation: maybe a little pointless. Also: cold. Very, very cold this time of year in St. Paul. Goose bumps on top of goose bumps wasn't remotely erotic.

So my husband could be scampering in the snow almost anywhere (car wash, DMV, bake sale, winter carnival), doing anything (washing cars, braving state employees, buying brownies, watching a guy chainsaw a likeness of a Dairy Princess from a block of ice), which meant that I was on my own when it came to solving the mystery of Jessica's weirdness. Well, on my own besides the cop, the zombie, and the other vampire I lived with.

"I imagine she'll have gone for a nap," Tina said with a vague expression. Oh, right. We were having a conversation. Luckily my tuned-out expression was the same as my tuned-in one. "And it's just as well the king was absent for your sister's visit."

"Ah . . . yeah. Good point."

Things were still tense between my husband and my sister. It had only been a few weeks since she'd kidnapped me, then dumped me in Hell and abandoned me with a "sink or swim" mentality. I swam, but she hadn't known I would.

My husband was many things; incapable of holding a grudge wasn't one of them. Sometimes it was like he *invented* grudge holding, except I know for a fact that my stepmother did.

Still, it made for tense get-togethers, which I loathed. "Guess Sinclair hasn't forgiven Laura for leaving me in Hell," I commented, because for some reason I felt like saying the obvious out loud.

Tina did that thing where she glanced at me and then glanced away, so quickly it was like she hadn't moved. "Mm-mm," was her typically low-key reply. And a couple of years ago it would have fooled me and I would have dropped the subject.

It wasn't a couple of years ago. "'Mm-mm,' what? 'Mm-mm, something smells delicious; oh, ham steaks, my fave!'? 'Mm-mm, damn skippy he hasn't forgiven her and he's secretly plotting to eat her'? 'Mm-mm, how can I prevent Betsy from knowing I wasn't paying attention and have no idea what we're talking about'?"

Tina thought it over for a few seconds before coming up with, "I never call you Betsy."

This was as close as I'd ever get to outsmarting her, so I was gonna take that as a win. "Yeah, okay. Good point."

"If you do not require my assistance at this time . . . ?"

"No, I'm good."

"Yes indeed," she said with a small smile.

"You silver-tongued devil."

"That, too."

"Tina, d'you like it here?"

Her big eyes got bigger and I had a "whoa, where'd *that* come from?" moment. One of those things I had no idea I was going to say until it was out of my mouth.

"I—yes."

"Oh. Good."

"May I ask, Majesty . . . ?"

"I don't know," I admitted. "It's just everybody's lives have changed in next to no time. Five years ago I didn't know you. Five years ago I was still alive and you were off doing whatever it was you did before we crossed paths, and I didn't know Sinclair. Didn't know I had a half sister, sure as shit didn't know she was the Antichrist. Didn't know I was destined to—"

"Take the throne."

"—kill the devil." What did it say about me that I thought of *that* first? Other than still being in denial about the whole queen-of-the-undead gig.

There was a long pause while I tried to read her face, which was just as much a waste of time as it ever was. Tina could outbluff Daniel Negreanu (Sinclair was a World Series of Poker addict). Her fair face, never terribly expressive, now seemed so still it was like she was playing Statues. Which she could also do really well.

"I don't," she said at last.

"What?"

"You asked if I like it here."

Oh. Right. I remember now. And shit. I knew she'd tell me the truth, but I'd hoped it was good news.

"*Like* is woefully inadequate," she continued. "I love my new life. And not merely for my own sake. I love *his* new life, too. Five years ago things were dangerous and we trusted no one and we depended only on each other, and my dear friend the king, the boy I loved from birth, pursued empty relationships and cared not if he lived or burned. And now . . . he does care. About many things. I love that. I love you. I love this house. I love your friends. I love our new lives, and I love the new lives your friends have brought into our home. It strikes me . . ." Her gaze went vague as she looked through me. "It strikes me that I can live a very long time and still be pleasantly, continually surprised. I love that, too."

"Oh." Hmm. She'd just told me this incredible generous thing and I'd better come up with something a little better than "oh." "That's great. I'm . . . that's really great."

"Do you have any other questions?"

"Nope."

She nodded and started to turn away from me. "Then I'll take my leave? Yes?"

"Sounds like a plan."

Well! That was unexpected. And nice. It was almost enough to make me forget why I'd started the conversation in the first place. Which was . . . uh . . .

Jessica! Right. Tina was feeling fluffy and Jessica was up to something. Busy, busy, lots of mysteries to unravel and Hell would wait.

It's not like it was going anywhere, right?

# CHAPTER
# THREE

*I shoved the swinging door that led to the kitchen. So far* there hadn't been a hilarious sitcom-type swinging-door face smash, but the year was young. "Jess? You in here? Listen, I'm a little worried about you and because I'm incredibly intuitive I realize something's wrong and want you to know that whatever it is, you have my full support and attention and, oh, *what the hell?*"

Marc Spangler, MD, looked up from yet another revolting kitchen experiment. This time he was freezing, dissecting, and refreezing mice. Did you know frozen mice don't smell like much of anything? They don't. Probably because they're so little. Or because of the cold. Was he doing that out of kindness to those of us with enhanced senses in the house, or was the freezing thing specific to his gross kitchen experiment and, dammit, *my kitchen*! Which was also his kitchen since he lived here, too, but still.

At least I didn't have to ask where he was getting his test

subjects. Since every old house on the face of the earth has mice, this solved two problems at once.

"The kitchen? Again? We eat in here! Well, the others eat, and the vampires drink, and Sinclair and I occasionally have sex in here! Aw, dammit, that was out loud."

"Ha! Knew it. Jess owes me fifty bucks. Besides, you banned me from the basement." Marc was blinking at me over a tidy row of teeny corpses. "You said it was like living with Igor . . ."

"It was! Is. No offense," I added, because there was nothing sadder than a touchy zombie whose feelings were hurt. God, the moping. The *angst.* Zombie angst . . . would that be zangst? Will that be a thing now?

". . . knowing I was skulking around down there doing sinister experiments, creating then destroying abominations, tracking dirt . . . which is stupid, by the way. I don't skulk."

Of course, knowing that the zombie you lived with was experimenting on dead rodents created a whole new problem. It almost made me yearn for the days when he was *skulking*

(*because he does he does so skulk his denials are big-time bullshit he skulks therefore he is*)

in the attic, all hidden and ashamed and furtive, full of zangst. Like Quasimodo if the attic was the Notre-Dame Cathedral, our puppies were the gargoyles, and Quasimodo was a cute dead gay doctor.

"I can obsess over their brains," my cute dead gay doctor said, indicating the row of teeny fuzzy dead bodies, "or yours."

"Yeah, we've been over this. Theirs, obviously, but couldn't you be a little less creepy about it?" I let the door swing shut behind me and edged toward the table. Everything was meticulously laid out; I had to give him that. Instruments neatly lined up, shiny-sharp. The sterile field all set up (guess he didn't want the dead frozen mice to catch an infection). Marc all scrubbed clean and shiny right down to the latex gloves. It was the neatest, sterilest (is that a word?) operating field I'd ever seen. *In my kitchen.* "I don't think that's too much to ask."

"What?" he asked, defensively. He was wearing a pair of scrubs that had been washed so many times, they were like fuzzy barf-green velvet. He'd cut his black hair super short again ("The Caesar," he called it, "or the George Clooney, circa . . . anytime, I guess. He really got bogged down with one style, didn't he?"), which pulled attention to his dark green eyes and pale (even before he died) skin. He was about my height—six feet, give or take—and lanky, and his face was made for smiling; grins took years off him. Not that he would age or anything. No. He'd . . . rot. But only if I wasn't paying attention, apparently? I was still vague on the details. The horrible, horrible details. I made him a zombie, except it wasn't me. God, I hated time travel. "Betsy? What?"

"Hmm?"

Marc, used to me staring vacantly at him while I pondered, got to his feet, neatly dropped the pile o' fuzzy corpses into the biohazard bag, snapped off his gloves and dumped them, too, tied the bag off, then went to one of the sinks, rooted around beneath, emerged with Clorox wipes, and proceeded to wipe down the table. (I know, probably shouldn't have fussed so much about the mouse massacre on the table, but come on! Mouse massacre! On the table!) Finished, he disposed of the wipes and crossed the room to go for the freezer. I definitely wanted out of there before I saw what was up for Revolting Kitchen Experiments, Round Two. "This isn't anything new, you know," he reminded me.

"You killed yourself less than two months ago," I retorted. "It's incredibly new."

He laughed and I smiled. Marc had a high, cheerful laugh and I loved hearing it. "Point."

"What . . ." I stared, then tried not to look so terrified. I wasn't afraid Marc would go all zombie feral in the night and try to suck my brains out of my head with a curly straw ("Don't be a dumbass, Betsy, a curly straw would take too much time. I'd definitely use a straight one, one of those big fat ones they give you for bubble tea."), but he definitely had some new, creepy habits in death. Undeath. "What . . . uh . . . are you going to do . . . uh, now?"

He opened the freezer door. Peered inside. Reached in to the shoulder (damn, that freezer was deep) and emerged holding . . . oh God, the horror . . . holding . . . "Check it out."

A bottle of vodka.

"Oh. Uh, very nice." I was inwardly rolling my eyes. Tina's vodka obsession was contagious. Lovely. Too bad her willingness to overlook most of my bad habits and terrible decision-making wasn't.

"Stop rolling your eyes," he said impatiently, crossing toward me. "Look."

I looked. "Stoli Elit," I read aloud, "Himalayan Edition." I squinted. "That font looks expensive."

"It was!" For some reason, he sounded delighted.

"Three thousand bucks?" Good thing Marc had hung on to the thing; I might have dropped it. "Are you kidding?"

"I hid it behind all the corpses," he continued gleefully. "Genius!"

"Genius," I acknowledged with a shudder. When? When would roommates saying things like "I hid it behind all the corpses" become commonplace? Was I rooting for the answer to be "never" or "any minute now"?

But he was right; no one—*no one*—would look for it there. In fact, knowing there was a big weird bottle of incredibly overpriced hooch in there *with* scads of mice Popsicles made me want to poke through the freezer even less. "But Marc, I mean, it's none of my business, but you can't afford this."

My best friend was rich, and I'd married rich, and my father had made an excellent living before engaging in the Midlife Crisis Jaguar vs. Garbage Truck battle and losing, so money had never been that big a deal, but still. Marc wasn't rich, had never been rich (air force brat, and unless your dad was, I dunno, King of the Generals, that didn't make for a cushy lifestyle), and was still hip deep in student loans last time I checked.

Hmm. Did he still have to pay those back? Nobody knew he'd been dead, however briefly. Kind of how some people knew I'd been dead and some people assumed it was some sort of nasty practical joke, and the government was years behind on the paperwork anyway so I just sort of plowed ahead and nobody bugged me about it. But Marc was still a person, according to the government. Social security card, birth certificate, lack of death certificate, tax forms—all that was still good.

But: he'd been dead. He was *still* dead. It was something to think about.

"Other than a car—which my dad helped me buy—it's the most expensive thing I've ever gotten."

"Well, as long as you're happy with it. MGM was out of Grey Goose?"

"No. It's a present."

"Oh. Ohhhhh." I took another look at the long slender brown and gold bottle—and for that price, the gold font should be actual gold. For that price, they should come to your house on command and pour you a shot, then tuck you into bed and read you a story.

Sure, the bottle was pretty, and the vodka was probably top-notch, but booze was smoothies was milk was Shamrock Shakes was tap water was anything but blood. I was thirsty all the time. Only blood helped; only blood quenched any of that raging permanent thirst. That didn't stop me from binging on liquids all night. I couldn't get drunk on booze anymore, though. Odd that Marc would drop so much money on something he knew, to me, might as well be ditch water. "That was really nice of you." If not well thought out. *Gah, next time just a gift card for DSW, Marc.* "Thanks a lot. I can't wait to—"

"For Tina, idiot."

"Oh." Whew! "Idiot" was a little bitchy, though. Not inaccurate, but still. "Why? What'd she do?"

"Her birthday's Friday." He said it without reproach, because he knew me and he knew my Swiss-cheese memory. True friends expect nothing from you. That's what made them so terrific.

"Get out!" I had to admit, I was intrigued. How *did* a hundred-and-fifty-year-old vampire celebrate a birthday? The standards (Sky Zone Indoor Trampoline Park? Water Park of America? Chuck E. Cheese?) were probably out. Midnight bowling, maybe? Midnight golfing? "How old is she?"

He grinned and carefully tucked the bottle away. "I asked, and got the 'a lady never tells and a gentleman never asks' speech."

"And you reminded her you were all the way around the world from being a gentleman?"

"Didn't have to; she already knew. Anyway, it's no secret she loves vodka, even if why she loves it *is*."

I nodded. It was a mystery, because as I said, nothing slaked a vampire's thirst but blood. Anything else was at best a waste of time and at worst just made the thirst worse. That didn't stop Tina from hoarding vodka like Smaug hung on to gold and oh my God, I just made a *Hobbit* reference. I had to stop watching TV with Marc. Like, now. *Right* now.

But back to Tina and her vodka hoard . . . I figured it had to be something from her old life, something that reminded her of better, simpler times. Or maybe she just really liked vodka. "It's a great present, but she's gonna freak a little. She'll know how much it costs. And if she doesn't, she'll find out pretty quick. She'd want you to save your money."

"Why?"

I opened my mouth but nothing came out—rare! It took a few seconds but I finally managed. I hadn't been prepared for Marc not to know why he shouldn't blow wads of dough on booze for dead Southern belles. "Why? Because . . . because it's your money. I mean, it's—you earned it. You should hang on to some of it." When that didn't seem to be getting through, I added, "Uh, right?"

He gave me the saddest smile I'd ever seen on his open, friendly face. "What am I going to spend it on?" he asked quietly. "A wife? Children? A mortgage? Retirement savings?"

I opened my mouth again.

*Don't make a stupid joke don't make a stupid joke do not make fun of this do not make a joke to hide the fact that you suddenly feel guilty and awkward.*

I closed my mouth. Took an unnecessary breath. Then added, "You quit your job."

"Sure." He was nodding. "I couldn't risk going back to the ER. Someone was eventually bound to notice I was dead."

I nodded back. That was definitely the risk you took when you worked with doctors and nurses and EMTs. He hadn't even gone to give notice in person. Just called up his boss and gave her the "family emergency" line. Which wasn't a line, come to think of it. Dying was definitely a family emergency. At the least, it should be a get-out-of-jail-free card.

"Okay, so you're—uh—not earning right now." It wasn't as much a problem as it would be for a regular dead person. But Sinclair didn't charge him rent—didn't charge any of these freeloaders rent and it was just now occurring to me that I'm technically a freeloader so I'm not going to make a fuss— although Marc regularly contributed to the smoothie fund. When he wasn't in scrubs he lounged in old jeans and various tattered T-shirts; he was like a gay . . . a gay . . . I couldn't think of the word that meant the opposite of cliché, but that was what he was. No mincing, no hair products, no reality television. He had a crush on Benedict Cumberbatch, but who didn't? Shit, *I* had a crush on the Batchman; Marc and I were proud Cumberbimbos. So Marc's expenses were low, but still. "So that's maybe a good reason to save your money?"

Marc shrugged off my nosy concern. "I'm earning. Tina set

up a WebMD kind of thing for me. Patients can contact me through the Web page to ask me things, and I diagnose online."

*What a terrific way to get sued.* "Okay."

"She's also offered to put my name out there for off-the-books medical care."

*What a terrific way to get arrested.* "Okay."

"She had a bunch of great ideas, actually," he added, clearly warming to the subject. When had he and Tina become BFFs? They had a lot of nerve going from roommates to really close friends right in front of my eyes like that. All that time in Marc's trunk, maybe the fumes were getting to the poor woman. "We're still figuring stuff out, but there's time. I mean, none of us are going anywhere."

"True," I allowed. It should have been depressing, but I thought it was comforting.

"Plus, Sinclair paid off my student loans."

"What?" I squawked. I wasn't annoyed, but I was definitely surprised. Sure, Sinclair had the dough to spare, and he wasn't miserly, but it's not like he and Marc were especially close. Even if the answer to "why did he do that?" was "why not?" why wouldn't he have said something? It wasn't a secret or anything. Right? "How'd that happen? He just walked up and gave you a check?" *That* could have been an interesting conversation to eavesdrop on.

"Actually I'm not sure it would ever have occurred to him," Marc explained. "He's a big-picture guy. Stuff like student loans slips right under his radar. But that's exactly the kind of thing Tina keeps an eye on. She's a details girl."

"She is, even if she hasn't been a girl in over a century."

"Yeah, but a lady never tells . . . anyway, I'm pretty sure it was her idea and once she brought it up, Sinclair thought it was a fine plan. He'd never miss the bucks, and it must have appealed to his sense of . . . not justice, exactly. Compensation?"

"You mean like in a 'sorry my wife made you a zombie in a horrible dystopic future that probably won't happen now, thanks for being such a nice guy about it, and don't spend it all in one place' way?"

"Well . . ." Marc giggled a little. I loved that sound. It was such a cute, breathy noise out of a guy who was one hundred percent masculine. "Pretty much, yeah. So . . ." He pointed to the freezer. "I wanted to do something extra nice for Tina's birthday."

"Her birthday!" I cried, mystery solved, and now delighted instead of startled. Sure, I hadn't had a clue her big day was this week. And sure, that wouldn't surprise Tina. Or anyone. But I knew when I had done wrong and was adult enough to make amends. Nothing would prevent me from making this slight up to her. Tina did so much for me and I did . . . uh . . . next to nothing for her. We needed a party! We needed a plan! We needed to remind Laura that this was about my making amends and Hell would have to wait just a bit longer until I solved Jessica's problem and threw Tina a party and my God, this might be the greatest day of my life.

It also answered my "wonder if Marc had to pay off his loans" question.

"Okay. I'll get back to that in a minute. I've still got to track Jessica down—"

"I can't believe you're even doing that. It hasn't been very long since the Incident."

I shuddered. "Don't talk about that. Don't even think about it."

"I don't want to," he admitted, "but it haunts me. I'm pretty sure it's going to for a while."

I shook that off. This was no time to get sidetracked by something besides the thing I wanted to sidetrack me. The Incident was days in the past. If people would quit bringing it up, we could all move on.

"*Anyway*, once I get with her, then I'll get back with you and we'll plan the centennial of Tina's eighteenth birthday, or whatever it is. I promise I won't forget." I was already headed for the door. "You can count on me!"

Marc was staring after me. "This is as motivated to get to the bottom of mysterious happenings as I've ever seen you."

"Thanks." In a seizure of generosity, I ignored the implication.

"I mean, being killed didn't do it. You still sort of stumbled around fucking things up and being all clueless and everything."

"Thanks."

"But now you've got the focus of a Lasik machine. It's awe inspiring!" He was leaning against the counter, absently rubbing Purell into his hands. We kept a gallon-sized jug of it by the main sink. "And a little terrifying."

"All right, time to move on." Argh, I had been so close to a clean getaway. And now *this*. I turned to face him. "Look, I was never the kid you were."

"The kid I was?" Marc asked, blinking in surprise. Apparently he'd been expecting a different reaction. "You never knew me as a kid."

"Yeah, but even without knowing you as a kid I know you were into D&D, and you'd pay extra money to watch *Star Wars* in a theater when you could get it for free pretty much anywhere on the Web, and you gobbled up the *Game of Thrones* books like they were—were—"

"Iced milk and raspberries?" he prompted.

I rolled my eyes. "Yeah. Like that. And it's cool and it's one of the things that makes you *you*, but I wasn't like that. D&D made me long for the peace of a coma or a concussion or anything to get out of figuring charisma points. Not only have I never seen a *Star Wars* movie in a theater, I didn't think the *Phantom Menace* stuff was so bad and—see? You're shuddering. You're making my point that we don't have much in common."

"Okay, we're going to circle back to your *Phantom Menace* blasphemy, but for now, I don't see how you can judge how I was as a kid based on . . . oh, hell, as much TV as we've watched together, and the movies I dragged you to—"

"Those *Riddick* movies are the worst."

"Shut up, don't talk about Vin like that; but it's not about whether you were into sci-fi or fantasy as a teenager. Doesn't matter if you loved it or hated it, you *know* there's magic. It's not even a question of faith; you know magic exists. And you know you can do it."

"I don't," I replied shortly, "and I can't. Vampires aren't magical. Neither are werewolves. Something happens to vampires when they 'die'—their systems slow down and as a result of that, they develop other abilities. Werewolves, they're another species, it's not magic. It's biology that most people don't know about. Hell isn't magic, it's another dimension, one I know fuck-all about. If anything, all this stuff is *science*, which was never my best subject."

He was nodding along with my terse lecture, but I could tell I wasn't swaying him. "All that stuff aside, Betsy, you recently discovered you can *teleport*. That you can break a whole bunch of laws of physics for funsies. You were already strong and fast and durable—"

"Please stop making me sound like a four-pack of double-A batteries."

"Okay, sorry. But you were already in a great position to explore all the cool things that happened to you, and now, presto, change-o, you can teleport."

"Only the one time," I mumbled. And yes. I heard the lameness in that comment.

Marc ignored me, probably wisely. "This is an ability that many people would be thrilled to have, every single person living in this house included." His face had lit up and he was waving his arms around in his excited agitation. "Why wouldn't you be all over that?"

"Because nothing's free, Marc." I crossed the kitchen until I was right in front of him and caught his flailing hands. Held them in my own, made sure he was looking at me and listening, really listening. "And some things—even if you *can* pay for them, maybe you shouldn't."

"What you're doing now," he said gently, shifting my grip—I let him—until he was gripping my wrists, "isn't working."

I stared at him. Yikes, was he bringing the zombie mojo or something? Was that even a thing? I couldn't look away. "It's the only thing I've got right now," I finally said, and he let go of my wrists and turned to the sink.

"Not the only thing. And if you look at it another way, this is nothing new. All you have to do is what you've done since you woke up dead. Suck it up and get it done."

"Easy for you to say." I was trudging toward the door.

"It's not, actually. You could get out of it if you really wanted, but you're choosing not to." He rubbed in more Purell and sort of waved me away, as if I were a six-foot-tall mosquito. "Just tell Laura you only agreed to help her to get her off your back," was his parting advice, which I ignored, and rightly. It wasn't *my* fault there was a crisis around here every ten minutes, a wonderful chaotic weird crisis. I was only one vampire queen, dammit! I was doing the best I could.

What? I *was*.

# CHAPTER
# FOUR

*A flight of stairs and several hallways and doors later, I found* Jessica in her room up to no good. Not "are you hiding up here because it's your turn to change a poopy diaper?" no good but clandestine-research, followed by hurriedly-shoving-papers-under-the-bed-when-she-saw-me no good.

"Jesus!" She finished shoving papers and glared up at me from her spot on the floor beside her and DadDick's bed. "Scared the hell out of me."

"Uh-huh, and that's not furtive at all. Jess, what's going on?"

"What? I'm just sorting. And thinking. And then more sorting. Yes." She got to her feet and began prowling around the room. She'd stuck a clipping in her back pocket, but I couldn't think of a subtle way to grab it other than tripping her, sitting on her, and emptying her pockets. For which I would pay and pay and pay. I was stronger and faster; Jess was smarter. Just the thought of all the terrible things she could do to me was enough to make me feel guilty for even thinking of assault as a way to get to the bottom of this, however careful I would have been. And even though she'd made her view on being turned into a vampire *mucho* clear before I cured her cancer (long story), I could absolutely see her nagging a vamp into turning her just so she could keep punishing me through the centuries. Also, the tripping and sitting and pocket rifling wasn't a nice thing to do to a best pal. It's very wrong that I thought of that one last.

She looked startled, but that could have been the 'do—she kept her black hair pulled back so tightly her eyebrows were always arched. Her manicure (lime green, urrgghh) was chipping, something pre-twins/not-insane Jess would never have allowed, and her T-shirt had splotches on it that, luckily, were only spit-up formula. (I hadn't given one thought to enhanced vampire senses + newborns = gross and really, I should have. Ohhhhh, I should have.) Her jeans were so faded they were nearly white, and she was annoyed that skinny jeans were out again. She was so painfully thin (when carrying Thing One and Thing Two, she'd looked like a tent pole someone had hung a bag of volleyballs on), any jeans she pulled on were skinny jeans, even just a few weeks after popping twins.

"Why are you in here?" she barked.

"Because I'm lonesome?"

Jess snorted but didn't kick me out. "Mm-hm."

I sidled closer to the bed but knew I was no match for Jessica's chaotic pile-everything-into-a-box-beneath-the-bed filing system. For a modern businesswoman, she was a Luddite when it came to paperwork. A big fan of old-fashioned file cabinets and long plastic containers that she stuffed with newspaper and mag clippings, she still shopped at Hallmark, for God's sake.

Unless I was willing to sneak in here when she and DadDick were out, or sleeping the sleep of the deeply sleep deprived, rummage endlessly through decades of clippings while trying to figure out which story had grabbed her interest (I wasn't), or worse, which story was missing and now riding in her back pocket, I'd have to finesse it out of her. Subtlety, that was key.

"Tell me what's wrong or I'll sit on you!"

"What?"

Okay, I could see it now. My finesse sucked. Time for a new tactic. "So, how's my mom?"

"Huh?" Jess had at least ten IQ points on me, which anyone overhearing this would assume was a testing error. "What?"

"My mom. Who you went to see." Wait. Whom? Whom she went to see? Gah, Sinclair was rubbing off on me in all the wrong ways. And now I was thinking of Sinclair rubbing. Must not . . . be distracted . . . by thoughts of . . . hot husband . . . "With the babies you forgot."

"Oh. I didn't . . ." She waved vaguely at me. "You know."

"I *don't* know, Jess, you postnatal weirdo. What's going on? You look like someone clipped you with a brick."

"Don't be a dope. Nobody's been near me with a brick."

Sighing at the effort this was taking (vampire queen/best friend's work was never done), I plunked down on the queen-sized bed she'd had for a decade. Jess was indifferent to her riches (the wealth was impressive, but her shitpoke father had earned it all, making it much less awesome in her eyes) and formed deep emotional attachments to restaurants, pals (we've been friends since junior high), and beds. (Also, DadDick and the babies, I assumed. Before you accuse me of vanity, I listed myself second on that list.) So the bed didn't so much sag as suck me in, like quicksand in a quilt. But I was used to its ways and kept both feet on the floor.

I really liked Jessica's room. It was the most modern in terms of setup and decoration, the carpet a deep caramel, the walls tan, the furniture all light wood (blond wood?). The wallpaper was red and tan and there were red accents all over the place, including the quilt and several picture frames.

And gawd, *when* would she stop displaying the one of us on my twenty-first birthday? Drunk off my ass was not a good look for me. Jess looked cutely rumpled and was grinning into the camera while hoisting a daiquiri-filled plastic cup, her arm slung around my shoulders in what looked like camaraderie, but in fact she was keeping me from pitching face-first into the floor.

I was so much more than rumpled; I was sweaty, and my face was so flushed I looked like I'd sworn off sunscreen before napping in a tanning bed. My T-shirt was more stained than a new mom's, making it difficult to make out the lettering ("Step Aside, Coffee, This Is a Job for Alcohol"), but worst of all was the expression on my face. One eye was half-closed, my mouth was hanging open like a dying trout's, I was giving Jess the side-eye stink eye (she had just cut me off, which unfortunately did not prevent the vomiting doomed to start an hour later), and basically looked like a crazy cat lady in her youth, pre-cats.

And it had pride of place on the wall! I could only pray that once the twins were sleeping more, Jess would update their walls with baby pics, a new-parent phase I was actually looking forward to. I wanted to pull an Anne Geddes, draping the sleeping babies over all kinds of strange surfaces and then snapping away until I had enough for a calendar.

I wriggled on the bed, trying to get more comfortable without actually getting slurped in. Sinclair and I slept on a—wait for it—superking. Yeah. I know. But the thing was doomed; we went through a half dozen a year. Was there such a bed as a super-duper-king?

"Did somebody come up to you and say something? Are—nnf! Stop it, bed, I know all your tricks . . . are you getting audited? Were you meeting a new boyfriend?" The last was completely out of character, but Jess was a sleep-deprived mom now, and they were crazy.

"Yes. But it'll be fine."

"Wait—yes?" Oh God! In a moment of carelessness one of my feet had left the floor! I shifted my weight until I had them both planted again. Might be time to make a break for it. "Which yes?"

"I've got to go," she replied, laying off the pacing in favor of darting to the door. Her fingers went to the clipping barely peeking out of her pocket, checking to see if it was still there. "I'll take the babies to see your mom."

I was so startled I shifted my weight and both feet left the floor. "Good God, woman, you are *losing* it! You've got to tell me what's wrong. Okay? Jess?" Her hand was on the knob . . . her body was through the door. "You get back here, young lady!" Normally I could have crossed the room and blocked the door before she got anywhere near it, but normally I wasn't being inexorably devoured by Bedzilla. I was reduced to wrenching myself upright with superhuman strength to escape, finally reaching the door only to almost knock the vampire king on his ass.

"Aw, fuck!"

Sinclair beamed. His vampire reflexes had saved him from my vampire klutziness. "Darling! You missed me."

## CHAPTER
# FIVE

**"Missed you? I didn't know you'd gone out until half an** hour ago."

"Your loving words soothe my soul."

"I know that look, perv."

"I adore your affectionate pet names." He reached for one of my hands and pressed a kiss to my palm, which, I had discovered in the last couple of years, was a sizeable erogenous zone.

"I have no time for sexual shenanigans right now," I warned the ridiculously gorgeous man smiling at me even as the tingles started in my palm and radiated . . . um . . . downward. "Something's wrong with Jessica."

"Ah. Laura's been here, then?"

"No, of course not. Okay, yeah, but that has nothing to do with this."

"Hmm."

"Something's really wrong," I insisted.

"Hmm?"

"And it's Tina's birthday, did you know? I didn't know. She's, what, a century and a half?"

He fake sighed. "They grow up so fast."

"So we have to celebrate that, too." I got A Look and defensively added, "What? We do."

"For the first time since you've known her? Really, my own? You are now compelled to acknowledge a birthday you have not once—"

"I know, I know, it's overdue. And see, that proves my case! You are proving my case for me."

"I devoutly hope not."

"She does so much for us, you know."

He nodded. "I do know." And then, in a teasing mutter, "I was unaware *you* knew." All the while we were wasting time with idle yakking, he had a hand on the small of my back and was gently steering me toward our room, where our superking lurked. Meanwhile, Jessica was getting away!

"Also, and I'm bringing this up again because I'm pretty sure you didn't catch it last time, I have. No time. For sex. Ual. Shenanigans." Probably shouldn't have split "sexual" into two syllables, if my husband's stifled giggle was any indication.

*(Oh my god I love that giggle he only started with the giggling when he started sunbathing without fear of immolation and every time every damn time I hear it I want to tickle him or something to get him to do it again and how did I not notice I'm now flat on my back in our bed?)*

"Dammit!" He'd literally swept me off my feet and plunked me in the middle of the superking. As I reared up on my elbows in prep to escape, he plunked himself in the middle of the bed, right on top of me. What little air there was in my lungs (I sometimes gasped or yawned or breathed out of force of habit) whooshed out. "Ggggnnnn!"

"Ah, darling, your sexy moan sets my libido aflame."

"Ged. Gedduh. Gedduh huck offme." I groaned and tried

to elbow him away as he pressed me further into the mattress. Why the *hell* was the theme of the week beds devouring me? Was that . . . was that supposed to be a metaphor for something? Like I had time to ponder *that*. "Gnnn. Dyin'."

He was giggling against my neck and marking me with little nibbling kisses and all at once I cared a lot less about Jessica's mysterious errands and more about getting out of my underpants.

"What's got you all sexually charged? Besides being a man and being conscious."

"Don't generalize, darling," he chided.

"Yeah, yeah . . . answer the question."

"It was so wonderful." He pulled back until our faces were inches apart, his eyes—a brown so deep they were almost black—gazing into mine. His dark hair was only slightly mussed, thick with a tendency to curl under at the ends, and his skin was utterly pale, not the slightest sign of a flush. So he hadn't been feeding. It had to be something else.

Oh.

Oh God.

"No." I shook my head so hard I made myself dizzy. Sinclair jerked back enough so that the ends wouldn't tickle his face and laughed at my "No-no-no."

"The only thing marring its perfection was your absence, my own."

"Never. I told you. Never again. I'm not doing it ever again. It's dumb and it's cold. Horribly, horribly cold."

"It is enchanting," he corrected me, now mouthing the tender, shivery spot just behind my ear. "Horribly, horribly enchanting. I was enchanted."

"Are you drunk?" I asked, staring at the ceiling while the tips of his deep brown hair brushed the side of my jaw. "I know it's impossible but we've done the impossible before and it would explain a lot. I would actually wish you were drunk over what you were really doing. That's what a bad idea I think that is."

"The fairyland spectacle of the St. Paul Winter Carnival enchanted me."

"And also, your dick?" Because there was definitely something enchanting pressing against the top of my thigh.

"It was all so wonderful," he moaned, pressing a kiss to the hollow of my throat. "How could you resist the sensual allure of the Moon Glow Pedestrian Parade?"

"Pretty damned easily."

"Not to mention the Snow Slide."

"Sinclair, it's a carnival celebrating the fact that Mother Nature tries to kill us every winter. Why the hell would I ever—wait, Snow Slide?"

"They should rename it the Sublime Slide," he said and oh God I think he was serious.

"You went on the Snow Slide?" And why the *hell* wasn't I there with a camera? And a video crew? He was right, I should have gone if only to have the means to make a looping video of the vampire king riding down a hundred-foot snow slide over and over and over, maybe shoving various children out of the way as he repeatedly cut in line. Baring his fangs at their avenging mamas. Then up and down and up and down again. My kingdom for that gif. "Okay, you've made the impossible happen. Fine. But I still don't regret not going to the cold weird sleet rodeo, or whatever they're calling it this year."

"I also indulged in the Beer Dabbler. Did you know they have over a hundred and fifty breweries plying their wares?"

"But you hate beer."

"And they have a blood drive."

"But you love—aw, nuts." I groaned. "Tell me you stayed away from the blood drive taking place in the middle of the day at an outdoor carnival celebrating the things water does when it gets below freezing." In fairness to them, how could they expect a vampire to take over the Snow Slide, sip beer, and then rob their blood drive?

"Of course I refrained," he said, pulling back and looking

offended. "You know I only drink from you or ruffians we subdue."

"Okay, I know you're an old man, but really—ruffians?" I yelped as his sharp teeth grazed my neck and his tongue followed, soothing the sting.

"Ninety is the new thirty," was his muffled reply.

I snorted. "What this all boils down to is, ice sculptures make you horny."

"Well, yes," he admitted.

"I remember when *I* made you horny."

"An ice sculpture of you would satisfy all my sexual needs."

I laughed as I shivered; I couldn't help it. The mental image was just so hilarious and gross and cracked. "I hate you."

"In fact," he replied, lips ghosting over mine, "you adore me."

"I'm pretty sure I can do both."

"Did you know"—he pulled back and gazed down at me—"ice is much more beautiful in sunshine?" He said this in a low voice, a serious tone, like it was a delicious secret he wanted only me to know. "It's like light made solid."

*This. This right here. This is why. This is the answer to everything, every time.* "I love you." I sighed.

He smiled. "Yes." Then struck at viper speed, his fangs punching into my jugular. We both groaned, me because being penetrated in any way by Eric Sinclair was my favorite thing on earth, and him because the smell and taste of my blood was his favorite thing on earth.

*It is, oh it is, my darling, my Elizabeth.*

*Less thinking. More boning.*

*Ever the insatiable romantic.*

Here was a man, a brilliant, ruthless, dead man, who lost everything almost a century ago and spent decades alone as a result. Okay, that's not fair—Tina had never left his side. But she wasn't a true partner, more like a beloved aunt. She had been a friend of his family for generations; they had known what she was and gave not one shit. Along came yours truly, bitchy and pissed about being dead, with no interest in being Elizabeth, the One, and not just because the whole thing was just too, too *Matrix*.

*Dear Vampire Prophecy, every single movie about a Chosen One called, and they want their plot device back.*

To say I had been happy to make Eric Sinclair's acquaintance would be a bigger lie than *just the tip, just to see how it feels*. I had fought him every baby step of the way, even more so after he tricked me into making him king. Not that tricking me was ever a challenge. I still resented it, though, and it had taken a while to admit to myself I was in love with the controlling, ruthless asshat.

The ruthless jerkass had been patient. The ruthless asshat knew time was on his side.

So here we were, married in the eyes of vampires and, eventually, the State of Minnesota, boning on our superking in the late afternoon, winter sunshine splashed across the bed. I probably don't need to explain that the first thing Sinclair had done in our bedroom was rip all the curtains down.

He drank from me and divested me of my clothes at the same time, a good trick and one I'd had cause to celebrate before. I grabbed a fistful of that thick dark hair and jerked his head up, then bit him, hard, in the sweet spot just to the left of the hollow of his throat. Warm heavy blood trickled into my mouth, which should have been revolting and wasn't ever, not once. I think in a lot of ways that's the worst thing about being a vampire: I am doing things I know are disgusting and/or wrong and can't stop. Or won't stop.

His hand gently cupped my right breast, long fingers curving around the nipple while he buried his face in my hair (strawberry shampoo + Sinclair's love of fruit smoothies = irresistible) and trembled while I drank.

I pulled off and gasped (how many more years would I need to be dead before I stopped reflexively grabbing for oxygen?) while his thumbs stroked the undersides of my breasts.

Sinclair knew the undersides were much more sensitive and responsive, because he was a clever, clever man. I arched into his hands while fumbling with his—oh. Oh, that was good. That was *excellent*.

*How do you do that? How do you get both of us naked without me noticing?*

*I would tell you, but you have insisted that hearing of my decades of sexual conquests "like, totally squicks you out."*

*I have not! Okay, but I probably didn't lead with "like." Stop that. Stop laughing in my head.*

He didn't. Bastard. Thank goodness Sinclair was the only one I could hear in my head (vampire queen perk, except when it wasn't), because he was enough of a handful. Headful?

I reached down and found his lovely long length as he gently kneed my legs apart, his fingers slipping through the curls between my thighs, stroking so lightly it was more a brush of fingertips than anything else. And thank goodness, because the brush alone was enough to send me through the ceiling.

Sometimes we spent hours exploring each other, indulging in edge play until we were both shaking like we were enduring malaria relapses. And sometimes we didn't.

He slid into me with a sigh and I could actually feel my eyes roll into the back of my head, which, for reasons unknown to me, my husband found intensely erotic.

*Oh yes. Oh yes, ah, Elizabeth . . .*

*Mm-mm. I wanna drive.*

*?????*

I gripped him with my thighs and rolled us over until I was on top, which was fun on a superking and a potential for broken bones on a twin. Then I was grinning down at him while his hands slid down my back until resting just above my ass. He shifted beneath me and grinned back.

*Go on, then.*

*You bet.*

I rocked against him, slowly at first, adjusting to the

intensity, then leaned forward to grip the headboard and sped up. He'd thrown his head back, unconsciously (or not?) baring his throat, my bite already healing and his neck covered with drying blood. I ran a finger through the blood trail and he shuddered and flashed his fangs. I pressed one with the ball of my thumb and it pierced like a needle, that fast and that sharp. When he sucked, I felt it between my legs.

And speaking of between my legs, terrific things were happening there. Sinclair was quite tall, with big hands and big feet, and yep, that cliché, at least, was true. The former farm boy was *built*. This will sound hokey beyond belief, but it was like he was built just for me, only for me, and me for him and only for him, and no one and nothing else would ever be that suited to us.

He was gripping my hips hard enough to bruise and thrusting up, forcing a gasping moan out of me. I leaned forward far enough for his tongue to flick across my nipple, then jerked back.

*Wanton tease.*

*Was that wanton, or wonton? Are you craving Japanese food?*

*Chinese food, my lovely idiotic darling—ow!*

*More where that came from.*

*Oh, please yes.*

I smiled. "Now who's wanton?"

"It seems—it must—be me." Every pause was punctuated by a thrust and it was like feeling his cock in the middle of my chest. Which probably sounds awful but was pretty swell. I could feel my orgasm start to sneak up on me. With Sinclair, I often had stealth orgasms. It would feel far away, like I had to work a lot harder to reach it, and then all of a sudden . . . surprise! There it was.

"My God, my God, don't stop. Ah, God, Elizabeth. Look at you." Sinclair lived to break the third commandment, now that he could without feeling like he was gargling hydrochloric acid. "Look at you."

I ignored that; I could be doing him wearing a Hefty bag

and a baseball cap and he would find it insanely hot. Instead I focused on my stealth ninja orgasm, which was still pretending it was waaaay off in the distance. It reminded me of that scene from *Monty Python and the Holy Grail*, when Lancelot is running to the castle to kill pretty much everyone inside, and the guards watch him run and run, and he always seems far away, and then all of a sudden he and his sword are *right there*. Yep, I'm comparing my orgasms to a goddamned Monty Python movie. It makes sense that I'm dead. I *deserve* to be dead, what with all that going on in my head while having incredible sex with a sexy vampire king.

Speaking of the king, he was giving me a somewhat incredulous look, no doubt picking up on the Python weirdness going on in my brain.

*Are you—?*

*Never ask me. Never.*

He shrugged in my head (yep, that's a thing) and tightened his grip on my hips, which was fine with me. I leaned in again, let his mouth barely brush my nipple, and when I jerked back it pulled a groan from both of us. When I heard the creaking, I realized I was holding on to the headboard so hard I was tearing it loose. I didn't care, and Sinclair didn't care, and the headboard definitely didn't care, but it was a distraction. Let go or let loose?

I let loose—yanked the thing free and tossed it to the left. Probably should have thought that through a little more, since it took out the bedside lamp and the side table on its way to the floor. The crashing and thumping and broken glass worked like a hormone shot on Sinclair, and now I was riding him, brushing splinters out of his hair, *and* cornering my orgasm while he laughed and shook beneath me.

*. . . you are . . . you are . . . ah . . .*

*Oh, hush up.* I tried a scowl. It didn't take. He knew his laughter delighted me.

*Do not dare to stop.*

*Dude, I didn't let our antique cherry headboard stop this. Nothing short of a nuke dropped in the kitchen will stop this.*

*I loathe when you call me dude.*

*Don't care. Do. Not. C—*

Surprise!

*Nnnnn . . . ninja orgasm . . . ahhhh . . .*

*Oh yes oh God oh my Elizabeth oh—what? Did you—what?*

*( ) . . . ( )*

*Are you thinking about ninjas right now?*

"Shut up, coming, I'm still coming," I slurred, and his hands gripped, brutally tight, and then

*( ) . . . ( )*

he was, too. The timing was outstanding, because I could watch his face while I came down from mine, just as he rose to his. His eyes, which had been narrowed in concentration (and consternation, when he picked the Python out of my thoughts), now widened and his eyes rolled back. It was unfair, dammit, it was hot when *he* did it. When I did it, I suspected I looked like I was drunk off my ass or struggling with the *People* magazine crossword.

*Please. Please, my love, my all, please. Stop thinking. Right now.*

"Bossy," I gasped as he arched so hard only his head and heels were touching the mattress.

"Nnnnnfff," was his rebuttal. Pretty good, considering.

When he came back down, literally and figuratively, it was to tug at me until my face was tucked into the hollow of his shoulder while he stroked my back with hands that shook.

"C'n I start thinking now?"

"Dunno," he mumbled. "Would not dare assume—ouch!"

"More where that came from."

"So I devoutly hope," he replied, and I could hear the smile in his tone. He pinched me back, but I let it go. One of us had to be the mature one. A sad, sad day when it was me.

# CHAPTER
## SIX

**"So, about Jessica."**

Sinclair groaned. "Please. I never beg, unless it is for you, or to you, and I am begging now. Allow me to enjoy more than thirty seconds of postcoital bliss."

"We've got to talk about how you talk. 'Ruffians' and 'postcoital bliss' . . . I dunno. Sometimes I despair."

"As do I," he muttered, seizing my wrist before I could tickle him in the ribs. "Knowing you as I do, I have resigned myself to twenty-eight seconds of afterglow and . . ." He stared at the ceiling for a few seconds. "End afterglow. Proceed."

"How do you do that? You don't have a watch."

"Decades of needing to know precisely when the sun rises and sets has left me with an excellent sense of time." He brought my wrist to his mouth and kissed the underside, teasing the veins with his tongue for a second. "That is a skill it would be useful for you to learn."

"Don't start something you can't finish, tongue boy." I yawned. "And can't I master making lumpless gravy first?"

"Come now, you have escaped death, and Hell, and Jessica's wrath any number of times. You survived the Incident. You can do this," he said encouragingly. "What time is it? Look at the sunshine on the bed, look at the shadows, and tell me the time."

"How would I know?" I complained. "This place is like Vegas, there aren't any clocks." There really weren't. There was a creaky ancient grandfather clock on the main floor that hadn't worked for, hmm, when did we declare independence from England? Yeah. It had been awhile. Everyone had laptops and cell phones. I assumed millennials didn't actually know what a wall clock *was*.

Sinclair sighed. "Darling, you're a creature of the night—"

"Except when I'm a creature of the day."

"—and should at least pretend to be interested in things like sunrise, sunset, and—hmm, I had a third, and it escapes me—ah! Helping the Antichrist run Hell."

"That's it. I'm out." I sat bolt upright like Frankenstein's monster coming alive on the table and started to swing my legs over the side. "I don't have time to have this—unnff!"

Sinclair, the sneaky bastard, had snaked an arm around my waist and yanked me back before I could flee. "Stop wriggling. Are you frightened because you feel you must do this alone?"

*No, I'm frightened because it's fucking absurd I'm faced with this at all. Have any of you met me? This whole thing was ridiculous from inception.* I glared at the wall, since he had now spooned behind me and my glare of hate couldn't reach him. Too bad my glares of hate didn't ricochet. "I'm not frightened. Not exactly. Jeez. It's not like that."

"Because you know I stand ready to assist you in this, as in all things."

*I'll bet.*

I loved my husband, all right? I had killed and died for him.

But he was not the king of the vampires by accident. He had grown up poor and loved, and he'd started over after he asked Tina to kill him. He never wasted an opportunity and he never backed off; he was like a pit bull, he never dropped a bite.

Sinclair *did* want to help me, I knew that. But he also wanted to get his fingers into the smoking hot Hell pie. (Oh God. Terrible metaphor.) And there was a good chance he would give in to his dark side, his Fred Flintstone side, and try and take over the place. All the while determining it was for my own good and that he was doing it for love.

And he would have been. But. This was a man who forbade me to work. *Before* we were married. When I still loathed the sight of him. And then was mystified when I laughed my ass off. He was as modern a monarch as he knew how to be, but that didn't mean we both didn't still have some growing to do.

And something else—when did I turn into the mature, farseeing one? I didn't approve of *any* of this.

"I know you want to help," I said carefully, "but this is for Laura and me to figure out."

"Ah." He stayed relaxed behind me and pressed a kiss to the back of my neck. At least he wasn't hocking loogies into my hair. "And will you?"

"What?"

"Figure it out."

"The minute I find out what's wrong with Jessica and also plan Tina's surprise party."

He laughed. Sinclair didn't do the ha-ha laugh thing. It was more like a deep chuckle that rumbled through his chest. You felt it more than you heard it. "Oh, a surprise party, now? Yes, that will certainly eat up still more of your time."

I elbowed his arm off me and flopped over on my back and let his last comment go. "Something's wrong, and I couldn't get Jessica to tell me. And then she left again on another fake errand."

"Jessica has many errands, none of them fake so far as I know.

She keeps a close eye on her business," he said approvingly. "I would have offered her some investment advice, except I have the niggling sensation that she may have more money than I. But if you were concerned, why didn't you stop her?"

"Her bed ate me. And then you did."

He shuddered. "I cannot imagine the crippling back pain they must awaken with."

"Knock it off, farmer boy. We didn't all grow up sleeping on two-by-fours."

"Nor did I, but back support is a must."

"It really isn't, and come on! You could sleep on a bed of nails and wake up refreshed and ready to bang, and can we get back to my thing now?"

"You can only avoid this for so long."

"That's not the thing I wanted to get back to. And yeah. I know," I replied glumly.

"At the risk of boring you with observations I have repeatedly shared with you—"

"Oh boy. Really hate when you start sentences with that."

"—the longer you avoid your responsibilities, the more difficult it will be to perform them."

"I *know*." I did. But it was *so* hard to wrap my brain around. Five years ago I'd been an administrative assistant, avoiding my father and stepmother as needed and trying not to strangle colleagues who thought the sign on the copy machine

**(IF JAMMED DO NOT FIX YOURSELF! IF JAMMED FIND ME! I WILL KILL YOU IF YOU DO NOT OBEY! YOU WILL NOT BE MOURNED! THE COPY MACHINE PEOPLE HAVE QUIT SENDING PEOPLE TO FIX IT!)**

didn't apply to *them*, oh, *hell* no.

Now I was dead and a reigning monarch, happily married (a huge improvement over resentfully married), with a houseful of friends and family, fending off death threats and resigned to living through the next several centuries with highlights *and* lowlights. Oh, and I was supposed to help run a dimension that was an afterlife of never-ending torment for billions.

In over my head didn't begin to cover it. In over my head wasn't even on the same planet as my new responsibilities. The same universe. The same galaxy! Wait, which one was bigger, galaxy or univ—never mind. My point: the whole thing was fucking *ludicrous*.

"I can't tell if I need your help yet," I finally said, breaking the long silence. "But if I figure out that I do, I promise to come get you."

He shifted, and I knew he hadn't gotten what he'd wanted. But I also knew that he was content to wait for me to ask. In this, we were well matched, since I normally had the patience of a toddler hopped up on Oreos, while Sinclair had the patience of a trap-door spider: *Come on over, take your time. You know I'll get you eventually.*

That shouldn't have been comforting, but it was.

# CHAPTER
# SEVEN

***"How did your father die?"***

Of all the ways I imagined Jessica would start, that wasn't anywhere on the list.

I'd finally pinned her down, and the usual list of suspects was in the kitchen, enjoying a postsmoothie afterglow. It was just short of midnight, all the babies (Fur, Burr, Thing One, Thing Two, BabyJon) were miraculously asleep, and the adults—dead and alive—were awake.

She'd wriggled on the hook, Jessica had, which told me that I should go ice fishing with my mom pretty soon. I hadn't been in years, but we used to go all the time. I hadn't thought I'd missed it so much, but fishing metaphors only cropped up when I was craving something fresh-caught, or Mom's company, or her ice house. Since I had zero interest in a salmon smoothie, and the only time I saw Mom lately was when I was dropping off BabyJon, or she was, clearly it was past time for mother-daughter time.

Also, my mom's ice house was terrific. It was red and white, shaped and painted to look like a tiny barn, and heated with propane. She could haul it onto the lake with a ball hitch and her Ford Escape; took about a half hour to get everything set up. Inside there was room for three; a Coleman stove for soup, cocoa, and mulled wine; four rods with rattle reels—the good ones, with the wide spools—the drill, scoops, and nets; and a padded chest for sitting, filled with blankets, hats, and extra gloves. It could be ten below, and we'd be toasty inside, sipping cocoa and watching bobbers, and when I got bored I could go out into the temp village and see what was what.

See, that was the best thing about ice fishing, the way a temporary town would pop up almost overnight. I always found it fascinating that Lake Mille Lacs (and other cold places, probably, I dunno, I'm not a geographer), while great for boating in the summer, took on an entirely new identity in the winter, sprouting towns of ice houses. So you had neighbors, and you saw the same people every season, but only for a couple of months or so. And when spring started to get close, the village gradually disappeared until there was nothing left to mark its passage besides tire tracks and iced-over holes.

And then for all of spring and summer and fall, the lake was just a lake. It wasn't a community, and no one had much interest in getting to know the tourists. And then winter would come back, and . . . and it would be a town again.

The only drawback was the way the ice tended to settle, sometimes with a shudder, and you remembered that this was a hobby that could kill you. But the same is true of bowling, so live dangerously, dammit! Embrace life!

(Was all that a metaphor for something? I hoped not. Unless it was a metaphor for how much I missed ice fishing. In which case, it was pretty perfect.)

Anyway. Back to Jessica. Cornering her had been tricky, mostly for the reasons I was complaining about earlier, to wit: it's not nice to brain-rape your best friend and force her to

vomit up all her secrets. But if she wasn't avoiding me out-
right, she was physically absent from the mansion, doing who-
knew-what. DadDick professed to know nothing, and since I
figured he was running on about four hours of sleep on a good
night, I believed him. It was possible DadDick didn't know
his own middle name.

But at last she fell into my clutches and could not escape.
I knew this because when I walked into the kitchen for midnight smoothies, she was waiting and greeted me with, "I have
to talk to you. Right now." Ha! She should have known she
couldn't escape my grasp for long.

And she'd started with asking me how Dad had died. Like
she didn't know. Like *I* didn't know.

More worrisome, the others—had she called a meeting?
sent out a memo?—were watching me like it was an ordinary
question, up there with "Are we friggin' out of ice *again*? It's
Minnesota in winter! Is it some kind of ironic joke? Is anybody
listening to me?"

I gaped for a few seconds and fumbled for the answer that,
to me—and I assumed to them—was obvious. "I—you know.
You know what happened, you all know what happened." I
looked around the butcher-block table at all of them. Jessica
and DadDick looked tense, but they were new parents, so natch.
Tina looked politely curious, but that was her default expression. Marc was wide-eyed, but he was always up for family
gossip of any sort, or anything that would engage his interest
and thus stop his rotting. DadDick was on Jessica's left, idly
scraping at what looked like a pureed peach stain on his T-shirt.
And Sinclair, immaculate in Armani gray, was on my left and
watching Jess with an unblinking gaze. He was in socks, his
concession to the late hour and informal setting.

"Dad and the Ant were in a car accident," I continued,
wondering why I was explaining stuff they all knew. "He got
the gas mixed up with the brake—I inherited his brains, so
I get how that happened—and plowed into the back of a

garbage truck. You"—pointing to Jess—"you were in the hospital, and you"—to Sinclair—"you'd been kidnapped; my badass vampire husband was overpowered by a little-old-lady librarian."

"Not that little," Sinclair muttered, the memory still rankling.

It had been a terrible time. Like, Black Death terrible. My father and stepmother were dead in a silly accident, and their double funeral had been held where mine would have been, earlier, if I, as the "corpse," hadn't woken up pissed and vamoosed. (Wait. Since I was literally a corpse, the quotation marks might not be necessary.) Being back in that funeral home had been awful beyond belief. I could still see their poster-sized pictures at the front of the room, Dad with his vacant country club grin and the Ant looking like a blond piranha, pineapple-colored hair standing tall. And I was pretty sure her eyes followed me. There was no escaping that poster.

No coffins, by the way. No chance. The bodies had been burned beyond recognition. I thought about my father, weak and nonconfrontational to the end, and my stepmother, Antonia, who threw his money at charities so she could plan balls and be the prom queen all over again. My return from the dead had horrified both of them. Their deaths had left me feeling bad that I didn't feel bad.

Jessica had been battling cancer from a hospital bed, a tormented DadDick (except he was Nick then—this was before I screwed up the timeline—he was Nick and he hated me almost as much as he feared me, and he was right to do both) only occasionally leaving her side to arrest bad guys.

Tina had been out of the country, making sure the European vampire faction—who had come to town to wreak havoc and went out on the toes of my Manolos and Sinclair's Louis Vuittons—were playing nice across the pond.

My mother hadn't gone to the funeral, and not just for obvious reasons. The accident had orphaned BabyJon, my father's son by the Ant. I didn't know it at the time, but BabyJon was about to become my son as well as my half brother. The accident made me his legal guardian, courtesy of my wish for a baby of my own, granted by my cursed engagement ring. It had been a monkey's paw deal. Fucking antiques.

Sinclair had also been nowhere to be found. Vanished. I didn't know it at the time, but he'd been kidnapped by a librarian; I thought he'd bailed on our wedding. Marjorie, the librarian, had been a tremendous pain in my ass, and killing her had been kind of fun. The blood rush I got from slurping down her life force like it was a blood-stuffed cream puff helped me cure Jessica of her blood cancer. Yeah, I know, but at the time it all made sense. Don't ask me to do any of it again; I don't even know how I managed it the first time. It was a perfect storm of supernatural nutjobbery.

Oh, almost forgot—when all that awfulness was going on, I was also planning my wedding. So, stressful.

To sum up: worst time of my life, and I was essentially alone for all of it.[1]

"No coffins, though, right?" Jessica asked carefully.

I barely heard her. I should have been paying attention, I knew that, but now that I'd started thinking about that dreadful month it blotted out everything else: unnamed babies, avoiding the Hell work-study program, Sinclair's new terrible habit of playing in traffic . . . gone. It was all gone.

Instead I remembered the eerie double funeral. I remembered feeling guilty because I wasn't sad. I remembered feeling completely alone and it had nothing to do with their deaths and more to do with the sick friend and absentee husband.

I had confused and annoyed my father before I died; I had

---

[1] All the gory details and then some can be found in *Undead and Uneasy*.

horrified him after. And try as I might, that was all I really remembered of him: his confusion, his dismay. His horror.

"The bodies," I said, "had been burned beyond recognition."

"Oh."

"But it was her, and it was their car, and it was him. I mean, they had their IDs—mostly melted but good enough for identification—and the cops traced the car registration and they were on their way to a thing they were known to go to."

"A thing?" Marc asked.

"Some charity something or other." I waved off the specifics. One of the Ant's "look at me, I *didn't* peak in high school and this latest gaudy party proves it!" balls, most likely. (A *ball*, for God's sake, like she was Cinderella and my dad was a balding prince prone to indigestion if he had too much dairy.) They could have been on their way to shave kangaroos for all I'd known; it didn't matter. They were on their way, they never made it, the end. "So . . ."

Marc was leaning in, concern writ large in his green eyes. "Are you all right?"

"Hmm?" *Betsy your father can't make it Betsy your father is stuck out of town Betsy your father had to miss it Betsy your father loves you he's just very busy Betsy your father is moving out Betsy of course it's not your fault Betsy I'll keep your father's name but I won't touch his money Betsy we don't need it Betsy your father your father your father your father . . .* "Sure." I had to make a concerted effort to be an active participant in the conversation. In older movies, the heroine can often rely on someone to slap her, or at least shake her, to get her to focus

*(PAY THE FUCK ATTENTION, YOU DIMWIT, THIS IS IMPORTANT)*

but I preferred to skip the middleman and shake my own shoulders, metaphorically speaking.

"Right!" Jessica visibly jumped, Tina's eyes widened, and Sinclair arched an eyebrow. That came out a bit louder than I'd intended. "Uh, right. The whole thing was such a cliché it was pretty absurd. Which is not something you should think when a parent dies, I know.

"Anyway, it was his midlife crisis—I think it was my dad's third Jaguar and second midlife crisis—meets garbage truck equals kaboom. They had those urn things at the front of the room, with the posters sort of looming over them. Over all of us, now that I think about it." I tried, and failed, to suppress the shudder. "No graves, no headstones." Which was hilarious in a really awful way. I had a headstone and here I was. They didn't, and they were gone, baby, gone.

"And a few days after that, you saw the Ant's ghost, right?"

"While Sinclair and I were having sex," I recalled glumly as my husband let loose with an almost imperceptible shiver. Whatever the female equivalent of losing an erection was, that was what happened to my junk when the Ant showed up: my lady parts had Closed Until Further Notice. Seeing ghosts was another vampire queen "perk," and yes, those are ironic quotation marks.

"But not your dad."

"What?"

"Never your dad. You haven't seen your dad's ghost." She was speaking with a peculiar intensity, practically pinning me in place with her bloodshot gaze.

I could finally see where she was going and wasted no time reassuring her. "Well, no, but there are trillions of dead people, and I haven't seen all their ghosts, either." Either because they had the good manners to leave me the hell alone, or they couldn't find me or didn't need me.

I was fine with any of those, by the way. The ghosts who did find me wanted something. They always wanted something. Sometimes it was easy. ("Yeah, you don't know me, but your dead wife moved the money you embezzled to the Caymans, and also, she says everybody knows you're wearing a rug and you should stop kidding yourself.") Sometimes not so much. ("I don't care how many mailmen you killed! I'm not going around to their next of kin and bitching about how it was society's fault that you ended up with a hate-on toward the U.S. Postal Service.")

Frankly, I was *glad* my dad hadn't popped by to ask for a favor. And not surprised. My dad hadn't exactly been known to seek out my company. I figured, in death, wherever he was, he kept the habit.

"And you didn't see him in Hell."

"Yes, but again, that's not a clue or anything." Why was Jessica not letting up the intensity? I felt like I was sitting in the witness box on trial, which made her Sam Waterston, except her under-eye circles were darker. "I wasn't in Hell very long and, again: trillions of dead people." Whom I was successfully ignoring so far, thank God.

"Yeah. Mm-hm."

I looked at her. Everyone else looked, too. Then they all looked at me, with various degrees of "what now?" expressions. My answer wouldn't have reassured them ("I got nothin'. Maybe another round of smoothies? Take the edge off?").

Jessica cleared her throat, so we were expectant. But she didn't say anything, so we went back to the waiting game. I saw Tina sneak a look at her cell phone, which made me wonder how long we'd been there, how long we'd have to stay there, and what time it was. Which Sinclair picked up on, because he looked annoyingly smug as he pointedly did *not* look at his phone while no doubt calculating the time to the nanosecond. Asshole.

She cleared her throat again, because she apparently wanted to meet with us so we could listen to the phlegm follies. "The thing is, I saw your dad three days ago."

Jessica had spit that out so abruptly we all sort of froze. My mouth opened, but nothing came out. It opened again—dammit, I had to come up with something, this butcher block needed a leader!—and I managed to squeak, "The hell? What?"

"Your dad. I saw him downtown on my way to meet my

accountant." I nodded, more at the accountant thing than the dad thing. And if it was a money meeting, she meant downtown St. Paul. Jessica was rich, but not idle. She was careful with her money and demanded accountability from accountants, and everyone else who worked for her, or for her money. DadDick loved this, and after the twins were born he encouraged her to get out of the house as often as she could, though these days she could keep tabs on her money gang from her laptop and cell phone. All that to say she tended to her business and her bucks, which was nothing new to me.

Seeing my dead father, however, was.

## CHAPTER
# EIGHT

*"Jess, I love you, but that's nuts. My dad's dead. You couldn't* have seen him."

Marc coughed. "Ah, that doesn't exactly mean . . . well . . . anything. Not around here."

He had a point, which didn't make Jessica correct. But yeah, I'd noticed death wasn't really . . . you know . . . *death.* More like a time-out from God, who eventually relented and let you back in the game. God: the original tough love.

It did make me wonder if Satan was going to pop up again, though. If anyone would come back from death solely to cause trouble, it'd be the Lady of Lies. Sure, she talked a good game about being sick of existence, about having the first and most thankless job (apparently not prostitution) in the history of human events and needing a permanent vacation, about being burned out because Hell had a shit HMO and no paid vacations. But in spite of all that, I couldn't picture her staying off the checkers board. Not for long, anyway.

(I don't know how to play chess, so I am reduced to checkers metaphors.)

"I did see him, though." Jessica took a breath, then slowly let it out. "And he saw me."

"No." I felt my irritation rise and squashed it. "He didn't. D'you know how I know this?"

"Maybe just let her finish?" Marc suggested. "And then start shooting her down?"

I ignored the crazy talk from the zombie. "I know this because my dad was an ordinary guy whose idea of excitement was cheating on my mom and bringing a doggy bag to Country Buffet so the last trip up all went for next day's lunch. That's the guy who got into a dumb accident—the kind that happens every day—and was killed and is now dead and has remained dead all this time. It's not a mystery. It's not a conspiracy. It's nothing we have to jump into and fix."

"Really?" DadDick asked, genuine surprise in his voice. "I kinda thought you'd be all over this." Marc was nodding as he continued. "It's just the thing to keep Laura off your—"

"Do *not* bring Laura into this," I snapped. "Not a word of it."

"Your dad saw me," Jess continued, like I hadn't just explained she'd seen something impossible and was therefore wrong and, frankly, owed me an apology for freaking me out and wasting everyone's time. And, ah, God, if the Antichrist caught wind of this . . . "Our eyes met—"

"Across a crowded room," Marc hummed.

"Yes, shut up now, our eyes met and when he recognized me he took off in the other direction. Flat-out jogged away from me."

Okay, that *did* sound like my dad, an Olympian-level avoider. And it wouldn't have been the first time he physically fled from confrontation. It wouldn't have been the first time he physically fled from Jessica. But of course it wasn't Dad. Because, as I previously mentioned: *dead.*

*(Except not really, not in this house, not with this group, and it's pretty plausible if you just stop and think about it for—)*

"Shut *up*!" I looked around the table of startled faces. "Sorry. If it helps, I wasn't talking to any of you."

"It *does* help," DadDick said, stifling a yawn. "Thank you."

"So." Jess took a deep breath. Don't know what she was all stressed and twitchy about; I was the one dealing with her hallucination. "Having known your father as long as I've known you, so, for almost two decades—"

Marc grinned. "Thanks for doing the math for us."

"We need a chart of some kind, something that shows at a glance who has known who for how long and under what circumstances."

"On it." Marc whipped out his phone and tapped it. His to-do list was horrifying, starting with the name: *Things to Do So I Don't Rot.*

"—I knew who he was and what he was doing and went after him."

Heh. The idea of Jessica barreling down the streets of downtown St. Paul as my dad frantically backpedaled to get the hell away from her was several layers of hilarious. All the more so because, as I mentioned, it wasn't the first time. When she found out he blew off my eighteenth birthday to take the Ant to Cancún, she chased him through the Mall of America food court, screaming as he scurried. People called the cops. They were both banned for a year. Jessica dated one of the cops who arrested her, for three months. It was the best birthday ever. There's been a special place in my heart for Orange Juliuses ever since.

"He got away," Jess was continuing in a voice heavy with regret. I was still lost in the fog of nostalgia and barely heard her explanation. "He must've zigged when I zagged or whatever. So I went to see your mom. For real this time."

Poof. Nostalgia fog burned off in a half second. "You had

a hallucination from sleep deprivation and decided to get my mom involved?" I asked sharply.

"I thought she'd have some ideas," she replied. I couldn't help but notice she had yet to apologize for anything. "And she did. She had no idea what he was up to—she assumed he's been dead this whole time, just like we did—so she suggested we ask the person who would know."

"No."

"It'd be easy."

*Tread carefully, my own.*

I ignored the voice in my head. A well-adjusted, confident, kinder woman might have had trouble shutting Sinclair out, but I had years of practice long before I formed a telepathic link with a vampire. "Wrong. Still no."

She leaned in and reached for my hand but, as I was invested in being a grumpy bitch, I pulled it back before she could grab me with her long, bony, spidery fingers. She still needed a mani, but she had time to go bug my mom? "Betsy, I know it's awful to contemplate, but don't you want to know? For certain?"

"I do know. He's dead. This isn't a mystery, Nancy Drew."

*Elizabeth. Please. Consider your words.*

*No sale, big buy, and quit nagging in my head.*

"You made a mistake, it's understandable, you're exhausted." I decided to quit waiting for apologies. I could take the high road for once. I guess. Probably. "We're just gonna pretend we never had this talk."

"Are we going to pretend we never had smoothies, too?" Marc asked. "Because then we could just make more."

Jess let loose with an annoyed snort. "Look, I get that your default is to turn a blind eye toward this stuff, just like Marc's is to make jokes when he knows people are getting uncomfortable—"

"It's true," Marc said, nodding. "That's what I do. It's practically a compulsion."

"In your case, it's a defense mechanism you'd perfected by the time you were in high school—"

"Do *not*," I warned, "try to psychoanalyze me. Not unless you want some right back."

*Elizabeth.*

"You run away from everything. You're still running. I don't think you should, this time."

"*Not* your call." God, this was turning into a vampire-friendly After School Special. "Jess, you're telling us you've been scurrying around behind my back with this crap for the last three days?"

"I wanted to help you," she said in a low voice.

"Wrong. This is about you—how your life has changed and how it scares the shit out of you."

*Elizabeth.*

*No, I'm on to something here. Tina and I were just talking about how everyone's life has changed in next to no time. This is part of it and proves she's wrong and be quiet in my brain now!*

"You have DadDick in this timeline, you're a mom, for God's sake, but part of you thinks it's not going to last. Part of you almost wants to make sure it doesn't last. You can't focus on that, that's the really scary stuff, which, for somebody who lives with a bunch of movie monsters, is actually pretty impressive. So you're gonna focus on this to avoid facing your new responsibilities."

*ELIZABETH.* The internal shout made me wince.

"I'm *what?*" The external shout also made me wince. I wasn't alone this time, either; Jessica's voice went so high all three of the vampires cringed. In the mudroom a few feet away, Fur and Burr woke and started yapping. Dogs all over the block were probably yapping. "What the fuck did you just say to me?" She'd leaped to her feet so quickly I barely registered the movement. I guess sleep deprivation sped up her reflexes. Or rage did. "You of all people? Accusing me of dodging responsibility, you silly bitch?"

"Proof!" I shouted, pointing a shaky finger at her. "Proof I'm right, you—you haven't even named your spawn! Even after the . . . uh . . . the Incident."

Oh God, the Incident. I couldn't believe I'd brought it up. A measure of my desperation or evidence of suicidal ideation.

Look, bottom line, nobody got hurt. That's what people keep overlooking.

# CHAPTER
# NINE

THE INCIDENT

***I beat Jessica to the basement with minutes to spare, and***
thank goodness; I needed every second. I was in such a rush
to get away from her avenging fingernails I nearly tripped on
the step and flopped down the stairs. But our dank, dark
basement, with the crumbling cement, stained floor, and cob-
webs making it look like a scary movie set, was going to be
my sweet haven. The gross, filthy place had multiple exits.

*Oh, basement, I've been wrong about you all this time and will*
*start making amends right now. Thank you for saving me! I promise*
*to find a mop and wipe the floors. Or something. Nothing's too good*
*for you, basement, my dearest friend and finest ally.*

"What's going on up there?"

I screamed and nearly fell down the stairs for the second
time. I'd been so terrified I hadn't realized I wasn't alone. Marc
was blinking up at me, wearing smudged scrubs and snapping
off rubber gloves.

"I banned you from the basement!"

"Yeah, I know."

"Remember the Igor conversation?"

"Sure." My zombie pal was supremely unconcerned. He nearly yawned. Once again, I had to think that the people I really wanted to intimidate with the vampire-queen thing never were.

"I'll deal with your insubordination later."

"Ooh, very Bond villain," he said approvingly.

"You could at least pretend to be intimidated," I muttered.

"I could," he replied with a cheerful grin, "but I don't think I could pull it off. Actually I'm glad to see you. I wanted to talk to you."

"Later." I hurried down and resisted the urge to tackle him out of my way. "Gotta go, please shove over. I mean it, Marc, *move.*"

He stepped back while shaking his head. "What? You didn't burst in here to bust me for Igoring in the basement, so what the hell did you do now?"

"Oh, that's nice! Blame the victim."

"You are the polar opposite of a victim."

"Thanks?" *I have no idea how to take that.*

"Betsy, what did you do?"

"Tried to help! That's all I ever do, because I am a considerate roommate and hardly ever complain that Mustard and Ketchup have basically stolen my best friend."

"You constantly complain about that. I think Mustard and Ketchup are your worst names so far. Just confess and maybe I'll take it easy on you. I can't promise anything about Jessica, though."

"It wouldn't have hurt them." I sulked. Gawd, new mothers. So freaking paranoid. "It would have been a huge time saver. And it would have made my life easier, so I never did get what the problem was."

"Wait." Horrid suspicion was dawning on Marc's face. "Is— no. It can't—not even you would—is that why you were looking for a Sharpie a couple of hours ago?" Before I could answer he plunged ahead, mouth full of damnation to heap on my highlights. "You were gonna write 'Ketchup' and 'Mustard' on the babies' foreheads with a Sharpie?"

"No, I was gonna write 'Coke' and 'Pepsi' on their foreheads with a Sharpie. A scented Sharpie," I added, "for which, *again*, nobody bothered to thank me. Those two can get pretty ripe. Every little bit helps. Do they make deodorant for babies?"

"Deo—I—you—" He shook his head. "No, I can't let myself get distracted by your dumb questions. I've got to stay focused. Let's face it, just come out and admit it: you wanted to brand the babies."

"*Label* the babies." How could I be the only person on board with this terrific plan? "Don't even pretend you can tell them apart. Jess and Dick say they can, but I'm pretty sure they're just trying not to look dumb."

"Yeah, because that's their biggest problem right now. Not looking dumb. Not crazy vampire queens scribbling on their babies with scented markers."

"Marker, singular." And strawberry scented, which I didn't add because nobody appreciated me.

"I should haul your dim ass up those stairs and hand you over, you twit!"

"Yet another betrayal," I sniffed. We'd been hurrying through the basement while I figured which exit would keep me free of knife wounds the longest. "What a surprise. That'll teach me to stick my neck out."

"Stick it out much further, Jess will slash through it."

"That's the truth," I muttered.

Believe it or not (and I wouldn't have, if I hadn't seen it; the absurdity was immense), at the far end of the basement was a door, a door that led to a secret tunnel connecting our basement to the river. Sure, it was five below out and I had little interest in hanging riverside in subzero weather, but that would be a Caribbean vacation compared to what Jessica had in store for me.

"I'm gonna have to sleep out there, aren't I?" I muttered aloud, asking but not really.

"Oh yeah," my heartless zombie replied. "At least overnight. And it's so stupid, Betsy. You're so stupid."

"I'm what?" Jesus! How many insults was I gonna have to take this week? "Marc! You know Sinclair made you promise to stop pointing out my intense dumbness."

"Yeah, but when you use words like 'dumbness' and scurry around scribbling on babies, you make it impossible. And if you'd quit avoiding Laura, if you'd quit lurking in the mansion desperate for distractions to keep you out of Hell, the babies would be (relatively) safe and we could be in Hell right now, getting a tour or figuring out a new chamber of horrors or cornering Ferdinand and Isabella and asking them to defend the Spanish Inquisition."

"All of those things sound terrible. And what do you mean, 'we'? Aw, no. Come on, Marc. Not you, too." Why was everyone so fascinated with my new part-time job? Why did they think co-running Hell was something I should jump on right away and bring them along for the ride? Were they all crazy? It was *Hell*. What about any of it meant super cool road trip? "You can't mean it."

"I absolutely mean it, you dope!" he shouted, which I found startling. Not the dope thing; we both knew he was smarter than me. But Marc didn't raise his voice often, so when he did, I paid attention. As much as I ever paid attention to anything. "Don't pretend you don't know why."

"Marc: I absolutely do not know why. Where's that secret lever? God, that's not a sentence I thought I'd have to say twice in three years."

"Betseeeeey," the zombie lurking in the gloom with me whined, "boooored."

"Shut up," I snapped, drawing on my vast reserves of

patience. Anyone overhearing this would assume we weren't friends and possibly were plotting each other's murder. "Or the next time you kill yourself to avoid turning into Future Psycho Asshat Marc, I won't accidentally reanimate your corpse."

"No, press lower."

I jabbed irritably at the fourth brick down in the wall.

"*Lower.* It means the opposite of higher."

"I *am*, it's not—oh." There was a distinct *clack!* and the super-duper secret hidden doorway swung back, revealing a tunnel filled with overhead lights automatically flicking on even as we stared. "Ta-da!"

"Yeah, you eventually followed directions, good work, Bets. But like I was saying. Bored. Bored, bored, bored. I'm ready to shoot a wall, here."

"No more BBC *Sherlock* for you," I warned, which was the biggest bluff since "no smoothies for me, I'm getting sick of them." Marc and I were tremendous Cumberbimbos, long may Benedict Cumberbatch reign. The glorious velvet-voiced bastard had even gotten me hooked on *Star Trek* movies. Benedict, not Marc. Marc's voice was perfectly nice but he was no CumberBetsy. And for a *Star Trek* reboot (I'm not a fan of the genre) it was pretty good. Way too much screen time for Spock and Kirk, but I was used to suffering for my crushes. I'm embarrassed to say how often I've contemplated biting my Cumbercookie. Turning him, even. Then he would be mine! Forever and ever, his velvety voice and long neck and long legs would be mine and we would rule the world!

Um, but those kinds of thoughts were not good, and Sinclair was likely to kick up a fuss, so thus far I had resisted the sweet, sweet lure of BenBatch's sweet, sweet neck. His throat was a foot long, for God's sake! The man was made to be chewed on!

"You know what happens when I'm bored," Marc, the eternally nagging zombie, was saying as we gazed down the tunnel. It was chilly. It led to the frozen river. I had zero interest in venturing down there, but less in being stabbed.

And yeah. I did know. Marc had zero interest in eating brains, but his own brain needed constant stimulation or he'd be a walking corpse for real. Right now he looked fine—very fine; I'd always thought he was super cute—and as he had killed himself with an overdose, his body had no grotesque wounds. He had no real scent, either, whereas before he'd smelled like clean laundry, dried blood, hair product, and Mennen Speed Stick. As a zombie living in close proximity with the vampire who (kinda) raised him,[2] he smelled like a piece of paper. Not offensive, but not especially memorable, either. As long as he hung out with me, he'd appear so recently dead—really recently, like, thirty seconds dead—as to seem alive.

That changed when he couldn't keep his mind busy with puzzles, experiments, marathon TV sessions, smoothie sessions, animal autopsies, and puzzles. He once spent a week working a fifty-dollar jigsaw puzzle that was just a pile of Dalmatian puppies. Plus the thing had been cut from two sides, not just the top, making it really hard to figure which end was up. And it had the same picture of a zillion Dalmatians on the back, tilted ninety degrees. I took one look and fled. For days every time any of us closed our eyes all we could see were black-and-white puzzle pieces. The horror. The migraines. You can't imagine.

All this because, as a zombie, my personal zombie (not a title I ever thought I'd assign anyone I knew, ever), Marc craved brains—his own. He needed to stay sharp. Boredom and ennui sped up the rot. He refused to be a doctor anymore, not trusting the occasional stiffening of his joints if he wasn't getting enough stimulation, so he referred to himself as a kind of supermedic.

I had to admit, I had nothing but admiration for how he

---

[2] Gory details—and they're plenty gory—can be found in *Undead and Unfinished*.

was dealing. I hadn't done half so well. Sometimes I worried I still wasn't.

"I don't think taking you to Hell will help your zombie-ness," I said, appalled. Truthfully I had no idea what Hell would do to him. And no interest in experimenting with him to find out. At all. No.

"Yeah, but it couldn't hurt, and you kill a couple of birds with the same rock."

"Marc, okay, first—gross. Second, I don't even know how I would get you there. I *just* learned to get myself there—and back, but that was after wandering around the place for what felt like *weeks*. What if I can't get you there? Worse, what if I can, but can't get you back?"

"My risk," he replied firmly.

"Too big of one," I said, just as firm.

"I'll sign a waiver."

"I'm not giving you a waiver to sign, you zombified crazy person! We're going to forget we had this conversation."

"Mm-mm." He was looking at me with his usual focus, as if I were a disease he'd just diagnosed. Which maybe wasn't that far off—it was my fault he was a zombie, after all. Just like how in the old timeline, it had been my fault he had become the thing in everyone's nightmares, the monster under all the beds. Just thinking of it made me want to vomit. "You say that a lot. And it never works."

"Look, we need to talk about this later. I have to . . . oh." I'd started to take a step down the hallway and froze. "Oh God."

He cocked his head but couldn't hear what I did, and even I had barely caught it. Footsteps racing up to the door I'd almost fallen through. Footsteps that abruptly stopped. "Fine! You *stay* down there!" The door shivered in its frame as Jessica unleashed a wood-splintering frenzy. "You stay down there until you die again! Idiot! Pull that Sharpie shit again and I will beat you until candy comes out!"

Lovely, just what I needed, a new title: Betsy Taylor, Undead Piñata. Much better than Betsy Taylor, Registered Republican. I sloooowly relaxed as I heard the footsteps retreat, then turned back to Marc. "So. You want a field trip to Hell, huh?"

"In so many words, yup."

"We never talk anymore."

"We talk constantly." He was grinning at me and easing the door to the tunnel closed. He knew I wasn't river-bound, not anymore. He also knew I was trapped like a rat.

"Still. I've neglected you. Let's catch up."

"Because you know you're stuck down here for hours."

" 'Stuck,' oh, Marc, that hurts!" I put every ounce of whiny hurt into my tone that I could. "Why would you want to hurt me?"

"So. Many. Reasons."

"I'm thrilled to be in this cement-lined, dusty, spider-infested shithole with you." I slung an arm across his shoulders, turned him around, and started walking him back to the other end. "So! How's the dating going?"

"Fine until we get to the 'I'm a Virgo,' 'Hey, neat, I'm a zombie' part."

"Superficial men." I shook my head. "What's the world coming to?"

He laughed at me, but that was fine. I had it coming.

# CHAPTER
# TEN

**"Do you even know how many harmful chemicals lurk inside** the average Sharpie?" Jess was raging, physically restrained by DadDick, who looked a) wide awake and b) like he wished he was anywhere else.

"Not the scented ones," I whined. "Is it more than three? It's probably more than three chemicals."

"Oh good God." Sinclair had his eyes closed as he pinched the bridge of his nose. "Madness reigns." Then, at Tina's near-imperceptible flinch, he added in a mutter, "Apologies." She shrugged and smiled; she loved—as he did—that these days he could break commandments with impunity and still be welcome at church. A lesson for all of us! Or something.

"And excuse me for wanting you to get on the stick and name your babies already. Pretty soon they'll be in kindergarten and when the teacher asks their name they'll be all 'sorry, Mom hasn't filled out that paperwork yet.' "

"Pretty soon?" she snarled. "That's five years away, asshat."

"No!" I was on my feet, too, and as I stepped forward Sinclair's hand closed over my biceps and he gave a not-especially-gentle yank backward. "That is *my* word. You're not allowed to use that word. Take it back!"

The State of Minnesota, it must be said, was disturbingly laid-back about naming babies. I guess they figured that the mom in question had just squeezed a human (in Jessica's case, two of the li'l suckers) out of her body, so maybe cut her some slack on paperwork?

The babies had to be *registered* within five days, not necessarily named. And all the naming chaos aside, the question I couldn't avoid: registered for *what*? *Register* is a noun and a verb: we sign guest registers, we register for wedding gifts and domain names, we register cars and boats, we register to vote and when we hit a mountain summit . . . and now we register babies, I guess? Good God, for *what*? What weird creepy thing did they need a statewide baby register for?

Anyway, if you register the babies but haven't named them within those five days, Baby Girl Berry and Baby Boy Berry were the names that went on the dotted line. Jess and Nick then had forty-five days to change Baby Boy and Baby Girl to *anything*, for the love of God, just pick *something*! If they waited longer than forty-five days, they had to pay extra.

Needless to say, Jess and DadDick didn't give a tin shit about what they had to pay. Also, when had I become surrounded almost entirely by millionaires? That was troubling, because it meant I was the white trash of the mansion. Hell, the neighborhood; this was Summit Avenue in St. Paul. The governor's mansion was across the street! How had I let that happen?

Anyway, it had been weeks and the babies were still Frick and Frack. Or whatever we were calling them that day. Salt and Pepper hadn't gone over well, probably because of the whole biracial thing. Sprite and 7-Up were greeted with derision bordering on rage. The reaction to Rocky and Bullwinkle will never be spoken of again, though DadDick did take me aside to quietly mention he thought Batman and Robin were the best so far. My faves: little Manolo and little Blahnik.

"Are we fighting about your hallucination, you bugging my mom for no reason, Sharpie ink, or how much you hate government paperwork?" I asked, trying and failing to wrest myself from Sinclair's clawlike grip. The man hung on like a velociraptor. "Because with all the yelling I can't deny I might have lost track! Which makes me even madder!"

"We're talking about deflection as it relates to the modern vampire queen." Marc, piping up helpfully, got a double glare from Jess and me.

"No, we're talking about how Betsy puts the dumb in dumbass," Jessica snapped.

"That doesn't even make sense!" was my outraged rebuttal, followed with the ever-intellectual, "and you have barf in your eyebrows!"

"Oh." DadDick, who'd been holding Jess back, peeked around her, let go with one hand, rubbed his thumb across her left eyebrow, then said, "It's just a little spit-up."

"Gross," was my revolted comment. I know. I was being a megabitch. Realizing it didn't make me want to behave, though; it just made me as mad at myself as I was at her.

"I just had two babies!"

*"We know."* I threw my hands up in the air. "It's all you talk about. And what, being a new mom means you don't have five seconds to look in the mirror?"

"Yes," she replied, relaxing in DadDick's grip. "That's exactly right. I don't expect you to get it."

I groaned. "Oh, please. Not this again. Come on. Come *on.* Please not with the 'I as a parent now understand all the mysteries of the universe, which you, poor babyless imbecile, will never, ever be able to grasp with your babyless mind and which is why your poor babyless existence is forever doomed to be unfulfilling, you poor idiot.'"

"Well." Jess coughed. "That's pretty much it."

I glared and was casting around for a rejoinder when I saw the corner of her mouth twitch. Then she did the awesome thing I could never resist. When Jessica was trying not to laugh, she sort of swallowed it. That's the only way I can describe it: her mouth would twitch and she'd fight the smile, and while she fought the smile the giggle would start to rise along with (weird!) her left eyebrow, and pretty soon her face was wrinkled up like a baked apple and the giggle would escape anyway, and now I was giggling, too, which was a helluva lot better than screaming.

"I just wish you could hear yourself sometimes," I managed and got a hold over the giggles. I was glad something had ramped down the tension, but we still had crap to sift through.

"Betsy, I literally have a ten-dollar bill for every time I've wished the same of you."

I waved that off. "Yeah, yeah."

"Oh, here comes the 'I'm fine, it's everyone else who has to change' attitude."

"And here comes the willing victim! Poor Jessica, saddled with Betsy, which is just so stressful, it must be the hour of the martyr yet again—"

"Martyr?" she nearly shrieked. "If only I could, but you've been hogging the cross for *years*. Should we make a list of your 'problems'? Let's see, eternally young—"

"Thirty is not—"

"—eternally cute—"

"Again: thirty! *Cute* is not a word to describe a woman in her thirties. I'm not going through eternity with the 'cute' moniker."

"—a house full of minions to carry out your every dumb command—"

"Minion," Tina said. "Singular. And if I may shift the discussion—"

"—married to a bangin' sexy vamp—"

"It's true, Betsy," Marc said, "you are." To Sinclair: "You are!"

"You never have to worry about the bills—"

"Right back atcha, Jess."

"—you've got superpowers—"

"Being able to walk outside at noon is *not* a superpower!"

"Enough of this. *Now.*"

Like that, the temp in the room dropped ten degrees. Sinclair hadn't even raised his voice, but the whip-crack tone got everyone's attention.

"Be seated and pretend to be a grown woman."

I had no idea which of us he meant, but it didn't matter. I sat so quickly I wasn't actually aware of a conscious decision to sit. The only thing to make me feel better was seeing Jess had dropped, too.

Sinclair settled back into his seat as well. "Tina," he said, and she turned her head at once. "You were saying . . ."

"Ah. Thank you, Majesty." She turned to me. "I should like to explore the circumstances surrounding your father's 'death.'"

"Don't use quotes," I said irritably. "I can hear them, you know. It's my dad's death, not 'death.' Because he's dead."

"As you like, Dread Queen." Her tone was respectful, polite, and very, very careful. "Please elaborate. There was a funeral, but no bodies. His car was involved, and his identification was found. The assumption by police and the coroner's office was that he and his second wife were killed instantly. Your stepmother, Antonia, *was* killed. Yes?"

"Yeah." As I'd already relived, I'd seen her ghost a few days later. I would not think about what that meant about my dad.

"What about the autopsy?"

I must have looked blanker than usual, because Marc helpfully piped up. "There may not have been one. The ME could have requested one—they have to if the cause of death is in question. Maybe nobody thought it was."

"Mm-mm. Possible."

"If there was one," he added, "the State of Minnesota

requires the Ramsey County ME to file the death certificate within five days of the death."

I stiffened and the angel on my shoulder instantly started yammering. *Don't do it. Don't. You're the better person and now's your chance to prove it!*

*I'm not, actually.* "Good thing the coroner keeps up with *his* government paperwork," I said snidely and ducked in time to avoid the glass Jessica hurled at my head. "Ha! Too slow."

"Stop that!" Tina snapped, which was unheard-of. I decided that for yelling at the queen she would pay the ultimate price and started to sink into a massive sulk. "Was there an obituary?"

Distracted, I thought for a second even as Jess and Marc were shaking their heads. Then I remembered, and I knew why they'd been so quick to answer in the negative. Not only was there not an obit, there hadn't been a word in the papers at the time. Which was how Marjorie, the eight-hundred-plus-year-old vampire who'd caused all my problems that week, tripped up. She told me she'd read a blurb in the paper about the crash, explaining her presence at the evening service and how she'd come to express condolences.

Which was a pretty mean trick because there had been nothing in the papers. Marjorie knew about the funeral because she'd kept tabs on us, was causing trouble everywhere she could, and had the suicidal gall to put her hands on Sinclair and lock him in a cross-covered coffin with no plans to come to her senses anytime soon. And she'd celebrated the insanity by showing up to my dad's funeral to giggle inside while she consoled on the outside. Just remembering this crap was getting me pissed at her all over again.

This is a terrible thing to say about killing an old lady, a librarian no less, but that was one I enjoyed. She'd thrived for almost a thousand years, but fucking with my man ended her wrinkled ass. It was like she hadn't even cared that she was ruining my wedding! No way could I tolerate that level of sociopathy in someone who wasn't a roommate. Didn't she know it was *my* day? Night? Whatever?

"Nothing in the papers, no obit," I agreed.

Tina had her phone out to take notes. Marc called her iPhone 'the Precious,' although he confided to me that she loved her phone far more than Gollum obsessed over jewelry. I found that equal parts terrifying and hilarious.

"I know your father earned an above-average income in his lifetime," Tina said, "based on things you have mentioned over the years."

"Yeah, he had his own consulting company." Consultant. Was there a vaguer job description? It suited my dad perfectly.

"Yes, and did you inherit?"

". . . No." At the polite silence, I jumped back in with, "That doesn't prove anything, because I didn't expect to."

"Dick," Jessica muttered to the table. Entirely against my will I warmed to her a bit. She'd been outraged at the time, even more so when she realized I wasn't in the least surprised he'd left me in death what he'd given me in life: nothing.

"He left it all to his son?" Christina Caresse Chavelle asked, because you could take the Southern belle out of the nineteenth century but you couldn't take the nineteenth century out of Tina. I love how she didn't even sound surprised, like disinheriting females was a standard thing.

"No, I don't think so. I mean, I'm BabyJon's legal guardian now and I'm sure I would have seen some kind of paperwork naming him as an inheritor." Was that the word? Inheritor? Or maybe just *heir*? "Or, if there was, I would have ignored the paperwork, which Sinclair would have found while he was snooping—"

"Darling, helping you organize your finances is hardly—"

"Shut it, Snoopy McSpy, we both know you can't help yourself." One of those things that had aggravated the piss out of me a couple of years before but which I was slowly becoming resigned to. It wasn't so much that I didn't care anymore as that I didn't mind. There's a difference there. A teeny one, but still. "I'm right, aren't I? No financial paperwork. Just the baby. I inherited my brother," I finished glumly. I did not regret that. Not one goddamn bit; I loved BabyJon not least because he was my only chance at motherhood. But it sounded so bleak to hear it out loud. I'd wished for him, and it had killed my father. I wanted a baby of my own, and it had orphaned my brother.

I shook myself out of the sadness semicoma and continued. "Dad's finances were always a snarl. He and my mom would fight about money when they weren't fighting about him treating marriage vows like marriage suggestions. He had offshore stuff, I think, and lots of money tied up into various funds. We lived well, but he was always bitching about being pulled in too many directions. So . . ." I looked around the table of sympathetic faces. Nope. No sale. I didn't want any fucking pity. And my father was dead. End of story. "So that doesn't prove anything. That doesn't mean he hid all his assets before ditching the Ant in death, only to pop up downtown a few years later and sprint away from Jessica."

"Insurance?"

I shook my head. I didn't know. At the time, I'd cared about two things: BabyJon, and that I didn't feel worse our father was dead. If there had been some—and he must have had key man insurance at the least—it hadn't trickled my way. It wouldn't have gone to my mom, either. The Ant, then, and since she died with him . . . what? Where did unclaimed insurance money disappear to? The ether? The Internet?

"Well." Tina set her phone on the table, folded her hands, and looked at me. "This is very curious."

"It's really not."

"I can begin looking into this for you at once, but of course—"

"No."

*Elizabeth.*

I turned to Sinclair. "I said no." I looked around the table.

"Not a single person in this room has time for this shit. Not one of us. And even if you did, it's none of your business."

"My own," the king began gently, "will you not consider—"

"I—I forbid you from looking into it, Eric." His eyebrows arched; I only called him Eric when I meant business. To Tina: "Both of you. I'm not allowing it. No."

A heavy, stressful silence, broken when Tina bowed her head and murmured acquiescence. Sinclair took a few seconds longer, and things were mighty tense while he considered my order.

A lot of people didn't get that I wasn't the queen because I'd married the king. Sinclair was the king because he'd married me. I was foretold; how about that for a joke on the universe? Sinclair was incredible and wonderful and maddening and lovely and one of tens of thousands of vampires. He was a king because he married the queen, and there was only one queen: she be me. If we were insane enough to file taxes as vampires, my name would be in the Head of Household box.

After a decade or two, he inclined his head toward me. "Of course, my queen. It will be as you say. We are yours to command."

I blew out the breath I'd taken and then forgotten about. I probably shouldn't have seemed so obviously relieved, so "oh, thank God, what would I have done if he'd said no?" but I couldn't help it. To his credit, he said nothing but the corner of his mouth twitched upward.

"All right," I said. "Okay. We're all on the same page, then."

Marc shook his head and DadDick piped up with, "Not even close."

Yeah, well, close enough, anyway. Crisis over.

"We're not, though," Jessica said quietly. "Yours to command, I mean."

Crisis back on. "Don't I know it," I snapped. "If anything, it's been the other way around ever since you kidnapped my plant in eighth grade Health."

"You had no right to take that magazine hostage," Jess retorted. "Something had to be done; you were going power mad."

"Kidnapper!"

"Hoarder!"

That bitch! I got aggravated just remembering. Some schools made students pretend to mother or father an egg; ours used little rosemary sprigs in pots. I'd refused to lend Jessica *Seventeen* magazine's prom issue and she had retaliated by kidnapping my plant, then sending me misspelled ransom notes with rosemary clippings ("Proof we have your sprig! Give up the magazine or your plant won't live to garnish anything!"). I'd refused to negotiate with terrorists and took the D in Health, then wore my dishonor proudly, like last season's Choos. To this day neither of us can stand the sight or smell of rosemary.

"Look, if that's supposed to mean you're gonna waste your time on this frivolous crap, then that's what you'll do, because if you say you'll do a thing, Jessica, then you'll do it and it's one of the things I usually love about you. But *they*"—jerking my thumb at the vampires—"can't help you."

"Yeah, I caught that when you pulled the queen card, not an overreaction at all. I don't need their help, you megalomaniac," she snapped back, "and if you're going to be such an ungrateful, miserable twat—"

"I am not miserable!"

"—then fine. I'll stay out of it."

"Good!"

"Fine."

"Okay."

"Yes."

Crisis averted again.

"But just because we're not digging doesn't mean you can hide behind denial, even if that's your default."

"Hide!" I gasped; that one genuinely hurt. Didn't she understand I was basically forced to secrete myself from the

Antichrist and, by association, Hell? That wasn't hiding, except for how *secrete* was a synonym for *hide*. How did she not get that? "Oh, very nice! As if I'd—whoa."

And just like that, the Antichrist was storming into our kitchen. We'd been so caught up in the argument, which felt like it had been raging for a year, no one realized she was there until she was *right there*. It was easy to surprise me, but seeing Tina *and* Sinclair looking like someone goosed them was startling.

I shouldn't have been surprised; as a half angel (apparently Lucifer used to be a good guy), Laura had inherited the ability to teleport herself anywhere as long as she did it from Hell. And she'd learned pretty quickly how to pop into Hell. Reason #261 the devil sucked: "physical contact" with a "blood relative" facilitated the "magicks" (ugh, I hate when they misspelled it on purpose, you could actually hear the *k*) of interdimensional teleportation. In other words, the Antichrist had learned how to teleport by slapping the shit out of the vampire queen. Sometimes I feel like my entire life after death(s) is one long punch line.

"You." Laura stopped dead and rapidly shook her head. There was a tiny pattering sound and white and yellow things in her hair. They were—were those eggshells? Yes. Yes, they were. She had eggshells in her hair and some of them were falling to the floor in her agitation. Someone had lost their damned mind and egged the Antichrist. "You!"

"Me?" I squeaked.

"I can't. I can't do it alone. I probably can't even do it with you. They're finding ways to get out of Hell and I can't make them stop."

New crisis avoided. Old crisis: back on.

## CHAPTER
# ELEVEN

*"What happened?" I reached up to brush more eggshells* from her hair.

"What does it look like?" she snapped, jerking away from me. Which, for Laura, was the equivalent of kicking me in the shin. If someone bumped into her, *she* apologized. I'd seen it. Hell, I'd bumped into her. (Once with my fist.)

It was so annoying. The Antichrist was just one big, constant, never-ending annoyance. I went through most of my life assuming I was an only child and, unlike other only children (Jessica, Marc, others I knew but didn't live with), I never once wished for a sib. Laura had met my expectations and then some: younger sibs, I had quickly discovered, were a pain in the ass. (I won't waste anyone's time with Laura's theories about recently discovered older sibs.)

"You were egged in Hell?" I guessed. It was impossible, but the only thing I could come up with based on the evidence. Just picturing it made me want to laugh and then vomit from terror. The dead had eggs? *Hell* had eggs? I—what? No. I can't. No.

"Of course not," she said impatiently, flicking her fingers through her hair. Anyone else covered in eggs would look like they'd refused to hand out candy on Halloween and had been punished accordingly. Laura, frazzled and out of temper as she was, looked like she was in the middle of an expensive beauty treatment. One that worked. "I forgot my eggs in the trunk." At my blank expression she elaborated: "Eggs. In subzero temperatures."

"So they got super cold?" I guessed. Unless she was the chicken who was supposed to sit on them, I had no idea why she'd care. Also I was positive the Antichrist had more important things to do than sitting on frozen eggs. I mean, she did charity work all the time but surely she didn't have to stoop to stooping over eggs. This is why I distance myself from charity work. You figure you can get away with just writing a check, and then they show up with frozen eggs for you to sit on.

"Liquids expand when it's cold," she said with exaggerated patience. Or maybe it was regular patience and just really getting on my nerves. "Opened my trunk. Ka-boom. Last straw."

"Okay. That happened to me once with an avocado. I was going to make guac for Jessica's Super Bowl par-tay and forgot one of the avocados in the trunk."

"Betsy . . ."

"The thing was like a rock the next day. A dark green rock with a light green center that used to be a vegetable except it's really a fruit. Anyway, I was scared to thaw it out—would it work? Would it ruin the guac? Would freezing have rendered it toxic? So I just threw it away. I felt bad wasting food," I assured the frequent volunteer at soup kitchens, "but didn't have much choice, you know?" There. My anecdote would show that I empathized with her problems as a caring older sibling while at the same time demonstrating my—

"I don't care. I don't! Betsy!"

"Hmm?"

"I need you!"

Hmm. It was almost like she was trying to communicate distress or something. "Do I want to know why you were driving around with frozen eggs at midnight?"

"As I said." She puffed an errant hank of hair out of her eyes. "Last straw. And why do you always focus on the least relevant part of a conversation? Listen to me. They're sneaking out, Betsy. What if they all leave?"

"You're talking about the dead people in Hell?"

"The souls in Hell," she corrected, lightening up just a little. "We have incontrovertible proof that the soul lives on after the body dies. Proof!" She smiled and became even more teeth-clenchingly beautiful, which I knew because I was making a concerted effort not to grind my fangs. Laura Goodman looked more beautiful in faded jeans, an old "This Shirt Built a School in Africa" T-shirt, and Uggs, boots that had never been more aptly named, than I did after locking myself inside a Sephora and commanding the makeup techs to have at me. Oh, and let's not forget her egg-riddled hairdo. I had no idea where she'd ditched the parka. If she'd come directly from Hell to her egg-riddled car, maybe she hadn't needed one. "I always had faith."

Huh? Oh. We'd been talking about eggs, then avocados, and then souls, and now . . . faith? I guess? I was impressed she was able to follow all the threads.

"I never doubted," she assured me as if I had accused her of big-time continual never-ending doubt, or called her Skeptic McDoubtypants. "But we *know*. We have proof!"

"Our word isn't proof." I said it as nicely as I could, because showing the world our trials and tribulations of late had zero appeal. In a future that will never come to pass, I ruled the world. And it was a huuuge downer. What little I'd seen of the other, ancient, grumpy, zombie-raising, Sinclair-killing me had been more than enough. And maybe it had started from something simple; maybe all I'd wanted was to share with the world that, yes, there was life after the body died and, thus, hope. "People don't know who we are, and shouldn't, Laura."

She ignored this, so the bright-eyed enthusiasm continued unabated. "And there are so few of us who *do* know! If we could convince the rest of the world, things would change overnight! No more wars, no more murders."

*Oh boy.* "People not knowing if there's a God is not what causes murders and wars," I said carefully, because she was glowing like a zealot-turned-lightbulb. "At least, not all the time. I promise you, Laura. I *promise*. There will always be war and murder because there will always be assholes. They are not an endangered species."

She pooh-poohed my cold, hard, pragmatic worldview with a flap of one pretty, pale hand. "That's to worry about some other time."

"Got *that* right."

"But enough is enough, Betsy. I think we both know I've been more than patient."

"That's true," I had to admit. *Dammit.*

"So now. Now I have to insist you keep your promise and help me. Otherwise . . ." Her voice faltered, then steadied. "I—I'm lost. I am." She reached out and clutched my sleeve, and I didn't pull back. How could I? I'd behaved badly enough already. Also, those big shiny blue eyes were getting to me. The Antichrist had the vulnerable thing down to a soft science. "Please."

Sigh. Yep. The time had come. And even if it hadn't, I now had a very good reason to shelve the whole Dadgate thing. She was right. It wasn't fair. I was old enough to know that fair wasn't a guarantee, and young enough to want to keep trying anyway.

I turned without a word and she followed me back into the kitchen (we'd fled to the sanctuary that was the Peach Parlor to have our convo).

"Betsy! You have to," she was saying as I pushed at the

swinging door, and, God, the woman just would *not* let up! It was an intensely annoying trait that didn't remind me of me *at all* and that was my story and I was sticking to it. "I know you have a lot of claims on your attention—"

"It's true," I agreed.

"I never said you didn't."

"Also true."

"But I need you. They're *leaving*."

I nodded and then we were both forced to take in the kitchen chaos.

In the few minutes we'd been in the other room, the babies had woken and been taken downstairs, Fur and Burr had woken and been let into the kitchen, Sinclair had made a horrifying discovery, Tina was feeding Thing One a bottle while looking for a phone charger, Marc was laughing as Fur and Burr frisked about beneath the table while licking his ankles, Jessica was poking Marc to keep his attention while holding Thing Two, and DadDick had dozed off. Also, he was a sleep drooler, so . . . gross.

"Elizabeth!" Sinclair thundered, stooping to snatch Fur or Burr to his chest. They were black Lab puppies, as identical as two peas. Or pees, in the case of not-yet-housebroken puppies. I knew I was reaching the end of my endurance when pee jokes seemed hilarious. "This will not be borne!"

"I know," I hastened to assure my deeply fretful husband. "You're right. It's not acceptable."

"We are out *again*." He glared around the room but no one was meeting his gaze, so he settled for fixing it on me. He was quite tall but when he was irked it was like he grew a foot. Or maybe that was just a side effect I felt when cringing away from his ire. "Look at this."

He held out an empty canister and shook it at me like it was a Tupperware maraca.

"Oh. You're talking about . . . about the snacks for the puppies? Right?"

"Homemade," he emphasized while Fur or Burr ran to him to be picked up as well. He stooped, plucked up the other puppy, then went back to towering over me while they fought each other for the privilege of licking his chin. "Their homemade nibbles and kibble—"

I giggled. Couldn't help it.

"—are gone and we lack some of the ingredients so I cannot make more and that is intolerable."

"I think 'intolerable' is exaggerating maybe a little."

His eyes widened in horror, then narrowed. "It's as if you do not care at all that my darlings had to eat store-bought dog food."

"It is," I agreed, stomping the urge to murder him a lot. "It's exactly like I don't care." Wow. Like I didn't have enough Dadgate incentive to get the hell away from the mansion.

"They require meat protein! Not meat by-products. Not stale dog food shelved for a minimum of six months, riddled with road kill. The rule is very simple, Elizabeth. If I will not eat it, the babies shall not."

"I have never once seen you gobble a dog biscuit, but you give them to the puppies all the—"

"Do you *want* them to develop allergies?"

"Nope." I was rubbing my temples and had a thought: God, was this how people felt around me sometimes? Like they wanted to choke me out just to get some peace and quiet? Naw. "Please stop shrieking."

"Hey!" Jessica hissed. Thing Two had finished the bottle and was nodding off; Thing One was already conked out in Tina's arms. "You keep it down! Sinclair, shut up your pups."

"I will if you will," the vampire king snarked.

"Burn," Marc pointed out (he can't help himself) and I giggled (I couldn't, either).

"If those puppies and any of this ruckus wakes up these babies . . ." Jess warned.

"Impossible," Sinclair scoffed. "Your infants do not sleep.

They lapse into temporary food comas." He leaned in and poked Thing Two's chubby little arm. Thing Two blew a milk bubble and lapsed deeper into sleep. "See?"

Jess took an affronted step back. "You got lucky."

"Ugh, stop it, both of you. Play nice or I will never leave this kitchen," I threatened. "Or I'll leave right now. Whichever you don't want to happen, that's what I'll rain down on your heads."

"Actually, whether you want her to stay or not doesn't much matter," Laura began after a pointed throat-clearing, "since Betsy and I were just on our way to Hell."

That got their attention. It got everyone's attention. There was a long pause and I realized everyone in the room, with the possible exceptions of Temp Coma Girl, Temp Coma Boy, Fur, and Burr, were waiting for me to explain why I wasn't, actually, going to Hell. At least, not anytime this week.

"No, really. I'm going. We're going." I sighed and said it. "We're going to Hell." Hearing myself say the words was surreal. So were their expressions.

"Ah . . . my own . . . you cannot. Do you not remember?" Sinclair put the wriggling pups back on the floor, where they raced to me and started sniffing my penguin slippers. Argh. "In light of the dearth of acceptable dog treats, you pledged to help me bake many batches of Cinnamon Bun Bites. Don't worry," he added, as if anticipating horrified protests, "we shall use whole wheat flour."

"Nope. We absolutely didn't pledge anything. And frankly, I'd almost rather go to Hell for the rest of the week—"

"Might take longer," Laura interjected.

"—than help you bake. I love you, Sinclair, but . . . no."

"I get that. We all get that. But I think you're forgetting the, um, secret freezer thing we discussed regarding the other secret thing we discussed," Marc added, jerking his head toward Tina in what I assumed he thought was a subtle head movement. "You can't leave right this minute. You said you'd help me with stuff."

"Marc, are you talking about my birthday?" Tina asked with a delighted smile. She'd been rocking the sleeping baby, and had fed it, then burped it, like a pro. Now she was cuddling it almost absently, like she knew all about babies and was confident enough to multitask while jiggling one. I wondered about who she was before she died. Maybe she'd been a mom. She sure was great with kids, and me. And she adored my husband like a son or a little brother. There were so many things I didn't know and, while there was no shame in ignorance, mine was because I'd never bothered to ask. And that *was* shameful. "You are such a darling man! But please. No fuss. I insist."

"Don't fall for that," DadDick mumbled, cracking one eye open and blinking at Marc. "That's a trap."

"Duh," was the sophisticated reply.

"And don't forget about your, uh, family issue," Jessica said. "The thing we were just discussing. A lot. Loudly."

I almost wept when I heard all this. I couldn't believe that, despite the argument, despite our differences and the terrible things we'd said, they were all still trying to support my cowardice and give Laura reasons why I couldn't go to Hell. Even though they all (rightly) disapproved of my cowardly bitchiness, they hung in. Knowing I didn't deserve support like that made it all the harder not to bawl until I was hoarse and hiccuping.

"It's fine, guys. Really. It is." Thank goodness I no longer cried actual tears, or they'd be streaming down my face, and who needs to worry about chapped cheeks on top of everything else? "Laura's been a good sport, but the time has come. And I gotta be honest, I'm not sure why I resisted for so long."

"Because it's Hell?" Marc suggested, getting answering nods from DadDick and Jessica.

"Well, yeah, but I've run offices in my old life, Hell probably isn't much different. Come on, it can't be any harder than running . . ." I tried to think. "Than running . . . uh . . ."

Marc rolled his eyes. "Are you trying to remember the

name of the nightclub you inherited after killing Marjorie and then did nothing with?"

"Anything sounds bad," I said petulantly, "when you say it like that." After killing the librarian who'd snatched my sweetie, I'd inherited her property. Vampire law. Which made sense, because standard laws of inheritance wouldn't apply so well to dead people who didn't age. Anyway, I'd been informed I owned a nightclub, I ignored it for a couple of years, and it was eventually sold. I think.

Laura giggled, then shot me a grin. "My faith in you is unshaken."

"We both know you're lying. Let's get a move on," I told the bemused Antichrist. "Hell won't run itself. Will it? Probably not. Which is why I'm going there. *We're* going there."

"I thought you'd fight this at least another two weeks," Laura admitted, shaking her head. "In fact, this is more than a little suspicious."

"That hurts, Laura," I said with as much dignity as I could, given that I was in flannel jammies and penguin slippers. Don't judge; vampire queens didn't always glam up and go clubbing during the witching hour. Not when it was this fucking cold out. "You're family; you know we can always depend on each other."

"Consider me reassured," she replied with an openly disbelieving expression on her face. "I can't imagine what you're going to Hell to *avoid*. Do I want to know what dreadful thing is going on in your personal life?"

*Your personal life, too, little sister,* I thought but didn't say.

# CHAPTER
# TWELVE

**There's this thing that happens in books and movies when** the heroine (*moi*) stumbles across something weird (my entire postdeath life, and also senior prom) and can't figure it out (all the time, any of the time) and is a slave to being overwhelmed (like that time my dentist kept hounding me to come back so he could finish the root canal—that guy was *obsessed* with teeth).

And every time, *every damn time*, this idiotic, often pointlessly gorgeous heroine, for whatever dumbass reason (afraid others won't like her, afraid others will notice she's turning into a slavering zombie, afraid she'll get audited, afraid they'll stop inviting her to parties, afraid she'll be deported, afraid she'll get slapped—and by this point, the audience is *itching* to slap the silly bitch), every time, she keeps it all to herself until the mysterious secret in question blows up in her face. Blows up in everyone's faces.

The terrible secret, now hideously exposed, nearly gets her

killed or straight up does get her killed (if you're like me, you're actively rooting for her miserable death by now). If it miraculously doesn't, it's only because it's the end of the movie when she explains to everyone what the hell's been going on and, weirdest of all, they don't fall upon her and murder her in a fit of "why didn't you *say* anything, you silly bimbo?" rage.

Every. Damn. Time. Go on. Test my theory. Stream a handful of horror movies and watch how stupid the heroine is. It's almost as bad as sci-fi movies featuring scientists who are Just. So. Dumb (*cough* *Helix* *cough*).[3]

Not *this* idiot heroine, boys and girls. Nope. I pretty much always know when something is over my head and can't wait to fob it off onto someone else. This has been a habit of mine since . . . oh, about first grade. I have always owned my uselessness. Which was why I'd been avoiding the Antichrist like I was getting paid. But acknowledging my complete uselessness for a job didn't always mean I should avoid the job. I'm bad at washing dishes by hand, too, but when the dishwasher broke . . . hmm. I'm not sure who handled that. I know we started using plastic cups for smoothie time, and there were a lot of explanations from individuals about why it wasn't their problem, and then more threats, but if I'd had to, I would have stepped up. Same with pledges to younger sibs and otherworldly realms.

The time for cowardly scurrying into corners was over. Now was the time for cowardly scurrying into a realm I knew nothing about and had no business running.

Right, then. To Hell! But in a good way!

Laura, who never flaunted her abilities, simply walked out of the kitchen, where she presumably vanished. Or kept walking out until she got back outside to her car; I dunno, I hadn't even noticed when she'd arrived. Not my job. I, on the other

---

[3] I'm aware nobody does the *cough* thing anymore. Shut up.

hand, since my middle name should have been Flaunt, gave my pals a cheery wave. "I'm off! Don't wait up." As exit lines went, it was lame, but I hadn't had a lot of prep time.

Then I dramatically disappeared.

Except not.

I'd thought this was mind over matter, I had gotten myself back from Hell just by thinking about it a few weeks ago. (Maybe it had worked more because of my desperation to get away from the Ant, the worst spirit guide *ever*.) But I was still in the mansion, dammit, while Laura was probably halfway (or all the way) to Hell by now, and several of my alleged loved ones were trying not to smirk. The babies, at least, were respectfully silent except for the occasional milk-snore.

"Well." I took a long look around the kitchen. "That was anticlimactic."

"Perhaps physical contact with the objects with which you focus your no-doubt formidable concentration?" Sinclair began in a helpful murmur that barely held back his snicker.

Of course! Dorothy's shoes! How could I teleport without Dorothy's silver slippers? I'd been a fool to try. Also it was weird that these were the problems I faced these days. I left the kitchen, came back, hollered, "Okay, bye! Again!" darted back down the hall and up the stairs, then all but flew into my room. If I wanted to get back and forth from Hell—and I did, I wasn't going to be an exchange student and live there, and I sure wasn't going to do the Hell equivalent of lunch at my desk—I needed to focus.

In other words, I needed Dorothy's silver shoes from *The Wizard of Oz*. The enchanting book, not the terrifying movie. I kept them in my closet, in the safe along with my marriage certificate (and gawd, Sinclair had bitched about that *incessantly*, saying we were already married in the eyes of the undead, which meant, as you can imagine, jack shit to me), my (useless? maybe?) social security card, and some of Sinclair's paperwork, I dunno, looked like stock certificates and stuff.

JPMorgan Chase stock was worth a lot, right? Especially when you bought it in 1955, when it was the Chase Manhattan Bank? And Coca-Cola stock from 1919 at forty dollars a share had probably aged well, too. Wait, how old *was* my husband again? Maybe his dad had really liked Coke.

No time for distractions, dammit, and no time for paper millions or government-issued ID; I needed something much more valuable. I tapped in the code ("sink lair sucks") and popped the safe, spotted the gleaming beauty of my unreal shoes, yanked them out, then slammed the door before the baggie of diamonds—did diamonds even come in red?—could fall out.

No time to get distracted by pretty colors; I had to get focused on my pretty shoes. They weren't really there, you know. They weren't real. They were my will, a piece of my wanting made solid by . . . what? I didn't know. Magic, I guessed (note the lack of *k* in *magic*, please). Or science so advanced and beyond my understanding it might as well be magic.

It goes like this: as a card-carrying member of undead royalty, I could travel back and forth between dimensions. Hell, it seemed, was one such dimension.

Wait. I've got to back up. It wasn't just because I was a vampire, or any of the hundred thousand (or however many there were; we were still working on a census) vampires on the planet would be zipping back and forth to Hell. I could do it because my half sister was the Antichrist. Which made *no* sense, because we were related through our father, an ordinary man who was now dead. Whoever my half sister's mother was should have had zero effect on *my* otherworldly abilities.

See? It's like I've been warning for ages. Any attempt to apply logic to this supernatural stuff was pointless. Not that I didn't try. Okay, I didn't try. But I thought about trying. Sometimes.

Anyway, some of the religions were right, Hell was a real place. (Which called into question: which religions? And if some of them were "right," did that mean others were "wrong"? Also, I was using quotation marks too much.) Not one near the planet's core, but an actual place nonetheless, one hardly anyone got to until they died. Except lots of dead people didn't go there. They went somewhere else (Heaven? Dairy Queen?) or didn't go anywhere (hung out where they'd died, occasionally tracked me down to demand favors, and that was just the ones I knew for certain). The whole thing was migraine inducing.

But knowing this, any of this, wasn't enough. It can be tough work, overcoming a lifetime of conditioning that assured me, over and over, that I could not teleport, Hell wasn't a job share, every bit of my afterlife was over my head, and knowing there is life after death solves little and explains exactly nothing.

Thus: the shoes. The pinnacle of my ambition, the Holy Grail of footgear, Dorothy Gale's silver shoes. Not ruby red, mind you. In the book, they were silver. MGM fucked with that because a) it's inherent in movie people to fuck with great books (*cough* *My Sister's Keeper* *cough*) and b) red = pretty! Honestly, movie people should just get it over with and have "Now I am become Death, destroyer of worlds" printed on their business cards.

I slipped them on and, because they weren't real, they fit me perfectly and didn't pinch even a little bit. Then I clicked my heels three times and murmured with wide, hopeful eyes, "There's no place like Hell, there's no place like Hell, there's no place like Hell," except not really. Once I had the focus, I didn't need magic words. I thought, *This is so, so stupid. I can't believe this even works.* And shut my eyes.

And, a second later, opened them in Hell.

## THIRTEEN

*"Well, one of the Taylor sisters takes her responsibilities* seriously and, in a shocking turn of events, it's not my step-daughter. It's the Taylor girl *I* gave birth to."

Just like that, I wanted to shut my eyes again. And maybe gouge them out. Followed by the completely sane decision to ram knitting needles into my ears. "Proof, like I needed it, that this was such a bad idea," I muttered, glaring at Mrs. Antonia Taylor, she of the pineapple hair (in height and color) and complete lack of maternal instinct. "Shouldn't you be screaming in agony in a lake of fire somewhere?"

"It's Monday," she replied, like that was an answer.

I was uneasy, no surprise, given where I was and who I was talking to, but putting that aside, I'd forgotten the worst thing about being in Hell: my telepathic link with Sinclair didn't work here. It had been so upsetting last time, I'd shoved the unpleas-antness right out of my head. If denial and repression were Olym-pic sports, I'd clank at every step what with all the medals.

And here it was again, here I was again, remembering the worst reason why Hell was Hell.

It was amazing how fast I'd gotten used to the impossible. I had gone three decades without Sinclair but these days he was the air I no longer breathed. Not being able to feel him inside me[4] was like losing a tooth. One of the important ones, an incisor or something. When I was younger I used to dread the inevitable loose teeth and subsequent losses, mostly because my mom was a fan of the "tie one end of a string around the loose tooth, the other around a door handle, then slam the door" school of thought. (Don't judge; it was surprisingly painless. Didn't make the whole ordeal any less stressful, though.) Once the slackass tooth was gone, I'd constantly tongue the hole where it used to be, unable to stop prodding the spot even though it felt weird. Now I kept reaching for that mental link, knowing it was gone but unable to leave it alone. Sinclair was like a tooth in my brain, only now he had been yanked like a cavity. Wait, cavities aren't yanked. And it isn't one of my better metaphors, either, so insult to injury.

"See, Antonia?" Laura had met her biological mother around the time she met me, and wasn't comfortable calling her Mom. She'd also rejected my many helpful suggestions (Jerkass, Homewrecker, Bilbo Bag, Knockoff, Fake Tan, Fake Boobs) and finally settled on Antonia, spoken politely with a dash of warmth. "We're already making progress."

"We are?"

Laura had appeared out of the ether (more on that in a minute) and walked up to slide an arm around the Ant's waist. The Ant looked startled, then almost-but-not-quite relaxed. See above, no maternal instinct. Also, I wasn't sure the Ant understood unfeigned affection. "I knew you were wrong when

---

[4] Not like that! Pervs.

you said Betsy was a sociopath with tacky highlights and no sense of social responsibility."

"Tacky?" I yelped. Then: "Oh, are you actually lecturing me on social responsibility, you odious bitch? You told me you were glad you were dead when I told you about Obama!" Ugh, that reminded me of how Jessica's awful dead parents had reacted, shades of "I can't believe we're dead and missing this!" I had no right, ever, to the moral high ground, which was another reason Hell was awful. I was the best of a bad lot around here.

Except for Laura, of course, who worked at being good, frequently failed, and always came right back to dig in again. Even though it seemed to me that these days she valued good mostly as a terrific way to spite Satan, she still worked at it. I admired the tenacity, while owning the fact that I wasn't up to it.

"Let's not fight," Laura interjected, which was ironic because she wasn't fighting at all. Now that she'd gotten what she wanted (she'd never learned to be careful what you wish for, a tiresome lecture for another time), namely, my presence in the pit, she had perked up. Way up; I hadn't seen her looking so carefree in more than a year, and I ignored the stab of guilt that brought. "Let's just get to work."

"How?" That wasn't my usual dumbassery. I genuinely had no idea how we would make anything happen. We were standing in a big bunch of nothing. Not fog, not darkness, just . . . void. I couldn't feel anything under my feet, but I was standing. I was taller than the Ant in Hell, as I had been in life, but again, we weren't standing on anything. To add to the illogic, the Ant didn't even have a body anymore! She was here spiritually, but Laura and I were here in soul *and* body. We were in the middle of a blank slate and I was in no mood for metaphors, even though the metaphoric slate was also a literal slate. (And when had I become so obsessed with metaphors?) What were the rules?

Worse, I had a good idea about why the place was blank,

why it was just a big old bunch of nothin', which was making me uneasy as shit.

"Yes, well." The Ant let loose with a pointed cough. "Good point, Laura. Enough time has been wasted." This with a typically unsubtle glare at me. I shrugged it off as I'd been doing since the Ant first tsunami'd into my life when I was a teenager. "So. Where do you want to start?"

I stared at them, then at the nothing, and managed not to scream, "How the *fuck* should I know?" into their expectant faces.

"I—I don't—what? I don't know. Maybe . . . maybe with the ones who are leaving? Or the ones who haven't left? Or—where *is* everyone? Aren't there supposed to be a whole bunch of souls down here? Wait, not 'down here' since we're not underground, it's not Dante's Inferno or anything. I—" I cut myself off before I could finish with "I got nothin'," cringing at how idiotic I sounded.

"They're all here," the Ant replied, answering one of my questions at random, "all the time. Hell has layers. Just because you can't see everyone doesn't mean they aren't here."

Layers made sense. It was a concept I could grasp pretty easily and I was pretty sure Hell was designed with that exact thing in mind. On one of my trips ("one of"—argh, cue drawn-out groan) to Hell I'd seen all kinds of souls being punished.

An aside, not to come off as a creepy voyeur (like there was any other kind), but getting a glimpse of Anne Boleyn cutting off Henry VIII's head while he begged her forgiveness for knocking her up with Queen Elizabeth I was just too good. I wanted to linger and say, "Oh, so we've learned a little more about biology in the last five hundred years, you fat fuck? That's right, it's the sperm that dictates a prince or a princess, and the sperm comes from the guy! Meaning you! I know you don't know who I am! Your hair is stupid! Hey, Anne, how about you pull another Red Queen and off with his head again?" Luckily I had been a model of restraint and just walked on without commenting.

My point, I just now remembered, was that on *that* particular trip, Hell was like a hive. The biggest, most complex, and fucked-up hive I'd ever seen. Each little cell contained someone's personal Hell and they stacked up so high and so wide and the events in the cells just went on and on . . . boggling, the whole thing. Just trying to ponder everything going on was enough to make anyone's head pound. Glimpses were all I got, and all I wanted. On that particular trip, anyway.

On another trip, Hell was a waiting room with ready-to-burn-out blinking fluorescent lighting, and the only thing to read was years-out-of-date magazines. Unpleasant, sure, but again—a concept I could grasp, context I was familiar with.

So maybe that was the key. Maybe the trick was to set it up however we want, in the best way we can think of, using relatable symbolism to help our (okay, my) tiny minds grasp ungraspable concepts.

Okay. Well. I'd never tried to run Hell, but I'd been fired more than once, and I'd had to take over more than once from someone who'd been fired. And the first thing I always did in a new job was . . .

"How did Satan do it?"

. . . figure out what my predecessor did, then refine. "I don't suppose she left us lists. Or suggestions for organization. You know, like how when you're in a new job, the person you replaced left contact info and lots of memos explaining day-to-day ops. Anything like that around?"

"At last, intelligent observations," the Ant muttered, as if I didn't have super vamp hearing and wasn't standing four feet away. "I knew if I waited through enough years you were bound to—"

"Oh, shut up. Look, you were the old boss's secretary or whatever—"

"Yes, or whatever," came the dry reply.

"—so you can take us through her routines and kind of go

over the day-to-day running of Hell, right? That's why you got right up in my face the second I showed up."

"There's no place I would rather be less than right up in your face," she sniffed, "and you know perfectly well why I was the first one to show." Ugh, so true. Last time I was here, everyone I thought of eventually showed up, called to me by the force of my bitching. "I've got very little interest in helping *you*," she added, all disdainful and pissy, but the fidgeting gave her away. In Hell, as in life, she was inappropriately dressed a good decade younger than her age: too-tight navy blue miniskirt, polyester blouse in an eye-watering floral print (yellow roses against an orangey-red background or, as I like to call it, *ow, my brain*), black wedge pumps (blech, wedges, they're ugly and they always remind me of the terrible disco era which *never should have been allowed to happen*), de rigueur black stockings. Bright blond hair piled high, too much green eyeliner and shadow, lipstick just a little too orange and bright to be flattering. If it had been anyone else, I would have assumed she was forced to dress like that as penance for her many sins in her wicked life, but it wasn't anyone else and I knew she thought she looked perfect.

But she still couldn't keep her hands still. When she got nervous or edgy, she'd run her hands all over her clothes and hair, sort of patting with fluttering fingers to make sure everything was in place. Which would be understandable if she did it once or twice. But those hands were constantly moving. It was dizzying.

"What's got you so—" I began, deeply suspicious, when my phone buzzed against my hip.

Wait, what?

I plucked it out and stared. A text from the vampire king: *I trust all is well. Return at once if you require assistance.* Classic Sink Lair. I ran it through my translator and got, *I'm sure you're seconds away from an epic screwup so I'm ready to haul your delectable ass out of the fire and won't tease you about it later except I probably will for a little while and I lurrrrrv you sooo much!*

Awww. What a sweetie.

The implications took a few seconds to hit, but when they did: "Whoa." I had been slow to embrace texting. Not to go on an old-lady rant or anything (if you're over thirty, thirty is the new twenty; if you're under, thirty is the new ninety), but texting was pretty much destroying civilization. As with Jessica's bed, I'd been gradually sucked in (I only started hauling a cell phone around in the last three years) and even now, I sent maybe five texts a month, and those along the lines of *How can we be out of ice AGAIN? What is wrong with all of us?*

But my telepathic link with Sinclair didn't work in Hell. Which he knew, and had handled with his usual pragmatism.

"Whoa," I said again, not at my creative best. "I can get texts in Hell? AT&T, I have once again underestimated your vast scope and reach."

"Yes, the antitrust laws were put in place for a reason," the Ant replied. "Monopolies aren't good. Unless you're running Hell," she added quickly in response to my dumbfounded expression. "Then they're fine."

"No, I just—I had no idea you knew what antitrust laws were." I myself was a little vague on the subject. Something about making companies play fair, right? Hell didn't need antitrust *anything*. Hell didn't have to compete with any other entity.

"I had an existence outside of *this*," she snapped back, gesturing vaguely at all the nothing.

"Yeah, I know the words to that song," I muttered in reply. "I pretty much *wrote* that song." But back to more important things: what to text back. A smiley face? A winking smiley face? Emoticons were a bit lacking when you factored Hell into the equation. I settled for *All's well so far.* I would not abbreviate. I would not OMG or LOL, no matter how TSTL I was. *You* was never *u*. *Are* was never *r*. Nevernevernever. "Okaaaaay. That's done. Also, how the hell was that even possible?"

Identical shrugs. Great. The so-called experts didn't know, either. Was it how Hell interpreted my bond with Sinclair? Was it like the shoes that didn't exist—it was a tool that helped me figure out the un-figure-out-able? Or did it simply mean that Hell had AT&T towers? Oh, my, yes, we were the perfect bunch to move in and take over. Nothing could go wrong. It made me think of a lost friend, Cathie, who'd had that same thought shortly before being murdered in her driveway and, the minute she figured out what had happened to her, haunted me until I found her killer.

"Never mind," I said, trying for comforting and managing to be just dismissive. "We'll figure it out later. Or we never will."

Laura was nodding. "Yes. I agree. It's probably that one."

"Um. Which one?"

"I'm not saying," she replied with a stubborn shake of her head. "You'll get even more irritated."

The Ant made a rude noise and, much as it pained me, she was corrected in her snorting. "I'd love to take offense and debate that, but when you're right you're right." I sighed. "So. Now what?"

"Now you give me a hug, you silly bitch," said the dead woman behind me. I turned, surprised, and saw a ghost I'd thought was gone forever. Unlike every other surprise in Hell, this one was welcome.

# CHAPTER
# FOURTEEN

*"Cathie!" I couldn't hide my delight, and my kind-of pal* grinned back. She looked different than the last time I'd seen her, well over a year before. In life she'd been a sallow, occasionally depressed blonde who had never done anything and never been anywhere (her own admission). Later, she was the second-to-last victim of the Driveway Killer.[5] (Yeah, I know, lame name. The peach parlor was the Peach Parlor and the serial killer who snatched blondes out of their driveways was the Driveway Killer. Sometimes Minnesotans are not creative.)

She'd announced her presence one random day by slipping into the backseat of my car and scaring the living shit out of me when I checked the rearview. Helpful tip: screaming at someone no one else can see is no way to convince people you

---

[5] We met Cathie and the Driveway Killer in *Undead and Unreturnable*.

don't need meds. That was also the day I learned never again to check my blind spot.

When I'd last seen Cathie, she was wearing the outfit she'd been murdered in, a faded green SeaWorld sweatshirt with the overstretched sleeves pushed to her elbows, black stretch pants, and athletic socks. No shoes or coat, which wasn't a big deal, she'd explained, since she no longer felt the cold, but still left her feeling not quite put together. Sock-footed for eternity; welcome to my worst nightmare. Cathie had a much better attitude, though. "On the other hand," she'd added, cheering up a little when she realized I could see and hear her, "I never have to shovel my driveway again. So who cares if I'm in yesterday's socks for eternity?"

After our awkward first meeting (I had so many of those it was almost boring), Cathie had nagged me until I helped find her killer. This was *completely* terrifying but ended up pretty great, since we managed to save the last victim before the killer could tool up on her. Also, Laura had gone all "from Hell's heart I stab at thee" and killed him. In his own basement! That was my first hint that Miss Let's Read from the Hymnal had a bit of a dark side. Which I should have seen coming because . . . y'know . . . *Anti*-Christ.

"You look great!" This wasn't saying something nice to someone you haven't seen in a while to prove you noticed their absence; she really did. Khakis, a pressed red button-down, hair pulled back in a neat ponytail (in life her ponytails were disasters trapped in scrunchies), black and tan oxfords. The pants were too long for me to check out her sock situation but I was betting Cathie had that covered, too. Her hands were stuffed in her pants pockets past her wrists as she slouched comfortably in the big bunch of nothing that was Hell right now. "Really great!"

I got an eye roll for my trouble, which was fair. "Ramp down the shocked surprise, will ya? Wasn't my fault I got murdered on laundry day. Besides, once you guys took care of my little 'if you wrong us, shall we not revenge' problem, I sure as shit wasn't going to haunt the earth in granny panties and a sweatshirt."

"The world is grateful," the Ant muttered, then she pulled Laura aside so they could whisper together, which wasn't alarming *at all*.

"Yeah, but that's how you looked the whole time . . ." I trailed off, remembering (if this was a movie, there'd be a flashback complete with memory-jarring soundtrack, a perfect time to go for a snack). One of the things I'd liked about Cathie was that, even after I'd solved her problem, she hung around. The others had all been "good job, thanks, quicker next time" and poof!

But Cathie was in no rush to move on, wasn't sure what her options were, and was dismayed to discover I had no idea. So she just hung out to chat and occasionally ran interference by dealing with some of the needier ghosts demanding my attention. It was pretty great; Cathie was one of those women who, after you talk to her for about a half hour, you know you're going to be pretty good friends with. As Heinlein put it, "You're an old friend we haven't known very long." I'm not a sci-fi fan, normally, but Heinlein did manage to write one book that didn't utterly suck.[6]

"Hell, no, I don't still look like that. You know those weren't actual clothes, right? And this . . ." She glanced down at her business casual attire. "This isn't a shirt and these aren't khakis and this—" Turning to show me, she then turned back. "That's not a clip holding up my hair."

"Impressive," I said, because it was. I've noticed a lot of dead people never figure that out. Or if they do, they've got no interest in taking advantage of it. Cathie could teach the newly dead a thing or two, even more impressive when you consider she was pretty newly dead herself . . . not even five years gone. "How'd you find me? How'd you even know I'd be here?"

Indifferent shrug. "Everybody knows." Which wasn't *too*

---

[6] *Friday.* It rocks and stands the test of time! Also, there are kittens, three-somes, and lottery winners.

terrifying. "And what are you asking me for, Betsy? You're the one who summoned me."

"Nuh-*uh*."

Another eye roll. "Really, vampire queen? 'Nuh-uh'? You don't think Hell's bad enough without you talking like you never escaped the trauma of middle school?"

"It *was* traumatic." I managed not to whine. Barely. "Besides, what's so bad about nothing?" I bitched, gesturing to all the nothing.

"Not having a clue what comes next," she replied so quickly and firmly it was obvious she'd been thinking about it. "And like I said—you summoned me."

"But I—" Then I realized, which must have shown all over my face, because . . .

"The light dawns! It's dim and flickering and will probably burn out any second, but it's definitely dawning for now. Better think fast before it blows."

I ignored the on-the-nose cattiness. And the fact that, once again, someone I might have wanted to scare at some point (just a little!) had absolutely no fear of me. It was as thrilling as it was aggravating.

"Aw, nuts," I said glumly. "I get it."

Cathie leaned forward and fluttered her eyelashes while clasping her hands together. "Is it possible? Can it be true?"

"Oh, shut up. I was thinking about you, and there you were." Fuck and double fuck! *Don't think about Jessica's parents don't think about any of the many vampires I've killed don't think don't think don't don't don't*

I groaned. "It's like that exercise where they tell you not to think about a white bear and *all* you can think about is white bears. Your brain starts crawling with white bears."

"Yeah. Ironic process theory and the Game." At my expression of surprise she added, "What? I was studying for my psychology degree when I got gakked."

"The Game?"

"Yeah, it's basically the white bear exercise, except it's a game."

"Helpfully called the Game?"

She grinned. "Yeah, I know. Anyway, the Game is the white bear exercise except instead of trying not to think about white bears you're trying not to think about the Game even as you're playing the Game."

"Oh, cripes." I pinched the bridge of my nose. "Please stop."

"And the presumption is that everyone in the world is playing the Game all the time."

"What?"

"Yeah, and you'll love this—it's impossible to not play, and consent isn't necessary at all." Cathie sounded positively gleeful. "And of course everyone loses. The best you can do with the Game is be the last one to lose it. There's no winning it."

"Pure and utter hell," I said, appalled.

"Yep." Cathie glanced around. "Seems fitting, right? But never mind the Game—which we've both just lost, by the way—let's get back to you summoning me without the vaguest clue how you did it or even if you could do it."

"Hey! I'm doing the best I can."

"No. You aren't."

Well. That shut me up, but only because she was right. I settled for prepouting, in which I was preparing to pout but would hold off to see if a full-blown Defcon 3 pout would be required.

Cathie sighed and shoved her hands even deeper into her pockets, which I hadn't thought was possible. If those things were cut any deeper she'd be grabbing her kneecaps. "So, let's see. Once again, you had no idea what you were doing, and while blundering around in your fog of ignorance—"

"Oh, come on!"

"—you did something inexplicably supernatural by accident, and then were shocked and amazed at what you hath wrought." At my puzzled blinking, she elaborated: "Major in psych, minor in English lit."

"I thought you were a horse trainer."

"Part-time. Try to stay focused, you adorable moron."

Adorable? I'll take it. Too bad the word following it wasn't quite as flattering. I looked down and scuffed a toe through the nothing. My kingdom for some dirt to kick. Wait, no! *No dirt. Don't think about the white bear and don't think about dirt. Maybe I can't summon dirt. Maybe I can only summon people, which is fine because I don't want dirt. Hell will be dirt free, I think.*

"Oh, Betsy, *jeez.*" Her tone was annoyed, but thank goodness her expression was fond, something along the lines of *I can't believe I like you, as you're a significant dumbass who will only bring me trouble.* "You've had the vampire gig how long now?"

"Not long," I said defensively. "In vamp years I'm a preemie, dammit."

She ignored my whiny argument. "Still with this? No clue about what you can do and what you should do? You're doing what you did when we first met, stumbling around and eventually succeeding in spite of yourself."

"I think 'succeeding' is the key word in that sentence."

"No, 'stumbling' is. Come on, what have you been *doing* for the last couple of years? Besides accidentally—you'll never convince me it was on purpose—ending up helping your whacko sis run Hell?"

"Plenty!" the Antichrist snapped back, rushing to my side and leaving the Ant standing with her mouth hanging open in mid-bitch. "You don't know what we've been going through. It's inappropriate for you to take her to task. And I am not a whacko!"

"Oh, goody, you're here, too." Cathie eyed the Antichrist, unimpressed, and I had to swallow a giggle when I recalled how Laura kept insisting Cathie stop haunting me and go to her King (it never occurred to her it wasn't cool to push Jesus on the horse-training atheist daughter of Jews). "And I meant whacko in a nice way. You *did* kill my killer. I'm not ungrateful. It's just—"

"What?" Laura snapped.

"I think there's something wrong with you," Cathie said bluntly. "Something really, really wrong. And before you jump to conclusions, it's not an across-the-board phobia of all things supernatural. I like your sister the vampire, and I liked the werewolves—" She cut herself off and turned to me. "How are they, by the way?"

"Gone," I replied, "but in a good way."

Boy, that was for sure. In the old timeline, Antonia-the-werewolf died taking a bullet for me. Werewolves were tough, better believe it, but the movies lied—if you blitz through their brain with a nonsilver hollow-point, they can't heal from that. Antonia had been a colossal pain in my ass, but I never wanted to see her brains spray across the wallpaper. I wouldn't have wished that on the Ant, never mind someone named Antonia who *didn't* have it coming.

And her lover, Garrett, did not handle grief well: he killed himself about a minute later. That was the shit cherry on the poop sundae that was my month.

Cue a clueless vampire queen tripping through the centuries in both directions and I returned to a timeline where Antonia was dead, and in Hell, but rescue-able. (Yeah. That's a thing now: people can be snatched out of Hell. I . . . don't understand.) And a very much alive Garrett determined to ride me (so to speak) until she was back with him.[7]

I settled for the Wiki version: "They wanted to see a bit of the world, get away from the nuttiness. Garrett's old-fashioned, so they send postcards." It had been so long since I'd gotten a handwritten communiqué on paper, at first I thought they had been kidnapped and I was reading a ransom note.

Cathie laughed. "Yeah, can't blame them for that one. It's

---

[7] Garrett's relentless determination to rescue his sweetie from Hell can be found in *Undead and Undermined*.

concentrated nuttiness in your mansion, that's for sure. Can't tell if you're the source or you just exacerbate everything."

"Excuse me," Laura interrupted, so much ice in her tone I wanted to dump it in a glass of Coke and fix myself a refreshing beverage, "but you were telling us there's something wrong with me."

"No," she replied shortly. "I said *I think* there's something really, *really* wrong with you."

"But why?"

Cathie stared. "Seriously? You've got no idea why I might be a little edgy around you? None at all? You're drawing a great big blank?" She glanced at me. "Huh. You guys look a bit alike—same coloring—but you've got more in common than I thought."

"Yeah! Shows what you—wait."

Before I could work out the insult tucked into the compliment, Laura was on top of it. She managed a self-deprecating shrug and a smile ninety-five percent of the planet would find irresistible. "It's the Antichrist thing, isn't it?"

"No," Cathie snapped. "It's the murderous temper coupled with magic and no-actual-checks-on-power thing. Or do you not remember why the Driveway Killer is in Hell, where he spends eternity being choked out with belts when he's not balancing Louis XIV's books?" She sighed and anticipated the inevitable blank looks. "One of the most expensive and corrupt courts in the history of human events. Half the expenditures weren't even written down, much less tracked, so Pryce can never get the books right. He's a murdering accountant being tortured by women who look like his victims while knowing he can never balance the books he's charged with."

"I'm sorry, I'm not . . ." Laura shrugged again. "Who?"

"Yeah. That? That's why I think there's something really, really wrong with you."

BACK IN THE DAY, KINDA . . .

**"Down here!" Cathie called, and darted into a closed wooden** door.

I was starting to get used to the smell of the refinery—we'd been driving around the neighborhood a good twenty minutes, after all. But Cathie was right, it blotted out everything else. If he was killing women in his basement, I couldn't smell it from the kitchen. I couldn't even smell the kitchen from the kitchen.

Laura and I hurried down the stairs, which were predictably dark and spooky until Laura found the light switch. Banks of fluorescents winked on, and in the far corner we could see a woman with messy, short blond hair, tied up and gagged with electrician's tape. Her outfit was, needless to say, a mess.

"Ha!" Cathie screeched, phasing through the wood-burning furnace and zooming around in a tight circle like Casper on Mountain Dew. "Told you, told you!"

"It's all right," Laura said, going to the terrified victim.

"You're safe now. Er, this might sting a bit." And she ripped the tape off the woman's mouth. "It's like a Band-Aid," she told her apologetically. "You can't do it little by little."

"He's coming back—to kill me—" Mrs. Scoman (I assumed it was Mrs. Scoman, the lady gone missing from her driveway three days before) gasped. "He said he—was going to use his special friend—and kill me—" Then she leaned over and barfed all over Laura's shoes.

"That's all right," Laura said, rubbing the terrified woman's back. "You've had a hard night."

"If those were my shoes," I muttered to Cathie, "I wouldn't be able to be so nice about it. Thank God she wasn't wearing flip-flops."

"Oh, your sister's a freak," Cathie said, dismissing the horror of Shoegate with a wave of her hand. "I've only known her a couple of days, and I figured that one out."

"She's different and nice," I said defensively, "but that doesn't make her a freak."

"Trust me. Having been killed by one, I recognize the breed."

"You take that back! You can't put someone like Laura in the same league as the Driveway Asshole."

"Will you two stop it?" Laura hissed, struggling with the tape. "You're scaring poor Mrs. Scoman! And I am not in the same league as the Driveway Asshole."

"I just want to get out of here," the bound woman groaned. "I want to get out of here so bad. Just my feet. I don't care about my hands. I can run with my hands tied."

Then I heard it. "Move," I told Laura. "The—we have to go now."

Cathie darted up through the ceiling and vanished, doubtless on top of the recon. Being murdered sucked, but the ghost gig had its compensations.

"What?" Laura asked.

I started to rip through the tape with a couple of tugs,

tricky because I didn't want to hurt Mrs. Scoman worse than she was. "The garage door just went up," I said shortly.

Cathie swooped back into the basement. "He's back! And, boy, he is freaked out. Keeps muttering about the damn foster kids, whatever that's supposed to mean."

"Hurry," Mrs. Scoman whispered.

"Please don't throw up on me. If I do it any faster or harder, I could break all the bones in your hands."

"I don't care! Do my feet! Break my feet! Cut them off if you have to, just get me out of here!"

"Carrie?" An appropriately creepy voice floated down the stairs. "Do you have friends downstairs, Carrie?"

"Oh, great," I mumbled. "The killer has arrived."

Cathie pointed at the man—I couldn't see him because we were more under the stairs than beside them—walking down the stairs. "Time's up, motherfucker," was how she greeted him, and damn, I liked the woman's style. What a pity he couldn't hear or see her!

"Why did no one think to bring a knife?" Laura asked the air.

"Because we're the hotshit vampire queen and devil's daughter, and we don't need knives. Unless, of course, the bad guy ties up his victims with tape. Then we're screwed." Ah! I finally got her feet free and went to work on her hands. Because she would have had to run past the killer to escape, I gently shoved her back down when she tried to scramble to her feet. "It's okay," I told her. "We've got it covered. We really are the hotshit—never mind. I'll have this off in another minute."

The killer turned and came into the basement. Saw us. (Well, most of us . . . not Cathie.) Looked startled, then quickly recovered. "Carrie, I told you no friends over on a school night."

"My name isn't Carrie," Mrs. Scoman whispered. She wouldn't look at him.

Cathie stepped into his chest and stood inside him. "Asshole. Jerkoff. Tyrant. Fuckwad," she informed him from inside his own head. "Loser. Virgin. Dimwit. Asshat. God, what I wouldn't give to be corporeal right now!"

"It's overrated," I mumbled.

"I can't believe this loser's face was the last thing I saw."

And can I say how *weird* it was that she was talking from *inside* him? Blurgh. One of those laugh-so-you-don't-cry moments.

"You aren't the foster kids," the psycho nutjob killer said, looking puzzled. "I thought the kids at the end of the block broke my window again."

"Score," I said under my breath, tugging away. I'd figured if the killer got home while we were still there, he'd see the window I'd broken (*so* satisfying to smash) and assume pesky kids, and wouldn't immediately flee the state. And it wasn't like he could sic the cops on us. "What did I say? Huh?"

"Yeah, you actually had a good idea," Cathie snarked. "And we're not calling the police right this second why again?"

"Why did you kill those women?" Laura asked, the way you'd ask someone why they picked a red car over a blue one. "Why did you steal Mrs. Scoman?"

"Because they're mine," he explained, the way you'd explain about owning a shirt. Everyone was being all calm and civilized, and it was freaking me the hell out. I could smell trouble. Not a huge talent, given the circumstances, but it was still making me twitchy as a cat in heat. "They're all mine. Carrie forgot, so I have to keep reminding her."

"Psycho!" I coughed into my fist.

"Did you really," Laura began, and then had to try again, "did you really strangle them until they pooped, and then make fun of them after you stole their clothes?"

"Laura, he's crazy. You're not going to get a straight answer. Look at him!"

Unfortunately, looking at him didn't help: he looked like a lawyer on casual Fridays. Nice, clean blue work shirt. Khakis. Penny loafers. Not at all like the slobbering nutjob he obviously was. "Look at him!" was not good advice.

Then he fucked himself forever by saying, "It sucks when you get the bra off and find out they don't have a decent rack. I don't mind them lying about that other stuff, but tell the truth about your tits, that's what my dad used to say. Otherwise, it's like lying."

Then, of course, he was dead, because Laura leaned down, picked up a chunk of wood off the pile, and broke his head in half. I screamed. Mrs. Scoman screamed. Even Cathie screamed, but I think she was happy. I wasn't. I was in hell. I think Mrs. Scoman thought so, too.

**"Had I known you'd be so ungrateful,"** Laura sniffed, folding her arms across her chest, "I might not have bothered."

"Uh-huh. At least that doesn't make you sound petty and unstable. Look, I'm not sorry the creep is dead, all right? But you went off and it wasn't because you felt bad for my situation, or Anna Scoman's, and it wasn't even because you were scared. You went off because you wanted to, because you could, and afterward you pretended nothing had changed, that you were the girl your adoptive parents raised and not your mother's daughter. That—that's willful blindness and it scares the shit out of me."

Loooong silence to that. It was one of those "I don't know where to look so I'll let my gaze bounce all over the place like a Ping-Pong ball" moments. After what felt like twenty or thirty hours Laura came up with her rebuttal.

"I might have known you'd end up in Hell," she said with a sad shake of her head. "I begged you to move on."

"Mm-hm," came the unmoved reply, and I felt a jolt. Because Cathie had a point; Laura was hiding. And when someone pointed out something unpleasant about her behavior, she just burrowed in deeper and went with her default: *I am a good person surrounded by evil doing the best I can.* I recognized the behavior. I ought to; who'd know about that defense mechanism better than me? (I realize I just insulted myself while complimenting myself, but it's okay. I'm an enigma.) "That's how you're going to deal? You're gonna gloss over everything I just said so you can focus on something irrelevant?"

"The destination of your eternal soul is not irrelevant," Laura snapped.

"Cram it sideways, Damien," was the unrepentant retort. I blinked hard and fast to keep my eyes from widening so far they were in danger of falling out of my head. One of the reasons Cathie and I got along so well was our identical inability to show respect or keep our mouths shut.

"You understand you're under my dominion now, right? It's not smart to antagonize me."

So . . . wait a minute. When she got pissed, Hell was her dominion, but the rest of the time it was the "sisters all the way, ruling Hell together, couldn't do it without ya!" chant. Hmph. But in the interest of not wanting the Antichrist to find a chunk of firewood and bust my head open, I refrained from commenting. Also, Cathie had proven she could take care of herself. Except for the getting-murdered thing.

"Yeah?" Cathie replied, unimpressed. Probably because she *was* unimpressed. "I know the new boss. Who is not, despite what the Who said, the same as the old boss."

"Yeah," I agreed, more to be saying something than actually contributing because, uh, what? I was not a fan of the crapfest that was seventies rock, and thus had no use for The Who, Zeppelin, the Grateful Dead, Zappa, etc. I tolerated Springsteen, the Talking Heads, and Pink Floyd because they stopped sucking in the eighties, but as for the rest? Pah. This had been a huge bone of contention with past ex-boyfriends. Then I fell in love with a dead senior citizen who thought Glenn Miller was edgy.

I dunno. The baby boomers were gonna change the world, but instead they gave us cable television while never shutting up about how terrific it was that their parents unleashed hippies upon the world. My gross prejudice had nothing to do with the fact that I'd seen a pic of my mom at Woodstock and she might have been topless, waving her arms over her head as she flashed peace symbols with both hands while demonstrating that she didn't touch a razor. It looked like she had a couple of baby rabbits nestled in her armpits.

I opened my mouth to make peace when the Ant again drew Laura aside and started up with the urgent whispering. I could have heard her if I wanted. Supervamp hearing, yippee. But I'd spent years *not* wanting, so I turned my attention back to Cathie.

"It's not that I'm not happy to see you," I began carefully, a veritable mistress of tact.

"Oh, here we go."

Yes, she was right to be suspicious. "It's just that things are pretty nuts right now what with the—uh—regime change, I guess you could call it? So maybe give Laura time to find her sea legs. Hell legs. What-have-you." I cleared my throat and changed the subject. "So, did you do it?"

"What?" Cathie seemed inclined to follow my change of subject lead if her yawning and scratching were any indication. I had no idea if ghosts got tired, or itched, so I kept my mouth shut.

"You said you wanted to see the world, remember? When you explained you wanted to go walkabout for a bit. You said in life you'd never even been on a plane."

"Oh!" She brightened. "I have now."

Argh, so—many—sarcastic—TSA—jokes. Must—fight—my nature—argh—sarcasm stroke—imminent—

"Ow, you're putting too much pressure on my incredibly

juvenile sense of humor," I groaned. "Ghosts having to get through TSA to fly? Or not, I guess; if they can't see you, they can't frisk or wand you, right? You just walked on and hung out in the plane for the duration and followed everybody off when it landed in . . . I dunno . . . Rome? Paris?"

"Dallas, actually. You worry," Cathie told me, sounding composed yet bemused, "about the weirdest things."

I was about to refute that when my phone dinged again. I fished it out for a look.

*Twins missing. Return at once.*

"What?" I gasped, clutching my phone so hard I could hear it start to creak. I loosened my grip before shards of metal and glass could be driven into my palm. "Oh, Jesus!"

"He's not here right now," Cathie said helpfully, "but maybe you could leave a message with that one?" Jerking a thumb in the Ant's direction, who bristled at "that one."

I barely heard her, and by then Laura and the Ant had broken off their chat and looked over. "Betsy?" the Antichrist asked, concerned. "Something wrong?"

Yes, and I had no idea what could have happened. Missing? How could they be missing? Okay, the mansion was disorganized on the very best of days, but it wasn't like the babies could hitch a ride outta the chaos. When you put them down somewhere, they stayed put. "I have to go. Laura—I'm so sorry—" I held up the phone to show her and was relieved when I saw her eyes widen and her expression go from long-suffering to stricken.

"Of course. Yes. Do you—should I come with?"

The Ant snorted. "Laura, you're a credit to my gene pool but still far too naïve. Obviously Betsy has set up some kind of 'fake emergency-text me in half an hour so I have an excuse to leave' thing."

"Sure, because I had complete confidence in my wireless plan and totally planned on being able to send and receive texts *in Hell*," I snapped back. Thinking: what a brilliant idea! If the

twins weren't missing I could have stolen it. Babies wreck everything. "Do you even hear yourself anymore?"

"Do you? You made a promise, and I don't care what the
made-up reason is, or even the legitimate reason, you're going
to stay here and keep your word."

I didn't remember moving but at once I was in her face.
"Who do you think you're talking to?" The Ant leaned away
from me without moving her feet and her mouth went tight.
"You don't give the orders here. The moment I killed the devil
your job title changed to Annoying Nobody, so how about you
shut the fuck up and let the grown-ups talk?"

The Ant glanced over at Laura . . . and Laura didn't come
to her defense physically or verbally. My stepmother's mouth
went tighter (her lips were almost inside her mouth by now)
and she forced herself to meet my gaze. "Apologies," she managed. "It seems—it seems I did forget. Who I was talking to."
A wintry smile. "It won't happen again."

I opened my mouth to really let the bane of my adolescence
have it

*Why are you having a pissing match with the Ant when your
best friend needs you?*

then turned to Cathie instead. "I'm sorry, I've got to—"

"Duh. Of course you do. If it's all right, I'll stick around
here. Not that I wouldn't get a kick out of seeing your gang
again, but when you get back here you're gonna need all the
help you can get."

I nodded and began texting back. *Coming.*

The Ant had recovered because she let out her trademark
inelegant snort. "Really, Cathie. Not necessary though it's
adorable that you offered your help. I'm sure my daughter and
that other woman—"

"I'm right here and you know my name, foul temptress of
middle-aged men!" I nearly screeched.

"—will let you know if they require your assistance."

"Go fuck yourself," Cathie replied pleasantly, which was just so wonderful I almost burst into tears of admiration. "That's for 'that other woman' to decide." She turned slightly and gave me her full attention, which was intimidating and reassuring all at once. "Whatever's going on topside—yeah, I know we're not actually underground; old habits, y'know?—you'll eventually be back here. And you'll have more people offering to help you through the regime change than you can shake a stick at."

"Absurd saying," the Ant muttered to Laura, who only shrugged in reply.

She ignored them and stayed focused. "Plenty of souls around here will come across as just soooo helpful and respectful and pretending there's nothing in it for them, and that's fine, that always happens in times like this."

"Times like this?" my sister asked, amused. "This is unprecedented, a once-in-a-million-year—"

"Regime changes aren't even a little new," she replied, bored, and then got back to me. Meanwhile I was so impressed that she fearlessly blew off the Antichrist *and* her horrible, horrible mother I was giving serious thought to kissing her on the mouth. I was sure Sinclair would understand. "But remember, fanged blondie: I helped you when I didn't have to, when there was nothing in it for me, and I did it long before anyone here had even heard of you. And I'm willing to do it again. So." One more shrug for the road. "That's all."

"That's plenty," I replied, a genuine smile lifting my spirits for the first time in what felt like days. "I'll remember, Cathie. And I'll see you again soon. For now, though . . ." I glanced down at my silver shoes. "There's no place like—I dunno. Wherever you hang your hat?"

Not terribly catchy, but good enough.

# CHAPTER
# SEVENTEEN

**"If I were Jessica's weird babies,"** *I mused from our toolshed,* "where would I go?"

Where indeed? Where were the hot spots for humans younger than milk shelf life who are plagued with incontinence, can't roll off their belly or back without assistance, and can't talk? Also, what the fuck was I doing in our shed?

My teleportation skills needed work. Also my sexual, social, political, and cooking skills, but first things first. Of course I hadn't been practicing a newly discovered skill that would probably take years to master. Puh-leeze! People might see me and leap to the conclusion that I planned to help run Hell sooner rather than later. I was lucky I hadn't landed in Minot, so the toolshed wasn't the worst. Except ugh. Toolsheds.

I started picking my way through/past dirt (bagged and otherwise), the rusted hulk of an engineless push mower (do they even sell those anymore? and if not, how old was our very own ticket to lockjaw?), mouse poop (should maybe tip Marc

off about the treasure trove of test subjects), and various gar-
den implements until I was outside. The shed was so yucky I
was actually pleased to find myself outside in bitter cold, shivering and shin deep in snow.

I trudged my way around the side of the house to the front,
climbed the few steps, and then remembered I didn't have my
purse and thus was keyless. So I shivered and started knocking
on our immense front door.

"Guys?" Rap-rap. "It's me!" Pound-pound. "I'm here to save
the day! Or something." Kick-kick. "Please let me in? Guys?
Hellooooo?" Kick-pound-kick-pound.

All right, enough of that. Yeah, I could have kicked the door
down. But the snobs over at Big Bill's Door Repair ("We're always
open, so your doors aren't!") were getting downright nasty about
all the work we'd been calling them for, something about how
our house was a national treasure and we should treat it better
than we were and how was it possible for a mahogany door to be
forced off its hinges twice in the same week . . . I don't know, I
wasn't paying attention. Big Bill liked to nag, and I liked to tune
out, so it was a perfect relationship. At least from my end.

"C'mon, guys," I, the powerful, feared vampire queen,
begged, trying not to whine. "C'mon, it's cold! I got your text
and here I am! Guys?" And . . . yep. Completing my week of
awful, it was starting to snow. "Please? Hello?"

Then, way too late to take any pride in it, I finally had a
good idea.

*Sinclair?*

*Beloved! Where are you?*

*I'm on the front porch! Dying! Of all the days to wear a short-
sleeved shirt! Let me in already!*

*Yes, yes. Ah . . . yes.* Was incipient hypothermia making me
dimmer than usual or did the vampire king sound distracted?
Like it was almost too much trouble to pay attention to our
pesky bond? *Trot around to the back, my own. The kitchen door is
unlocked.*

*Trot around back?* I made zero effort to keep the annoyed outrage out of my brain. *You* texted *me, asshat! And I have never, and will never, trot! I'm giving serious thought to beating you to death for suggesting it!*

*I cannot yet come down to let you in, as I have my hands full preventing Detective Berry from calling the—ow.*

*Ow?*

*He is really quite—ouch. Quite adamant—hmm, that one will ache for a bit—about calling in the authorities. Tina and I are attempting—ouch. To, er, dissuade him. Ow. We would prefer not to—ouch—hurt him. Oh, now, that one will take at least an hour to heal—stop that this instance, Detective Berry!*

For a second all I could do was stand on the porch, frozen (internally and externally). *Is DadDick hitting* you? *Why are you letting him hit you?*

*It's fine,* came the soothing thought. *He cannot truly hurt me, and I think it may be helping his stress levels.*

*Stress levels! He thinks he's stressed now? He hasn't felt anything yet! We'll find his weird babies but that doesn't mean he should be tooling up on my husband.*

*Better a few punches than the alternative,* came the sharp retort. *Do you not agree, my own?*

I didn't answer, too busy stomping around the side of the house. Well, trudging—the snow was deep in places. Not trotting, though. Definitely not trotting. And I knew what Sinclair was alluding to, and I didn't like it. Not at all.

It's complicated, and annoying, and it doesn't help that I still don't truly understand all of it myself even though I was *there* for all of it. But here goes.

A long time ago (except it wasn't, not really, not in terms of *time* or anything), Sinclair and I had—had—oh, fuck, there's just no nice way to say it: we raped DadDick's brain (except he was Nick then). He'd found out things we'd rather he hadn't, and we made him forget those things for the greater good. And just because you do something terrible for the greater good doesn't mean you're a) right or b) *not* a dangerous asshole who should be locked up for everyone's peace of mind. Trouble was, sometimes the vampire mojo doesn't take. Or it does, but eventually breaks down. Or it does, and eventually breaks *you* down. Or one too many vampires try to mojo the same poor schmuck (cough) and the forced suggestions kind of fight each other.

Bottom line: Nick remembered very little, except that he had become terrified of Sinclair and me. Which was a sensible thing to feel, believe me. Before, we'd been almost-friends. I'd gone to the cops for help in my prevampire life,[8] met Detective Nick Berry, and through me he met Jessica and they started going out. Since Jessica is wonderful, and Nick is wonderful, and I was peripherally involved *at best*, they quickly fell in love.

That's where it got all kinds of nasty and terrible. Nick couldn't reconcile his love for Jess with his terror for me. Couldn't understand how the woman he loved could overlook her best friend's unsavory bloodthirsty side. No matter what I tried, how hard I tried to rewin him over, he always remembered the brain-rape and how helpless he'd felt. How terrified and alone. And I didn't dare try *another* mojo to make him forget any of that.

Eventually Nick had made Jessica choose: him or me. That time she chose me. I won't deny being gratified as well as surprised . . . I'd *thought* she'd probably pick me. But I hadn't been one hundred percent sure. And "winning" hadn't felt as good as I thought it would.

Then I accidentally changed the timeline, and when Laura and I came back from the future, *this* version of Nick had somehow figured out how to choose us both. Or had never felt the urge to force the choice. He'd never been mind-raped in the new reality, and had no trauma to try to jettison in order to achieve happiness. Old timeline = Jessica was single

---

[8] Deets are in *Undead and Unwed*.

and ready to mingle. New timeline = Jessica smells like baby barf and looks happy when she doesn't look exhausted.

All that to say it was no surprise Sinclair was letting DadDick smack him around, *especially* if it kept his mind off a) calling the cops and b) being mojo'd. Sinclair and I would willingly eat our own arms off before ever trying that again. It gave DadDick a sizeable advantage, even if he didn't know it.

"Hellooooo, the house!" I called and got a big fat nothing for my trouble, possibly because I was still outside. Or because they'd forgotten all about me after *commanding* me to return. To which I'm compelled to say: oh, Goddammit! I go to all the trouble to escape from Hell (okay, *escape* wasn't the right word, *fled* was the right word)—and that only because of Sinclair's tersely urgent text—but I was here, and obviously DadDick was too busy playing one-two-punch with my husband to care that I was back, no one cared I was back, so no one was down here to greet me with talk about how prompt I was, or how driven (or frozen) I was. Phooey. Phooey × 1,000. Next time I'm in Hell, I'm turning off my cell.

I heard unfamiliar voices coming from the kitchen (aha!) and practically yanked the screen door off its hinges in my urgency to get inside. As Sinclair promised, the inner door was unlocked and opened easily into the mudroom. At once I was warm, though still shivering, and bent on ignoring Fur's and Burr's delighted slavering and yipping.

Well. I wasn't made of stone. I didn't *entirely* ignore them, just paused for a few seconds to pat their sleek black heads. The fact that they were penned up in the mudroom, alone, told me how serious things were. Somebody was always willing to watch them or play with them or nap with them or take them outside for walks; those two fuzzy extortionists were hardly ever alone.

I lunged for the toy box on top of the washing machine and extracted a couple of Sinclair-approved dog toys, making a determined effort not to look at the price tags. We had money, but some things were just too ridiculous, and an "educational" dog toy designed to go into a puppy's mouth and be slobbered on was at the top of the list of things to be ashamed of because we paid lots of money for them. I stooped, scratched Fur (or Burr) behind her ears and gave her a squeaker, then gave Burr (or Fur) the other one. As they gnawed happily I made my escape into the kitchen.

"H'lo, Onnie!"

I stopped so abruptly the mudroom door swung back and almost hit me in the ass. I stepped farther into the kitchen and gaped at the unfamiliar children seated across from each other at the kitchen table—they looked about four or five— and managed to come up with, "My name's not Annie."

"Duh," the other one snorted.

The first one—the girl—scooched up in her chair until she could lean across the table and smacked the other one— the boy—on the fleshy part of his upper arm. "Nuh-uh, you can't! Not s'posed to say that to grown-ups."

"It's Onnie!" the boy protested. "She's barely a grown-up."

"That's okay," I said quickly, before things escalated. The tiny boy's return glare was terrifying. "It's not the first time someone's said that to me. It's not even the first time this month."

The boy stopped glaring at his sister (I figured, had to be), then beamed up at me. "Okay, I know, but it wasn't nice so I'm sorry now, Onnie Bets."

"Oh, super splendid. That's just terrific. Glad we've got it all worked out."

They beamed at me, showing lots of bright white baby teeth—what Tina calls milk teeth. Which always sounds equally cute (milk! harmless yummy milk) and scary (teeth! teeth in milk? no one wants teeth in their milk) to me. They were both dressed in some sort of shiny overalls, deep blue for the boy and pastel blue for the girl, and the shirts underneath were also blue. They were shoeless and sporting thick white socks, and they seemed quite comfortable on the kitchen chairs even though their little chubby legs dangled quite a ways from the floor. They had pale skin, with lovely rosy gold undertones, and enormous dark eyes. Their features were nearly identical, with small noses and pointed chins, though the girl's black, kinky hair had been pulled into braids and the boy's hair was clipped short.

I'd seen those features before. Sure, I had.

No. I hadn't. I was mistaken. It had been a long day and I was mistaken. These strange children were absolutely not who I thought they were. Because that was impossible.

With that thought firmly in mind, I again engaged the little charmers. "Um, don't take this the wrong way, kiddos, but who the hell are you? And what are you doing here?"

Identical, epic eye rolls. At me. So eye-roll-ey it was like their gaze had weight. Their incredibly familiar gaze with weight-bearing eye rolls. Yep, I'd seen *that* look before.

No, I hadn't.

"We *did* this," the girl said.

"We did," the other one said with a nod.

"Okay, *we*," I began, "didn't do anything. I don't think. Seriously, who are you? Because . . ." Because there was no way they were who I thought. Except what other explanation was there? Man, these little kids better speak up or I'd press charges for . . . I dunno, trespassing? Being a toddler with extreme prejudice? Insulting my intelligence but being so adorable about it I was charmed instead of enraged? Yes, the police, definitely. They should be called, like, *now*. Then the overall-wearing cuties could answer some questions downtown, by God! "You look familiar," was my incredibly weak finish.

"'Cuz we *are*."

"Familiar," his sister added. "I'd like a cookie, please."

"Me, too," the other one added, a look on his face like the most brilliant thing ever was happening right now. "And also milk? Please?"

"We don't have any—"

"Mama keeps them up there." Pointing to the cabinets across the kitchen, the ones above the main stove. Far, far out of reach if you were a shortie in overalls. "The sugar st'sh."

"Stash," the other one corrected. "Staaaash."

"I said! St'sh."

"And you know about the stash," I concluded, officially giving up, "because somehow you're Jessica's babies."

"*Not* a baby!"

"We'll be four in this many months!" the other one added, just as hot under the collar, if they'd had collars instead of T-shirts. She showed me a hand of splayed fingers. "That's the *opposite* of being a baby."

"Opposite!" the other one cried, equally annoyed.

"Jeez, sorry, calm down." *Argh, don't say* jeez *to little kids!* I put my hands on my hips and shook my head at them. "I'm sure there are some parental rules about why you can't have a cookie out of the super-duper secret sugar stash—"

"There is."

"Are," her brother corrected.

"But that's why we have *you*, Onnie Bets."

"You think cookie rules are dumb," her brother added. "And they are!"

That sounded legitimate. Food rules in general had always struck me as dumb, unless you had diabetes or wanted to land a modeling contract. "How d'you know what I think about any rules, never mind rules specific to cookies?"

"You told us a zillion billion times. You're always sneaking us yummies. Duh. Hey!" He rubbed his arm and glared at his sister. "I can't help it! She's dumb sometimes."

"He's right," I admitted. "I am. I'm just going to sit down." What to do? Scream for help? Tell Jess and/or DadDick? Go to any lengths possible to *never* tell Jess and/or Dick? Maybe I should ask Thing One and Thing Two. They seemed pretty bright.

(This is how things are now: I seriously consider taking

advice from small children who haven't mastered wiping their own butts but seem to know all about things I can't grasp.)

"Okay, you guys? I'll get you both a cookie. And milk. D'you like smoothies? We can have smoothies."

"Banana-strawberry?" Thing One begged.

"Your shoes are pretty and shiny," Thing Two observed, earning a place in my heart for all eternity. "Strawberry for me, please."

"You can have all the smoothies you want," I recklessly promised (what did I care? they weren't my kids so the ensuing sugar rush wasn't my prob), "but you have to stay here for a minute. Okay? Just . . . stay right here. Do not move from those spots. Stay put and when I come back it's all cookies, all the time. I have to go—" *Terrify the shit out of your poor parents.* Uh, no. "I'll be right back. Just stay put. Okay?"

"Okay," they chorused.

I started for the swinging door that led to the main hall, then stopped and looked them over again. "You guys are—you're pretty neat. You know?"

"You say that all the time," Thing One said. He sounded bored but gave me a lovely smile for my trouble. It almost made up for the shit storm I knew would follow.

"It's nice, though," Thing Two added. "You're always nice to us, except for that time we spilled paint all over your—" At Thing One's squeak of distress and frantic head shake, she changed tactics. "Never mind."

"Oh boy. It had something to do with my closet, didn't it? And the shoes therein? Don't answer! This part of the conversation never happened. I'll be right back. Stay!" I added, then got the hell out of there.

# CHAPTER
# EIGHTEEN

*I could hear the argument before I was even halfway to the* room.

"—the cops *now*."

"Dick, think on this for merely a moment."

"I don't have time to think! Okay, that came out wrong. You know what I mean. Every minute we don't call the cops, whoever took the babies is—is—" I hurried as I heard DadDick's voice break, then steady. "They're getting farther away. I should have called for help twenty minutes ago."

"I think Tina and Sinclair have a point," Marc cut in tentatively.

"Of course you think that!" Jessica snapped. "You think your new bestie is pretty damned perfect."

"Do you *really*?" was Tina's delighted response. "That's so darling, Marc. You're so darling!"

"Ugh, stop."

"Think on it for one minute," Sinclair coaxed. "How could

an ordinary person make their way into our home and steal your infants without one of us noticing? Save for my queen, we were all home. We have searched from attic to basement—"

"Yeah, some of these stains are never coming out," Marc muttered. "How would you even get dead spiders out of scrubs, anyway?"

"—and turned up nothing. Your children's disappearance must be supernatural in nature. At best, involving the authorities will do nothing save slow our investigation and raise questions among your colleagues you do not wish to answer. At worst, you risk exposing us."

"And that's what it's all about, isn't it, you self-interested son of a bitch?" Jessica hissed. "Covering *your* ass."

"Covering all our asses, yes," was the quiet reply.

"Get the *fuck* away from that door. Dick didn't want to hurt you too much, but I don't have that problem."

"I believe you. Please think about what you're doing."

"Last chance," I heard, and I put on a burst of speed because whenever Jess used that tone, something that inevitably led to neighbors putting their house up for sale was about to come down hard.

"All right, thtop it!" I'd managed not to wrench yet another antique door off its hinges while getting inside the room, where the gang was staring at me with wide eyes. "Come on, you guyth. I go to Hell for half an hour and you all loothe your collective thit?" Aw, man. The lisp was back and I should have expected it. I got a good look at Sinclair's bloody nose and whirled on DadDick. "Not. Cool."

"Not my finest moment," he replied, and his sincerity went a long way toward my decision to postpone the plan to drown him in Tina's vodka. "Betsy, you don't under—"

"*You* don't under. I found the babieth." *No time to preen. But damn! They called me for help and I solved the case in about ten seconds. They are so lucky to have me! I'll remind them later.* I saw Sinclair catch that one, and his relieved expression gave way to a smirk. I, a paragon of maturity and cool-headed thinking, ignored it. "Tho it'th okay now. Thit! Hate the lithp."

"You—what?" I hadn't thought it was possible but DadDick's eyes went wider, hopefully because of my announcement and not because he couldn't understand me.

"The babies?" Jess gasped, trembling so visibly DadDick at once pulled her into his arms. "They're back?"

*I don't think they ever left.* "Right downstairs." Ah, excellent. The blood was already drying and I could talk, so I showed off a little by throwing another *s* in the mix. "Come see! Heh. 'See,' not 'thee,' did anybody catch that? I'm definitely getting a handle on this. Thisssssss."

"Now's not the time for the narcissism parade," Marc pointed out. Which was just crazy. There was always time for that particular parade.

Clearly unbelieving (*that can't be right*) but hopeful (*why would Betsy lie about this?*), DadDick and Jess stampeded into the hall and down the stairs. I scrunched my sleeve down past my palm until I could hold the fabric in my fingers, then reached up and carefully used my sleeve to wipe the blood off Sinclair's face.

He caught my hand and pressed a kiss to my fingertips. "My thanks."

"It was good you didn't hit back." I paused. "I guess. Come on downstairs. You won't believe this. Also your theory that it wasn't a random baby-stealing dude just happening to wander by and snatch them was dead-on."

His lips twitched into a wry expression. "I will not like what I see, will I?"

"I honestly have no idea," I replied, because it was the stone truth. "See for yourself. You guys, too."

We hurried back to the kitchen in time to hear Jessica's shriek. Yep, she'd found the preschoolers and wasn't at all pleased, and who could blame her? There was only so much stress a new parent could take before—boom. Meltdown.

I shoved at the swinging door and ducked inside before it could swing back and break my nose. The others, still behind me, were gonna have to fend for their own noses. "Jess, I know, and you're right to be freaked, but—"

"Look at them!"

"Yep. I get it. But the thing is—huh."

Jessica was pointing at the preschoolers, who were—when did *that* happen?—babies. Babies lying on the smoothie counter and starting to fuss. Babies who were definitely not preschoolers anymore.

"They could have fallen!" This while she and DadDick were scooping them up and cooing at them. She whirled on me, which made Thing One (?) let out a startled squeak. "You just plunked them on the counter and *left*?"

"They weren't on the counter when—uh—I'm not actually sure what's happening here. But whatever I did, I'm very sorry. Unless you're glad. Then I'm proud of what I'm not sure I did." I turned to Sinclair. "It's not my fault! I told them to stay," I whined.

Although. Technically they had.

# CHAPTER NINETEEN

*"The important thing is,"* Tina began, *"the little ones are* home and they're safe."

They weren't so little when I saw them last, but I kept that to myself. I wanted to get Sinclair alone and explain what I'd seen so we could decide together what to do about it. Ironic, that I was doing that annoying trope where the female lead keeps an important secret to herself until it's Almost Too Late, but there was a lot more at stake here than Jessica's roused maternal instinct. And ugh, I just heard myself. What in the name of all that was (un)holy was I becoming as I approached my midthirties?

Something to obsess over later.

"Yes, thank . . . *God.*" Sinclair really loved being able to break that commandment. I think he and Tina must have come to an arrangement, because though he knew it hurt her, she didn't glare or complain or give him the "I knew you when you were still in diapers, buster, so quit showing off" look. "That is, of course, the most important thing, quite right."

"And they're fine, too. Right, Marc?" Jess asked, kneading and worrying the corner of one baby blanket until it began to fray. Her gaze, wide and anxious, never left Marc's face. "They're fine?"

"Completely," he assured her, putting away his steth and other medical goodies. Tina had bought him an old-fashioned doctor's bag in which he kept meticulously cleaned instruments and Tic Tacs (he had a horror of rotten zombie breath). The first thing he'd done was give both babies a thorough once-over, then let DadDick and Jessica feed them their 6:25 p.m. bottles (soon to be followed by their 6:45 p.m. bottles, because those li'l buggers were bottomless yawning pits of hunger). "I can't find a thing wrong with them."

*Then you're definitely not looking hard enough.* Actually, now that I thought about it, there likely *wasn't* anything wrong with them, at least on a physical level. Too bad it wasn't as simple as that.

"Okay. So." DadDick smiled down at Pepsi, watching with a sort of concentrated raptness as he/she guzzled. "What happened? And could it happen again?"

"And what do we do if it does?" Jessica added, cradling Coke. V-chip them? Recalling how my Sharpie plan had been received, I decided to keep that thought to myself, too.

The irony was neck deep. I was doing that thing I saw movie characters do all the time: I knew something about the zombies/plague/weird babies/sentient dogs/robot lizards trying to take over the world and rather than helpfully cough it up, I was keeping secrets. I had become the thing I loathed: the useless, dim, hysterical horror movie heroine.

"One thing at a time," Tina soothed. "I think the best thing for now is to—"

Jess ignored her, locked eyes with Sinclair, and said it straight-out: "So what's the policy on turning kids into vampires?"

Decades' worth of cool self-control was probably the only reason Sinclair's jaw just didn't unhinge. My jaw, however, was now on vacation and my mouth was so wide a dozen bees could have flown in and had a meeting.

For a long moment no one said anything. Since I'd literally rather die than let a silence hang too long, I was the first to break.

"Where did that come from?" I managed (after three tries, which had sounded like "whuh? muh? derp?"). "The babies being gone? Because they're back. And they're fine. Marc just explained how they're fine. You trusted him to deliver them, so we all know you both trust his medical opinion despite . . . despite stuff happening." At the casual compliment (except it wasn't so much a compliment as a statement of fact), Marc dropped his gaze and smiled a little at the floor.

"I'm just curious," Jess clarified, as though she often wondered about vampires being babies or vice versa when we all knew her thoughts on the subject. Shit, she'd been dying, actually *dying of cancer*, and had made it clear she was not, not, *not* to be turned. By anyone. Under any circumstances. She hadn't known at the time—no one had known; I hadn't even known—that I'd accidentally cure her but she still made it plain she expected to die human and remain dead. "Just . . . just wondering. About things. Things I hadn't ever really wondered about before."

"Do you think someone stole your infants to bring them to another vampire to turn?" Tina asked, her face twisting with such dark emotion she wasn't at all pretty for those few moments. "Because that would be unconscionable and we would never, *never* allow—"

"No, I don't think that. I think Sinclair had it right." She nodded at him. "I don't think a regular person could have come in here to take them for *any* reason, never mind fetching them to a vampire for a midnight snack." DadDick visibly shuddered at her words and clutched Pepsi closer. "But I'm wondering how we can protect them, going forward."

"That is not the way," Sinclair said, and thank goodness, because I was about to say the same thing but much, much louder.

"Okay," she replied steadily, "but why?"

*"Why?"* I repeated, much, much louder.

"Is there, uh, is there an official policy?" Jessica looked around at us, clearly prepared to wait all night for an answer. "Or something?"

Sinclair looked at me. Which was unnerving, because, um, like *I'd* know? Oh. Right. Queen. "I have no—" I began, only to be cut off by Tina.

"Jessica, when was the last time you slept?" This in a lovely, gentle tone that didn't have even a trace of *also, have you lost your fucking mind?*

"I don't know," she snapped. "What day is it? It's not because I'm tired. You guys know it's not because I'm tired."

"Exhausted," I corrected. "I get tired explaining why Payless sucks. I get tired when I have to buy ice because there is a ton of ice outside, all the time, through May. You're not tired. You're exhausted, and why wouldn't you be? It's no wonder sleep deprivation isn't considered cool even among torturers. It's true!" I added, like they were getting ready to contradict me. "You know a torture is bad when *guys who torture* are all 'hey, man, you'd better back off, that's going too far.'"

Jessica shrugged. "Like I said. It's because I'm thinking about things I've never had to think about before." I could sympathize, really. I hated when that happened to me.

"You cannot actually want your infants to become vampires," Sinclair pointed out, sounding all reasonable and not a little aghast, which was good on him because I knew he was horrified. I could feel it, all the horror.

"No, I wouldn't want them to be like this for all eternity," she said, looking down at Coke.

I shuddered. Eternity as a newborn! A crying, shitting, nonverbal creature the size of a bag of flour who would only give negative feedback. *Argh, kill it, kill it with fire!* They could make that their new family motto.

"Has it ever been done?" DadDick asked, so suddenly I'd

almost forgotten he was there. Jess tended to fill a room when she was wound up. I'd almost forgotten *I* was there.

No answer from Sinclair or Tina. And his thoughts, I couldn't help notice, were carefully blank. Unlike mine, which were usually blank but not because I was trying.

"So, that would be a big fat Yes," Jessica guessed, going with that whole "silence signals consent" thing. "It *has* been done before. So what—"

"The creatures were destroyed," was Sinclair's deadly quiet reply. "Immediately. Those who made them were also destroyed. Slowly."

I suppressed a shiver as I watched my husband. *Remember when we used to have pleasant conversations in this kitchen?*

*Not really, Elizabeth. No.*

"Okay!" In my intent to bring this awful chat to a close, I spoke a little too loudly, if everyone jumping (except Coke and Pepsi, glutted and now in milk comas) was any indication. "If there isn't an official policy, there's definitely an unofficial one, one that I am behind a hundred percent. No babies turned into li'l fangers. No preschoolers, either. And no elementary-age kids. And middle school sucks; who wants to be twelve forever? For that matter, high school sucks, too, and it'd be beyond evil to condemn anyone to a lifetime of smelling like Clearex and sexual frustration. Except maybe sixteen should be the, what d'you call it, the cutoff?" I looked around the room. "Should someone be writing this down? And speaking of writing things down, I have to go back to Hell. I only left because of the text, but now that the babies got back (heh, get it?), I have to go back, too. I'm sorry." I was speaking directly to Jessica now. "I'm not running away from this particular weirdness so much as leaving because I have to address a different particular weirdness."

"Yeah, yeah." She flapped a hand at me. "You'd better, I guess, although we don't really feel safer knowing you're down there doing stuff."

"It's not *down there*," I began to explain for the ninth time, "it's a whole other dimension."

"And listen, about your dad—"

"Don't worry about it," I cut in, because yikes! How'd we get back on that subject? "I know you haven't had any time to look into this, I mean—"

"Well, a solid twenty-four hours, which is—"

"—I've only been gone, what? Half an hour? But I'll come back later and we can—"

"—not nearly enough time but I *was* able to figure—"

"—figure out . . . what to . . ." I trailed off as Jessica's words sank in. "What now? How long was I gone?"

"A night and a day," Tina replied, watching me carefully, "and now it's night again."

"No. No, that's not—" I stared and, since I couldn't think of anything else to do at that moment, stared more. And they were all looking at me like *I'd* been the one to lose track of time and not crazy, new-mom-hormonal, sleep-deprived Jessica. "Is it? That can't . . ."

Sinclair's big hand gripped mine and he gave it a light squeeze. "It seemed like much less time in Hell?"

"It was half an hour in Hell! Oh, hell. I mean, the hell with Hell. Argh! You know what I'm trying to get across."

"Vaguely." The corner of his mouth twitched, but he squashed the grin. "So in addition to mastering your new-found ability to move your physical body to and from another dimension, it seems you had best adjust to, and understand, the time issue as well."

"I didn't even know there *was* a time issue! How the hell am I supposed to address it? Don't even get me started on understanding it."

"By allowing me to attend you," was his soooo smooth reply.

I yanked my hand away. "Aha! I see your subtle game, Sink Lair; you're not fooling me."

"The *b* in *subtle*," he began with a mournful sigh, "is silent. As we have discussed."

"Back off, Grammar Police."

"Would that not be Pronunciation Police?"

"Don't try to confuse me!" Alas, too late.

"Never mind that—what's subtle about Sinclair saying straight-out that he wants to go to Hell with you and take some of the burden off your bony shoulders?" Marc asked with honest curiosity.

"He just wants to take over." Weird how I snapped that like it was a bad thing. "All right, I'll deal with that, too." My brain waited hopefully, but no idea was forthcoming. I'd deal with my lazy brain later. It would be punished! Everyone would be punished! "I have to go." Not least because Jess apparently had a Dad update. Pass. "You know you can text me if you need me."

"Yeah, about that," Marc began, and Tina's eyes lit up. I could actually see them widen and get sparkly the way they did when she came home with a bottle of peanut-butter-flavored vodka.

"Yes, how interesting! And how fascinating, my queen, you must tell us how—"

"No idea." Better nip that in the bud right now, the thought that I could actually be a helpful source of information for them. "Seriously, you guys. I've got no idea. And hanging in the kitchen isn't going to help me get one. I'll be back in—" A day? A week? Ugh, no idea, everything was horrible, life was horrible, Hell was horrible, Jessica's weird babies were horrible, my vampire king husband angling for a supernatural corporate takeover was horrible, ugh *ugh UGH!*

*I just really, really need to get the fuck out of here right now I have to have to* have to—

# CHAPTER
# TWENTY

*"Oh, now, what is this shit?"*

I was back in the big fat nothing that was the pit, Hades, the place where you could never find your receipt and even if you could, Hell doesn't take returns.

I'd wanted to be back in Hell—or at least gone from that kitchen. And I was. Blink! Jeannie and her pink outfit of scarves and air (and her disturbing habit of referring to an air force major as "Master") had nothing on me. Too bad I had no real idea how I did it. More of that "Hell and its rules are shaped by the force of your will" bullshit? The force of *my* will? What, like, think positive? *Don't think you can run Hell . . .* know *you can!* What? No. Nothing was that easy.

Could those business seminars I'd endured for various office jobs have been right all along? Communicating with Tact, Diplomacy, and Professionalism . . . do I have to say what a waste of money that was for management? Almost as much as the bucks they shelled out for Conflict Management Skills for Women. Should I hang some of those motivational posters in Hell? *Be the Bridge: Problems become opportunities when the right people join together. Excellence: Some excel because they are destined to. Most excel because they are determined to.* Are they also determined to end a sentence with a preposition? Because that's what they're doing. Show me *that* poster, thanks.

"Oh, look," a familiar, bored voice drawled behind me. "It's back."

I whirled and glared at the Ant. "What the hell is going on in Hell?"

"You aren't tired of hammering that stupid joke over and over yet?"

"I will *never* get tired of hammering stupid jokes," I retorted. "Now tell me what's going on. How long was I gone? And how come I was only here for a few minutes but the gang said I was MIA for a day? And what's up with the weird babies?" This was why I hadn't said anything to Jessica or DadDick about what I'd seen their babies do. Because if there's one person on the planet who loathes my stepmother more than I, it would be Jessica, who loathed her with all the power her love and loyalty brought to bear.

The Ant had, after all, been the one to tip me off to the problem with Jessica's pregnancy[9] and the strangeness therein; I assumed she'd also know what was up with Oil and Vinegar. But there was no way I could have said, *Something unprecedented and terrifying is happening to your children and the only one who might be able to help us is a woman you and I both despise and have never been nice to, but, no big, I'll go play Twenty Questions with her in Hell and maybe she'll be helpful and maybe not. Later, bitch!*

Uh. No. If I had, Jess never would have let me go back to Hell without her, and taking my best friend to Hell was not

---

[9] The Ant was uncharacteristically helpful in *Undead and Unsure*.

happening, *ever*. And she wouldn't have forgiven me for going without her.

"Oh, now you want my counsel?" The Ant was cupping her elbows and shivering as if she were cold, which she totally wasn't. She was also tapping one foot, which I assumed was to remind me that a) she was Very, Very Busy and b) she still had terrible taste in footgear. "That's nerve. I thought since you killed my boss I was now the—how did you put it?"

"Annoying Nobody," I reminded her, then realized I wasn't helping myself. "Um, I think. I dunno, it was so long ago." *Maybe.* "Look, just cough up what you know about this place, okay?"

"No," was the predictable answer, and there it was, the thing I loathed more than pleather: the Pout. The Pout had precipitated my father filing for divorce, cruises to tropical islands, my father's second marriage, and various shopping trips abroad. And that was just the stuff I knew about. It was the Ant's mightiest weapon (aside from her stiff hair, which, I was pretty sure, was bulletproof from all the product she shoveled on) and one that never failed to work.

On my *father*.

"Don't even," I warned. "I will rip your lips off your face. Then throw them on the ground and stomp on them." What ground? Hell was still a big pile of nothing. I was undaunted; for the purpose of lip stomping, I'd find a way to make Hell have a ground again. Have an up and a down and a right and a left, too, if it came to that. "Look, you think I don't know this sucks? I'm well aware this sucks and I'm just as horrified as you are to find out we're still in each other's lives."

"That," she replied grimly, "is impossible."

"Ha! You remember how appalled you and Dad were to find out I'd come back from the dead? As a vampire, no less?"

"Yes," was the short, stiff reply. "Nightmare."

"For me, too! You think that was any kind of fun for me?

You think that was my plan? Because that was not my plan, Antonia; in no way, shape, or form was any of that my plan."

She opened her mouth to retort, but I was off and running.

"Being run over by a Pontiac Aztec on my thirtieth birthday after I'd just been fired was not my plan. Hearing my skull shatter—it sounded like ice cracking, by the way—was not my plan. Coming back as a vampire was not my plan. Coming back as the foretold *queen* of the bloodsuckers . . . wait for it . . . not my plan! And that's just the stuff that happened that first *week*! That insane amount of insanity was all *before* I found out about the Antichrist being a blood relative and Satan looking like Lena Olin and—and—and me messing up the timeline and time travel and the cold, frozen netherworld of the future and Ancient Me and helping run Hell!"

"Yes, yes, you have problems. We know. *We all know*, because you never shut up about how put-upon you are with the money and the happy marriage and the minions."

"I don't have minions," I said, sulking a little. "I have help-ers. Like . . . like Boy Scouts. Boy Scouts on a liquid diet possibly for eternity. And what the *fuck* would you even know about my marriage?"

"Do you think this is what I wanted?" she snapped back, gesturing at all the nothing while ignoring my very sensible question. "I'm well aware of what a skull sounds like when it shatters, or did you forget I died almost exactly the same way?"

Um. I kind of did. Forget, that is. The garbage truck had pancaked them. Yeah, *them*. Because there were two people in that car and one of them was definitely my dad. It never occurred to me to wonder how much of the fatal, devastating accident my stepmother remembered. It was horrifying even to think about, never mind quiz her about. Even more horrify-ing: of almost all the people I knew, the Ant was someone who could empathize with some of the less-than-great aspects of my life after death.

The Ant! Why does the universe hate me and want me to be

sad? Because *could* empathize wasn't the same as *would* empathize. In fairness (groan), I had zero interest in empathizing with her, either.

And, oh good God, she was still bitching. "Do you think it was my plan to be possessed by the devil, to have her run my body for a year?"

"I thought you were more upset about how no one noticed you were possessed," I admitted. It wasn't funny, except to me. It was actually pretty vindicating: she was so awful, no one noticed she'd been possessed by the evilest thing in creation.

The smirk fell off my face as I realized that was something else we had in common. I'd read the Book of the Dead in a misguided attempt to learn more about vampires and their nature and what I could expect in the future.[10] I'd turned evil for a bit and raped Sinclair, who had been delighted for every second of it.[11] That was an awkward conversation, later.

More empathy, ugh. And at the worst possible time. I couldn't afford to feel anything for the Ant except my usual exhausted contempt. Anything else only made complicated matters even more difficult.

"And did you think—" Oh, good, the shrill bitching was helping me back off from the momentary empathy. "Did you think it was my plan to have *another* baby in my thirties?"

"Forties," I mumbled.

"And die in my late thirties?"

"Forties."

"And find out that my daughter—the one I'd been forced to carry for nine months and squeeze out without so much as a Tylenol, never mind an epidural—was the Antichrist?"

---

[10] The Book of the Dead was written on human skin by Ancient Betsy in the future, was taken to the far-off past by the devil, and ended up in Betsy's possession. Everything in the Book comes true, but unfortunately anyone who reads it for any length of time goes insane.

[11] And that's not all she did. Check *Undead and Unappreciated* for the rest.

"Well, I had to find out she was my sister, and also the Antichrist." Speaking of, where the hell in Hell was she? Where was anyone besides This Woman? "So we can both relate, so what? This isn't further proof we should go get coffee together or something, right?"

Judging by the expression on her face, the Ant found that concept as repulsive as I did. Whew! "And before you ask," she continued, "my daughter had to tend to something back on earth." Wow. I've lived long enough to have "back on earth" be a true, literal thing, something I barely blinked at. "She has many responsibilities and demands on her time."

"So do I!" I cried. "*So* many. Speaking of, Jessica's babies—"

Nostril flare at the name. I stomped on the urge to take off her shoes (which weren't really there) and beat her to death with them (which was impossible) and then set the shoes on fire (tricky, since the shoes *and* the fire didn't exist). Ultimately futile, sure, but sooo satisfying. I think.

"Keep your bigotry out of this," I warned, which was like telling Cinnabon to keep their sugar out of anything.

"I am not a racist!" she cried, contradicting many, *many* of her actions, conversations, and boldly stated philosophies. "We're very supportive of all their causes. For years we donated to the—ah—"

"Can't remember the name of the charity you use for a tax break? That's not surprising. Not even a little tiny bit."

"You're as bad as I am—"

"*You take that back!*"

"—with your one black friend and—"

"Wait. What?"

A snort, followed by an eye roll. "Sorrrry. African American friend."

"No, that's not what I take objection to." And never would. I'd made that mistake once, and as a consequence Jessica almost fed me my own face. *My parents and grandparents and greats and great-greats and great-great-greats were not African! We were from*

*Jamaica! This PC shit is going too far! Don't assume you know where my family's from because I've got more melanin in my skin cells than you do, you silly bitch!*

*All right, all right! Say it, don't spray it. Sorry.*

The Ant cut through my stressful flashback (it was so real! I could remember the feel of her fingers as she seized my shirt and twisted, giving it the fabric equivalent of a purple nurple). "Oh, you know what I'm talking about. You've got your one African American pal to cement your street cred but you don't hang out with any other—"

"Stop. Talking." I took an unnecessary breath (it didn't calm me but the dizziness helped me focus). "You're awful. And nobody says 'street cred' anymore."

"Sorry. I'm not up on current slang."

"And that's what you're apologizing for, which sums you up perfectly. But shut up already, I've got bigger problems than you and isn't *that* a crying goddamned shame. Jessica's babies turned into toddlers and then turned back. Except everybody else thought they left the house, then *came* back. I've got no idea what to do about that."

She beckoned my petty concerns forward in a "hurry up, out with it" gesture.

"And . . . that's it." I thought about it. Yep, that was the sitch in a nasty little nutshell. "There's no more to tell. Isn't that enough? Any ideas?"

"Several."

"About Hellman's and Miracle Whip?"

"Who?"

"The *babies*."

"Yes, kick them out of your lives. All of them."

I was surprised I was surprised. I've never been what you would call a fast learner. Or even a medium-speed learner. "Okay, now can I have a suggestion that doesn't reek of sociopathy?"

Another shrug, one that barely concealed her impatience and

boredom. "Don't do anything. They'll adjust, the way they've had to since you didn't have the common decency to stay dead."

"Yes," I agreed, "that was ill-mannered of me." Ill-mannered? Sinclair was rubbing off on me, and not in a sexytimes way.

"They're fine. You're fine. You know what the problem is. Just explain it to their parents."

"Right, because it's just that easy." Wait, was it? Naw. That was not how life worked. How my life worked. "And where is everybody? Not that I want a crowd, but it's so odd to be standing around in nothing having awful conversations with you." I gestured to the nil of perdition. "There should be billions milling around."

"They're here. You'll see them when you wish to see them. That's all."

I gritted my teeth at how she said "that's all" like it was the entire explanation and there was no need for further discussion. *That's all.* Cripes.

My stepmother rubbed her temples and looked like the Before picture in a Pepto-Bismol ad. "Think of it like a chest of drawers. You know exactly where your socks are even though you can't see the socks. And before you squawk about how it can't be that simple, you're wrong. Because I have to break it down *so* far in order for you to get it, it *is* that simple."

I had to give it to her; when she explained Hell that way, it was a concept I could grasp. "Then why are you here? I wasn't thinking about you; I didn't accidentally summon you." In fact, it was probably time to get back to the Game. *White bear, white bear.* Except I was thinking *DadDadDadDadDad.* The whole time she'd been reading me the race riot act: *DadDadDadDadDad.*

She looked away. "Where else would I be?"

"Uh . . ." Oh God, no. Please. No more empathy for the Ant. It went against everything I believed in. And everything she believed in. "Okay."

"I was always going to end up here."

"You were?" The way she said it made me a little sad. Like she was stuck and there was nothing to be done. Which exactly described my father's second marriage. (Yeah, I know, very meow. I literally cannot help myself.)

But was that even correct? She had been the devil's right hand. Satan had been fond of the Ant as undivine vessel for the Antichrist, and they both cared about Laura, which made the Ant one of the few souls (?) Satan could absolutely count on to keep the Antichrist's interests front and center. Satan was gone or dead or whatever, off to Heaven or another Hell or a dimension we didn't know about or just total nothingness, but that still put Laura (and me to a *much* lesser extent) in charge. So was the Ant really stuck here? Was she staying by choice? Did she just hang around in all the nothing, waiting patiently for Laura or me to turn up?

Wow, any more parallels to her marriage to my father and I wasn't going to be able to shake the feeling that Everything Happens for a Reason. Also, ugh.

"Of course I ended up in Hell," she said with a sigh, in response to my polite "You were?" "I led a married man into adultery." At my uncomprehending look, she elaborated. "It's a sin." Then she snorted, "Presbyterians."

First off, I knew it was a sin, I just didn't think many people these days truly thought they would go to Hell for treating their marriage vows as marriage suggestions. Second, my religion was none of her business. Third, I had no idea *she* was religious. Or moral. "It, um." What the hell to say to that? Any of that? "You know the saying. I mean, it wasn't all you." This would kill me. I would literally nice myself to death, and for the Ant, of all people. Death was coming. "It takes two to, uh, adult. Be adulterous, or adulterate. Whatever. You weren't in it by yourself. In fact, you weren't even married, he was. So he was the actual adulterator. Right?"

A sullen shrug, but the way she peeked at me out of the

corner of her eye while refusing to look straight at me was almost cute. "We made mistakes," she finally allowed.

I accepted the olive branch (which was more like an olive twig, or maybe the pit) and went back to what I really wanted to know. High time, even if I didn't have a hidden agenda. Because being stuck in Hades talking about my father's marriage with my stepmother . . . if I'd had any doubt we were in Hell, that would have cleared it right up.

And again, because this was starting to bug me, I was here . . . without Laura! Unfortunately I didn't have a leg to stand on in the "how come you punked out on that thing we agreed to do together?" department, due to my avoidance shenanigans. Still, it was annoying. Laura was supposed to be the better (wo)man, dammit. Never in my life, not once, had *I* been the better (wo)man. Why would anyone expect me to start now? Frankly, their unreasonable expectations were kind of a burden.

*Because it's your responsibility? You're not just a queen, you're the* older *sister.*

I shoved those thoughts away so I could get back to what I needed to discuss. "Yeah, speaking of adulterating and all that came with it . . ." I made a show of looking around. "Where's my father?"

A silence that could, at best, be referred to as uncomfortably awkward was my only answer. It took me several seconds to realize she wasn't going to say anything. That this might not be a conversation, but a monologue. An uncomfortably awkward monologue.

I cleared my throat and tried again. "Did you understand the question? About Dad?"

"I've got no time for this. Neither do you."

And she turned her back on me.

# CHAPTER
# TWENTY-ONE

*Okay, this. This, um. This was not how I'd expected the* discussion to go. I'd expected her to tell me right off where she thought Dad was or that she had no idea and her husband's whereabouts were none of my business. Not avoidance, which—I had to give the Ant credit—wasn't ever her style. In fact, she went out of her way to avoid avoidance, always delighting in being blunt and confrontational, whereas in any confrontation you'd find my dad in the other room, and sometimes the other state. She was the yin to his yang, the Demi Moore to his Ashton Kutcher. Wait. Never mind.

The "conversation" we were having was like prepping to tangle with an arsonist, only to realize you were tangling with a burglar instead. You had to think up entirely new rules to deal. You had to understand that what you thought would get burned would instead get stolen. I'm giving way too much thought to this metaphor, possibly because the conversation was *freaking* me *out*.

"Neither do I? Neither do I?" Repetition worked pretty well with the Ant; she was like a parrot that way. "Is that what you think? Not your call." I made a determined effort to ignore how my stomach plunged and kept at her. "And you're not the one who gets to tell me what I do and don't have time for. In case you missed a recent shift in power dynamics, I outrank you. Which means you're going to make time."

She snorted. "That's convenient. You spend weeks wiggling on the hook like a whiny worm—"

"Gross. Don't make fishing metaphors if you don't know dick about fishing. And could you turn around? It's so unsettling to argue with your shoulders."

"—and telling everyone who would listen that you're not suited for this job, right up until you want to use the perks to pull rank."

Damn. "Good for you," I said with grudging, *painful* approval. "You're still going to have to make time."

"Why would you think I know?"

I nearly fell down, for a couple of reasons. In her capacity as the Executive Assistant from Hell, the Ant had answered questions I'd had on other trips here I hadn't been able to get out of. But even putting that aside, the Ant, in life, had always known my dad's whereabouts pretty much all the time. She was always aware of the karmic retribution that is when you marry your mistress, you create a job opening. (My mom had pointed that out to her with gleeful fury.) I couldn't imagine she would be much different in death. So far no one I'd met was different in death. The fact that she even asked me that question showed the size of the wall she'd just slammed between us.

"You must know," I replied, shocked. "You're the expert on Hell since Satan quit/got her ass killed. And even if you weren't, you died with him. And—and if you 'woke up' here or whatever by yourself, you could have found out. You and Satan were practically besties. She could have done the Hell equivalent of making one phone call and finding out for you."

"She did say I was her favorite unholy vessel," the Ant mused. Even while stonewalling me, she managed a second-hand compliment.

*I could learn from this woman.*

Naturally I banished that thought the instant, the *second*, it surfaced in my mind like a fart bubble in a bathtub.

"Billions of souls," the Ant was saying, because it might have started as a monologue but had eventually turned into a conversation. "Needle in a haystack. And it's none of your business, anyway."

This was the—what? The sixth or seventh time this week I was so staggered it took me a minute to remember how to talk. Some people found shock upon shock to be exciting, a ticket to an adrenaline high. I . . . did not. I liked my adrenaline highs to come from sample sales and banging the vampire king. And maybe smoothies.

"None of my business? Oh God, anything but that!" I cried, horror-struck. "You mean there's actually something *to* this? No! No, you're doing it wrong, it's all wrong, how can you not know how this goes after all these years?"

She twitched a little, alarmed. "I don't—"

"This is how it goes! This is how it's *always* supposed to go! You're supposed to mock my black friend's sleep-deprivation-fueled conspiracy theories and say something faux-supportive yet racist, like how it's not her fault but the more babies she has, the more welfare checks she'll get or something just as terrible and then I'll lose my temper and you'll remind me what a burden I was on your husband."

"But she's rich. Why would she need to go on wel—"

"*I don't know!*" Really? That was the part of the expected response she was going to focus on? "Racism isn't logical, for Christ's sake! But you've gone all squirrelly and that is freaking me right out!"

"I'm right here," she pointed out. "No need to scream."

"Dammit dammit dammit!"

"You were right."

Well. Those were the magic words that took the wind out of my sails, so I forced myself to get a grip before my rant could gain momentum and become sentient. "Okay. Thanks for that." Had I ever heard those words from her? Maybe, if one of her charity-bim pals dared her. Or if she had a fever. A really high fever. Like, boiling-point high. "Which part was I right about?"

"Your time is your business and it was inappropriate for me to tell you otherwise. But my time is *my* business, and I don't have any for this."

"Again: this is not how this conversation goes. You're supposed to—to—" Wait, why was she smaller? Was she—? She was! The pineapple-haired bitch was walking away! "Antonia, where do you suppose you're going? Antonia? Ant?" Farther and farther away, the nothing was swallowing her even as I watched. "You get back here this instant, missy! This isn't over and we aren't even close to done. Don't make me hunt you down! You think I won't? I'll hunt you like Khan hunted Kirk!" Oh, jeez, did I just yell a *Star Trek* reference at my dead stepmother? That was it. Marc's biweekly sci-fi movie marathons were hereby canceled. "There's no point in running, you know. You'll never escape me so you should just suck it up and accept the fact that—annnnnd you're gone."

I was standing by myself. Entirely by myself. In a Hell dimension populated by billions, I'd managed the trick of being alone. I had no idea how to feel about that. I had no idea how to feel about the fact that I had no idea how to feel about *that*, either.

The worst part was, the entire confrontation had settled exactly nothing. I'd forced myself to ask the question, something unthinkable only a few hours before. By asking, I was forced to acknowledge (to myself if no one else) the fact that his death was not, perhaps, what it seemed. So I'd sacrificed my complacency for next to no gain.

Shit, maybe my dad *was* in Hell and just didn't come when I wanted him, knew I was playing (and losing) the Game but keeping well out of sight. No question at all, that would have been one hundred percent in character.

He'd been a lousy father. It was hard even to admit that and had taken years for me to acknowledge, never mind face. It didn't help that I felt guilty complaining when so many people had it worse, endured fathers who beat them or sexually abused them or stole from them or killed them. Jessica's father had been much worse; I couldn't imagine enduring a tenth of what she'd been subjected to. I tried to count my blessings but I always fetched up against an undeniable fact: all my father's sins against me hadn't been out of anger. They'd been born of indifference, which somehow hurt the worst.

Men who knew me briefly and sometimes not even that long had been more interested in my life, more helpful and concerned, than he had been in three decades of what Jessica dubbed "kinda parenting." When I was younger I wished he'd care more. Or, if he did, show it more. By the time I was in my late teens I'd given up on that as a hopeless fantasy (like my fantasy of Christian Louboutin deciding I was his shoe muse and designing pair after pair for me *only for me* ALL FOR ME, ALL OF IT!).

Instead I'd indulged in different wishful thinking; I wished for a different father. Childish, I guess. But I had clung to it for years and even now it was a tempting thought.

Another father, and now I was thinking of some of the older men I'd known over the years. Such as the retired mailman who'd lived across the street from my childhood home. He'd leave cupcakes in our mailbox sometimes, which I found hilarious and delicious. Mr. Reynolds had been rising before dawn for over thirty years and, though retired, couldn't shake the habit. So he'd filled his mornings with baking and was always leaving Mom and me mailbox goodies. Mom hadn't been able to resist reminding him that it was a federal offense for anyone but the owner or the PO to put things in mailboxes, and being retired didn't shield him from federal law. But she said it with a smile on her lips and a dab of frosting on her chin. Today that would probably come off as creepy, but back then we didn't worry about it and it worked out fine; the treats were always delicious and Mr. Reynolds didn't push boundaries any further.

Or someone like the priest I'd run into not long after waking up dead. The father had always been nice to me even though he knew what I was. He was upset when a member of his flock staked me, even though he was one of the reasons I'd been in danger in the first place. He'd shown more anxiety over my staking than my actual father had about my fatal car accident. What was his name? Mark something, no, I was getting him mixed up with our Marc, I think it was Father Mark and whatever happened to that guy that father *that Father Mark Father Mark Father . . .*

# CHAPTER
# TWENTY-TWO

*"Hello, young lady!"*

I didn't move for a few seconds. Just took a couple of deep unnecessary breaths. *Okay. It appears to have worked. Turn and confirm . . . I guess that means my old neighbor is still alive. Or in Heaven. Because the guy talking to me isn't a postal worker turned postretirement cupcake god.*

I turned. Saw the small older man—old enough to be my dad and, yep, I admit to a few dad issues—and smiled. "Hiya, Father Mark."

"Markus," he corrected with a smile. "You were always terrible at names. All of our names."

"Oh, who cares?"

I did, kinda. Maybe one or more of them was here, too, but I hoped not—they'd all been young, younger than me, younger than Laura.

And I was happy to see a friendly face in Hell. Before Cathie showed, it had been the Ant and Jessica's parents and

Laura and they'd all had harsh words for me. Like I wasn't struggling, too!

Father Markus looked just like he had when I last saw him, and it was clear he still thought of himself as a priest, even here. Black suit, white collar. White fringe of hair, but otherwise bald. Small brown eyes that scrunched when he smiled, as he was now. Small, neat hands, simple black dress shoes that were neatly shined. And the white collar. My gaze kept going to it.

"You were expecting me to be in a T-shirt and Bermudas?" he teased.

"Ugh, what an image to shove into my brain, why would you *do* that? It's just weird to see a priest down here. Here," I said again, correcting myself. "We're neither up nor down. Sorry. Old habits."

"I do it, too. It sure feels like 'down here.'"

"Why *are* you here?" I glanced around, which was dumb. It was just him and me. And the Ant, probably lurking back in the fog of nada while ignoring my call. Oh, and let's not forget, never forget, the billions of souls also lurking (at least the ones who hadn't taken advantage of the confusion brought on by new management and vamoosed). "Are you a hostage?"

"Hostage denotes value," the priest replied cheerfully. "I have none."

"I doubt that. A lot."

"Don't let the collar fool you; I was always just an ordinary sinner."

"But technically we all are, right?"

His eyes gleamed with momentary approval, as he knew I'd been an indifferent Christian in life. A believer, sure, but I'd never been one for getting up early on Sundays. Like most of my ilk, I'd always assumed that whatever issues God had with me could be worked out . . . eventually. Not today, though. Maybe not tomorrow. "Yes, we all are, but I broke my vows."

I chewed on that one for a few seconds. Tricky ground with a priest. Most of them took that Bible stuff pretty seriously and, in an age where texting *OMG* was technically a sin, he could have ended up here for any number of reasons.

Off the top of my head I was thinking big number six: thou shall not kill, no matter how tempting it was or how stressful your day or how much easier it would make your life (I'm paraphrasing). Father Markus helped plan murders—except the Brood Mariners only targeted people who were already dead. Is it murder if the person you killed was already (un)dead? He hadn't formed the gang (it was like *West Side Story*, except it wasn't a love story, it wasn't a musical, and instead of dancing they staked vamps) to do anything malicious. He—they—truly thought they were doing God's work.

God hadn't weighed in, but I had. Which was why the Blond Wormers had disbanded.

"It sucks that you're here—"

"That disappointed to see me?" he teased.

"No! A bazillion times no. But I'm not sure you belong here."

I got a stern look for that. "Of course I do."

"Come on, Father. You were one of the good guys. You put yourself in danger to round up the Blini Wanderers—"

"Blade Warriors." He sighed.

"—those annoying teenaged emo vampire killers—"

"Emo?"

"How long have you been dead? Never mind," I said as he opened his mouth to answer. "We'll be here all day. *Is* it day? Don't answer! An emo is a kid with a terrible attitude about life, which isn't new, but these kids are often right, which is. The kid who says, 'He's too good for me,' and you want to be all, 'No, no, don't talk like that,' except you know the kid's right. Emos never cut their bangs, and they write long, meandering poems about things they have no reference for, like death or prolonged suffering or using too much fabric softener. I'm generalizing," I added when his eyes started to cross from the info dump, "and I'm sure they're not all annoying. It's just, all the ones I've met are." Minnesota emo kids liked Orange Julius almost as much as I did, and there were always at least two in front of me and one behind me in line. Sometimes in the middle of the day! (Emos don't have to go to high school, apparently.) Also, maybe Orange Julius = existential deepness?

"Basically—it's okay, I'm almost done, I swear it—basically it's the 'these kids today' lament with a healthy dose of black hair dye. That, and the only thing worse than an emo who wishes they were a vamp is one who kills vamps and then writes a really long poem about it using phrases like 'burning ice' and 'sunlight of shattering cold.' Except that might not be quite it . . . wait, did I get goth mixed up with emo again?"

"I know you're trying to help me understand, but I'm more confused now."

Yes, I often had that effect on people. "Never mind. My point is, you saw what you thought was evil and you wanted to face it; you saw badness in action and the orphans you took in off the streets—"

"Not all of them were orph—"

"Details, Father! We can't get mired in details! You made them into a team and gave them all the wooden stakes they could stab with and helped them say their prayers, when you weren't helping them track down and kill psycho vampires."

"Again, I realize you're trying to help me, but I'm not at all comforted."

"That's because you keep interrupting me! You did all that stuff except you didn't, not really. Someone else was pulling all your strings, we know that now."

"Yes," he said, mouth turning down in a sorrowful bow. "Now."

"Will you please ease up on yourself? The gang and I fixed it, evil was punished, and when it was all over I owned a nightclub, called Scratch." By vamp law, when you killed one of us, you inherited all the vamp's stuff. Tina had explained the somewhat savage tradition ("Vampires don't have families to whom they can bequeath their belongings.") and, like most things vampire, it was unpleasantly hilarious. "Except I don't anymore; we sold it. You did what you did and I did what I did and—"

"—we're both here."

Yep. That about covered it. "And you're here because you knew you were supposed to come here when you d—how did you die, anyway? If it's not too personal," I added. Ah, the tricky etiquette of asking a Catholic priest how he died and went to Hell.

"You know that sushi that can kill you if it's improperly prepared?"

"I think so." I'd never much cared for eating bait when alive, so sushi wasn't my strong suit. But there had been that *Simpsons* episode . . . "Cuttlefish?"

"Puffer fish. The preparation is stringently controlled and the chefs are required to undergo years of training."

"I would hope so, what with them wanting to feed their patrons poisonous fish," I prompted, "that *might* not kill them *if* the chefs paid attention in school?"

An approving nod, which cheered me up. Ugh, I definitely was dealing with father issues this week.

"After the Blade Warriors disbanded, with Jon going on to write books, Drake getting his prosthetic feet, and Anya headed to the Olympics—"

"Okay, I want us to stay on track but I'm going to want to get back to that stuff you just said."

"—I found myself seeking new challenges. We were wrong to kill vampires but I admit to missing the thrill of the chase."

"Adrenaline perv," I said affectionately. "So you took a look at your life and said, 'I know! I'll eat poisonous fish! That's a sure way to solve all my problems!'"

"Indeed." Father Markus shrugged and smiled.

"I can't believe you accidentally killed yourself with a fish."

"Oh, I didn't. I had a heart attack on the way to the restaurant."

I stared at him. "You mean we've been talking about bubblefish—"

"Puffer fish."

"—for, like, an hour—"

"About one minute."

"—and it didn't have much of anything to do with the story?"

He shook his head, brown eyes full of resignation. "I should have known better than to go anyway. *Fugu* means 'river pig' in Chinese."

"It does?" No kidding around: I was grossed out.

"Oh yes. The emperor of Japan isn't allowed to eat it, can you imagine? It's considered far too risky; it's against the law."

"If the emperor of Japan is determined to chow down on poison on a plate, maybe they should let him. Maybe you don't want someone with impulse control issues and a need to take risks running the country. Natural selection could just run its course on that one."

I got a disapproving frown for that tone. "Be that as it may, the liver is considered the tastiest—"

"Because gross."

"—as well as the most poisonous."

"Of course it is." I wanted to wring my hands and wail. "And people still line up for the privilege of sucking down river pig with their green tea? God, we're all so stupid. Humanity is screwed."

He laughed at that. "Not at all. But we've definitely got our work cut out for us."

# TWENTY-THREE

*"If I haven't mentioned it before—"*

"You've brought it up several times on our walk."

"—this is Just. So. Stupid."

I'd gotten tired of standing around in all the nothing during our chat, so I'd taken the priest's elbow and started walking. And that was when it happened: I opened my big mouth and accidentally did something that at worst would make everything worse and at best would only raise more questions.

And it had all started soooo innocently. My own fault for dropping my guard. *Whitebearwhitebearwhitebear.*

"This place would be a lot easier," I had stupidly bitched, practically yanking Father Markus in my wake, "if it was organized."

"Yes, well. I imagine that's why you're here."

"Me and my sister," I corrected him. "Or my sister and I; Hell is probably teeming with grammar police so don't you dare report me. Anyway, we're comanagers. Except she's not here, still."

"Your sister."

That was odd. He said it so flatly and gave me a look, something like "why would you say something you know to be false," except that couldn't be it because a) it wasn't false and b) how would he know if it was?

"Your sister," he said again, like he thought maybe I didn't hear him from a foot and a half away.

"Yes, after I, um, did the thing . . ." And now I was on tricky ground again. Father Markus was in Hell for doing what he thought was right. My sins were so much greater than his and yet I was one of the people in charge. How to just blithely rattle off my Satan-murdering antics? "After that, after we—I mean I—after I—" *Tongue, stop flopping down on the job and help me form words and actual sentences! Don't make me bite you while I'm chewing gum!*

"After you freed the Morningstar," he prompted.

"Yeah, after I freed her by freeing her head all over her— I'm not sure *free* means what you think it does, Father."

"The Morningstar paid a heavy price for his—"

"Her, when she looked like Lena Olin."

"—dissatisfaction."

"You sound like you felt sorry for her."

"A heavy price," he said again, forgetting (again) that I was only a foot or two away. "He, or she, or what-have-you, could have returned to God's grace at any time. Pride prevented that."

"Uh-huh. So she was stuck with the job because she was too proud to tell God, 'Hey, sorry about the whole war-in-Heaven thing, can you prodigal me already?'" A million years running the pit? More? And all she had to do at any time was cough up an apology to a deity basically made of sunshine once you were forgiven? "Boo hoo."

"For shame, have you no compassion?"

"For the devil? So you don't remember anything about me at all, do you?"

He ignored that. "All this time and I had no idea *prodigal* was a verb," the priest mused. "But back to the Morningstar. She had fallen, it was true, but there was a way back. It was known to her but her pride prevented her escape as effectively as any jail."

*Yeah, this is soooo fascinating.* I made my eyebrows do that "please continue, I'm hanging on your every word" thing while mentally preparing to stake the Ant to an anthill after burying her in a mound of Sweet'n Low.

"The Morningstar, for all her power and deeds, was to be pitied. Ironic, really, because in part I am also trapped here by my pride."

"I thought you were here because you had a coronary on your way to eat river pig."

"Yes. But the devil often spoke to me through the voice of my hubris." He hung his head. "If not for my pride, I might not have led the children into sin."

Pity prickled the back of my throat and I had to cough. "Yeah, she was a bitch that way." *Argh, don't say "bitch" to a priest!* I coughed again. "And you're being too hard on yourself. Like I said, you thought you were helping. Maybe you *were*, even . . . when I took over the undead reins, horrible mass-murdering jerkweed vamps were the rule, not the exception."

"You have changed that?"

"Tried. Trying, I mean. Attacks and murders and overall vampire nastiness are going down, but it's more because they're afraid of Sinclair and me than because they want to be good and not bad. Most of the vamps accept me as queen now. Not out of any huge love for me," I added, lest he get the wrong idea, because love was definitely not the factor in *any* of that, "but because they're starting to realize they have no choice. None of us have a choice. We're all trapped together. Uh, in a nice way?"

"Baby steps," he suggested, and I had to smile. "You were telling me about the Beast."

Had I mentioned the Ant? Anything was possible, except . . . ah. "You're talking about Laura."

"The Antichrist, yes." He was giving me that odd look again. "You're expecting her to return?"

"Sure. Like I said, we made a deal. Actually I should have been here a while ago, but stuff kept coming up." *I kept making stuff come up.* "And the first thing we're doing is getting rid of all the nothing." I waved irritably at all the nothing. "Hell was a waiting room and then it was a beehive. Now it's nada central and it's making me nuts."

"How would you organize it?"

"I dunno. It's one of the things Laura and I have to figure out. Like I said, it's my fault we haven't yet," I added with what I knew was a guilty expression. "I kept stalling."

"You're here now. If *you* had to choose, how would you do it?"

"Oh, I dunno, maybe by having it be any setup *but* this." For some reason that reminded me of an early Halloween ep of *The Simpsons*, when Lisa reads Bart "The Raven": *Darkness there, and nothing more.* "D'you know what would have been scarier than nothing?" Bart asks her, then answers, *"Anything!"*

So then. What was more efficient than nothing? Anything would be an improvement. Even if it was something that didn't work, at least we'd know about something that didn't work. "It doesn't have to be complex," I continued, thinking about my old office jobs. Thinking about the shopping I would do when I called in sick for my old office jobs. "Something people can grasp, something I can grasp. Like a gigantic filing cabinet. No, that's idiotic. Like—a mall! Hell should be laid out like a mall! Complete with 'You Are Here' signs."

"Yes, that sounds sensible."

"Sensible? I'm a goddamned genius!"

Father Markus winced, either because I'd blasphemed or

my fingers were sunk into his arm like claws. I loosened my grip and he staggered a little. I steadied him and kept babbling. "I'm sorry. But listen! So many people think malls are hellish anyway, so it's relatable, organized, *and* terrifying. The stores are individual hells for various people. They don't have to stay in their little stores; they can go out and about.

"The food court will always smell wonderful—you'll be able to smell your favorites all the time—but they'll always be out of what you want to eat." I was thinking of the Mall of America, thirty-five miles from our house, and all the things I loved and hated about it. Thumbs up: Orange Julius and Barnes and Noble. Thumbs sideways: the amusement park. Thumbs down: the enormous parking lot. No matter where I parked, I always ended up as far away as possible from the stores I wanted to check out and had to walk for what felt like hours. And then walk back.

"Some of the stores could be actual stores, like Apple or Sephora or Aveda. But they'll never have what you want. Apple's Genius Bar will be an Idiot Bar staffed with people who will never be able to answer your question or fix your problem. Aveda will have product, but nothing that suits your particular hair problem. Sephora will only have, I dunno, orange lipstick and bright blue eye shadow. Hugo Boss will never have your size and neither will Macy's. And the stuff they do have in your size will always add ten pounds to your face and be in your least favorite color and feel weird against your skin. The movie theaters will only have out-of-date movies and the projector will break down at the good parts." I was getting downright giddy. The possibilities for torturing people were *endless*.

Father Markus was starting to smile, so my enthusiasm was infectious or he was relieved to find sensation returning to his arm.

Trapped in my genius idea, I kept babbling. "We could have an entrance just for the new people—or maybe that could be the function of the anchor stores. In real life, lots of people park by the anchor stores and use them as a jumping-off point. And no matter how long you've been shopping, by the time you want to go back to your car you realize you're as far from your anchor store as you can be and still be in mall property.

"And we'll add insult to injury by making the damned endure the gigantic parking lot and all the walking, so it'd be unpleasant before they even got to Hell. And the security office would be where Laura and I hang out while pretending to work and—oh my God, as we walk Hell is forming itself into a mall behind us, isn't it? *Isn't it?*"

"I haven't looked," he admitted, "but there's definitely something going on behind us. I learned very quickly not to look over my shoulder in Hell. You wouldn't think it possible but what's coming up behind is always worse."

Fuck that. I turned and looked.

# CHAPTER
# TWENTY-FOUR

**"You must be pretty excited."**

"Well, it *is* nice to see you again, and doing so well. It's not the first time I've been glad the children didn't kill you."

"That's not what I meant. And besides, they did, but the Bling Waddlers couldn't keep me down for long."

"I decline to rise to the bait, young lady." He'd been looking out over the amusement park, which was set in the middle of the Hell mall. The lines were hideous, the park employees were sullen, the food was either too cold or too hot or too stale, and the smell of vomit from woozy ridegoers lingered. Ever had stale popcorn after riding a ride that flipped you upside down? *Glurt!* "I know you know they're the Blade Warriors. I'm not going to keep reminding you."

"You caught on a lot faster than my friends and family," I admitted, sipping an Orange Julius that tasted like water. *Was* water, I was pretty sure. I had to laugh at the old saying (people in Hell want ice water). Water *was* Hell when you wanted a frosty, tangy, sweet Orange Julius. Coke was Hell when you wanted lemonade. Steak was Hell when you wanted couscous. I could go on, but won't.

We were seated at the far end of the food court, looking out over the Hell mall. Yes! Seated! Tables, a place to sit and have a convo and people-watch. Hell was finally becoming civilized.

And crowded! Because that was the worst thing about malls. However a necessary evil gigantic shopping plazas were, we endured them a lot more than we enjoyed them. The Hell mall would always be crowded bordering on claustrophobic. I didn't see anyone I recognized, either waiting in a never-ending line for a ride that was under repair, sitting at one of the tables staring dejectedly at cold rubbery fries, or behind the counter handling food they wanted no part of. Several of them were sneaking glances my way, but no one came over. Did not blame them.

They didn't have to come to me, anyway. Nobody did. And I didn't assign anyone to do anything, but the mall format was taking care of that. Hell had employees, which I'd always unconsciously known but was only now remembering. It wasn't staffed entirely by damned souls. The human resources office probably had a file cabinet stuffed with demon résumés. "It kind of looks like Hell almost . . . runs itself? Is that right?"

"It can. But only under the proper dominion. There needs to be a—how to put this?—a guiding hand. Which it now has."

"Wait'll Laura sees this! She'll be super impressed by what I've managed to accomplish entirely by accident." I was practically rubbing my hands together. "Accuse me of shirking, will she? This'll show her."

"About the lawless one," Father Markus began.

"Are we back on the Ant again?"

"Your sister. You have of course noticed that this realm has been a void until you put your mind to changing it, yes? From the moment the Morningstar went to her reward—"

"Not sure it was a reward." Also, where does an unrepentant unforgiven fallen angel go after goading a vampire with great shoes into killing her? Not Heaven. Definitely not Hell. I think my earlier theory—that she just let herself go into nothingness—was the answer.

"There has been nothing at all for weeks. Or centuries, I'm not sure." He made a vague gesture encompassing the amusement park, using the hand that was holding his flat Pepsi (if the lack of carbonation wasn't bad enough, the priest was a Coke man all the way). "Time is different here."

"Ugh, really? The 'time moves differently in Hell' trope? Yawn."

"What is a trope?"

I took another sip and watched the employee working the ice cream stand, where the only flavor they had left was spumoni. "It's like a TV or movie cliché, I guess. Or a stereotype. It's something that, when you see it, you know exactly what that character or situation is going to be. Like the sexy librarian trope."

"But librarians *are* sexy."

I waved that nonsense away. Despite (because of?) that particular trope, every librarian I'd ever seen had crow's-feet like canyons and wore thick support hose to control the varicose veins. "You're a priest, what do you know?"

Father Markus laughed so suddenly it was startling. "I suppose that's my cue to say something like 'I'm a priest, not dead' except—"

"You *are* dead!" I replied, giggling. Luckily the dead guy was also giggling, so it wasn't as insensitive as it could have been. "Okay, fine, you think librarians are sexy. How's this for another example . . . you're a trope."

"But I'm not on television or in the movies."

"Yes, but you're a symbol of organized religion in an unlikely place where I would not expect to find aid, and you're friendly and helpful."

"That's a trope?"

"Yeah, and it's a boatload better than the evil unhelpful priest trope."

"There's an evil priest trope?" he repeated, horrified.

"I think we're losing focus."

"That's terrible!"

"Focus, damn you and your librarian-loving ways! We're not going to wonder about tropes, we're going to wonder about why time's different here, remember? I wonder how Satan handled it. Or is she the one who made it like this? That would be so her, making time be all—uh—whatever the opposite of linear is, that's what she did to it. Just to make things more difficult for me!" I paused. "Okay, I hear it. Her decision probably didn't have anything to do with me. Or much to do with me. What d'you think?"

"I don't think it has anything to do with you."

"About *Satan*. About how she did it, or why she did it."

Father Markus shook his head. "I rarely saw the Morning-star."

"The devil didn't have a sit-down with all the newcomers? You must have met her at least." Maybe that had been the Ant's job. "No 'Welcome to Hell, flogging to the left, delousing to the right, and you'll never finish the paperwork' sort of thing?"

"Well, yes, but we weren't sitting. I was hearing Eva Perón's confession—"

"I don't want you to get off track but we should circle back to that later."

"—and she came right up to me and asked just what I thought I was doing."

"And then the flogging started!"

"No. She laughed when I explained. Then she said—"

" 'Begin the flogging!' "

"No. She said it was brilliant. Then I said I was sorry for her—"

"So *then* flogging started."

"No. I'm not sure why you're obsessed with my flogging. I was never flogged. She just laughed again." Father Markus paused, thinking about it. "I didn't expect her to have such a sense of humor. Which was naïve, I know. Who would laugh more than the devil herself? She's seen everything of the human condition and lacks our Father's compassion. She must have found nearly everything funny."

"Uh-huh. She said you were brilliant?"

"No, she said giving hope to the damned was brilliant. She said I could raise their spirits just enough for her to stomp on them again. And so she gave me the run of the place."

"The better to get to the stomping, no doubt. I can't say I'm surprised. If she was slowing down time in Hell to have sit-downs with all the souls, however brief the meetings were, no wonder she was so grumpy. No time off? No sick days? God must be the worst HR head ever. And you never answered my question."

Father Markus tried another sip, grimaced, then pushed the cup full of room-temperature flat pop (the Hell food court was always out of ice) away with a sad look. "I don't recall you asking me a question."

"About how you must be pretty pleased. You know. Relatively speaking. This." I gestured. "All this. It proves Catholics are right about Heaven and Hell and all that. It must be vindicating. Right?"

"I think," he began slowly, "that 'pleased' and 'vindicating' aren't the words I would use."

"Except that doesn't really solve anything. Hell exists, so what? That just raises a fuckload more questions I think God better get around to answering. Does that mean there's a Purgatory? What about Jews? Are any Jews down here? There must be."

"*Must* be?"

"You know what I mean," I snapped. "Not 'must be' in the

sense that they're here because they are Jewish, ergo 'see you in Hell, yarmulke boy!' And if there's Hell, there must be Heaven, too, right?"

"Oh, definitely," the priest said with a nod. "I haven't been there yet, but I've heard about it from people who have."

Intriguing! And deeply confusing. "How does *that* work?"

"There's an exchange program."

"No, you didn't."

"Pardon, my dear?"

"You did not just say there's an exchange program between Heaven and Hell. Between Germany and the U.S. I get. We had a German exchange student when I went to high school and she was pretty cool. She was one of the few people in that school who appreciated my shoes. That's something I can wrap my head around. I can't wrap my head around exchange programs and field trips to and from Hell." But even as I said it, I realized how stupid I sounded. "Except that's what I've been doing, isn't it? Field trips."

"I think so."

I spoke slowly, the way I did when I was realizing something and verbalizing it at the same time. "And I can't do that anymore. Can I? This isn't a place to visit and forget about when I leave; this is my responsibility."

The priest's gaze was steady. "I think so."

I nodded and sipped my Orange-Julius-that-wasn't. I should have been scared and angry, realizing that. But instead I felt relief. It was good, it was so very good to finally face the thing I had been so carefully, obsessively avoiding. And it wasn't like I had to do it alone. I never had to do anything alone again. I'd changed the timeline and obliterated Ancient Betsy, that worthless tyrannical bitch, to ensure it.

"Will you help us?" I asked, straight-out, no fucking around. Father Markus was in or out. I'd understand if it was the latter but hoped for the former.

"I'll help *you*."

"Oh. Sure, I get it, you don't know Laura that well."

"That's not what I—"

"Would you like a refill?"

We both looked up and there was the Ant. She was still wearing her awful outfit but now had a small gold name tag pinned just below her left shoulder with her name: "Antonia." A round white pin with black lettering on the opposite side read, "Serving seven billion and counting!"

"There are no refills in Hell," I replied almost without thinking.

"Correct. That was a trick question." She was holding a clipboard and looking from the priest to me to the priest again. "So I should put your father down—"

I nearly spilled my Orange Not-Julius. "He's not my father. I mean, he's *a* father. Just not mine. My father, I mean." Was I saying "father" a lot? Did they notice? "Right, Father? Who is not my actual father? Faaaather father father."

She kept going like I hadn't interrupted her and, for once, I was grateful. "—as a consultant?"

"Yeah, sure, put him down. Wait! Let me elaborate: put him down as a consultant. Don't insult him or anything." To Father Markus: "Thank you."

"And thank *you*," the Ant said after scribbling something on the clipboard. She made a point of looking around the Hell mall. "Very well done, Betsy."

"It was an accident," I bragged. Wait, why was I proud of that?

"Yes, I assumed. You're off to a good start."

Why, *why* was her praise cheering me up? God, this place was so insidious, making me feel things I had never felt and never wanted to felt. I mean feel.

"It still smacks of being way too simple. The fact that this is how it really works. It's almost anticlimactic."

"I'll never understand why people think anticlimactic is bad," said the damned priest who used to help orphans kill vampires.

"Yeah, I'll bet you don't, Father. But this place . . . you believe you're supposed to be here, so here you are. Same with my Ant—"

"Your aunt?"

Over the Ant's annoyed huff, I replied, "Long story, no time. Same with her, same with Henry Tudor, same with the guy over there allergic to ketchup who's only allowed to eat ketchup . . ." We all shuddered at the far-off retching noises the poor bastard was making. "If we're here because we want to be, can we leave? I mean, I know I can, but could you?" To my stepmother: "Could you?"

"Yes. I think," he added. The Ant said nothing, just stood there with her dorky clipboard and shifted her weight from one foot to another. "There are souls I've spoken to here that I no longer see."

"Yeah, but billions. Billions of souls, right? Of course you couldn't be expected to remember 'em all."

"Correct. But it's not difficult to track down someone here. It's not a planet with a defined area like Earth, it's a different dimension with different rules, as you're busy discovering. I do think people are leaving."

I nodded, remembering Laura's warning. *But I need you. They're leaving!* "Yeah, that's part of the reason I'm here."

Puzzled, Father Markus tilted his head. His small dark eyes were bright like a sparrow's. "I don't understand. Some souls are leaving when they're ready to move on. When they've learned. Or been forgiven. Or forgave themselves. Or repented. They're—"

"There's a lot to take in," the Ant cut in, almost like she didn't want the priest to keep clarifying for me. Which was nuts; she wanted me up to speed ASAP to ease some of the burden from poor precious Laura's delicate creamy shoulders. "I think you've done very well in a short time." That explained the praise, too. Should have known it wasn't entirely sincere. "Once you actually showed up," she added in a mutter, because she was, after all, still the Ant, no matter how pleasant and helpful she was being. Or pretending to be. It was almost a relief to hear the knee-jerk insult.

"All I can tell you, Betsy, is what I learned myself not long after I arrived here." Father Markus kept forgetting his drink was nasty, because he again picked it up and again put it down without sipping. Torture! Oooh, I was a genius. "It has been the joy and sorrow of my afterlife to find that there are more questions than answers. The only thing I have learned is that I have much to learn."

"Yeah, I learned that, too. Way before I died, even."

"There are Muslims here, and Jews. I've debated theology with Sikhs and Baha'is and I've heard confession from atheists and Taoists and Lutherans."

"Bet the atheists are pissed to be here."

"You'd be surprised. Some of them were relieved. Not to be in Hell, but that people they'd known who'd judged them for their beliefs were *also* in Hell."

Heh. "Okay, that's funny." What? It was.

"This is not a dimension set aside solely for Catholics who believe in a concrete Heaven and a concrete Hell and an Almighty Father and a Devil and punishment and redemption. It's for everyone and I don't know why. I may never know why. And there are children, too."

I was so startled I sucked in a breath. "Kids? Aw, no. Don't tell me that."

"Not being tortured, not damned," he reassured me. Tried to, I mean, jeez. I wasn't sure I could be reassured, though he'd get points for trying. The whole idea—toddlers in a food court that wasn't childproofed!—was horrifying. "They didn't sin, how could they, the precious ones? But here they are. What does that mean? And there are people who absolutely deserve to be punished for quite some time, if not forever, who *aren't* here."

"Like my dad!" Wait. Did I say that out loud?

"It's puzzling." I was relieved he'd let the dad comment pass. "Like Jewish vampires being burned by crosses. One of the Blade Warriors' victims. It shook me and I could never get it right in my mind. I'd hoped to find the answer to that here, as well, but so far I haven't."

I remembered, vaguely. They'd told me about it before they disbanded. They'd tracked and killed an old-school vampire, one who had a taste for rabbinical seminary students, men as well as women. He'd been old enough, and experienced enough, to give them enough trouble that one of the Blind Worriers ended up in a wheelchair. They got him down, finally, and killed him. The cross worked great, and they'd brought buckets of holy water, which was even better.

Afterward, they realized he was Jewish (I was a little surprised his victim predilection didn't tip them off). Which raised all sorts of problematic questions. *Why* did the cross work? Why did any of it work?

"Oh, not that suggestibility thing again." I managed, barely, to keep from rolling my eyes. This had come up before, and I'd dismissed it before. It was either too dumb for me to understand, or too sophisticated.

It goes like this: vampires couldn't stand crosses or Bibles or what-have-you because in life, they had believed the books and comics and movies. Stephen King's *Salem's Lot* was inserted so far into popular culture that even people who didn't read the book (or read Stoker's *Dracula* or watched *Buffy* and *Angel* on TV or read the *30 Days of Night* graphic novels or went to the movies to see *Shadow of the Vampire* or *The Lost Boys* and shut up, that was a great movie!) knew how to kill vampires. Ergo crosses hurt. So even if you were a Jew or an atheist in life, a cross would burn you once you turned into a vamp.

Which, again, *makes no sense*. It was so dumb I spent a lot of time deliberately not thinking about it. Unfortunately (or maybe the opposite?) Father Markus had zero interest in marinating in ignorance.

"I think there are *many* dimensions out there. I don't think we'll ever know how many or what it means or even how they came to be. Perhaps not even how *we* came to be. If we can come to grips with that, if we can accept the thought that after an eternity of trying we still won't have all the answers, there's hope."

Hmm. Interesting thought. And possibly depressing as shit; I'd have to think about it. Also, did "we" mean he and I? The Ant, he, and I? Just me? Just him? Him and the demon standing behind him? (Not that there was one.)

"So . . ." Gah. I'd had about all the theological chitchat I could take for one day. Or one hour or one year or however long I'd been here this time. "To answer the question I asked *ages* ago, you don't have to stay here, probably?"

"But I will." He touched his collar, as if reminding himself it was still there. "Can you think of a place more in need of a sympathetic ear? And we need to set up a rotation schedule for those keeping an eye on the children."

With a jolt, I realized the Mall of America—my model for Hell Mall—had a day-care center. And again: *children*? I didn't care that they weren't being tortured, I had to look into that. If BabyJon—*ohgodpleaseno*—died, would he come here? Who would look after him and play with him and sneak him maple sugar candy?

I shook the horrifying thought off with a determined effort. "I appreciate that, Father. But stay or go, I can put in a good word for you with . . ." Whom, exactly? The devil was dead by my hand. (My hand, my other hand, my feet, my teeth—toward the end I was lashing out with everything I had and I'm still kind of astonished I pulled it off.) I couldn't imagine the Antichrist would care about a sinful priest—one willing to help us, no less! or help me, anyway, which was almost as good—and if she did, what could she do? Send him away? Where? Back to "the real world"? The Heaven dimension? Could she banish a sinner to Heaven? Could we call God on the phone (cue Joan Osborne and her intensely annoying song "One of Us" and, no, Joan, God wouldn't be a stranger on the bus, and He wouldn't be anything like a holy rolling stone, either; *God*, I hate that song) to ask for leniency? And how would that phone call go? *Hey, God, how's it going? Can you believe so-and-so won the Super Bowl? Anyway, we've got a defrocked priest down here, he's a pretty good guy, really, and maybe you could let him trade up?*

"Maybe you don't have to spend an eternity here," was all I could come up with.

My stepmother let out another trademark inelegant snort. "I'm sure Father Markus is touched by your vague offer to help in some undefined way."

I scowled. "Careful, or I'll put you on amusement park barf detail." The shudder I received was more than satisfying. And speaking of being satisfied . . .

"I've gotta tell you guys, this is pretty nifty. I've gotten a lot done." They opened their mouths and I went on anyway. "Yeah, yeah, by accident, but who cares? The point is, a lot got done." At her eye roll I revised. "Some stuff got done." Another eye roll—her optic nerves were gonna go into spasm if she kept that up. "All right! A tiny amount of stuff kind of got done and there's ever so much more to do, yes, fine, I get it. But cut me some slack. I (eventually) stepped up and (finally) took action and frankly, I think I deserve a smoothie break!" My hip buzzed and I reached for my phone. Perfect timing. I wondered how long I'll have been gone from the mansion this time.

*Babies gone again. Your father is alive.*

"Oh, fucking *fuck*," I nearly shrieked and then nearly died of mortification. "I'm so sorry," I added at once.

"I've heard those words once or twice," Father Markus said, eyes going teeny as he grinned. "Even before I got sent to Hell."

"Trouble at home again." I noticed the Ant hadn't phrased it as a question.

"Yeah. My friend's weird babies keep disappearing except not really. But I think I know what to tell her. At least, in a way that won't result in her permanent nervous breakdown. Or my decapitation."

"I understand."

"No, you don't."

"No," he admitted. "I don't."

I stood, ready to empty my tray, when I realized all the garbage cans were full because of course they were. I set the tray back down. "I have to go . . . do you have to go find your Hell? Is one of these stores for you?"

The Ant immediately started flipping through pages on her (magic, right?) clipboard. "I can answer that for you. I've got it here somewhere . . ."

"I can, too," he said politely then turned back to me. "No, I don't have to participate. My penance is to forever offer counsel and be rebuffed nine hundred ninety-nine times out of a thousand."

Sounded grueling. But knowing Father Markus, reaching that one soul kept him going. I admired his dogged compassion, even if I couldn't match it.

"I just don't want you to get flogged or burned or whatever you don't want to have happen to you."

"Not all penance is of the body. I prefer a flogging to despair," he admitted. "I prefer it to nothing, to be honest."

"Come on, how bad can nothing be? Getting lashed has to be way worse."

"Even if I just wandered around the food court and no one ever laid a hand on me, it's eternity, Betsy. You don't have to be burned or flogged forever to realize it's punishment."

"Oh." Wow. Hadn't thought of it like that. What a depressing thought. "Good. I think." I clipped my phone back to my hip. "I'll be back when I can."

"Oh, we'll be here," the Ant said with annoying cheer.

"Again with the threats," I said, and I vanished with the smug thought that, in Hell, getting the last word felt soooo good.

# CHAPTER
# TWENTY-FIVE

*"All right, everybody calm down, let's just keep it together* and I don't understand why I keep ending up in the damn toolshed!" Beyond ridiculous. I ruled over the vampire nation, traveled through time, and Hell was starting to bend to my will, but I couldn't seem to avoid toolsheds as I traveled through space and time? Why does every cool thing in my life have to be tempered with something ridiculous?

At least I knew the routine by now as I trudged through the snow to the side door, helpfully (hopefully?) unlocked as it was last time. Then I'd hose Jess down with sedatives until she was calm enough to hear my theory about how the babies weren't actually gone. They were just gone. Not *gone* gone, just gone. Nothing to worry about! Probably!

Better work on my soothing explanation. But before I could begin, I heard a car slow and pull into our driveway. I prayed it wasn't someone from outside our inner circle of strange—let it be Mom, let it be any one of my roommates, let it be a former Bloat Wonderer, anything but a stranger because I could not handle being fake-polite to an underage cookie salesman.

Wish granted. It wasn't a stranger. It was *two* strangers. Two teenage strangers and what the hell was this now?

I watched them climb out of Sinclair's concrete gray ("For the final time, it is silver, Elizabeth!") Lamborghini, also known as Elizabeth, I Love You but If You So Much As Scratch This Car I Will Not Touch You for a Month. I don't have the strength to go into how ridiculous boys are about their toys, except to say that my husband didn't appreciate how I shrieked, "You're driving a gigantic electric shaver!" and then laughed so hard I fell down.

Still, despite my chortling contempt of Sink Lair's toy, the fact remained that a couple of strangers had been dumb enough to a) steal Eric Sinclair's concrete-colored midlife crisis (I figured he was on his third crisis by now) and then b) were insane enough to return to the scene of the crime.

They chattered at each other as they started for the front steps with the affectionate familiarity of family or close friends and as I approached I could see how closely they resembled each other. They were about the same height, tall, lanky, all lean limbs and casual grace. They were both in jeans, the girl in dark green and the boy in jeans-colored jeans. She was wearing a beige silk T-shirt, with the short sleeves neatly rolled up about an inch, and a simple gold chain around her neck. No makeup except for frost-colored lipstick, which, incredibly, she made work. If I so much as tried a sample of that at Sephora, I'd look like I was succumbing to hypothermia. This would easily be enough to hate her on sight, but she threw me such a brilliant, beaming smile my pissyness couldn't get a firm hold.

The boy glanced where she was looking and grinned at me, too. He was wearing a black T-shirt so faded it was closer to gray, which read, "Everything is easier said than done." They were both in narrow black running shoes that didn't have laces or Velcro or anything to keep them tight on their feet. I sidled closer to get a better look at their gear, which looked to me like a loafer and a sneaker had a baby.

Well. Time to aggressively get to the bottom of this. "Uh . . . hi?"

"Uh . . . hi back?" the girl replied.

"Hiya!" her brother added, flapping a wave in my general direction. "Managed to 'port into the shed again, huh?"

"Did not," I said automatically, revising the rest of my opening statement, which was going to be, "You two dolts better get your ass out of my driveway before my husband eats you and, yeah, I mean that as a literal threat," because *what the . . . ?* They knew about the teleporting? And my annoying inability to escape the gravitational pull of the shed? "Uh, what are you doing here?"

"We live here."

"Nuh-uh!" Unless . . .

*Babies gone again. Your father is alive.*

Oh. Huh. Still, best to be sure. Probably not a good idea just to grab them and march them into the house and then call a smoothie seminar. Or, as was more likely, grab them and march them around the house, through the (unlocked?) side door, and into the kitchen after fighting our way past Fur and Burr. I wasn't putting myself through all that unless I was *sure.* Although who the hell else could they be?

Just the fact that I was thinking, *These teenagers are obviously teenage iterations of Jessica's newborn twins, duh,* was a testament to how much things had changed. It was getting to the point where if something incredibly strange and unexplainable *didn't* happen, I felt itchy and out of sorts.

My long silence got the teens thinking, apparently, because the girl—she and her brother looked about sixteen—spoke up. "We might have to break out the hand puppets for this one." But—and I'm not sure how she pulled this off—she said it in such a nice way that I wasn't offended. Okay, not too offended.

And the other one said something in reply that I didn't catch at all: "Onniebetty likes keeping it stripped to the bones." And even though I had only the vaguest clue what any of this was, again, the delivery was so pleasant and kind my annoyance was having a hard time catching fire.

"Just give me a few seconds," I snapped. "If you guys know me, you'll know I'll need—"

"Ten minutes?" the boy guessed.

"Half an hour," the girl said with a nod. At my disgruntled expression they both grinned.

I knew this behavior. I had seen it before, many times. And, my suspicions aside, there was something about the two of them—

Of course! They looked like larger versions of the strange toddlers, only trapped within puberty this time around. They had the same pale skin with gold undertones, the same large brown eyes and foxlike faces (loved those pointed chins!). This time their hair was bristling into large proud Afros, which made their faces look smaller and foxier.

More telling, their mannerisms and tone were vintage Jess. I'd heard—and loved—that affectionate sarcasm for years. Hell, I'd been on the receiving end of it for almost two decades. I was a little embarrassed it had taken me this long to tumble to who they were. Then I gave myself a "give yourself a break, you're trying to run Hell" pass.

Even though I knew who they were I still stared. Even though I was pretty sure I had figured out how they kept doing this I stared. I had to. It was just so . . . enormous. So huge. And they were so . . .

"Oh, but you're so beautiful," I managed, and it was tough work croaking around the lump that was suddenly making it hard to breathe and doing weird things to my eyes. "You're so beautiful."

Which was awful. Like it defined them and was more important than, say, their ethics or their brains. I deserved the twin eye rolls! But all I could think was that my best friend and her husband had created a miracle × 2, and no matter what happened to any of us down the line, some part of my mortal pals would live on.

And not just endure: it would live on in two gorgeous, clever children who were gonna grow up to be King Cool and Queen Awesome going by their clothing *alone.* I had no illusions about my "normal" friends outliving me. It was so dreadful to have to face, I usually didn't.

Tina could do it; she could find the courage to make friends year after year only to lose them, always, year after year. Hell, she'd befriended the Sinclair family for generations. And despite that example, Sinclair couldn't or wouldn't do that, choosing to be alone until I'd stumbled (literally) into his afterlife.

Face it? That *at best* my dearest friends would get old and sicken and die? I couldn't even bear to *think* it; Jessica had made her wishes perfectly clear when she'd had cancer a while back, to wit: *If you turn me into a goddamned bloodsucker who has to serve you into eternity while never again seeing the sun and outliving children and grandchildren and so on, the first thing I will do is bite you in the face. Then I'll start with your shoe collection.*

Except now it was a teeny bit less dreadful. Now I could see her children and, through them, my friends. For a few seconds I had a glimpse of what the centuries yawning ahead would bring me and, for a few seconds, it wasn't terrifying.

"Maybe you should sit down," the girl said, moving to my side and holding out her drink. "Here, sip."

An Orange Julius! *How had I not noticed what they were drinking?* I actually swayed on my feet. "You stole Sinclair's car—"

"Hey!" the boy yelped. "Uncle Sink gave standing perm to snatch any of his cars."

The slang and abbreviations were annoying, but easy to

follow, so I could keep thinking out loud. "—to make an Orange Julius run—"

"Mine's strawberry."

"—to the Mall of America?"

"'Course," she replied. "What else on a Friday afternoon? Oh, and Macy's, you know. The spring shoe sale. Too many boots, don't bother."

"And Cinnabon," her brother added. "I won't face the weekend without at least two dozen Cinnabons, Onniebetty. Not with the Net flickering in and out like that. *Won't.*"

"My babies!" I cried and clutched them to me in a hug that left them both gasping and wriggling for their freedom. "Jess and DadDick will be so happy!"

"Oh." They pulled back and looked at each other, then at me. It was equal parts uncomfortable and exciting to be the subject of such focused twin regard.

"Oh," his sister added. "Um. You haven't had the misnomer chat with Dad yet. He doesn't like that, you know."

Her brother whacked her on the elbow and glared when she yelped. "That hasn't happened yet! They have to kill the prob themselves." He turned to me. "Never mind. And about Uncle Sink's car . . ."

I snickered. Couldn't help it. Uncle Sink, heh. Oh, all the ways I was going to casually work *that* tidbit into conversation. How many times could I moan it during sex before he pulled out the spider gag?

The girl arched eyebrows at me and looked exactly like Jess had at that age, so yikes. "What are you chuckling at, *Onniebetty?*"

"Ugh, that's my name?"

"It's the closest we could get to saying 'Auntie Betsy' when we were babies. You don't even want to know what we call Big Bro—ow!" She glared, rubbed her elbow, and added in a mutter, "Never mind. Hasn't happened yet."

Big Bro? Could they mean BabyJon? God, was it true?

Were we one big happy family eventually? Or at least in the parallel universe these twin teens came from? That, too, was exciting and frightening. But a good frightening, if there was such a thing. The fear of knowing great things are coming, but not knowing exactly what, or exactly when, or how it will change your life.

"Uncle Sink lets us snag his cars, but maybe not tell Mom? That's the rule."

"There are sooo many things I shouldn't tell your mother," I agreed.

"Yeah, we actually have a list. Don't worry, it's a hidden list. We've also got stuff not to tell Dad. Much shorter list."

"He's fuzzy and it ruins alllll the fun," the boy agreed. "For our sixteenth he showed us all these icko classic movies. *Wheels of Tragedy*; *Mechanized Death*; *Highway, Bloody Highway*." He let loose with an exaggerated shiver. "Brought us to the morgue, even! Like we hadn't been there a dozen times helping you with . . ." His mouth snapped shut. "Nope."

"It's like he doesn't remember that it's the twenty-first century and the GPS/Net heads off just about any accident. Nobody even gets e-tickets anymore. The Net makes your car slow down if you get a case of the stupids."

"That's amazing!" I gasped, then shook myself. This was no time to get distracted. More distracted. It definitely wasn't time to beg them to tell me what was trending in boots. "Never mind. Listen. We have to go into the house right now because everyone thinks you've been kidnapped or are possibly on some kind of infant walkabout. We have to explain to your folks just how weird and wonderful you are . . . what?"

They were both smiling again. They had terrific smiles, I figured because of terrific orthodontists. "That's fine. We're okay to do that. In our house," she explained, nodding at the mansion looming behind us, "weird *is* wonderful. It's a synonym."

"Is that, like, a metaphor? I've been working on metaphors this week."

"Keep working. And don't worry, Mom and Dad will get it."

"They will?" I didn't want to worry the kids, so I managed to keep most of the doubt out of my tone. "Okay. They will. Right? Right."

"What choice?" the boy asked, looking, for a few seconds, older than his years. "That's how it is here."

"Point," I said. "Then let's get it done. We have to go around the side, I'm afraid."

"Nix." Jessica's son reached into his back pocket and then jingled something in front of my face. "They're called house keys and, nobody knows why, but you never have yours with you."

I resisted the urge to snatch them away. "Off my case, brat."

"Ease, willya? She's got stuff. It's not easy running Hell," his sister said, sliding a protective arm around my waist.

"I loved when you came to career day." He sighed. "Next time, bring more demons."

"I might love you two," I decided, "more than sandals in summer."

"We grew on you. Like lichen!"

Her brother snorted, then shook his keys at me again and started trotting up the sidewalk toward the door. "Move-move, ladies! Let's go have the Talk with the 'rents. Again. And then take a Cinnabon break."

"I should be more terrified," I confessed, following them.

"Plenty of time for that," Jessica's daughter replied with such a droll smirk, I couldn't help laughing again.

# CHAPTER
# TWENTY-SIX

*Here's the thing about vampire hearing. We can hear a pin* drop, but that's boring. (Who lurks in doorways listening for pins to drop, anyway? Creeps. That's who.) We can hear whispered conversations a floor away, sometimes a block away if the wind is right. We can hear a car pull in from the attic, or pull out from the basement. We can hear when Marc is experimenting and when he's just pacing, desperately wanting something to keep his dead brain busy. We can hear the babies snuffling in their sleep, we can hear them wake up, and we can hear Jess and DadDick stumbling through the house to warm bottles and go to them. Sometimes we can hear heartbeats.

But a lot of the time we don't want to. Speaking for myself, if I'm concentrating on hate-watching old eps of *Helix* (they've got to stop giving the Syfy channel money to make movies), I don't want to be distracted by Tina muttering under her breath two floors away as she struggles to reconcile one of SinCorp's many P&Ls.

So you learn to tune it out. Or try to. I could never get the hang of it until Tina took me aside and said, "Airport," like that was an answer.

It was! But it took me a while to get it. She pointed out that when you're in an airport, you're walking to your gate while lugging an overnight bag or a laptop, counting gates and glancing from café to bar to Starbucks to figure out what you want to drink before the flight boards. And there are hundreds of people around you, milling and chatting and running and walking and it's busy all around, and it doesn't matter. It's not upsetting or overwhelming or even interesting. It's just how airports are. And you don't care, so you don't hear them. You can just tune out all those conversations that have nothing to do with you and focus on getting to your gate with your Green Tea Frappuccino intact. And once I grasped what Tina was trying to explain to me, it became easy. I didn't have to hear the babies' heartbeats, or Marc's pacing, unless I wanted to.

All that to say that I did *not* need vampire hearing to hear Jessica's shriek when we walked in the front door, courtesy of her kid's keys: "Someone better find my babies *right goddamned now* or I'm going to get my husband's guns; call my lawyer; and take one of Sinclair's shiny, sexy cars—and everyone in the city of St. Paul will have a very bad day!"

The twins exchanged a look and started to sprint and I had great respect for their reckless bravery. I, meanwhile, had to actively resist the urge to scuttle back outside to the driveway, or at least cower in the hall, and followed.

"Jessica, be reasonable," my husband was pleading. "Leave the automobile out of it."

"Stupid, we're so *stupid*." I could hear every bitter word, and if the twins weren't in front of me, I would have crossed the length of the mansion in a heartbeat. It broke my heart to hear the savage self-hate in my friend's voice. "We knew it had happened before and we just—we just sat around until it happened *again*. And I know you texted Betsy, but what do you think she can do, exactly? We've figured we can't call the cops, but nobody's dropped off a ransom note, nobody's made a demand, our babies are just—just *gone*. Again! And even if we get them back, how long until they go missing again?" Her voice caught on sobs. "I c-can't live like this. W-won't live like this. It's too m-much—who the hell are you?"

This because the girl had gotten to the swinging kitchen door first, darted through, and threw herself into her mother's arms. I heard Jessica grunt and stagger back—the twins had their father's long legs—and got to the kitchen in time to see her arms automatically go around the intruder/daughter.

"It's okay, Mama." Jessica's daughter squeezed her in a fierce hug, eliciting a pained squeak, then pulled back and held Jess at arm's length. "We're right here. We're not missing. We're here. It's—nnnfff."

Her brother, right on her heels, and that was twice in five seconds Jessica nearly went sprawling courtesy of her exuberant offspring. DadDick was on his feet and moving to pull them apart. "Hey! Get off her, both of you. What are you doing here? How did you get in?"

"We didn't use my house keys," I replied, "I can tell you that."

*My own. As ever, you arrive in the nick of time.* My husband's deep relief came through like a baseball bat through fog.

*Dude, you are not even going to believe the story behind these two.*
*Doubtless. Stop calling me* dude.

"We're not missing." Jessica's daughter was patting her cheeks, the way little kids do when they're reaching out for someone they love, trying to get their attention. "We're not stolen. We're here, Mama, and it's all fine."

"This'll be tough to chew, Mom, but we're yours. Remember your freak pregnancy? It resulted in freak kids." The exuberant teen spread his arms wide. "Ta-da!"

"But we're *your* freak kids," his sister said, snuggling into

Jess for a hug, which my dazed friend automatically returned. "And there's nothing to be scared of. We're here even when we aren't. It's our nature."

On the one hand, I had to give them points for how quickly they were calming my pal. I hadn't thought that was possible without heavy tranquilizers. On the other, the things they were telling her made no sense, so it shouldn't have calmed Jess at all. But I didn't interrupt or try to correct them. I was too busy trying to think up a nonalarming way to explain what was happening.

"We can prove it." They were now directing their comments to their father, who had stopped trying to separate them but looked like someone had punched him in the kidney and followed it up with a gut punch. "We know everything about you guys. You've told us so many boring stories of your childhood. Boring because of the repetition!" the boy hastily clarified. "Not boring because we don't actually care how your childhoods were grueling and how good we have it and how when you were a little boy you had to sell tractors uphill in the snow while waiting for your trust fund to mature."

Jessica took in a deep breath, waited a couple of seconds, then let it out, along with, "I believe you."

"Oh, an example? Okay, when you and Dad were young and dumb—you believe us?"

"You, um. You look like a picture of my grandma. You look exactly like her. This might sound hard to believe, but for a second I thought you were her, time traveling to the future for some strange supernatural-related reason."

"It sounds one hundred percent believable."

The boy slapped his forehead. "Grammy Midge! We should have thought of that straight off." He turned to his father. "Elephant in the room? I look like her, too—it's fine, it's okay to say. Damn these delicate features! Why couldn't I have inherited your swimmer's shoulders, at least?"

"It's true. It's really—you didn't get taken. You didn't.

You're okay. You're—you're nice, too." Jessica burst into tears and elicited squawks as she squeezed the twins in a ferocious double hug. "And you're not freaked out. You're worried about your dad and me. You're not surprised by . . ." She waved a hand at the kitchen, encompassing the zombie, the vampires, the king and queen of same, the evidence of an emergency smoothie session, the freezer practically bulging with bottles of strangely flavored vodka, the other freezer stuffed with dead mice. "By this. Any of it. You're okay. You're really okay."

"Thank God you're finally here."

Finally? So I'd been gone longer than my time in Hell again. At least the others were taking it in stride, more because they were used to dealing with my incompetence than because they were resilient. Or numbed to the ongoing strangeness of their lives.

"It was like a season two *Game of Thrones* flashback," Marc whispered to me. "Y'know, when Dany finds out someone stole her babies? 'Where are my dragons?!' That whole season was just her yelling about her dragons."

"Time and place, Marc," I replied, making shushing motions, but alas. Too late.

"If you don't stop with the *GoT* references, I will punch your face into the back of your skull," Jess threatened in a way that seemed more than plausible. "There won't be enough Advil in the world to fix the resulting headache."

"Yes, ma'am." The zombie gulped.

"Stop scaring our zombie. And you two . . . how? How are you even here?" DadDick still looked stunned.

"Here it is, Big Papa, when a man and a woman love each other very much, sometimes they tell the vampires they live with to get gone for a while so they can practice private coitus—"

I burst out laughing, a slave to the boy's excellent smart-assery.

"You can skip the technical details," DadDick said, relaxing for the first time since we'd blitzed into the kitchen. I figured he, like me, had seen how like Jessica these two were, and it was almost better than a DNA test. "How are you doing this? Is it time travel? Oh. Huh."

"I know, right?" I asked. "You hear yourself say something that ridiculous and unreal, and you're only surprised that you're not surprised."

"Exactly." He turned back to the teens. "Is someone doing it to you?"

Vigorous nods. And the twins looked over at me.

"Whoa." I held up both hands like I was being arrested. Which would be the least of my problems right now. "Do not. Nope. You twerps aren't pinning this on me."

"We wouldn't, except for how it's all your fault."

And like that, all the happiness was sucked out of the room.

*"This!"*

"Ow," I mumbled. Jess's shriek was nearing supersonic.

"This is why we wouldn't ask you to be their godmother!"

"I didn't do anything! I am innocent and, also, I'm the one who *found* the little jerks. Twice!"

"Little? We're almost as tall as you are," the girl snapped.

I shrugged that off and turned back to Jess. "And what are you talking about, 'wouldn't ask'? You're not going to ask? You're not gonna name them and you're not gonna assign godparents?" I couldn't tell which one I found most appalling. Wait, I had it now. The one about me, definitely.

"This is not about soothing your insecurity!"

*Aw, come on, not even a little? She could soothe me if she really tried.* "Don't you remember me telling you how horrible the future was?"

"Vividly," she muttered, trying—and failing—to run a hand through her hair. She had it pulled back, and slicked back, so it wasn't budging for a while. When the screaming started, we all assumed the positions: Sinclair and Tina off to one side, watching with polite dispassion; Marc pulling back so DadDick could step up (for a hug; he knew better than to try to run soothing fingers through her hair); and me cowering by the sink. "The whole thing is still very, very vivid. Mostly because you wouldn't shut up about it."

"It was awful but fascinating. It's hard to picture me not being with Jessica like you said in the old timeline." DadDick gave his wife a squeeze. "I'm sorry there's no more Christian Louboutin to make your favorite shoes, but at least there's us and the babies."

I bit my lip so as not to let out something less than charitable ("You could have a thousand weird babies and none of them would replace Louboutin's genius, flatfoot!") and tried to stay on point. "Yeah, like I was saying, the future sucked hard and long—"

Jess slammed her hands over the girl's ears. "Not in front of the babies!"

"Ow, my tympanic membranes!" The riled teen shook her off. "Mama!"

"She's in all the advanced classes," her brother confided. "It's fine, Mom. We've heard this story a hundred times: You Almost Never Existed except for Onniebetty's Blundering. And she's said way worse than 'sucking hard' and—"

"Enough," Jess warned, and her son closed his mouth: zip!

*How? How is this my life?*

"I was tyrannical and gross and Sinclair was mysteriously absent and you were, too, and there were zombies, icky, drippy, rotting zombies, but remember how wonderful BabyJon was? Oooh, and handsome? Not that good looks measure goodness or anything but it's still worth noting. He was gorgeous. Because of me! Okay, because of the Ant and my dad, genetically speaking, but he was confident and strong and sweet because I raised him to be like that! So how come I can't be their godmother? If the spawn of the Ant can turn out terrific, your li'l sprogs can, too." Also, what exactly were the responsibilities that came with godmotherhood? I should probably get a detailed job description before I got further invested in being hurt that I wasn't being offered the job. The girl seemed savvy about footgear, so clearly my work with her had borne fruit, but the boy was a trickier read, though his fondness for Cinnabon and Orange Julius was a huge point in his favor. They were fearless and funny, which was even better. And maybe I was supposed to, I dunno, guide them spiritually? Or whatever? "Give me one good reason why it wouldn't work."

"I'll give you six. Vampires. Zombie—no offense."

Marc let loose with his "none taken" sigh. I admired how he didn't point out that the house zombie had safely delivered her weird babies.

"Ghosts. Dads who aren't dead. Dads who *are* dead. And—how many?"

Her twins each held up one hand, fingers splayed wide.

"We can help you out with that list if you like, Mama. Number six—"

"Traitors!" I clutched my chest. "Argh, your betrayal burns. Why? Why would you turn on your Onniebetty?"

"Because you ratted me out two years ago when I spent the night at—never mind."

"Look. Betsy." I could see Jessica visibly trying to calm herself. "I love you. There's not much I wouldn't do for you, but you've got to admit. You—and by extension we—live a dangerous life. Someone outside that, someone who knows about the craziness of our lives but who isn't necessarily exposed to it all the time, that's who we need to look after the babies in case the worst happens. If something happens to us"—gesturing to DadDick—"the last thing we should do, no matter how much we love the people involved, the last thing we should do is plunge our children further into the supernatural cesspool that is your life."

" 'Cesspool' is a little harsh," I mumbled, wanting to keep being offended but aware that she had a damned good point. Dammit.

DadDick stepped forward and took my shoulders in his giant cop hands. *Here comes a "stop it, you're hysterical!" slap. He doesn't even care that I'm not hysterical. He just wants to get to the slap. Police brutality in my own kitchen!*

"Betsy, I know this will be hard to hear."

"Because you'll slap me so hard my ears'll ring?"

"What? No. This is hard to hear because . . . are you ready? This is not about you."

"I don't understand."

"Exactly." He gave me a noisy smack on my forehead. Better than a slap, but also more confusing.

"If, God forbid, something dreadful happens . . ."

Both twins waved their hands. "We know, we know!"

"Shush." Jess spoke affectionately, if absently, and they obeyed. "Your mom's on deck."

"Jeez." I wasn't happy about this at all, and still wasn't sure where DadDick was going with the "it's not about you" crazy talk, but this was their decision and I had to respect it. And she had a point. My mother would be a wonderful guardian, but she wasn't far from retiring. If someone blew up the mansion one night in a blaze of bitchy retribution and the little ones somehow survived, Mom would be responsible for three babies at a time in her life when she would have been looking forward to grandchildren. She was always happy to baby-sit BabyJon, and she'd been over quite a bit to see the twins, but at the end of the day she knew the children weren't her responsibility. Except someday they could be.

Which, in an unsettling way, made Jessica's point. An elderly, single college professor was their best option. That's how nutty our lives were.

"I'm going to sulk about this," I warned, "for the rest of the week at least. And I'm going to do all sorts of passive-aggressive crap, like accidentally pouring all your nail polish down the kitchen sink and leaving you to deal with the mess. And the ensuing lack of polish."

"Agreed."

We glared at each other for a few seconds, then mutually looked away. A draw.

Meanwhile, sensing the worst part of the crisis was over, the girl had taken notice of Marc, who'd been watching the events with interest and in uncharacteristic silence since Jessica had listed him as a reason why I wasn't the twins' godmother. She must have picked up on that (before I did, but that wasn't such a trick) because she flopped down into the chair beside him with the air of someone supremely comfortable with her surroundings.

Marc tried a tentative smile. "Hello."

"Good job delivering us when Mom couldn't get to the hospital in time." This with a sideways glance at her mother, who suddenly couldn't return the gaze. Ha!

"Thank you. But everyone helped; it wasn't just me."

Well, phooey. Stupid Marc and his humane desire to play fair at all times.

"Hiya, Unk." The boy waved at him from across the kitchen, where he'd been chatting with Sinclair.

"Hello. Glad you and your sister aren't missing."

"That's all boring now. We've solved it."

"We haven't, actually, and you guys haven't explained how—"

"Yeah, yeah, how about this?" She leaned right into Marc's personal bubble, cupped her hand around her mouth, and whispered in his ear. (Good trick, too; I couldn't hear a thing despite eavesdropping.) His green eyes widened, then narrowed, and then he was on his feet and backing away. "No. No! Don't. I don't care. Don't you dare. I can wait. Do *not* tell me how *The Winds of Winter* and *A Dream of Spring* end."

"But the dragons finally—"

"No!" the zombie screamed and clapped his hands over his ears.

"Too bad." Jessica's awesomely evil daughter sighed. "It's pretty spectacular." She caught her brother's gaze and giggled, and then we were all laughing. It was the sharp-edged laughter that was *this close* to tipping over into hysterics (DadDick might yet get the chance to smack me), but we indulged anyway. It was impossible not to, and reason #742 why I loved where I lived and who I lived with.

# CHAPTER
# TWENTY-EIGHT

*"We call it shifting. Old stuff to all you guys by the time we* started kindergarten. For us . . ." She looked at her brother and they both shrugged. "It's how it is. How it's always been. It's our life."

"We were up to middle school before we tumbled that not everybody lived with vamps and zoms and weres." Her brother chortled. "In fact, hardly anybody did. Made for some strange-o sleepovers."

I shuddered at the thought of keeping everyone's nature hidden from various strange children all in some stage of sugar inebriation and, judging from the looks on Tina's and Sinclair's faces, they were having the same horrific vision.

"It's like your pregnancy, Mama."

"I don't really . . ." Jess shot a look at me and I gave her my "what?" shrug. "I don't remember much of it. Just that everything worked out. Mostly I felt like whatever was going on in—"

"Your uterus of the damned," Marc supplied helpfully.

"That everything would be fine," she finished after shooting him a glare that practically smoked. "Other people worried— Betsy's mom worried and then Betsy did, too, for a bit—but we . . ." She looked at DadDick.

His reply was slow and careful, as though he was considering every word before speaking. "It all turned out. And it was like any other pregnancy—back me up on this, Jess—in that mostly we wanted healthy babies. And like I said, it all turned out."

Sure, it did. But it was all the way around the world from "any other pregnancy." The way the Ant laid it out,[12] I didn't just accidentally change the timeline on my trip to the gross past (no air-conditioning) and horrific future (too many zombies). Moving myself from various dimensions of existence left me changed, and it wasn't just the vampire thing. I couldn't zap myself to and from Hell the first time I woke up dead; I couldn't do it a year after I woke up dead. I couldn't do it at all until a few months ago and the speed with which I started to get a handle on it was a little

*(terrifying)*

disconcerting.

So take my undead shenanigans + the Antichrist being a blood relative × Satan always ready to stir up trouble ÷ time travel = I am subtly changed, and by *subtly*, I mean *incredibly*. One of those things where if any one of those factors had dropped, we wouldn't all be in the kitchen talking to Jessica's newborns who could legally drive.

Long story short (ever notice how when people say that, it almost always indicates "this is gonna be a long story no matter how I tell it, so get comfy"?), even though Jessica was a regular person (comparably speaking), my physical proximity sort of rubbed off on people I spent the most time with. Marc wasn't

---

[12] See *Undead and Unsure*.

rotting because I was around. And Jessica's pregnancy, which only existed after I changed the timeline, was supernatural . . . or so scientific we lacked the understanding to get it.

A lot to take in, even for us. Having the twins explain their maybe-mystical, maybe-science-we-don't-understand natures to their parents was the best way to keep them calm and help them accept the chaos they had to *know* was coming.

Coming, hell. The chaos was here, and the chaos loved Orange Juliuses. The chaos was pretty damned adorable.

"Sometimes you were three months along"—she was prompting her mother—"and then the next day you'd be six months along. And a week later you'd hardly be showing and a week after that you'd look ready to—"

Her son mimed an explosion, complete with waving hands and those phlegmy blowing-up sounds boys can do almost from birth.

"Nobody who lived here noticed, because you're all under Onniebetty's spell, for lack of a word that actually makes sense. Grammy Taylor noticed, but only because she didn't live here."

*Grammy Taylor . . . awwww! Good to know my mom's still around in fifteen years. Except . . . um . . . wait, the twins aren't time traveling, they're twins from a different universe, so my mom might not be . . . damn, I'm getting a headache . . .*

"We're the same. You see? Your pregnancy was kinda the harbinger to our natures." They stopped talking and making explosion noises and looked expectant, as if that was all they had to say and we were about to assure them that, yep, we got it now, thanks for stopping by.

Tina cleared her throat. "Young lady, if you please, speaking only for myself—"

"I don't think so," I said.

"You're not alone in not getting this," Marc added. "I thought a medical/scientific background would help me. I was wrong."

"—could you elaborate?"

"Sure, Teeney Tina. Mama and Dad are norms," the girl said. "The only ones in this circus of a home. Everyone else— including us—is mystical or supernatural in nature. Mom was pregnant after Onniebetty—"

Marc snickered and I took the high road of maturity and only kicked him a little. "Nnnnf!"

"Serves you right," I muttered under my breath.

"—changed the timeline. Once Onniebetty was back, she was around for the whole thing. It changed us. In another timeline we don't exist—Mama picked Betsy, not Dad." Shooting her father an apologetic glance with Jessica's lovely brown eyes, she continued. "After the change, though, Dad never gave Mama the ultimatum, so we're here. But it's us through all the iterations of the timelines. In some timelines Mama didn't get pregnant for years. Or got pregnant much sooner. Any timeline where things didn't go *exactly* the way they did in *this* one means we're older or younger or not here yet. It's . . . I know it's a lot to . . ." She made a snatching motion with her hands. "It's a lot for your brains to grab. I guess the best explanation is that your newborn twins have shifted into a timeline where you and Dad coupled up much earlier."

"But you wouldn't be here? You wouldn't be alive?" DadDick's tone brought my attention back to him in a hurry. He talked like someone had a hold of his throat.

I got it, as much as a nonparent could grasp such a thing. It was one thing for me to have the "hey, when I left, you were out of Jessica's life forever, and now that I'm back you're not only here but you've knocked her up, weird, huh?" conversation. It was another for him to love his life with Jessica and the twins and realize that if one little thing had been different, he'd be alone.

Clearly his children were as alarmed by that tone of voice as I was, because in an instant they were up and at him with hugs and pats. It looked like he was trapped in a hurricane of gangly elbows and knees but it served its purpose: he calmed right down.

"It seems peculiar and way too unsettling but I promise, I promise—"

The boy took up where his sister left off. "—you get used to it, it's no big by our fifth; you're more disconcerted about Uncle Sink adopting four more Labs without telling you— never mind, I didn't say that."

"Four?" Uncle Sink said, delighted. "What an outstanding idea, how clever your children are, Detective."

"Absolutely not!"

"We're a little clever," his son objected.

"Not you, hon, of course not you, and, come on, Eric! We've already talked about how we can't take on more—we're getting off the subject." He turned back to his teenagers. "Can you control it? Can you—what'd you call it—can you shift back to newborn? Or—God forbid, I don't know if my heart could take it—ahead to your twenties? Or any time in between?"

"Nawp." He shook his head. "It just happens. In fact, I'm hugely surprised we're still here. We'll blip out pretty soon. That's what you guys said it was like. We just blink out and there's a 'pop' and—"

"From the air rushing into the space we just occupied. Science, hooray!"

"—and we're back to the age you'd expect."

"I thank you for taking the time to explain," Tina said with customary courtesy. "And none of this makes the slightest sense."

*Welcome to my world, honey.*

"Next time, bring hand puppets," Marc advised, which I should have found sarcastic but instead thought was a pretty great idea. Hand puppets would definitely help.

"Maybe next time you see us like this you'll be yawning

from how everyday it is," the boy said with a hopeful smile. His sister nodded so hard she had to steady herself against DadDick.

I tried to think about how these two could be any awesomer and came up *nada*. Well, maybe if they'd come back from the mall with Orange Juliuses for everybody. When I thought about how jealous I'd been of them even before they'd been born—I had been dreading being usurped in Jessica's life by incontinent, nonspeaking infants—it made me want to squirm.

Speaking of the delectable orange drink of the gods, he'd left his drink unattended. Foolish boy! I sidled closer; all the stress and shouty emotions had left me parched. That Orange Julius was my due, he owed me the rest, or at least a sip, and nothing would stop me from—*dammit*.

"I was just getting it for you," I whined.

"Nice try, vampire hag." The brat helped himself to a noisy slurp. "Ahhhh! Never have I had a more refreshing beverage, all the sweeter because you were old and slow. Reminds me." He tossed a silvery flash at Sinclair, who snatched it out of the air quicker than thought. "Thanks. Ace run, like always."

Sinclair clutched the car keys and we all heard the plastic crack. Not good; now he'd have to use the actual metal key to lock, unlock, and start it. "I demand the truth. You will be blunt, but no harm shall come to you." Were his . . . yes. His lips were trembling as he prepared to face catastrophic news. "Is my automobile intact?"

This was too much, even from Gearhead Boy. "You went from slutty loner to loving a lot of things besides me and it's making me nervous."

"By *nervous*, Onniebetty means *insecure*," the other brat piped up.

"You stay out of this; you're only a few weeks old. I'm serious, Sinclair. The cars, playing in traffic *without* the cars, Fur and Burr—"

"I forget! They jumped out of my mind, c'mon!" Jessica's son handed me his drink (victory! that brat was no match for my wiles or how I was just standing there like a blond lump) and started for the mudroom door. "Right now it's just Fur and Burr and they're still puppies in this timeline."

"Ooooh!" His sister was right behind him. "It's fun to see them again when they're babies," she clarified, like we'd insist on an explanation as to why they would want to play with adorable puppies. "They grow up so fast."

From Marc: "Wow."

DadDick: "Yeah."

From Tina: "She genuinely doesn't understand the enormous irony in those comments."

From me, since I finally caught on: "Oh! I get it. Irony! Heh."

But at the last second, she seemed to change her mind, because she turned and came straight at me. "You ratted me out when I was fourteen," she whispered, small, strong hands clutching my wrist as she leaned up and cupped a hand over my ear and her mouth. "But you didn't rat me out last month when the garage accidentally burned down."

"What?"

"Shhhh! So listen. It's not your fault. You wanted to help and they saw it and used it. But you'll do a good job. So don't worry."

"What?"

She spun away from me and charged toward the door. "I want a pup right now!"

"Wait, get back here," I commanded. "What were you talking about? And we've got more questions."

"Be speedy, then!" her brother shouted from the mudroom, and I wasn't sure if he was talking to his sister or to me.

"Get back here right now," I said in my best "I'm the queen so don't fuck with me" voice, which had the exact effect it did on Fur and Burr: no effect. Again: why couldn't I intimidate people when I really needed to?

The mudroom door slammed shut and I was reminded that a) they had no control over when and where they shifted, or to what age, and b) they'd expected to be gone already. And at once, though there was no logic to it, I knew they were going. The others didn't seem to pick up on it—or maybe were still brain-fried from the events of the last hour—because they were standing around staring at each other.

I rushed to the door and groped for the knob. "Wait!" I screamed, furious I hadn't thought of this sooner. I wrenched open the door. "What are your *names*?"

I was greeted by Fur and Burr, who were yapping and licking the faces of two newborns, who seemed surprised but not upset and only wriggled in an attempt to avoid canine drool instead of crying.

Aw, son of a *bitch*. Now we'd have to depend on Jess and DadDick to know their names. Which would involve actually naming them.

I wasn't going to hold my breath. Vodka and Orange Juice it was!

# CHAPTER
# TWENTY-NINE

*Jess had gone to lie down, and no one could blame her.* I felt like a nap myself. Perhaps ten naps. But maybe I should get back to Hell. I had to set an example for the Antichrist, after all. Big-sister stuff. Coworker stuff. I owed it to Hell to return to its Mall of the Damned. I definitely wasn't worried about the second part of Sinclair's text. Not a bit.

"She's gonna sleep," DadDick said, returning to the kitchen.

"Maybe you should, too," Marc said. He'd fussed over the babies, given them another quick exam, and assured all of us they were perfectly fine. They sure seemed fine. Their diapers didn't even need changing. "I'll watch them."

"Thanks, Marc." He scrubbed a hand over his face. "Christ. All that. I still can't take it in. Thank God they're okay, but I don't—sorry, Tina."

"Not at all," she murmured. "You're quite correct, it was a great deal to take in. Blaspheming seems appropriate. I have many questions."

"As do I." There was a pause as Sinclair ambled across the room and snaked an arm around my waist to pull me in until our hips bumped. "I suppose making some sort of schedule wherein we can refer to a list of questions for the twins based on whatever stage of their lives they shift into would be—"

"Completely fucked," I said before DadDick had to. "We're not making charts or lists, cripes. 'Hi, kids, happy twenty-first birthday and what'd you major in, anyway? Your cribs are all made up and ready for you.' No."

"Perhaps just think it over," he coaxed, smiling the smile that I always felt below the equator and when *was* the last time I got laid, anyway?

Too bad the smile was for DadDick, who was immune.

"Not now, please, you guys."

See? Also, "you guys"? *I* wasn't doing anything. He should have said "you guy." "Yeah, back off, Uncle Sink." Never let it be said that my horniness for my husband allowed me to stand by while my friends were being overwhelmed. "DadDick has had a tough few days."

*"My name is Dick!"*

"See? He's falling apart! He's bursting at the seams like an overstuffed sausage." Hmm. Not my best. "Wait, why are you yelling at me?"

"I've had enough of your obstinate refusal to call me by my fucking name."

"I think you should yell at anybody *but* me, *Dick*," I warned. *Elizabeth.*

"Quit that," I snapped, pulling away from him. "You're not in charge of how I behave even when I'm self-absorbed enough to pick the wrong time to get into a pissing match with a vulnerable, exhausted new father who insists on calling himself by the wrong name. Okay, that didn't come out like I planned. I'll rephrase. The thing is, Not-Dick, I can't be expected to—"

"Tina, Marc, Sinclair"—DadDick's knuckles went white

as he leaned on the back of a kitchen chair—"could Betsy and I have a minute?"

"Of course," Tina murmured, falling into step behind Marc and Sinclair, who were leaving in what could best be described as an undignified scramble. Cowards. "Please excuse us."

*Be kind to him, my own.*

*He started it!*

*You must be the mature one.*

*He's older than me!*

*Elizabeth.*

*Oh, go away. And get out of my head. Whitebearwhitebearwhitebear.*

*????*

*Never mind.*

The kitchen door swung back in and we were alone, except for Fur and Burr, who had done that puppy thing where they were playing then basically passed out to nap where they collapsed. Their fat little bellies huffed in and out with quick breaths because their puppy lungs were so small. I'd find it much cuter if it didn't remind me that their puppy bladders were also small.

That's Not My Name huffed, squeezed the back of the chair once more, then straightened and speared me with his exhausted, bloodshot gaze. Intimidating and, it must be said, a little gross. He looked about one half-step behind a nasty dose of pinkeye. Also: eye boogers. Sometimes I really appreciated being undead.

"Do you know why, Betsy?"

"No?" That seemed safe enough.

"Of course not. Have you ever once asked yourself why I would object so strongly to a perfectly nice name like Nick? Hmm? Elizabeth? Or should I call you Beth?"

"Please don't."

"Or Liz."

He was so cruel! "Ugh."

"Liza?"

"I think I'm starting to see your point. Your brutal name-calling has helped me see the light so let us never speak of this—"

"I don't like hearing it because it reminds me that in another life or timeline or parallel universe or whatever, I was enough of a dumb fuck to let Jessica go. I can't bear the thought of it. I have *nightmares* about it, get it? And yeah, this week has been tough but I'd rather be in the middle of this supernatural freak show—"

"Hey!"

"—than the alternative." He'd quit with the chair squeezing and had progressed to tile pacing. "I've got to come to grips with the fact that my babies are unlike any other children in the world, that they could be powerful or vulnerable or both. That's hard enough, but at least I'm here for it. I'm not trapped in a stupid decision that I would have made out of fear. Not even a decision, maybe a reflex from the sheer terror of being in your lives."

"But if that was true, it's not like you'd know it," I pointed out in a small voice. "You'd never have known. You can't mourn what you never had, and never knew you could have."

"But I do know it! Now, here, I'm aware of how close I came to missing all of this." He waved a hand but I was sure he meant his home, his friends, his babies, his smoothies, and not the toaster he gestured at. "And I'd appreciate it if you didn't remind me how close it was every time you deliberately let the wrong name fall out of your mouth."

Oh.

Huh.

"I suck," I said with pure sincerity.

He shrugged.

I decided to pretend he'd said something like, *No, no, that's crazy, don't beat yourself up,* and elaborated. "No, I do. That's awful. I've been awful."

"I wasn't debating the point."

I let it go; I had it coming and then some. "I'm so sorry."
I decided to do something nice and lined him up to take a
shot at me. "I guess you could say I wasn't thinking."

DadDick—sorry, Dick—let it go.

"You could also say I was really stupid and insensitive."

Hmm, still nothing. A gentleman *and* a detective! I
stopped trying to get him to insult me so I would feel better
and got back to the groveling. "I'm so sorry, Dick. It will never
happen again."

"Thank you," he replied, polite yet exhausted now that his
anger had been doused with the water that was my apology.
God, my metaphors were getting worse! How was that even
possible? "Appreciate you hearing me out. I'm going to go
make sure Jess didn't wake up and need something."

I caught his elbow as he turned away. "Dick, I don't think
I've ever said it, but I love you. I'd love you for your own
oddly named self even if you weren't in Jessica's life. But you
are, and so I love you for that, too. I double love you! And
what I've been doing—the name thing—it's a shitty way to
treat someone you care about. I'm truly sorry and I meant
it—it won't happen again."

"Thank you," he said again and smiled a little. I tentatively
reached for him and he rested his head on my shoulder for a
few seconds. We both pretended not to notice that he was
crying a little. Stress, I figured. Hoped. Because if my thought-
less asshattery had reduced him to such a state, I had a lot to
make up for.

No time like the present, even when you could accidentally
time travel.

# THIRTY

*Label maker in hand, I was deep into my project when Marc* walked in on me. I held a finger to my lips and he shrugged; he knew how it was with her. We'd need to be quiet, but not silent. Jess was a heavy sleeper even when she got a solid eight hours per. She was sprawled facedown on her bed right now, her exhausted snores muffled by her pillow. The Food Network was blatting away on the television near the wall across from her bed. Jess wasn't a foodie or close to one, but she liked the background noise of people chatting and cooking. Her mom had been far too refined to slime her manicured paws cooking for "loved ones" (the quotes were ironic), so the Watson kitchen had been the opposite of a warm, friendly room the whole family liked to congregate in. It was more like a lab that had been shut down for lack of funding.

"Huh," Marc said from the doorway as he glanced around the room. "This is new."

"Yeah, Dick and I had a thing."

"The name thing."

"Yep." God, had I really been that obviously offensive, or had Dick confided in Marc? Dumb question, even for me; it was both. Who hadn't confided in Marc at one point or another? Dead men tell no *et cetera*. "It's been a strange week for all of us. Whatever problem you're bringing to me, maybe it could wait?" Which was shitty, because I never hesitated to burden him with my silly bullshit.

Okay, new plan. After I made things right with Just Plain Dick, I'd offer Marc a friendly and attentive ear. Maybe both ears. This, of course, assuming I managed not to offend any other loved ones before the weekend. I'd better update my schedule.

"No problem. And I'm not bringing a problem, I just wanted to check on you. Because you're right, and even though I hate to feed your immense starving ego, your week has probably been the strangest."

I grinned. "Probably?" Then, "Aw, come on. Starving?"

"Like I said, hate to spoon-feed that insatiable ego you've got lurking in you. How's Hell?"

"You won't even believe it. It's actually starting to come together." What was that strange tone in my voice? It seemed familiar. I almost had it. What was the opposite of shame? Got it: pride. "Laura's gonna be psyched when she sees I finally made progress."

"Mm-mm. Once she got you down there she pulled a Houdini?"

"Well, yeah, but she's got stuff besides Hell to deal with. Her charity work alone eats something like fifty hours a week. She went down there—dammit, now I'm doing it again, Hell isn't down anywhere! But like I said, she went down there plenty of times without me."

"She did? Well, if you're looking for ideas about how to torture the denizens of your second home—"

I shuddered. "Please, *please* don't call it that. Most people, their second home is a cabin somewhere. Mine's Hell. I can't. No."

"You could make them play kill-bang-marry."

"Nobody plays kill-bang-marry anymore."

"How are they supposed to know that if you don't tell them? If the person in charge of Hell says playing kill-bang-marry is still a thing, then it's still a thing."

"Uh-huh, and every time we play, someone ends up crying." Meaning: *I* end up crying. It does my ego zero good to find out how many of my friends would rather kill me than marry or bang me. Tina and Marc want to marry each other ("A sexless marriage is the best marriage."), Sinclair wants to do all three to me in no special order, and *everybody* wants to marry Jess, because she's rich and low maintenance. A lot of my friends secretly want to be kept men. Or women. Plus, I didn't want to cry in Hell. Not in front of the damned—they'd never let it go. "No, it's too awful, even for people there to be tortured for eternity. I've gotta put my foot down somewhere, Marc."

"Okay, how about what's the most disgusting thing you've ever had in your—"

"No."

"I was going to say mouth!"

"Not much better, pal. A thousand times: no."

"Aw, come on, I'll bet someone who's been in Hell for a thousand years could come up with crazy stuff nobody's ever heard of."

"No. I wouldn't let you play that game with vampires and a zombie and a new mom; why would you think I'd okay it in Hell? Like I said, even that's too awful for Hell."

He shrugged but didn't seem put out. Usually he'd be in partial-pout mode if I shot down two ideas in a row. Odd, even for him.

"What's going on? Did you seriously come up here to give me terrible ideas you must have known I'd nix?"

"Only partly," he replied, leaning against the doorway to get comfy, his eyes crinkling as he smiled. "Mostly I'm supposed to keep you here so you don't run off. Teleport off. Whatever."

I froze in midlabel, then forced myself to relax. I had thought it was dumb delightful luck that Sinclair didn't start with the nagging the minute the newborns were newborns again. Not only did he not bug me, he'd left. I had assumed he was checking over his gigantic electric shaver of a car, but he hadn't come back yet. And that didn't bode well. And I wasn't thinking about the second part of his text. Nope.

"Ah, you're still here." Tina had appeared in the doorway beside Marc, who stepped aside to let her into the room. "The babies are asleep. All the babies." Ah. She meant Fur, Burr, Thing One, Thing Two, and my brother/son. At least that was what I hoped she meant. She was old enough to consider the rest of us as babies. Hell, she'd been Auntie Tina to Sinclair the first dozen years of his life.

The age issue aside, I felt a stab of guilt since I hadn't been able to play with BabyJon for days. I hadn't laid eyes on him in at least two. Maybe I'd been kidding myself and the reason he turned out so great in the future was because I didn't have time for him when he was little. An awful thought; I had to swallow the lump it brought to my throat. I was missing my brother's childhood and had no one to blame but myself. Other working moms made it work, ones with much less time, money, resources, supernatural abilities, and jobs from Hell where they couldn't set their own hours. I wouldn't consider "bring your brother/son to Hell" day, but there were other things I could do. Things I'd better do, or I'd wake up one night and BabyJon would be enjoying his prom. And probably resenting the nickname BabyJon.

Tina read my mind, because she was terrifying. "He adores you. And when he is older, he will honor your work."

That probably wasn't true at all, but she was a sweetie for saying so.

"Besides, my queen, you should—ah, perhaps turn off the television?"

Eh? Oh. That could only mean one thing. Tina wasn't a fan of the Food Network. She considered it torture porn ("I cannot enjoy any of those dishes unless I dilute and puree them. Why would I put myself through such an ordeal?"). However, she would occasionally keep Marc company in the wee hours and watch it with him. Which was how she learned of his deep abiding hatred of Giada De Laurentiis, a perfectly lovely woman Marc wanted off the air forevermore.

"It's 'spuh-GET-ee.'" Uh-oh. He had forgotten about everyone else in the room and regressed to yelling at the TV. "It's 'ri-ZOT-o.'"

We were too late. *You arrogant ass, you've killed us all!* Trapped, trapped like rats, unless . . . knocking Tina off her feet so I could be the first to escape wasn't very queenlike. Right? Dammit.

"Shut up, you many-toothed bitch, stop pronouncing stuff like that—'spah-GAY-tee,' 'moots-ah-RAY-la,' 'pan-CHAY-tuh' . . . you're from California, for God's sake!"

"It's quite legitimate," Tina corrected him mildly from her safe spot beside the door, ideal for a quick getaway. This. This was why Tina was still alive after well over a century: she always mapped escape routes, even in her own home. "Ms. De Laurentiis was born in Italy." *Why do you know that?* I mouthed, but only got a shrug in response. A respectful shrug, but still.

"Yeah, *born* there; it proves nothing, *nothing*!" Marc had progressed past yelling at the TV and was in full-on violent gesture mode. "Because right after that, the family picked up and moved to the States when she was . . . what? Eight days old?"

"Twelve years."

Seriously: why does she know that? Marc was the Food Network freak in our house. She was putting up with a lot of vampire torture porn to keep Marc company. They'd become besties right under my nose.

"Regardless. *She's from California*; the big move was decades ago; every other word she pronounces with an American accent. I don't even think she speaks Italian."

"Of course she speaks Italian," Tina replied, exasperated. At least their squabbling got the attention off me so I could work on the project some more.

"Nuh-uh, she speaks Italian *food.* Everything else: American accent. Because, again: California, lived there for decades. Giada should stop talking about 'spah-GAY-tee'; it's so pretentious." Marc turned a haunted gaze on me. "No one from California should ever be pretentious. And don't get me started on her disproportionately sized head."

"Easy there," I said warily. Marc was as a rule so easygoing he should have kept a surfboard in his room, but when his zombie dander was up, he was no one to fool with. Death, it seemed, left him a wee bit judgmental. And, as I'd already pointed out, it had been a nutty week, even for us. "She pronounces food that way probably out of respect for her mom, right? She's maybe from Italy?"

"My dad was from Germany and you'll never catch me singing 'Deutschland, Deutschland.'"

"Right. Okay. Marc, I think it's time you went to your happy place." Mine was the Manolo Blahnik brick-and-mortar store on Fifty-fourth Street in New York, which I modified only slightly in my head by putting a smoothie bar in the basement. "Which is good advice for all of us."

Before I could elaborate, I realized Sinclair was in the doorway with his mouth already open, clearly geared to lecture mode, when he stopped and looked, and then looked some more. "Hmm." While he hmm'd, Marc and Tina vamoosed without him saying a word. Jess, natch, was still snoring. I had to actively fight the temptation to label her.

"Here you are. I have need of you." That could mean a whole host of things, many of them delicious and filthy; others, smoothie related. Hell, it could even be vampire monarch business. But I was pretty sure it wasn't anything like that.

"Busy." I finished with the chest of drawers, then crawled to the bed and fished around beneath it, found Jessica's terrible filing system, and pulled it out.

"So I see, but there is something that requires your urgent attention." He was still holding his keys. Hadn't stopped in the kitchen to hang them up, then. He'd just disappeared on an abrupt errand, returned quickly, then come straight up to get me. Not good. "At once, if you please."

"What doesn't require my urgent attention these days? Besides, I'm not done atoning." I gestured at the room, and the bed, where I may or may not have succumbed to the urge to label Jessica.

His lips twitched but he swallowed his laugh, and most of the smile. "And I loathe taking you away from it because in this, as in most things, you are a delight."

"Most, huh?" I sat back on my heels and brushed my bangs out of my eyes, accidentally labeling myself in the process. Nope. Would not do for Dick to get the wrong idea. I unlabeled myself. "Listen, we can talk about the twins, whom I'm now calling I Don't Know His Name and I Don't Know Hers Either. And we can talk about how much you want to take over Hell for me and Jessica's refusal to name us godparents and anything else in a little bit."

"Elizabeth."

"Hell's doing great, by the way. As great as Hell can be, I mean. Not that you asked or anything."

*Elizabeth.*

Yeah, being scary and firm in my head wasn't any more effective, buddy, but points for effort. "I don't know how I did it, but things happened. I'll go back in a bit and more things will happen. I'm almost sure of it."

He had crossed the room, knelt, grasped my wrists, and lifted me to my feet. "Your father is downstairs."

"No. He isn't."

"He is, my love."

"Impossible."

"So are you, darling."

"It's a joke, right?" I could feel my lips twitching and realized I was trying to smile. "It's an elaborate April Fool's prank you're all in on, which you did months ahead of schedule to throw me off."

*I would never.*

I could feel myself starting to tremble and when Sinclair carefully pulled me into his arms I accidentally labeled myself again.

"How awful is it?" I asked his shoulder blade. I was hugging him back so hard I felt my fingers punch through the fabric of his shirt. Sinclair didn't move away or make a single sound of protest, but I loosened my grip anyway. "On a scale of one to ten? One being 'whoops, we were wrong, he *is* dead, we'll get the corpse out of your house right away' and ten being 'kidnapped by sinister supernatural forces and tortured by same for years, which is your fault and you'll be haunted by that for eternity.'"

"Come see for yourself." I pressed my ear to his chest. I loved his voice almost anytime but the deep rumble was especially comforting now. "I will be with you, my own. As will we all. You are not alone."

"Can't you at least give me a hint?"

*You must hear it from him.*

"He's been kidnapped? He's secretly a vampire? Satan found him and has been doing awful things to him because she didn't like me? He's dying and didn't want to worry me by being alive? He testified against a murderer and had to go into Witness Protection? Audited? An STD he can't seem to shake? What?"

He sighed and I clutched harder.

*Oh, my love. It's much worse than that.*

*Sinclair was right. If anything, he undersold it.*

"You're alive because you're alive? That's it? That's your explanation?"

My father had been over it twice and I still didn't get it, making it worse than that appalling endless time he tried to teach me to change a tire. So much rage. And grease.

We were in the Peach Parlor and my father looked great. At first I thought he'd been tortured somewhere nice, like Little Cayman, explaining the tan. Or locked up somewhere without access to junk food, like a farmers' market, explaining the fifteen-pound weight loss. Or held prisoner in the basement of a Neiman Marcus, explaining the smartly tailored dark brown pants, cream-colored dress shirt, silk tie with cream and gold accents, and Manolo Blahnik brown suede loafers. Argh, *Manolo Blahniks* on his treacherous feet! Why not just set my soul on fire and get it over with?

"Dad, what the hell?" I know. Lame. But it was the only

thought to pop into my brain. At least it was a complete sentence.

He'd gotten to his feet when I trudged into the parlor, but sat back down the second I came to a stop in front of him. No tearful reunion father-daughter embrace, then. Not even a handshake, given how he was clasping his hands together.

Dick had been standing near him in a faded T-shirt and his rubber duckie pajama pants, like a menacing bodyguard who'd just gotten out of bed. Which, in a way, he was. Once I was in the room he relaxed and went to sit on the love seat with Marc. Tina and Sinclair remained standing. Their carefully neutral expressions were terrifying.

"Your, uh, friend has been guarding me. Right?" Dad tried a smile. It didn't fit his mouth, and not just because he knew he was on the spot. He'd never had a roommate. He'd never seen the desire to live with people if you didn't need them to do things for you. "Afraid I'll run off?"

"Yes," everyone but me said in unison.

He looked rattled, but I didn't know if it was because of my friends' retort or my lack thereof. "Er . . . why?"

"Because you're a coward/chickenshit/dreadful man/runaway/scumbag," everyone said in unison (though they all picked different descriptions).

In next to no time I went from puzzled that he was alive to worried about what he'd had to endure to shocked when I realized he hadn't endured . . . well . . . anything.

"There's no supernatural explanation? No dramatic terrible weirdness that snatched you out of my life?"

"Dramatic terrible weirdness is why I had to leave."

"Had to leave?" I could only gape. Even I, occasional poster child for the self-involved, was staggered. "You didn't appreciate the drama *you* had to endure?"

"That's right."

"And you've been in St. Paul this whole time?" That was the part my mind kept reeling back to. He'd faked his death and hid, except not. How had I never noticed we were living in the same city? Okay, St. Paul wasn't exactly a small town, not with three hundred thousand live humans, nineteen vampires, an unknown number of ghosts, and one zombie (at last count, anyway), but still. In some respects, St. Paul *was* a small town in that many of us moved in the same little circles. (I was betting that was why he'd bumped into Jessica the other day.) It made me wonder if he'd wanted to get caught or if he was just lazy.

Once his fake funeral was over, Dad had gone straight back to his routine: making money, chasing women far too young for him, living in St. Paul, and pretending he didn't have a family. He'd moved his money around so he could still access it after a name change. He'd sold off some properties and bought new ones. He was unfettered in all the best ways.

If he ever got to Hell, the Ant would kill him.

"Let me see if I'm getting this." I saw him shift on the couch but had no pity for his impatience with my inability to grasp hideous behavior from someone who was supposed to love me. "There are no killers to apprehend, nobody to track down to avenge you? You haven't been kept prisoner in a farmers' market or Little Cayman?"

He blinked. "No."

"You just . . . took a time-out from your life? And mine? Wait." It hit me and I was a fool not to realize sooner. "*Not* just my life. Your other daughter's life. Your son's life. Your wife's. Your ex-wife's."

"The pressures on me"—he sighed—"were crushing."

"The Ant died in the accident, you selfish shit!" Talk about *crushing*.

"Language. And the accident wasn't my fault," Dad interjected. "I had the flu, remember?"

"No," I said shortly. I'd seized a peach throw pillow from the couch and started plucking at the tassels. Soon I was walking back and forth in front of him, shedding peach fuzz everywhere, keeping my fingers busy so I couldn't strangle him. I reminded myself this was no time for multitasking. "Of course I don't remember. You didn't talk to me much before you faked your death, either."

He blew that off. "I couldn't go, and you know Antonia."

*Better than you now, maybe.*

"She brought her hairdresser to the ball."

"Sergio or Esperanza?"

"The illegal who had sticky fingers."

Sergio, then. "So he didn't have his own ID but he nicked yours."

"Wherever he took it, or whenever, he didn't have time to pick through and take the stuff he wanted, so he grabbed the whole thing. Probably would have stripped the cash and cards and then tossed it. Hell, maybe your stepmother gave it to him to spite me for not going with her." He smiled, like a kid who was trying to impress his parents with something they found horrifying. "The accident was unforeseen, and it wasn't like correcting the coroner's ID would have brought your stepmother back."

"But . . . the dental records? You were both burned beyond—I mean, your wife and Sergio were burned beyond recognition. Would the ID have been enough? Wouldn't they have pulled dental records?" I mean, there was a reason I'd never questioned the fact that my dad was dead. It had seemed pretty definitive at the time, which, given my and mine's penchant for returning from the dead, was unforgivably naïve in retrospect.

He coughed into his fist, a dry bark. "I spread some money around. Not even that much, come to think of it. Nobody cared much." He glanced up at me and looked away. "Like I said, none of that would have brought your stepmother back. All I did was take advantage of a fortunate coincidence."

"Fortunate. Coincidence?" Was it possible I was talking too fast? Was that why he wasn't getting it? "Your wife. Died."

"Aren't you listening? I didn't plan the accident. She died, but it wasn't anything *I* did." Another quick interjection, like he knew what I would say and when I would say it. He'd rehearsed, then. I recognized the behavior as I'd seen it almost constantly since about the first grade. When Sinclair tracked him down and explained to his father-in-law that he *would* be visiting Vampire Central before skipping town, Dad had started marshaling his arguments. Anyone else would have been polishing their apology.

Okay, so it was clear (and awful) he didn't care his wife died. R.I.P., the Ant, and wow did I not want to feel sorry for her, but I did. No wonder she hadn't wanted to help me solve the mystery, doing everything short of jamming her fingers in her ears while chanting "nah-nah-nah, can't heeeeear youuuu!" She would have realized that instead of being devastated by her death, or at least unpleasantly surprised, her husband had turned it into a ladder he could use to escape. Which was cold-blooded on a level I had only ever seen in vampires. The really old, mean ones.

Appealing to his status as a loving husband hadn't worked; time to try something else. "Your son. Was orphaned."

"But left in good hands."

"*No*, Dad, *not* in good hands!" I couldn't remember the last time I'd lost it so quickly or completely. "You left him in *my* hands—what the fuck were you thinking?"

His shoulders had been going up in his trademark turtle-not-wanting-to-be-here pose, but that snapped him into sitting back upright. "Language."

"Fuck you! Fuck you! Fuck you! How's that? Here's more language: you are a craven shithead!"

"Please stop indulging in hysterics," he semi-begged. He didn't dare get up and storm out of a room full of lethal people glaring at him, any one of whom would have been happy to turn his femurs into splinters, but neither was he happy about having to stay in the room with his overly dramatic daughter and her tiresome awkward hysterics. "No need to be childish."

Yep. My head was trying to blow itself up; I could almost feel the pressure building. *Head, I sympathize, but you're not going anywhere.* "You haven't seen *anything* yet. You've got a lot of nerve being alive, Dad," I continued in a cold rage, "and also this is the last time I'm going to speak to you for a while so drop dead! Except don't, because you suck at it! And—and I hate you, and your wife is more horrible in death than she ever was in life." Lie. "And your hair is stupid, everybody knows you're going bald." Truth. For a few seconds I wished we were having this chat over the phone so I'd only have to contend with his asshat voice and not his asshat voice and face. One of the old-fashioned phones, which granted the user the ability to slam the receiver down knowing you partially deafened the guy on the other end with the crash. The future sucks sometimes. No one in their right mind would slam an iPhone.

He didn't say anything, so I kept it up. "How could you do this to Laura? All she wanted from you was to get to know you a little. You had no history with her like you did with me, so you'd have a fresh start. You'd like her, the An—" I cut myself off. Reminding my dad that the daughter who wasn't the vampire queen was the Antichrist might give him the mistaken idea that his shitty plan had been a good one. "She's nice, a lot nicer than me. And what about BabyJon? He's innocent." The Ant was harder to argue. "Doing it to me I kind of get. I resented the shit out of you and the Ant and never stopped letting you know it. But with BabyJon you had a fresh start. Instead of a bitchy disrespectful teenager, you could start over with a wonderful baby. Indulge in the 'this time I'll do it right' trope. Instead you bailed on everyone? Don't you see how shitty and selfish that was?"

"Stop acting like a child—"

I wasn't letting that go by twice. "Oh, and you'd know what that looked like *how*? You weren't around for most of my childhood and you're sure as shit not planning to be around for BabyJon's. And pointing out your grotesque flaws isn't acting like a child."

"—and look at it from my side." Ha! He couldn't think of an argument to what I just said, so instead he clung stubbornly to whatever asinine self-serving point he wanted to make. *Oh, Christ, was there where I got it? Fuck and double fuck.* "Trapped in a second marriage—"

"Trapped?" That was it. My brain was definitely going to implode inside my skull. Marc had told me the brain didn't have pain receptors, which was wonderful because I figured when it blew, it probably wouldn't even hurt. Wait, did he mean all brains or just my brain?

Dad was still mumbling excuses. "You know she only had the baby to get me to marry her. And she had the other one to make sure I wouldn't leave. For a while I thought it wasn't even mine."

"You—what? You—okay, first, *it* has a name. It's . . ." Jon something. John something? I called him BabyJon but that probably wasn't the name on his birth certificate. Shit! "And he's more than the bait in a trap. Okay, Antonia shouldn't have tricked you, but don't blame your son for her choices, or yours. Nobody stuck a gun in your ear and forced you to marry her."

"I'm too old to start over."

"Do you hear yourse—?" I cut myself off. He didn't, any more than I ever did. "You're the one who chose to bang the Ant *sans* birth control."

"She said she'd had a hysterectomy," he whined.

"Dad, she still got her period! Or did you think the Tampax was for making Molotov cocktails?" I clutched at my hair and managed—just—not to rip out whole chunks and then start on my scalp. "This is not the time for a lecture on how much you don't know about wives despite being married most of your adult life. You chose to marry her and to raise a kid together. What, you never planned on sticking around? Were you looking for an escape hatch before the ink dried on your marriage certificate?"

"No."

Silence. A bubble was coming up from somewhere, one I didn't want to surface. Because if he hadn't planned to ditch the Ant, and later the son, because of *them*, that meant the straw shattering the camel's back, the tipping point, was me.

"Were you even a little glad I didn't die for real?" The bubble had popped and it was as dreadful as I feared. And who was talking in such a small pitiful voice? Whoever they were, they should speak up; they sounded pathetic. "That even though I'd been run down like a skunk on a back road, I came back from that? I wasn't hurt or—or anything. I was—"

"A monster."

Hmm. Was he talking from a rapidly darkening tunnel? Or was the rage eclipsing everything but the need to pull his spine out through his ass and strangle him with it?

"It's nothing personal," he explained as I started to laugh. I think it was laughter. I was making weird noises, anyway. "I needed a fresh start. I deserved one, don't you think?"

*Bite him. Mojo him. Make him forget what he did, make him into the father BabyJon deserves. Or mojo him into taking a walk off the top of the IDS Tower.*

"Don't worry, Dad. I'll give you what you deserve."

*Bite him. Turn him. He'll be your slave forever, until you or someone else kills him; he'd never do it himself. Be his nightmare.*

My family was so silent I'd almost forgotten they were there. But I could feel their shock and outrage, and Sinclair was carefully staying out of my brain. Probably didn't want to shock me with what he was picturing doing to his father-in-law. Sweet, but unnecessary. There was no way whatever he was thinking was worse than what I was thinking.

"Y'know, I'm curious, Dad. What's your plan for when you grow old? With one wife divorced and the other dead? No friends—not that you had many—because of the whole faked-death thing? You removed yourself from your children's lives pretty thoroughly. It'll just be you out there."

A one-shoulder shrug. "I'll hire people."

"Uh-huh." I nodded; that was the response I expected. It would never occur to him to view a lack of friends and family as a crippling disadvantage. *Thank God, thank God in that one respect he and I are not alike.* "So you'll never have an accident? Never endure some unseen calamity? You can foresee every single bad thing that could happen to you and meticulously plan for each and every one?"

"Well, I . . . um . . ."

"That's what I thought. If you get clipped by a bus and pitched into a coma, anywhere in the world, the hospital will know exactly what to do, who to call? You won't spend your golden years rotting away in a state-funded nursing home? What if you end up with a cancer diagnosis? You'll foresee every single thing that could come of that and make all the provisions? Anything that might possibly go wrong in your life is one hundred percent foreseeable, if not preventable?"

He opened his mouth. Closed it. Opened it again. Nope. I'd put the brake on his brain.

I had him, and it should have been a triumph. "Because the thing about being a monster, Dad, is that I would outlive you by centuries, but would always have been in a position to keep you safe. I'm doomed—I mean destined—to be the top dog around here for quite a long time. If you lost all your money tomorrow, or ten years from now, I'd still be living with millionaires who would be able to handle any expense. Who would be happy to help you if only out of love for me.

"But that's gone now. You wanted a fresh start? You wanted to put the new family behind you the way you put the old one behind you? Congrats. Wish granted." I didn't crowd him. Didn't go near him. I would never touch him again. "Don't come back here. Don't reach out. Don't call. Don't write. If I see you again, or I find out BabyJon or Laura has seen you, I'll see you dead at my feet. I won't bother to do it myself, that's how much of a nothing you'll be to me. I'll delegate your murder like it was sorting recyclables: something so boring I couldn't be bothered to do it myself."

Pale (even for him), Dad rose, straightened his crease, and crossed the parlor to leave. He didn't speak to me. He didn't look at me. That was fine.

"One more thing. I want you out of town within the week."

He turned, eyes narrowed, a scornful smile riding his mouth. "What, you're the landlord for the city of St. Paul?"

My hands had snapped into fists at some point. I had to make an effort to loosen them so I didn't punch my nails through my palms the way they'd punctured Sinclair's shirt. "As far as you're concerned, yeah. You've got the whole rest of the planet to get old and die in. St. Paul is *mine*. Get the fuck out."

He walked out of the parlor without another word. I listened to him cross the entryway, open the door, step outside. Then I used Tina's trick. I pretended I was in the airport and he was a passenger who was a stranger to me, someone I didn't have to listen to, someone whose proper place was background noise. And I let him fade.

And I vowed to never hear him again, not even if I lived to be a thousand, which I very well could.

# CHAPTER
# THIRTY-TWO

*Peach. Peach everywhere, so much peach it wasn't just all* around me (we should repaint that ceiling), it was under me. I blinked and thought about that for a second.

Ah.

Somehow I'd gone from forbidding vampire queen ordering a dead-to-me father out of my city on pain of death to crumpled pitiful daughter shivering on the carpet and wanting Mommy.

A circle of concerned faces were looking down at me. This should have been creepy, or at least startling, but I was pretty numb. All I could muster was a kind of tired, faint curiosity as I stared up at them.

*Elizabeth? My own?*

"Easy," Marc said, pressing his hand against my shoulder as if I'd tried to rise, when I had no intention of ever leaving my new womb, the Peach Parlor. "Rest a second." A second? I planned to rest for a century at least. I wouldn't even need a bed. The thick, dusty peach carpet would be dandy. The mice would creep out at night and befriend me. I would be their queen.

"D'you want something?" Dick asked anxiously. His face kept appearing and disappearing over me as he paced and fretted. "A smoothie? D'you need blood?"

"I would like my mommy, please."

"Er . . ." He and Marc traded glances.

"I could call her, hon," Marc said, waving a finger at me. "Follow the tip, please."

"I don't have a concussion, Marc. I didn't hit my head." Did I? I was still a little fuzzy on how I got down here.

He ignored me and took my pulse, which was so laughable I didn't know where to start. "Oh, don't give me that look. Think I haven't memorized your undead RHR? You want me to call your mom?"

I shivered. No, best keep the awful truth(s) to myself for a bit longer. Mom would be upset and infuriated on my behalf before I got to the end of the tale, the part where I threatened to stomp her ex like a roach. *Note to self: do not tell Mom the end of the tale.*

"Perhaps some sugar-cookie-flavored vodka?" Tina suggested, which was quite the offer as it was her current favorite and they were discontinuing the flavor (despite her impassioned letter-writing campaign). Thank goodness. Bakery products and booze sounded good on paper, but the reality tended to be a disaster, and nobody wanted a repeat of New Year's Eve. "My queen? What do you need?"

Well, let's see. I needed a new dad. I needed to get out of running Hell. I needed to turn the Peach Parlor into my permanent lair. Most important: I needed to get my thumb out of my ass.

"I'm fine." Nobody said anything. "Really. I'm okay. I just wanted to rest. Very suddenly. I'm perfectly fine. *Apropos* of nothing, don't be alarmed if I never leave this room."

Sinclair smiled at me, dark gaze intent on my face, and it was almost enough to make me feel better. "If this is our room now, then it shall be so."

"Oh, Eric." Would not would not *would not cry*. "And you hate peach."

"I do. I cannot understand why we have not yet had this room redone." He glanced around with a frown, then returned his gaze to me. "Also I may murder your father if, for no other reason, than because he upset you so much you called me Eric."

*What? It's your name, isn't it? I call you that. Sometimes.* I could count those times on the fingers of one hand, but that didn't make his point, except for how it did. *And wanting to kill my dad is so sweet! I can almost feel myself melting into this horrible carpet.*

*I am quite serious.*

I gave him a warning look. *If I held back, you'd better, too.*

"I hate when you flaunt your supernatural mystic Vulcan telepathic link thing," Marc griped. "Could you please talk out loud now?"

Eric—sorry, Sinclair—obliged. *"Apropos* of nothing, when I have recovered from my worry, I shall tell you how proud I am, my dread queen. And . . . and . . ."

I groaned. "Go on. You know you can't help yourself."

"The *s* in *apropos* is silent."

"It was burning you up inside, wasn't it?"

He inclined his head in a slight bow. "I thank you for this indulgence, darling queen. Now perhaps if you—"

He cut himself off, and he and Tina both cocked their heads to the side, the motion almost doglike. I almost felt like smiling, it was so cute. They were like undead bipedal versions of Petey the Dog!

"Did you hear . . . ?" Tina murmured to Sinclair.

Sinclair had taken my wrist and was running his thumb back and forth across my sluggish pulse point. As he listened, he brought my wrist to his mouth and pressed a cool kiss to the vein. "Hmm," was all he said, which was just mysterious enough to be annoying.

"What are you guys talking about now?" Marc said, apparently satisfied that I wasn't going to expire on the spot. He had settled on the carpet beside me. "There's a lot of super secret vampire stuff going on in this room and I won't have it! What do you hear?"

"Nothing! Not one goddamned thing." I clawed for some self-control and lowered my voice. "I can't hear anything that man is doing. I'll never hear anything he does ever again. It's the airport trick, remember, Tina? Oh, stop it," I snapped as Marc started groping for my pulse again. "It's a vampire trick Tina taught me; I'm not out of my mind. At least no more than usual. So nope. I don't hear anything. And neither do any of you."

Tina wasn't paying attention, which was all kinds of aggravating. "It almost sounds like—"

Breaking glass and groaning metal. And was that shouting? Yep. Screaming, too, as different voices howled at each other. But that only made sense if . . .

I sat bolt upright, like Frankenstein coming to life on the table. "Where's Jessica?"

And then we were all scrambling to get outside and, not for the first time, I was glad the Peach Parlor was so close to the front door. Otherwise I would have missed the whole terrible, wonderful thing.

# CHAPTER
# THIRTY-THREE

*"Get away from there, you cow!"*

"Who are you calling a cow, chubbo?"

Distressing enough to overhear, but the follow-up crash, which sounded like a bag of bricks glancing off a window before grinding into metal, was also alarming.

As we got closer I was amazed to see my guess was close. Jessica had apparently woken from her nap, spotted or heard my dad, then rushed out of the house, hauled the lawn mower out of the shed, dragged it through the snow to our driveway, then somehow heaved it high enough to toss it into the car. In her struggles she'd broken a window. Since the thing was at least a third of her weight, I was hoping she hadn't also broken a bone. The whole endeavor wasn't as tough as it might have been, though, because my father is an asshole and his choice of car reflected that.

"Get that thing out of my Mustang!" Dad pointed, in case

Jessica forgot a) there was a Craftsman lawn mower in his car and b) she'd been the one to put it there.

"After all the trouble to get it in there? Why would I do that?"

I was used to gaping as a way to showcase my ignorance, so this was nothing new to me. But to see identical slack-jawed expressions on the others was gratifying. We probably looked like an illustration for *duh*. Dick in particular looked like he wasn't sure if he should rush to her side or applaud. (My vote: both!)

"Fine, you can explain it to the police, and then my lawyer." Dad let out a self-important huff and fished for his phone, lips pressed together so tightly they almost disappeared. "Let them deal with you."

"And you," she pointed out, panting slightly from her exertion. Cripes, the woman squeezed multiple human beings out of her love canal not even two months ago; I was impressed she was just panting *slightly*. Jessica smash! "Don't forget that."

"I'm telling you one more time, if you don't get that out right now I'll sue you for seven figures and—"

"What, Mr. Taylor? Sue me and what?" Jess was standing on the hood, hands on hips, glaring down at him. I knew she had no idea we were there. I was pretty sure she had no idea what city she was in. My friend was like Cate Blanchett in that *Hobbit* movie: beautiful and terrible as the dawn, treacherous as the sea. All shall love Jessica Watson and despair! (No, wait. That was *The Lord of the Rings*. Or am I thinking of *Elizabeth*? Cate Blanchett is the greatest, no matter what queen she's playing.) "Call the cops, excellent idea, don't forget to mention that you faked your death. And probably indulged in a little insurance fraud while you were at it. Be sure to bring that up, too."

While Dad stood there, stumped, Jess busied herself fussing with the lawn mower and at first I thought she was trying to shove it out of the way, not so much to obey my dad but so she could hop off the car. Then I saw she was up to something else, but couldn't quite . . . that was not what she . . . wait. Was she . . . ?

She was! She was starting the lawn mower! I couldn't figure it out right away because the context was all wrong. I'd seen Jess in a car lots of times. I'd seen lawn mowers lots of times. I had never seen Jess trying to start the mower she flung into my father's Mustang. Not once.

I knew Marc kept the thing in good working order, but it was also winter and the thing hadn't been started in months. Still, it was new and Jess had the unholy strength of the pissed-off, so the thing was giving it the old college try with every yank of the starter cord: *Nnnn-mmmm! Nnnn-mmmm!*

"You're mixing up my white-collar crimes with your pervert father," Dad finally snapped back. "Apples and oranges, young lady. Say what you will—"

*Nnnn-mmmm!*

"Okay. You're a self-absorbed dick; you didn't deserve your wife or your daughter or your son. The Ant you might have deserved." Jess was moving back and forth as she struggled with the mower. She couldn't make much progress, so the effect was that of a pissed-off windup toy. "And this car is a joke. Why not just paint 'Ask Me about My Midlife Crisis' on the side?" *Nnnn-mmmm!* "A friggin' Ford convertible in Minnesota in winter? With the top down, you silly fucker? Let's see, what else?"

"Say what you will about me, I never laid a hand on either of my children." Dad was looking up at her with one hand shading his eyes (not sure why—it was almost dark, gloomy enough that Tina could stay on the porch without getting burned), the other hand clenched in a fist he jammed into his pocket. "Your father, meanwhile, was the disgrace of the neighborhood and your mother wasn't any better."

"First off, he was the disgrace of the whole state."

*Nnnn-mmmm!* "Second, damned right. Third, don't pat your-self on the back because you couldn't be bothered to be around your kids." *Nnnn-mmmm!* "You *faked* your *death* and were dumb enough to hang around afterward. You look stupid trying to pull off morally indignant."

"Why aren't we helping her?" Marc asked in a low voice, though he needn't have bothered. Neither of them had a clue we were there.

"Because you don't help Van Gogh paint or Thomas Edison invent or Kristen Stewart scowl for the cameras," Dick said with an admiring sigh. "Adding another person is super-fluous."

"Awww." Marc rested his head on Dick's shoulder. "That's beautiful." Dick grinned and reached up to ruffle Marc's short hair. Tried to, anyway; sometime in the last day or two Marc had chopped it brutally short.

Meanwhile, Dad had gotten ready with his nasty retort when the engine caught (*Nnnn-mmmm—mmmmmmmmmmmmm-mmmmmm!*) and the blade started making horrible scraping sounds and bits of leather and fabric starting flying every-where. I was amazed and made a note never to buy any other kind of lawn mower because, *damn*, that was good design!

"I cannot bring myself to look away, though I devoutly wish I could," Sinclair said, appalled. "That poor automobile."

"And you know what? It sounds exactly like you'd expect a lawn mower chewing up a Mustang to sound."

"I have always been fond of the lady," Tina announced, "and am now making a mental note never to enrage her. Should I do so, however inadvertently, I will refuse to engage for my own safety."

As far as advice went, you couldn't beat it. I'd made the same mental note fifteen years before and it had stood me well.

Jess hopped down from the hood and made no move to stop my dad as he pushed past her. She even stepped back with a courteous smile as the mower started to belch smoke and the engine began to hitch (*nnn-ggkk!*). Dad stretched up to grab for the starter switch (tough to hit a moving target) while flinching all over the place as he was showered with bits of Mustang. The mower chose that second to give up on trimming the car and died with a final choked screech. After the unholy racket, the sudden silence was startling.

Jessica blinked when she noticed us for the first time, raised one shoulder in a "sorry, but you know what I'm like" shrug, and turned back to Dad, who looked close to bursting into tears. "All right, fun's over."

"*Fun?* I don't—"

"I meant my fun, shithead. Get off our property."

Dad had been reduced to waving his arms like an impaired traffic cop. "I can't, I have to—"

"Send a tow truck for it. Or don't; I'd love to find other tools to use on it. I think an electric drill could be fun. Either way, leave."

"But thanks to your childish tantrum I don't have a way to—"

"Bus stop is two blocks east."

"Bus stop?" he replied. From his aghast tone, you'd think Jessica had suggested he gouge out his own eyes. "I can't do that!"

She gave him a long look, then turned and started for the toolshed. I managed to restrain myself from clapping my hands and jumping up and down. What next? The aforementioned drill? A weed whacker? *Oh, please, please let it be the weed whacker.*

My father did something smart at last: practically sprinted down the driveway and onto the sidewalk. He didn't slow and after a few seconds I couldn't see him anymore.

Jess turned back toward the house, then nearly fell over Dick, who had raced to back her up after my dad pushed past her. Now he was on his knees and staring up at her like a

supplicant while grabbing the bottom of her shirt and tugging
to keep her attention.

"Jesus, you scared me!"

"Oh, please, please," he implored, gazing up at her with an
adoration most people showered on chocolate croissants,
"you've got to marry me."

Jess smiled but then glanced away. "Not this again."

Ooh, this again! It wasn't the first time he'd proposed but
after what had just happened, I knew it would be the last.

"How can I ever—? With anyone else, ever? You're so—and
this was so—" He gestured blindly at the car vs. mower showdown. Even though he wasn't speaking in complete sentences,
I knew what he was trying to convey. We all could. "Please,
you have to. Please, there couldn't ever be anyone else for me;
say it's true for you, too, and tell me yes."

"I suppose." She sighed. Then, because her fear of marriage
demanded at least one snarky remark: "Like I could find
another guy to put up with . . ." She made the same vague
gesture he had, which encompassed Mowerzilla, the mansion,
the rest of us. "Yes. I will. Of course I will. I'm sorry you had
to ask more than once." She bent to him, looped her arms
around his neck, and kissed him softly on the mouth. "Thank
you for asking more than once."

I had to glance away. It was so much wonderful, it was too
much wonderful after all the terrible. I didn't just feel like bursting into happy tears, I felt like blowing up into tears, detonating
into tears. Marc, too, was blinking fast and Tina had pressed a
small fist to her mouth to contain her happy whimpers. I turned
to Sinclair, who was doubtless shaking his head in bemusement
at our emotional antics, and saw his lips tremble just a bit before
his mouth tightened. In a week of weird, that was maybe the
strangest, and best.

"Holy shit!" It was happening right in front of me and I
still couldn't believe it. "Sinclair, are you *crying*?"

"Of course. And I'll thank you to keep your mockery to

yourself," he replied with perfect dignity. Dignity ruined when he sniffled just a tiny bit. "Damn. I suspect I will be hearing about this for quite some time."

I giggled and nodded.

"Yep." From Marc.

"Your suspicions," Tina said, "are accurate, as they often are."

He shook his head, then put an arm around my waist and pulled me in for a kiss. "Your dad is a fool." Another kiss. "And you are a wonder."

"Better that than the other way around," I replied and kissed him back.

# CHAPTER
# THIRTY-FOUR

*"You're going back to Hell right this minute?"*

"I've got one stop to make first." I had no interest in getting into that with Marc. With anyone. I didn't dare; if I talked about it before I did it, I'd talk myself right out of it. "After that, yeah. I'm going back. But only for an hour. Or three days. Haven't got the time thing worked out yet."

"Betsy, you've been through a lot in a super short time." Marc sounded more distressed than he did after a Giada De Laurentiis marathon. "People will understand if you hang here for a bit."

People. Oh, sure. And who were *people*? The ones stuck there? Laura? No and no. *People* was me. And, in fact, people would *not* understand if I didn't take care of this nasty business as soon as I could.

But it wasn't the time to explain that to Marc. It might not ever be the time.

"It's actually a good time to go." As he raised the eyebrows of skepticism, I backpedaled a bit. "Okay, 'good' might be an exaggeration. It's a not-terrible time to go, how's that? We've found out what's up with the babies, Dad's out of my life, and I actually made a little progress in Hell last time."

"But there's so much to ponder! There was a lot even before your dad stopped by under duress."

"Duress, huh?" I couldn't keep the smile off my face and turned to Sinclair. Jessica had spotted my father earlier in the week, but I knew Sinclair had done the rest: followed up, found Dad, tracked him. Figured out what he had done, cornered him like a rat. Produced him at the right time for me to confront him—when there was a house full of loved ones to lend emotional, physical, and mower-based support. "How'd you get him over here, anyway? I can't imagine he wanted to come."

"I appealed to his family responsibilities," Sinclair replied.

"Uh-huh, what'd you really do?"

"I appealed to his love of keeping his legs unbroken and his testicles unsmashed."

I nearly melted; so romantic!

"I just realized, your dad's a widower now."

I grimaced. "So?"

"He's back on the marriage market. Maybe your mom and dad will get back together—it's the dream of every child of divorce."

"Please stop," I groaned.

"And maybe you'll get a new brother or sister, too!" Marc enthused, which made me want to punch him and punch him and punch him. Before I could get started, we were interrupted.

"What are you guys doing in our room? Nope, don't care," Dick added as Marc opened his mouth to explain. "Go away. Jess and I need some alone time."

Marc waved that away. "You've got all night to have 'hooray, we're engaged' sex. You gotta check this out first."

"Whatever it is," Dick grumped, gently pushing past what he clearly considered to be an absurd number of people hanging out in his bedroom, "it can wait until—oh, cripes."

Jessica, who'd followed right behind him, snorted and rested her forehead in the middle of his back. "Saw it when I woke up," she managed, shoulders shaking. "Had to get moving after doing a quick check on the babies. Didn't want Betsy's dad getting away. But now I've got time to take it in."

"We all do!" Marc added cheerfully.

After years of trying to encourage me to be more organized, my mother gave up in despair, but not before indulging in a handheld, battery-operated label maker. Marc found it in the attic and took to it like a long-lost best pal. He'd burned through two days labeling experiments, experimenting on labels, experimenting on labeled experiments . . . he'd had a blast. I knew where he kept the thing, and after apologizing to Dick I'd popped into the attic to grab it and got to work.

PROPERTY OF NICK BARRY was on everything in the room: the headboard, the pillows, the quilt. The tops of the dressers, each individual drawer. The framed photos on the walls. The end tables, and everything on the end tables (books, box of Kleenex, lamp, bottle of lotion, *American Cop* magazine). The walls, the carpet.

"Do you like it?" I tried and failed to keep the anxiety out of my tone. "I meant what I said about not screwing up your name anymore. I wanted to show you, because sometimes I talk and never do."

Dick's mouth, property of Dick Barry along with the rest of his face, twitched at the corners and his eyes went very bright. "You did. It's great. You didn't have to go to this much trouble."

I was touched at how he was so obviously overcome. "It wasn't much trouble." Not compared to some of the other things I'd had to do that week.

"Really, really great," he squeaked. Squeaked? Wait, was

he overcome with tears of gratitude or trying not to laugh? Because it seemed more like he was trying not to laugh.

"That reminds me. I don't ever want to wake up and find PROPERTY OF NICK BARRY stuck on my shirt and in my hair." Jessica's hand went to her pocket and she extracted a small ball of crumpled-up labels. "What kind of savage are you when I can't take a nap without being labeled?"

"The worst kind of savage," I replied, brandishing the label gun at her. I'd left it on the dresser when Sinclair and I went downstairs to deal with Dad. It felt sooo good to have it back in my hand. Perhaps everything in the house needed to be labeled. "The kind with no remorse."

"Majesties, I wanted to advise you about the—the—" Tina peeked in the doorway, then let out a stream of giggles that were like verbal champagne bubbles. "Oh. Oh!"

"I was just telling her," Dick said, and why was there a warning in his voice? "I told her she didn't have to go to so much trouble and I thanked her and that's the end of it."

"What? Did I miss something?" I took another look around the room again. I was sure I'd hit everything.

"She's gonna find out," Jessica admonished. "Might as well be up-front about it."

"Find out what?" In my exasperation, I accidentally labeled myself again. "Dammit! Don't get any ideas," I warned, yanking it off. "My leggings aren't property of Dick Barry."

"Nor is what's inside them," Sinclair advised. He had the small, familiar smile on his face that I particularly loved, the "I can't believe this is my life now and it's so great" expression. "Nicholas's last name is spelled B-e-r-r-y like strawberry, not B-a-r-r-y like Barry Manilow."

I digested that for a second. Peered at the label gun, looked at alllll the misspelled labels. "I don't know what's more upsetting," I announced at last. "That I fucked this up so completely or that you know who Barry Manilow is."

"The latter," Marc said with a vigorous nod. "No question."

"You could have warned me," I snapped, glaring at Marc and my husband. "You both watched me do it!"

"Yeah," Marc agreed.

"We could have," Sinclair added. "No question."

"You both suck." I turned back to Dick Berry-not-Barry. "I'm sorry. I'll redo the whole thing."

"Oh, please don't," Jess groaned from behind him. "You made your point. We get the remorse at play here."

Dick hugged me so hard my feet left the floor for a second. "Yes, please don't. And Marc's right, Jess and I have the rest of the night. I want to check on the babies, anyway. Putting portable cribs in the kitchen was the most brilliant idea you ever had, Tina. C'mon, I'll make strawberry-banana-chocolate-chip smoothies."

"You keep wanting to add candy to our smoothies," Marc complained as they started out of the room. "At some point you'll have to admit that your healthy smoothie has become an unhealthy milk shake."

"Never! C'mon, hon."

"In a second," I said, though he hadn't been talking to me. I fired off a quick thought to Sinclair—*I need a minute with Jess, be right down after*—so he left, too, after pressing a kiss to my palm.

"Uh-oh," Jess said when we were alone. "Is it lecture time? Confession time? Worse, are you going to get mushy on me?"

"Me to know and you to find out. Why'd you do it?" I figured everyone else assumed her motive was petty vengeance on my behalf. But Jessica didn't do petty anything.

"Because I knew you wouldn't." Her arm went around my waist and she rested her head on my shoulder. "I knew you wouldn't kill him, and that's fine. I knew you wouldn't be able to make yourself hurt him, even, and that's fine, too. Before he faked his death, you could hardly bring yourself to incon-venience him; you'd never be able to hurt him. You took crumbs too long, and told yourself it was a feast. That *wasn't* fine, but there wasn't much I could do about it. And I just . . ." She raised her head and looked at me, mouth set in a solemn line. "I wanted to see him suffer, even if just a little bit. I wanted there to be an instant consequence, not whatever might happen in a decade or two. He was too ignorant of what you are now to be properly terrified; that'll come later, maybe. I didn't want him to get to wait to be freaked. I guess you could put it down to my need for instant gratification."

Yep. That was what I figured. I smiled at my oldest, dearest friend. "I love you."

"Well, sure. I'm terrific."

That one earned her a poke in the belly. She giggled, sounding not unlike the Pillsbury Doughboy, and then we were both laughing in a room riddled with misspelled labels.

# CHAPTER
# THIRTY-FIVE

*"I know you're in there!"* I lied to the intercom. *"Might as* well let me in. You're lucky I didn't just teleport right into your living room." Ha! Unless Laura's living room was in our toolshed, no chance. But I was counting on something besides Laura's ignorance of how I sucked at teleporting. It was new to her, too, and we'd both been feeling our way along. Until Laura decided she'd felt long enough. "I'll just hang around out here and give your neighbors polls. 'Who did you vote for last election and what's your policy on the undead and/or the damned?' You think I can't live my life from your lobby? I can make quite a comfortable life here, missy." And if she wasn't home, I would come back. And back and back.

This behavior was earning me a few odd looks from Laura's neighbors as they came out the door headed to wherever her neighbors go, which was in line with my sinister plan. I was in the lobby of one of the multistoried buildings belonging to the Atrium Apartments in Burnsville, a yuppie-clogged

Minneapolis suburb I once ruled as a former Miss Congeniality. I'd had to walk past the swimming pool and tennis courts
to get to her building, which was just annoying. I lived in a
mansion and didn't have a pool, I was pretty sure. There were
entire rooms I hadn't so much as peeked in. All right, I might
have a pool. But Laura's was out where people could find and
enjoy it.

The Antichrist had moved from her comfortable, unique
older apartment in Dinkytown (Minneapolis) to a bland yup-
pie hive, all part of her "now I'm, like, totally an adult so you
have to treat me like one, like, okay?" move after I'd killed
the devil. I should have realized then that the move was just
step one in her plan. I should have realized all sorts of things.
And maybe late really was better than never, but I didn't think
so this time. I think late was just late.

"Are you enjoying living down the hall from the Antichrist?" I asked a twenty-something woman clad in the official
Minneapolis outfit for office workers: a neat, plain suit (usually
in a neutral color, but occasionally an indulgence in navy blue
or red was all right), nude pantyhose, and running shoes. If
you missed a bus out here in midwinter, you could die. You
needed to be able to sprint to save yourself. "Your new neighbor doesn't throw loud parties, but she *is* the Son of Perdition.
Daughter of Perdition, I guess. The Bible got that wrong, too."

The poor thing, a redhead of medium height with pale
pink lipstick, smeared eyeliner, and a strained expression,
scurried past me, whipped out her keys, quickly got the door
open, and darted through.

I pressed the intercom button for Laura's apartment again.
"Wow, your neighbor sure can move when she wants. It's like
she thought I was a vampire or something. Speaking of, I
haven't fed in days. D'you have any neighbors keeping you up
late? Is the building manager a pain in your ass? Say the word
and I'll start to slurp."

*Bzzzzzzz!*

I smirked and opened the door. Sure, I could have broken into the place, but I was trying to be subtle. Subtle without the hard *b* sound. And the crack about feeding got me thinking. I hadn't fed in days, since I usually liked to snack with Sinclair (or on Sinclair). We tended to go trolling for rapists together as a way to keep our love alive. I was thirsty, I was almost always thirsty, but not (as Tina put it once, after which I begged her to find another way of putting it) gagging for it. (Why a Southern belle had picked up Brit slang I was determined never to discover.) Another queen perk: even newly risen, I hadn't needed to feed every night like most vampires. Now I was down to once or twice a week and suspected that could go longer. My time in Hell seemed to be extending the time I could go between feedings. An hour there, three days here, it was screwing with my system, but in a good way.

Could I feed in Hell? Something to ponder. And if I could, and did, would it be punishment for the damned, or reward? Could I chomp on Himmler, bin Laden, Bundy? Or, on the other side of that coin, Coco Chanel, Lincoln, Harriet Tubman? And did I want to?

*You should focus for this.* Yep. Good advice. Thanks, inner voice! You're always looking out for me. And by always, I mean rarely.

Hers was the fourth down the hall on the right. If I hadn't known the apartment number, a peeved Antichrist standing in the hall with her door open and her arms crossed would have tipped me off.

"Sorry to show up empty-handed, I couldn't find just the right plant," I said, pushing past her into the bland new digs. "Happy new apartment, symbol of your new life and the fucking-over of your sister. I didn't think a cyclamen would quite cover it." Too bad, too. I liked cyclamens. Their flowers looked like little butterflies and their leaves were a deep green that (almost) put Marc's peepers to shame.

"Half sister," was how she greeted me, "and watch your

mouth in my home." In fairness, I hadn't exactly been Suzy Good Manners, either, so I let the reprimand pass. "What do you want?"

"Oh golly, Laura, what don't I want?" I turned in a small circle in the middle of her living room, taking it all in. It was an open floor plan so I could see at least half the apartment in one glance. She was completely unpacked, and the place even looked a bit lived in. It didn't smell like new paint; it smelled like spaghetti and garlic bread. The kitchen was neat, but there were dishes (colander, plate, knife, fork, big wooden spoon, big plastic fork, saucepan, pot, lid for same) drying in the strainer, and I could feel the heat coming off the oven. "Well, let me think. I want to be able to enjoy a medium-rare slab of pork loin with a side of wild mushroom risotto without throwing up. I want Marc to quit stuffing the freezer with baggies of dead mice. I want to know when you found time to unpack and keep up with all your charity work if you were spending so much time in Hell struggling without my help. And, I dunno, world peace? Or at least world time-out?"

"Really." I had picked up a ceramic vase, painted with pink flowers and also stuffed with pink flowers, ugh. She took it from me and set it back down on the bookshelf (man, that woman had a lot of Bibles) with a decisive *clunk*. "You're here to yell at me about my work ethic? I help more people in a week than you have in your entire life."

"It's not my fault I was raised Republican."

"How did you find out where I live?"

"Aw. That sounds like you weren't planning on having me over anytime soon. You seem less than happy to see me."

"What tipped you off?" she snapped, crossing her arms and cupping her elbows. Her eyes were big and blue and anxious. Her flannel-lined jeans were faded, rolled at the cuffs and showing her ankles (tart!). They looked well-worn and comfy, as did her Abbott Northwestern Volunteer sweatshirt.

"Oh . . . everything." And then some. Too bad it took me

so long to put it together. "And Sinclair found out where you lived. I didn't even have to ask him; by the time I needed the info, he had it."

"Spying on me."

"Sure. He put a tracer on your car, too."

"He *what?*"

I giggled. "I know, what a scamp. A smart scamp. He didn't trust you. I did, and I'm paying for it now. I'll pay for a long time, I think."

Laura could never look ugly, but her mouth twisted and turned down and she came as close as she could while forcing out her question. "Why. Are. You. Here?"

I ignored the question, reaching for a stack of *Reader's Digest*s on her coffee table. "Wow, I had no idea anyone under forty read this." She didn't like me touching her stuff, that was for sure. I was mad, but sad, too. When had we grown apart? Easy: we had never been close, and not because we hadn't met until we were adults. Any thoughts that we had a loving sisterly bond were just more evidence of me fooling myself. I had always been good at closing my eyes to inconvenience.

"Took him about two minutes to find out where you lived. The vampire king sure gets around now that he can go out in the sunshine. He goes to church, too. They made him a deacon!" Laura actually gagged. I knew how she felt; the whole thing was bizarre. But Sinclair was thrilled to be a church-going fella again, and I didn't have the heart to tell him how funny it was. "How does that fit with your theory that all vampires, *moi* included, are inherently evil and sucky?"

"That there are many things I neither know nor understand."

"Truer words, little sister. I'm right there with you, by the way. There's all kinds of shit—sorry, stuff—I don't know or understand. For example, our father is alive." I was watching her carefully, and my heart sank when she didn't change expression. "You knew."

"Of course." She wore a small, scornful smile that looked wrong on her face. "You're surprised? You shouldn't be surprised."

"And it, what, slipped your mind? Or you could never think of a tactful way to bring it up?"

"I could never think of a tactful way to tell you it was *your* fault he had to do it."

"He didn't *have* to do anything, you bubblehead! It was his choice! All his bad decisions were his choice, just like yours are yours and mine are mine. How'd you find out? What, you went to see him? I know he didn't come see you, Laura."

A small flinch told me that last had been a direct hit. "My—my mother told me."

"Ah." Sure. I should have realized. Of course Satan had known what my dad was up to. She had made it her business to know everything about Laura. And it was why I was sure the Ant knew what Dad had done, because the devil would have told her. But I couldn't let myself be distracted by thinking of the Ant now. One family crisis at a time. "So you rushed to Daddy's side to tell him you understood his pain?" I watched her face as I threw that out there and saw that she hadn't. "No. You didn't have the balls to confront him. Can't really blame you for that one; I could barely bring myself to do it and I had help. Jessica saw him days ago and I spent every day since *not* thinking about it."

I paused, but Laura didn't say anything. " 'And then what happened?' " I prompted and got an eye roll for my trouble. "I'll tell you what happened. I did finally get my thumb out and had a chat with him and he's dead to me now. And if I see him again, that's literal. Just so you know. Please don't plan a father-daughter-daughter lunch anytime soon. It'll be a disaster even if he doesn't expect us to pay."

"You would do that, wouldn't you?" She was shaking her head, blond waves tumbling artfully. Man, I hated being the funny sister. "Kill your own father."

"Yep. And if I ever have to do it—" I cut myself off before an embarrassing noise—hysterical sob? choked laughter?— could escape. Could this be happening? Was I discussing patricide with my sister?

*It's happening,* the voice in my head affirmed. *Better face it. Don't turn away now. Waaay too late for that, honey.*

I cleared my throat "If I ever have to kill him, it would be great if you'd keep out of my way."

"Is this the part where you tell me that, contrary to centuries of legend, *you're* a good vampire?"

"No, it's the part where I remind you that you've killed, too."

"In self-defense," she said quickly.

"No."

She chewed on her lower lip and didn't reply. Girl needed to get herself some ChapStick if she was gonna chomp like that. Plus, winter in Minnesota was as dry as a desert. A desert! How fucked was that?

"What I really want to know is, were you always going to stick me with Hell? Or was that a recent plan, a 'that'll learn ya to kill my mommy' thing?"

She looked at the door, like she was really hoping I'd start for it soon. *Keep hoping, little sister.* I wasn't going anywhere until I'd said my piece, and maybe not even then. I might crash on her couch. For a week! She'd hate that. Unfortunately, I would, too. Talk about cutting off your sister to spite your face.

I hadn't come looking for an apology. Good thing, too, because I wasn't going to get one, I'd known that going in. That was all right. I wasn't going to give one, either.

"No wonder Hell didn't look like anything when I got there." I was trying for coolly accusatory, not sniveling. I remembered the vast reaches of nothing, how it had been pure void until I started giving some real thought to how it could be run by someone like me: lots of practical office experience, not much supernatural experience. "You hadn't been there much yourself. You never had any intention of helping me.

You never planned to have anything to do with the place. Hell didn't take anything from you because you wouldn't give anything."

"Yes."

I kind of liked that. No denial, nothing shrill. She just owned it: *yep,* which might as well have been, *gotcha!* As much as I wanted to wring her neck until her bright eyes bulged, I still liked her and wanted her to like me.

"It's not all about you, Betsy."

*What foolishness is this? And why did people keep saying that to me like they think I'll get it?*

"I don't understand," I admitted.

"It's not about me punishing or tricking you—"

"Though you are," I pointed out.

"It's about me saving myself."

"Oh yeah?"

"My life has been nothing but madness and murder since you stumbled into it."

"What?" The *Antichrist* was blaming me for her chaotic, crazy-ass life?

"Do you deny it?"

"Um, yes. I deny the living shit out of it. I didn't make you kill anybody. That was all you, sweetie, each and every time."

"Because of positions *you* put me in! I can't do God's work if you're constantly throwing me into the abyss!"

"Again: no one is making you do any of the things you did, are doing, and will do, sunshine. Those were your choices. You're all super keen on being treated like an adult; start by taking responsibility for your own life."

"My life was never meant to be serving as the right-hand stooge to a pack of unholy vampire vermin."

Wow, there was a lot to address in that comment. I went for the easiest one. "Your life? You were born into this, you gorgeous jackass! Your mom was the devil! *Is* the devil—frankly, I don't think that bitch is really dead! But that is a theory for another time! You were born the Beast. Me, I got chomped on by a pack of feral smelly vampires and woke up their queen. Apples and oranges, dammit!" Ugh, apples and oranges, my dad had said that. And probably in the same shrill, whiny tone. Like this confrontation couldn't get any more nightmarish.

Laura had gone pale, her lower lip getting ragged from all the chewing, but she stood her ground. It was as impressive as it was irritating. "Ruling the undead was your destiny."

"And running Hell was yours," I retorted. "Except you decided you didn't want to play. So you stuck me with it."

"You're not 'stuck'—"

"Will you cut the shit for five minutes?" I nearly screamed. "Who else? You won't, and I can't—but I have to. The labor pool is a little shallow, don't you think? We can't just leave Hell unattended. That's how you got me to finally go down there in the first place—you told me the damned were getting out."

She didn't say anything and my heart, which had dropped into my stomach, now fell to my ankles. "Oh God. You didn't."

She shook her head, but whether it was in denial or because she wouldn't discuss it, I didn't know. And in that moment, I lacked the courage to follow up. I knew she was, in her own way, as self-indulgent as I, and as determined to get her way, but I didn't think she'd go to such lengths.

Laura took a breath and let it out. "My mother didn't want this for me."

"And you think mine did? That's your argument? Why are your mom's desires more important than my mom's?" Before she could reply—though what she could have said I had no idea—I raced ahead. "Five years ago I was a newly fired office assistant. Now I'm running Hell—badly, but at least something's getting done—but this is all about how *your* life has gotten unacceptably chaotic? You—you—" For the first time I had a glimpse—more than a glimpse—of just how infuriating people found my innate selfishness. I could have slapped her. A lot. But I wanted to slap myself more. Because Marc had been right, days before. I wasn't a victim. Nobody made me come here. Nobody was making me stay.

"You know the dumbest thing? The laughable, stupid thing?" I asked, slumping onto the end of her couch. She winced, clearly assuming I was getting comfy so I could stay and yell at her for a nice long time. The truth was, it was flop down or fall down. "I knew. Even before I consciously realized what you were up to, people were trying to tell me. I just wouldn't let myself think about what they were saying. After all, you're the good one. Right?"

"Right," she replied firmly, which was the funniest thing to happen all day.

I had known. I just had no interest in facing it. Or, the truth: no courage to face it. Because in retrospect it was so obvious. Everyone around me had been dropping hints.

Father Markus: *I'll help* you.

Cathie: *It's the murderous temper coupled with magic and no-actual-checks-on-power thing. I don't trust her. You shouldn't, either.*

Sinclair: *You know I stand ready to assist you in this, as in all things.*

Hell, even Jessica's teenagers. *She's got stuff. It's not easy running Hell.* "She," not "we." Everyone knew I was kidding myself about being co-anything with the Antichrist. Everyone knew I was in it alone. They were just too tactful or kind or scared to explain it to me. And that was on me as well. I had to be approachable, and I had to keep an open mind. "Easier said than done" had never been more accurate, or annoying.

"I'm not here to fight," I told her, and that was true. Good thing, too. I was exhausted as it was. "Just to tell you that I'll do it. I'll take over your job, your destiny, the one you tricked me and lied to me to get out of. But . . ." I snickered, and finished: "But *you* do more good in one week than I have in my whole life. Right?"

And all at once, the Antichrist had trouble meeting my eyes.

I was almost sympathetic, because in that moment, for the first and last time, I saw our father in her. She was getting what she thought she wanted, and one day that would bite her in her perfect ass.

"But there are strings, Laura. You don't get to dump this on me and walk away without *major* strings. I'm giving you the same deal I gave our dad: we're family or we're not. This isn't something you can change your mind about later. And you can't half-and-half it, either. No flitting down to Hell to check on me or catch up on family gossip." Laura managed a sour smile at that one, and I smirked back. "Yeah, I know, not likely, right? But even if you were the type, that would all stop now. If you're giving up your birthright and dumping your responsibility on me, then *do it*, and do it all the way.

"You're done; you're out. Hell's not your inheritance anymore; it's not yours in any way anymore. You don't get to jettison the responsibility but keep the perks. No using Hell as a way station to teleport from point A to point B. Hell's mine now, which means you stay away. You want to pop over to Paris for a week in the spring, you fly Air France like everybody else. If I see you in Hell, I'm going to assume you're dead."

If I saw her in Hell, she might be dead anyway.

"I would never end up there," she said in such a low gasp it was more like a hiss.

"Then it shouldn't be a problem. Right?"

She nodded, surprised, and I could tell she was thinking hard. I was guessing she thought I'd put up more of a fight. She had no idea that after the showdown with Dad, this one was almost easy. Almost.

"Right," she said at last. "Agreed." She made an aborted movement with her arms and I realized she'd been about to hug me, then stopped herself. Of course. You didn't trick your sister into the worst job in the history of jobs, agree to denounce your demonic supernatural abilities while condemning her for stepping up, and then hug her. Just wasn't done.

"Anything else? Now's the time, little sister. I don't think we'll be seeing each other for a while."

"No." I barely caught it; she coughed and raised her voice. "No. There's nothing else."

"Yeah. You're right about that, at least." Then I slapped my forehead, because there *was* something else, something we'd both forgotten. Or I had forgotten, and she'd never cared about. "What about the ones who escaped?"

"No one escaped."

Yep. It was as bad as I'd feared. I knew she'd been desperate to get me to Hell, but I hadn't guessed how deep that went. "So you lied when you said souls were escaping Hell. That's what Father Markus—"

"Who?"

"Never mind. He tried to tell me that no one had escaped, that some souls had left by choice. Because you, what, left the gate unlocked? You just let them leave?"

Shrug.

"You didn't even have to, you stunning shithead! What, like I was taking attendance? You could have just *said* they were escaping; it's not like I would have known the difference."

"You wouldn't have, no." Again with the not-looking-me-in-the-eye. "I didn't count on—I hadn't expected my birth mother . . . to be helpful to you. She would have known the truth. I couldn't just lie about it; it had to be a real thing."

"You *did* lie about it."

I got another shrug for my trouble and had to shake my head at the whole fucking mess. "And isn't that the god-damned irony of the century. My age-old nemesis, she of the pineapple hair, being helpful while you were doing everything you could to fuck me over." I'd chosen my words deliberately, hoping she'd get angry, raise her voice, *something* besides the detached nastiness. In vain, sorry to say. Now that she knew she was getting what she thought she wanted, she just wanted the convo to be over so I would leave.

I had to shake my head. "Letting them out. Great. As long as you didn't do anything that's totally going to bite me in the ass later."

"I'm sure it'll be fine."

"Random souls wandering the earth? Good guys, bad guys, just set loose? Did you even keep count? Did you bother to get names? Or did you just tag and release?"

"It'll be fine," she said again, and for the first time I was afraid I would kill her. She was the Antichrist, but she was mortal. I could toss a Pontiac into a brick wall if I wanted; it'd be less than a second's work to snap her neck.

*No. No. No. You're the big sis, even if only until you walk out her door forever. Set an example. Besides, it's like Dad . . . let her live with her guilt. It should be nothing to you.*

No idea if that was good advice or bad, but I was going with it. I calmed down enough to reply almost calmly. "You're sure it'll be fine, huh? Why is that? Because you've never read a book or seen a television show or a movie? Because this shit always, always comes back. It always bites whomever in the ass."

"Maybe. Either way." A chilly smile. "It's now officially filed under Not My Problem. Your terms, remember?"

"It was three minutes ago, of course I remember."

"Impressive," she mocked.

"Wow, you're a bitch." I shook my head again. At least I wasn't shaking a finger at her in scolding-elderly-aunt mode. "How have I not noticed this?"

"Exactly," the Antichrist said.

"What, this is my punishment for not paying attention?"

"Exactly."

*Enough of this shit.*

I studied her while getting ready to leave. She was so lovely, and so young. And I had hopes that her close-minded religious beliefs would loosen with maturity. Because if not, the world could be in a whole lot of trouble. I didn't think this was the end of anything between us. The lengths she'd gone to in order to get out of her birthright showed me that. At *best*, she and I were on a time-out that could last years, decades.

And that could be bad, because while this confrontation might be done, and while we both assumed we were out of each other's lives for good, I wasn't sure it would be so easy or so complete. I had the feeling Laura wouldn't just eventually become a villain. She'd be the worst kind of villain, the bad guy who thinks they're a good guy, who is rock-solid certain they're in the right, and thus can justify every awful thing they do by telling themselves it's all for the greater good. Laura was almost as good as I was at justification. And, of course: Antichrist. She'd bear watching for that, if nothing else.

But I was confident. Or at least, not as horrified and despairing at our fate as I might have been. I wasn't alone; I had a mansion full of people who loved me and would help me with pretty much anything I needed. Laura didn't have that, and she scorned my resources. Her choice, of course. Just as it had been her choice every step down the line. She hadn't considered that, but I had.

"I'll send a plant," I said and turned to leave. She didn't walk me out, which was just as well. I was sad and angry, but maybe a tiny bit smug, too, and it wouldn't do to have her pick up on it. Because it wasn't all bad. Maybe, in time, it wouldn't seem bad at all.

I hadn't fed in days and felt fine. Teleporting was getting easier (though my accuracy still sucked). I'd commanded my father out of my life, as well as my sister, and agreed to take over Hell.

Hell was making me stronger. I bet Laura hadn't considered that, either.

It made me wonder if the devil *had*.

# CHAPTER
# THIRTY-SIX

*"Wow. Look what the dog barfed up."*

"I'm in charge now," I told Cathie, who was in the Hell Mall's Payless store, trying on sandal after sandal that didn't fit. (Hint: none of them would fit.) "You can't talk to me like that."

"I'm absolutely going to talk to you like that all the time," my "friend" replied. She was wearing khaki shorts that displayed knees that looked like scowling trolls, white anklets (why? why try on sandals with socks? even in Hell?), and a red sweatshirt with "I'd tell you to go to Hell, but I don't want to see you every day" in an oddly cheerful white font. "So you should resign yourself to that right now."

"How long was I gone?"

A shrug. "There aren't any clocks in Hell. It's like Las Vegas."

"Or my house." I pointed at my well-shod tootsies. "Luckily my magic shoes helped me get back."

Cathie stared at Dorothy's silver slippers, then looked back up at me. "You do know they aren't magic, right? And that they aren't even shoes? They're a physical manifestation—"

"—of my ability to travel between dimensions, something tangible to help me focus on decidedly intangible dimensional abilities, yeah, yeah. Now I need to think up magic shoes that help me teleport without getting the toolshed involved."

"Wow, do I not want a single one of your problems." She pulled a shoe box out from the middle of a stack as high as the deep end of a pool. The stack swayed like a rickety bridge in a hurricane, but miraculously didn't topple and bury poor Cathie under a pile of pleather flats. "Why am I even doing this?"

"Dunno."

She opened the box and scowled at its contents: flattering, comfortable sandals in just the right color. One was a size five, the other size ten. "You're back in a short time, probably, and you've got a 'well, time to roll up my sleeves' expression, which, by the way, you can't pull off. So your sister finally told you what's what, huh?"

"No."

"Oh." Cathie's expression was placid, and then her eyebrows arched in surprise. "*Oh.* Had it out, huh? Is she going to show up dead? Here? Ugh." She glanced down at her sweatshirt. "I really don't want to see her every day. My ironic sweatshirt has become an oracle, which is not normally what I look for in a long-sleeved garment."

I laughed. "I didn't kill her. But I forbade her to use her Antichrist superpowers."

"And she's going along with that?" I could tell Cathie was thinking about the serial killer Laura had dispatched with ruthless, capable efficiency in that poor woman's basement. And Cathie didn't know the half of it, or how many Laura had killed just in the short time I'd known her.

My sister could take all sorts of lives, supernatural and human, and in the past she hadn't considered killing vampires to be murder. But killing the killer, however richly deserved, *was*. And she hadn't hesitated.

"She's going along with that." For now. A problem for another day. Another decade. Or never, please God. She can stay on her side of the playground, I'll stay on mine. Except hers was now mine. "She got what she wanted."

"Yeah, well. You know what they say about that."

"Oh God," I groaned. "Don't tell me. I think that's the lesson of the week." Dad, Laura, even Satan. They'd all gotten what they thought they wanted, poor bastards. "When did my life turn into an R-rated After School Special?"

"The minute you were too dim to stay dead," was Cathie's smiling reply. She booted the last box of sandals away and stood, slipping on her loafers and following me past stack after stack of sandals that were all wrong. "I don't even know why I bothered."

"Again: I don't, either."

"Okay, I do. I was curious. Hell's been a void for a while and I was curious. At least it was something to do." We fell into step as we left the store and merged with the souls wandering around, shopping, running, being tortured, or all of the above. It would have been more upsetting (it was definitely off-putting), except plenty of them looked interested or intrigued and clearly *weren't* being tortured or punished. Exchange students? Tourists? A couple of them *were* wearing fanny packs. So much I didn't know. So much I'd better learn, and quick.

"Oh. Welcome back."

"The mother of the Beast," Cathie said without turning around as my stepmother came up behind us. "Don't fret, Toni. Betsy didn't hurt your horrible kid."

Toni? "What, you're buds now?"

"Uh, *no.*"

"No! We just have things in common. We know some of the same people."

Cathie let out an inelegant snort. (Redundant?) "She means we both want to help you, because you're bound to fuck up and will need support before, during, and after the inevitable fuckups."

This was how rotten my week had been: I interpreted that bitchy speech as stuffed with care and concern. My eyes welled, for God's sake! Or they would have, if I were still alive.

"Thanks," I replied, managing to keep it short and clipped. No one here but us ruthless rulers of Hell. "Um, Antonia?" My voice almost caught. I was so used to referring to her as the Ant that I had to think about what I was doing for a second or two. "I ran into your husband earlier."

The Ant busied herself with her clipboard. The three of us were now walking abreast past the theater, which was playing (with constant interruptions, as the film needed to be spliced again and again) *Star Wars: The Phantom Menace*, *Caligula*, *Superman IV: The Quest for Peace*, *The Astronaut's Wife*, *From Justin to Kelly*, *Cutthroat Island*, and *Sahara*. Which was just staggering. Movies so bad, they couldn't even be hate-watched? Diabolical.

"I said I ran into your husband earlier."

"Dead," Cathie muttered under her breath, "not deaf."

"I'm sure you did," the Ant replied, not looking up from the clipboard. "I didn't think you'd leave it alone."

Awkward silence. I gave Cathie the side-eye, and she gave me the "what? I just work here" look in return. God help me on the inevitable day when I have to give her the "get the hell out of here and, yeah, I hear the pun" look.

"So anyway, Dad's dead to me now. And, um, so's your daughter." It occurred to me that I wasn't the only one having a shit week. At least I was an active participant in all the awful. The Ant had to hear about it secondhand. "But they're both okay. I mean, I didn't hurt them."

"No, of course not." She looked surprised, like she'd assumed all along I wouldn't hurt them. Which was really,

really nice. "You gave them what they wanted. That's much worse."

Oh. Less nice.

"Did you want to know—"

A noise that might have been a snort, or a bitten-off sob. Please not the latter. Feeling sorry for the Ant flew in the face of everything I believed. "I don't, actually. Let me guess: he faked his death because one of his kids was a vampire, another was the Antichrist, another was going to turn into God-knows-what, he'd found out his mistress made a shitty second wife, and he wanted his old, simpler life back and knew he couldn't ever have that again. Right?"

"Pretty much." Yes, that was a succinct and devastating sum-up. What she didn't say was that she'd known he was alive, and why he was alive, and found it humiliating. And just like that, I didn't want to talk about it anymore and, better, didn't *need* to talk about it anymore.

"So what's next?" I asked, shuddering as we passed a gelato store where the only flavors in stock were rum raisin, black licorice, and bacon. Bacon! They took two of the most wonderful things in the history of terrific things to eat, bacon and ice cream, and merged them into one horrible entity. Maybe I was too soft for this job, because I instantly wanted to stock vanilla at least. Or at least pistachio.

"We were hoping you'd tell us."

"Oh." *Oh.* "Great!" *Fuck.* "Well. Let's round up Father Markus, and anybody you two think could help, and let's talk about what happens next. Letting Laura off the genetic hook and deciding to run Hell by myself has taught me that I can't run Hell by myself. I don't think anyone can." Well. Satan had, but I was pretty sure that was why she'd been such a huge, historical bitch.

"All right," the Ant said. "I'll get started. Father Markus. Hmm." And she clicked off, efficiency in a bad dye job and worse heels.

"What was that supposed to mean?" I asked, the opposite of surprised when the Ant didn't turn and answer.

"Oh, nothing." Yeah, not buying it. Cathie's tone was way too innocent. "Certainly not that you switched out one father for another, and kinda one sister for another. Not that you ever thought of me as a sister, but Jessica's alive. She can't help you with this. Uh, she *is* alive, right?"

"And kicking," I agreed, thinking of Mowerzilla and swallowing a chortle.

"Right. You can't have her here, but you can have me—someone who gets you more than the Antijerk ever did."

"Wow," I said, my tone pure admiration. Antijerk! How had I never thought of that? "You never did like her, did you?"

"I never did like her. Which was fine; I was never one of those women who has to be pals with everyone. You, though . . ."

"Recovering Miss Congeniality."

"Oh my God. Just when I thought I didn't have anything new to mock you with. Thank you. Thank you." She shook herself out of her euphoric haze and continued, neatly avoiding three men in business suits all having loud conversations on their cell phones, sharing TMI tidbits like, "But you said the rash would clear up by now!" and, "I said embezzle, not decapitate," while dodging other Mall-goers. Were they the ones being punished? Or was it the people who couldn't help overhearing? So much to know! "Laura maybe never loved you—and I'm sorry, she's an idiot. But you couldn't ever get close to her, either. For all kinds of reasons, and maybe none of them are important now. You couldn't warm up to each other, but you and I get along. I've—I've always really liked you. I'm glad now for the chance to help you, after everything you did for me."

"Mushy," I said, delighted. I was usually the one getting mocked for that.

"Shut the fuck up."

"If you cry," I teased, "then I'm going to cry. Then all of Hell will cry. It'll be sobfest of the damned."

"That's it. Offer retracted. You can wander off and die now. Or something."

"How'd you guess Laura meant to stick me with the job?" I'd accepted that the people around me had picked up on this faster than I, because I'd always known the people around me were smarter. But I wanted specifics. "I get now that you knew." I remembered how she'd been so dismissive of Laura from the start. How she'd been so quick to ride my ass for not understanding more about my supernatural abilities than the last time we'd spoken, years earlier.

Cathie laughed, but the sound didn't have much humor in it.

"Yeah, you got me. I'll admit it, I couldn't get over that you hadn't made much progress. In the time I saw the world twice over, you'd gone from reluctant vampire queen to . . . reluctant vampire queen. I remembered wondering just what the hell you'd been doing with yourself. Clinging to the decayed remnants of a normal life?"

Yep, she got me. "Pretty much."

"I figured you needed all the help you could get and I wanted to be there for it."

"Yes, but why?"

That brought her up short; she stopped so suddenly the mom behind her ran into her heels with her empty (?) stroller. "Watch it!" the mom (?) snapped, wrenching the stroller around us and rushing off. Cathie barely took notice.

"Why? You kidding?"

"I helped you, but it wasn't a trade. You didn't have to help me back. You sure didn't have to wait in the wings to help me with what you know will be a sucky, likely eternal, job."

Cathie shook off her shock and grinned at me. "You're kidding. You really don't know? Why am I surprised you don't know?"

"I haven't a clue. I know it wasn't just because after you were murdered, I was the only one who could see you and talk to you." Plenty of other ghosts had haunted me, and every one of them hadn't lingered once I'd solved their problem. "But I don't know what it is."

"Uh-huh. Well, it's like this. You didn't just offer to find the guy who strangled me with his belt until I shit myself," she explained in that odd, cheery tone most people used to describe why they thought baby bunnies were cute, "who then stripped me and made fun of my tits and dumped my naked body in a Walmart parking lot. He did those things to me because he was afraid of me, even though we'd never met, and you heard me—though your listening skills were, and still are, for shit. I was alone but you heard me and offered to find him."

I opened my mouth, but Cathie shook her head. "Shut up now," she said kindly, and I did. "But you didn't stick to that. And when you reminded me you had no lawful authority, that the most you could do was stall my killer until the cops showed, you demonstrated your resolve by preparing to let him stab you multiple times. You knew he couldn't kill you but you also knew it would hurt like a bitch because, hello, *stabbing.* And you didn't care. You wanted to stop him. You put your body between a killer and someone you didn't know, and that's such an integral part of your personality that you don't even remember making the offer, and you didn't expect anything from me in return. *That's* why. Oh my God," she added, horrified, "are you—you're not going to cry, are you?"

"No." I sniffed. "And thanks. That pretty much made my month."

"If you cry," she threatened, "I'll never offer to help you run Hell ever again. You'll have to screw it up entirely on your own."

"Noted. Not crying. Or if I am, they are tears of evil."

"Good," she replied, relieved.

We stopped at the food court and got in a long line—like there were any other kind—was Cathie thirsty? But when people saw me, they parted. Hmm. Head of the line, a fringe benefit of killing the devil and taking over Hell. It didn't seem like an even trade.

"Coke, please. Lots of ice."

"Cathie, you know that won't—"

"Here you are."

Whoa. I blinked at the beverage, instantly handed over by the twenty-something working behind the counter. Her hapless food court uniform fit poorly and was the most unflattering shade of orange I had ever seen. The three-inch-wide button on her uniform shirt read, "Low-Quality Food for High-End Bucks!" Yep, that seemed about right.

The drink, now. The drink looked great. The red and white cup with the Coke colors and logo, first half-filled with crushed ice, then filled to the brim with the sparkling chocolate-brown carbonated liquid, looked like an oasis.

"Thanks," Cathie replied with a heavy sigh and, at my curious expression, added, "I fucking hate Coke. Ever since I had a high fever in seventh grade and that was the only cold drink in the house besides water, which I also hate. Trust me, I'll always be able to get a Coke or a bottle of Dasani here."

I didn't want to laugh; it wasn't funny. But her doleful expression coupled with her usual no-punches-pulled demeanor made for a funny contrast. "I'll pull some strings," I promised. "We'll have you swimming in iced tea in no time."

"God, be careful what you *say*. That could literally happen to me here!"

Then I did laugh, and the woman I'd subconsciously (*please, God, please let it be subconsciously*) replaced as my sister laughed, too.

# CHAPTER
# THIRTY-SEVEN

*This time I found myself entire yards from the toolshed, ankle* deep in puppy shit. Woo-hoo!

Sinclair had fenced off a small area of the side yard for Fur and Burr, which he usually kept clean. But the li'l buggers had made some sort of sinister puppy pact and were quick to fill it up every time the previous week's poop had been scooped.

Determined to stay positive, I shook some of the real poop from my imaginary shoes and thought that there was a time such an abomination would have sent me into a three-day red rage. This time I would only indulge in a three-hour red rage. Later. I had to bring the gang up to speed, and then I had to indulge in an emotional collapse. And Tina's birthday party loomed, assuming I hadn't missed it. *Please, God, I need those things to happen and I need them in that order. I did you a solid this week! Don't make an enemy out of me! Thank you, Jesus, amen.*

I opened the kitchen door and stepped into the mudroom. It was a puppy-free zone, which meant . . .

*Welcome back, my own.*

Sinclair's thought had all the warmth of a hot chocolate on an icy day. I toed off the shoes I wasn't really wearing and popped them in the "Things We Got Dog Poop On by Mistake and Which Need to Be Cleaned, SINCLAIR!" box. Then I opened the mudroom door and found my family clustered in their usual spots around the butcher-block counter we used as a kitchen table. The smell of strawberries and blackberries hit me like a fruit-drenched wave. Jessica's ire was more like a wave of impassioned bitchery.

"Nobody has it worse than single moms. Don't bring up my money!" she added sharply before any of us had a chance to. "Hi, Betsy."

"Hi. I wasn't gonna bring up your millions and your ability to hire a fleet of nannies."

"Good! Though with all the goings-on in this joint, can you imagine a regular ordinary human person plunked in the middle of it—"

"—and I definitely won't bring up the fact that you're best friends with the vampire queen, who could assign vamp minions to dote on your weird babies."

"Why?" Marc asked, horrified, while His Name's Definitely Dick groaned and covered his eyes. "Why would you come back from Hell and immediately pick a fight?"

"Because I just got back from Hell?"

"It's not only single moms struggling with one income," Jess added, not to be put off her rave.

Yeah, one *gigantic* income.

"It's important, sure. It's a huge factor. But it's not about money; it's about societal expectations. If a single dad is out and about with his kids, women melt all over him."

"Like life-sized giggling butter pats," I suggested, heading to the counter to see if the greedy bastards had slurped it all or if there was enough smoothie left for me. I didn't trust the blender full o' blackberry smoothie. Blackberries were wonderful in theory. Big and fat and sweet and gorgeous, but pop one in your mouth and you realize the thing's all seed. "Oozing all over the single dads." Raspberry! Slightly less seedy! Yes!

"It's true," Jess continued, again despite the fact that no one was arguing. "We see single dads with kids in a completely different light than we see single moms."

My chauvinist husband and his sidekick, a recovering Southern belle, listened with carefully polite expressions. I admired Jessica's determination to break them down and turn them into her version of feminists, even as I had zero interest in helping her. The most I would do to assist was not point out in front of everyone that a single millionaire mom whose babies were only weeks old wasn't necessarily the expert on either a) motherhood or b) feminism.

So there it is, proof that I belong in Hell.

"Women see the dad at the park, they love it. They see the evidence of his fertility, they assume he's the main income in that household—most people don't think palimony—and they see he's also nurturing because he's at a *park* with his *children*, stop the presses, right?"

"Right?" Tina replied, no doubt hoping that was the answer Jessica wanted.

"Except it only goes one way. Because when a guy meets a single mom, the more kids *she* has, the more turned off *he* is. He's got zero interest in her fertility and assumes she's either divorced and on alimony or was never married and is a slut. Or figures she trapped the guy with her uterus. As for the fact that she's out in a park with her kids, that's what moms are *supposed* to do, right?"

"I don't want to get into a thing here," I began, cautious, as if someone had told me the kitchen had been booby-trapped, which in a way it had been, "because you make some good points—"

"But mothers *are* supposed to be nurturing," Tina said, the lovely moron.

Jess made a rude noise. "I *know*, Scarlett, but so are dads!"

And there it was. It wasn't about Jess finally agreeing to allow Just Plain Dick to haul her narrow ass to the altar, it was about the fact that Jessica's father was an unrelenting shithead pervert fuck-o of the highest order and though she'd been engaged for maybe a half hour she was already freaking out about it. So glad I got back in time for the meltdown.

Again: no question, I deserved Hell.

"I'm not sure we have time to get into this right now," I tried again. Which was bullshit, because I was pretty sure we did. For the first time in days, I felt like I could take a break. I just didn't want to take a feminist break, if that's a thing.

Jess shook her head. "You putzes are so lucky I'm exhausted."

"Yep," I agreed. Time to get off the sensitive subject of single moms and switch to the sensitive subject of a Southern belle aging. "Did I miss Tina's party?" At Marc's glare, I back-pedaled. "I'm sorry. Was it a surprise?"

"Not anymore," he said pointedly.

"Come on," I coaxed, "you weren't really planning a surprise party."

"Not anymore."

"In this house? You can't keep a secret around here, you know that."

Marc's grumpy expression eased a bit. Tina, meanwhile, looked both relieved (the single-mom thing shelved for another time) and pleased (aw, you shouldn't have!). "I don't want a fuss, Marc." Good, because wish granted, probably. Then she turned to me. "If there's to be any sort of celebration, of course we wouldn't indulge unless you were there to partake as well."

"So we'll put it off a few months," I joked. "I'll just say it now so I'm off the hook: happy birthday."

"Thank you, Majesty."

"No offense, and we're doing a lot more than just wishing you happy birthday, but can't we please make Betsy tell us about Hell?" Marc begged. "We're all *here*. The babies are in their milk comas. The adults are all awake at the same time and in the same room in the house at the same time." Hmm. Good point, a rare event. "And the dogs don't care."

For the first time I realized Marc was cradling a yawning Fur or Burr, and Sinclair had Burr or Fur in his lap and was slowly stroking the fuzz on the top of her head while she snored. "They sure don't. They're lucky they're cute. It's the only thing that keeps us from drowning them."

*Us?????* Sinclair clutched Fur or Burr closer to his body and actually leaned away from me. Please. Like I'd really drown them when I could just dispatch them with a well-placed stomp. Again: please. Like I'd ruin a pair of shoes for that.

"Sure," Dick said through a yawn, "regale us with tales of Hell. You're gonna win every single 'my day was worse than yours' contest from now on, aren't you?"

"Hey, I hadn't thought of that," I replied, pleased. The perks were few and far between, but they were adding up.

"Unless, of course, Her Majesty cannot discuss such things with us." Most people wouldn't have heard Tina's tiny pause between "with" and "us." Because she meant, *Maybe the vampires should leave the room and go have grown-up time somewhere else and you guys do whatever it is you do when we're not hanging.*

"Her Majesty definitely wants to discuss it with you," I assured them. "I've learned exactly one thing this week."

"Just the one?" Marc asked, raising his eyebrows.

"Okay, I've learned more than one thing but the thing I've internalized is—"

"Be careful what you wish for?"

(. . .)

"Okay, I've learned two things this week. Be careful what you wish for, and also, I can't do this by myself."

"Well," Dick said after a short silence. I appreciated how he didn't finish the sentence with "duh." "You know we're always ready to help."

"You might want to think that one over," I warned, hauling

a stool to the counter. I'd grabbed a glass and gotten the last of the raspberry smoothie dregs, and now planned to savor that while sitting on my ass. Goals, it was important to have goals. "Because starting now, helping me will mean more than occasionally picking up my dry cleaning."

"You never have dry cleaning," Marc pointed out.

"And if you did, we'd die a thousand deaths before picking it up, you lazy jerk," Jessica added.

"Stop, you'll make me cry." I wasn't entirely joking. I realized there was a third lesson for the week—okay, clearly there were many things to take away from the last several days, but the big three now included my realization that I'd been complaining about something that was actually pretty wonderful.

"I've picked a few souls in Hell to help me get the place back up to speed. If that's even the phrase, because I've got no idea what my idea of 'up to speed' will be. Stuff's gonna change. I'm just not sure what, or how. And the thing is . . ." I took a quick gulp. Now that I was back from Hell, I realized how thirsty I was. Sinclair picked the hunger out of my head and speared me with a steady, warm look.

*Perhaps we need to go hunting tonight.*

I shot him a smile that, though I was going for aloof and sexy, probably came out deranged and a little goofy, and continued. "You know how I'm always complaining—"

"Sure."

"Yes, you have several things to say at all times."

"Stop!" I shouted before Jessica, Tina, and Sinclair could add to the madness. "Will you let me be specific, jerkheads? It seems like the people I've always wanted to be impressed with my powers never are. But they're the ones helping me run Hell, and most of the rest are my roommates. And I think that's beyond excellent, because there's nothing worse than a dictatorial asshat being surrounded by terrified yes-men."

"Just ask Justin Bieber," Marc suggested, earning a smack

on the arm from Tina (who had a motherly soft spot for the li'l douchebag) and a giggle from Jessica.

"It used to drive me crazy," I admitted. "It *still* drives me crazy. Who wouldn't want to intimidate the Ant? But I think it's good that the people I want the most control over, sometimes—they're the ones who either knew me before I died or don't care that I'm the vampire queen. It's good that the Ant isn't scared of me. She'll be more of a help if she isn't terrified."

"A help." From Jessica.

"Yeah."

"The Ant." From Marc.

"Yeah."

"That's how you know it's Hell." From Jessica.

"*Oh* yeah." I grinned—I couldn't help it—and she laughed again, which got the rest of us started.

Tina was quickest to recover and got right to it politely but decisively, as was her way. "Majesty, have you been able to recapture the escapee souls?"

"Whoa, people escaped from Hell?" Dick looked around at us. "Where was I?"

"You might have been sleeping. You both were definitely, uh, sleeping." So of course we all knew by Marc's tactful pause that they'd been doing the "yay, marriage looms!" bang.

"It's fine. I didn't have to round up any escapees. And we gotta call them something else, since they didn't so much escape as act on the fact that Laura let them go to trick me into keeping the promise I stupidly, *stupidly* gave in a moment of weakness."

An uncomfortable, decade-long silence dropped. And that's when I realized.

"You guys knew. Or guessed."

"I respectfully request the protection of the Fifth Amendment," Sinclair said. Marc shrugged and Jess wouldn't drop her gaze, but it was sympathetic and not scornful.

"Cheer up," Dick said. "I had no idea."

I was already shaking my head. "You all knew. Most of you knew." I sighed. "Of course you knew." That was when I realized we weren't just talking about Laura lying about escapees. My, my, it was a week for me to stumble across realizations I would have tumbled to ages earlier if I had just *pulled my thumb out of my ass.* How much time did I waste, hiding from truths I couldn't face? Were lives lost? *Oh, please not that on my conscience, too. Please.*

*My love.* Sinclair's concern cut through my distress like Fur's sewing-needle-sharp teeth razored through his Kenneth Coles. *I should like us to withdraw.*

*Yeah.* I rubbed my forehead. *Yeah, me, too.*

"If Laura lied, the Ant probably knew that, too. Right?" Marc thought about that for a few seconds. "Oh, hell, of course she did, what a dumb question."

"Don't feel bad. Took me too long to figure that out. It was there in front of me and I still wouldn't see it. That's why she wouldn't leave Hell."

"No."

"Yes." I understood the identical looks of shock on Marc and Jessica. Dick was starting to look dozy and Tina and Sinclair wore their careful neutral expressions. "She was always there when I needed something and, let me tell you, that shit got on my nerves almost immediately. I even asked her a few times what she was doing there and she'd snark at me and then I'd kind of forget about it until she'd helpfully yet bitchily show up again. But she was always there when I needed something."

"She knew what the Antichrist was up to, and she still stuck around?"

"Yep. And now she knows Laura's off the paranormal grid. And the Ant's *still* in Hell. Waiting." Funny how that should have been terrifying, and wasn't.

I watched them think that one over, and I sympathized.

Laura Goodman, the sister who professed to love me, who when not killing or lying had judged me for dishonesty and murder and then tricked me into taking on Hell. Her birth mother, my mortal enemy and the scourge of my adolescence, meanwhile, went out of her way to help with the burden of shit she knew was headed my way. And she also knew what my dad had been up to and refused to say, partly to save her own pride, but also because she knew I'd be devastated.

"It's too much," I said, before they could comment, and burst into violent tears. In an instant, Jess's bony arms were around me in a comforting pointy-elbowed hug. "I don't understand what's happened." I wept while the others made distressing "there, there" noises. Fur and Burr both started awake and whined in sympathy, then began wriggling like worms on a grill to get down. Marc and Sinclair released them and they wasted no time rushing over to my feet and—yargh, needle-like puppy teeth!—nibbling on my toes in solidarity. I think. "I—I'm not sure I can live in a world where I'm in Hell, Laura and Dad are out of my life, and the Ant is looking out for me and protecting me."

"Shhhh, stop that, it's fine," Jess soothed. "I'm sure she's still completely horrible. You're just not looking hard enough."

"Th-thanks. That helps." I straightened. It *did* help. The Ant and I might have the uneasiest of truces, but we weren't even close to best pals. Despite her help of late, there were still plenty of things besides her fashion sense to loathe her for.

Sinclair had scooped up both puppies and deposited them
"Yow! Teeth!"
in Marc's lap, then reached for my hand. "The queen and I will take our leave of you for the evening, if you please." Not that he was really asking, mind you. "Marc, could I trouble you to let the darling girls
*Ugh.*
*Shut up, darling girl.*

out within the hour? And perhaps a walk?"

Marc flapped a hand in a "go along with your bad self, I've got it covered" wave, and I didn't deny being impressed. Sinclair rarely delegated puppy time. Yay, he loved me more than the puppies! Suck it, puppies!

# CHAPTER
# THIRTY-EIGHT

**No sooner did Sinclair boot the door shut than he had me** pressed against it, his lips kissing the hollow of my throat. I wanted to say something like, "Is that a stake in your pants or are you just happy to see me?" but managed a mere, "Nnnggn." His fingers, meanwhile, had gone to the waistband of my leggings and he skimmed a finger just beneath it, caressing my belly. I wanted to lean into his mouth and his finger. I wanted to lean in, period. I wanted to knock his ass over and do filthy things to him. Alas.

"Wait, *wait.*" I tried to wriggle free, which wasn't easy, as at that moment Sinclair was more octopus than man. "I want to—I need to talk to you about Laura."

"What a vile mood killer," was his reply, but he let me go.

"Since everyone in the universe knew what Laura was up to before I did, that means you did, too."

"Don't be silly, my own. Not everyone in the universe knew. How can you say that when you haven't met everyone in the—"

I cut that nonsense right off. When Sinclair wanted to avoid answering an uncomfortable line of inquiry, he seized on semantics. "Except you knew more. Everyone guessed she was lying, but you knew she had a plan to dump Hell on me." This time his back was against the door while I kept him at arm's length. Literally; I held my arms out and my fingers barely brushed his chest. "When did you know, how did you know, and why wouldn't you of all people warn me?" I made no effort to keep the hurt out of my tone. If I couldn't show all of me to my husband, and by extension the others, what was any of this *for?*

He reached for me and, because he'd been blessed with longer arms, cupped my chin in the palm of his hand. His voice was slow, deep. "How could I tell you that you had been maneuvered and tricked by your own sister?"

"Yeah, you're the only one allowed to do that to me." I tried to sound bitchy, but it choked off in the middle. In the beginning, our relationship had been based on trickery and mistrust. I was hypersensitive to it, even now, after he had proved again and again that I meant more to him than blood, more than his own life. "Isn't that how it is?" I had no interest in crying. I hoped my emotions were taking note of that.

He sighed, long and low. "How could I tell you what your own sister meant to do? That someone who was supposed to love you conspired with the author of all sin to trick you so you couldn't get out of your own way?"

I thought about that. "That answers why. How about when?"

"Weeks ago. We met at church and I made some educated guesses she did not deny."[13]

The thought of the king of the vampires and the Antichrist having a kaffeeklatsch at the local Presbyterian church was

---

[13] See *Undead and Unsure.*

hilarious or terrifying. Sinclair must have mistaken my look of confused horror as confusion, because he elaborated.

"I warned her—"

"Oh, please don't say it."

"—to be careful what she wished for."

"And there it is. The After School Special lesson of the week. At least it wasn't, 'Keep off drugs and stay in school.'"

"Pardon?"

I shook my head. "Forget it. And all this time I thought you wanted to help me with Hell so *you* could run it."

"That is not necessarily off the table."

"Nice try, but you're not as cold as you pretend sometimes. You wanted to help because you knew what was coming down on me."

"I suspected."

I snorted. "For you, pal, that's the same as anyone else saying, 'I knew and got it in writing and then got that notarized and, really, it was always bound to happen.'"

"Do I have your forgiveness?" His thumb slid along my sluggish pulse point and then he kissed that same spot. "I was not strong enough to hurt you. I am deeply sorry you had to endure what you did without any assistance from me."

And that was it, the real reason. I had to do it myself to know I couldn't do it myself. Sinclair waited until I made the connection, knew what I'd have to do, and then he backed me to the hilt.

"I s'pose you're forgiven. Too much of a pain to kill you and break in a new guy. Not that you're broken in. Yet."

"Yes indeed." He held both my wrists in his hands, then turned them over to kiss the palms. And then . . .

And then he . . .

*Oh.*

I hadn't even realized I'd broken the skin, but there were four little crescent-shaped cuts on each palm. In a week's worth of outraged fist clenching, it was bound to happen. I'd have healed already, but for the fact that I hadn't fed all week.

*Mmm. Speaking of . . .*

Sinclair was licking the blood from my palms, his steady gaze never leaving my face. I had a thought so dark with lust

*He's tasting me, savoring me.*

my knees almost buckled.

*You are delicious, my own.*

"Clean living," I said, and I absolutely did not gasp because I was in complete control and oh my God since when did my palm have a direct link to my clit? Did the bastard rewire me in my sleep?

*Some things will never be told.* He was pulling my sweater over my head and sliding my leggings down my thighs to my ankles. A few tugs and I was also divested of bra, panties, and knee-high nylons (shut up, I wasn't about to wear pantyhose under leggings). He pulled me in closer and the feeling of my bare skin pressed against his shirt and slacks was divine. His mouth was skimming my collarbone while a hand fisted in my hair, gently pulling my head back so he could nip and suck on my throat, his other hand sliding up to tease the undersides of my breasts. Sinclair had been the one to teach me that the undersides were a hundred times more sensitive to touch than the tops, which should give you an idea of the mediocre lovin' I'd had until we met.

"Too many clothes," I managed as his knuckles skimmed up to my nipples, and then he was rubbing his thumbs over them, coaxing them to stiffness. "A stupid amount of clothes. Far too many items of clothing are between us. Why? Why would you get dressed today?"

He chuckled and started unbuttoning his shirt. "To keep the respect of our boarders?"

"Roommates," I corrected, trying with all my might not to snicker. Boarders, heh. "Why? You're still dressed, I don't understand. Why would you hurt me like this? Get naked, my God, man! I can't put it any plainer!"

He was laughing so hard he staggered more than walked, and I decided enough was enough and helped him off with his shirt

"Ouch! Buttons!"

and pants, smiling at the clatter of buttons bouncing and his belt buckle hitting the floor. His slacks slithered down his legs and then I was yanking, and then one navy blue sock went flying, followed by the other. That left his navy boxers.

"I'm giving you the benefit of the doubt and assuming you didn't coordinate your socks with your underwear today."

"Your forbearance is sweeter than plum wine, darling."

Then we were finally finally finally horizontal, his weight pressing me into the bed, and just as I was readying a sarcastic reply his teeth broke the skin over my jugular and all I came up with was, "Nnnnn mmmm ggggnnn." I would never understand the miracle of feeding with Sinclair. The blood between us was finite, but even as he drained me I felt stronger by the nanosecond. And it would be the same for him when I pulled away and

"Ah! Elizabeth, oh Christ!"

returned the favor. His dark sweet blood filled my mouth and my nerve endings lit up like a casino.

I slid my hand down and gently grasped his cock, already hard and urgent, and palmed the hot silky skin. My hand slid lower and I found his balls already trying to draw up—it had been a long time. Hours. Days! How were we even still functioning?

He slid down my body, nipping and kissing as he went, his big hands easing my thighs apart as his thumbs found me wet, spread me open, and then his mouth was there, his tongue lapping at me and darting and teasing, in me and then out, delicately laving over my clit again and again and one of those damn sneaky stealth orgasms

*Fuck oh fuck oh God God God*

*Yes. Yes. Louder, oh. Want to hear you I need it. Need to hear you.*
caught me by surprise and I arched against his mouth, my
back leaving the bed for a few seconds.

Then he was back up with me, his chest pressing against
my breasts, his tongue sliding past my teeth and I tasted
myself and our mingled blood and as his lovely long length
filled me I

*GodGodGodGodGodGodGodGod.*

came again. He hissed in pure pleasure and started to move,
carefully at first until I subtly signaled my desire for him to
speed up by pressing my heels into the small of his back and

*Ow!*

urging him forward, faster, more. "Sorry," I groaned.
"Really don't need you to take it easy right n—ah!" That was
more like it.

*Oofta.*

*Please stop thinking that singularly unsexy word.*

*If you've got the brain power to use words like* singularly, *we are
terrible at this.*

He laughed and kissed me, nipping my lower lip and flicking the bead of blood away with his tongue. His thrusts were
getting steadily, wonderfully urgent and the friction buildup
was outstanding.

*Do not leave me behind again. Take me to Hell with you.*

*I had*

*???*

*some thoughts*

*Elizabeth?*

*on that oh oh oh oh ha can't sneak up on me again stealth orgasm
this time oh oh oh oh I'm ready for oh oh oh oh*

*???*

I shrieked when I came, mostly because it was make noise
or blow up. Sinclair hissed in my ear and I felt him throb and
then pulse. His lips chased mine for another kiss and then he
was groaning into my mouth

*OH GOOD CHRIST*

and shuddering against me, his joy in being able to break
a commandment without feeling like he was gargling acid
kicking one more gorgeous series of spasms through me.

We collapsed. Well, he did; I was already flat on my back,
so I didn't so much collapse as sink further into the bed with
a satisfied moan. Sinclair was mumbling something into my
hair that I didn't make out right away.

"Too long. Left it too long. Should have sex more. You will
kill me. You are killing me."

"Um, I'm sorry?"

"Why?" His head came up and I saw he was smiling and
flushed. "You're the only one I would allow to kill me. Do so
whenever you wish."

"Um . . . that's sweet, Sinclair."

The smile dropped off his face so quickly I was startled.
"I meant what I told you, my queen. Take me with you. It is
my duty to help you rule. *All* your kingdoms."

All my kingdoms. What a (horrifying? exhilarating?) thought.

"Yeah, I'm with you. Tina and Marc want to come, too. Jessica
and His Name Was Always Dick are the only sensible ones;
they've got zero interest in a field trip to the pit. Also they're
looking forward to having the place to themselves."

"And perhaps more babies as a result," Sinclair said, sounding singularly comfortable. I'd never known what a family
man he wanted to be until we were a family.

"But I've got to get better at 'porting. I've got to get better
at the Game—white bear white bear—and I've got to stop ending up in the shed." Sinclair's brow furrowed and I waited for
the inevitable questions (who could blame him? I sounded like
a crazy woman, possibly because I was one), but he let it all slide.
Instead he rolled over, pulling me with him and settling me
against him as we made like spoons in a drawer.

"When I've got a handle on that stuff," I said, still thinking
out loud, "that's when we can really get to work and not before.

I'm not trying to take you to Hell until I'm sure I can get us there and back and there and back without shed time. Or at least without consistent results. And I'm talking like it'll be easy, but it won't. It's likely gonna suck. But I've got you to help me with that, too."

"Always," he told me, his voice going deeper with satiated fatigue. "You are mine. I belong to you. Always."

"Yeah." I sighed, wriggling against him. "I figured."

"I should like to see Hell," he rumbled. "As a tourist, mind you. Or an overlord."

I groaned. "It's comments like *that* that make me think twice about getting you involved in stuff like this."

He chuckled. "Nonsense. I am there to serve you. It will be as you desire, as our life is here."

"As I desire, huh? Well. I had an idea of how it might go. Once I've got a better handle on things, I mean. Now that I've stopped railing against my dreadful fate and died inside and become resigned to—"

"Oh, Elizabeth," he said with gentle reproach. "It distresses me when you talk like that."

"I've been thinking about it a lot. Imagining it. Just the looks on your faces when you see it, if nothing else." I laughed. Laughed! Who knew resignation could be so freeing? Running Hell would always be a burden, but, as it had taken me far too long to realize, I didn't have to do it alone.

That's how you know the people who love you, I think. When they know helping you is a terrible idea, and they want to do it anyway.

I had never been so blessed.

# EPILOGUE

**We were by the escalators at the east entrance, looking down**
onto the Hell Mall. From there we could see almost the entire
amusement park, and the movie theater was directly across.
The damned were going about their business, waiting in lines
and arguing with cashiers and getting motion sickness from
Hell's roller coasters and terrible return policies. It was controlled chaos, miserable and busy.

Sinclair, Tina, and Marc just stared out at everything,
taking it all in. I could see Cathie, Father Markus, and the
Ant at a table at the edge of the food court, arguing about
something they seemed to feel strongly about. There were a
lot of big hand gestures and raised voices and the clipboard
was being waved around. The Ant noticed me first and gave
me a distracted wave; Cathie and Father Markus glanced over
and both gestured at me to trot over. The argument didn't
stop or even slow down. What now? Father Markus wanted

to implement mandatory mass? The Ant wanted to nix the exchange program?

"Guys, the Hell Mall." I raised my arm to indicate the entire place. "Hell Mall, the guys." I smiled at my family, who were wearing varying expressions (surprise, wonder, trepidation). "So! What do you want to do first?"